# CAFÉ PARADISE BOOK 3

# THE INHERITANCE

Patricia Comb

2QT Limited (Publishing)

First Edition published 2017
2QT Limited (Publishing)
Settle, North Yorkshire BD24 9RH
www.2qt.co.uk

Cover design Charlotte Mouncey
Cover images supplied by iStockphoto.com

Author website www.patriciacomb.com

Printed in Great Britain by IngramSparks UK Ltd

A CIP catalogue record for this book is available
from the British Library
ISBN 978-1-912014-48-4

For Pat Tatham, York, North Yorkshire.
Thank you for your support, encouragement and enjoyment
of Books 1 and 2. Your enthusiasm was inspiring.

# ACKNOWLEDGEMENTS

I would like to thank Catherine Cousins and all the staff at 2QT for their help with this book with special mention to Charlotte Mouncey for the lovely cover. As ever, my sincere thanks to Karen Holmes for her friendship and continued support in editing this final book in the Café Paradise trilogy.

My thanks to Mark Malley and Gary Smith for their help and advice on mistakes commonly made when people undertake DIY, (not by them) and their experiences hanging heavy chandeliers - happily successful in all their own cases.

Lastly, my thanks and love, as always, to my husband, Peter. Poor man he never knows from one day to the next which character he is going to journey through the day with.

# PROLOGUE

## *September 2013*

Walter Breckenridge watched as Elvis, his young sheepdog, made a wide sweep behind the flock of Swaledale sheep. Elvis began to drive them slowly down the field towards where his master stood holding open a gate to a sturdy pen made up of hurdles strapped together with baler twine. As the sheep approached Walter stood to one side.

'Lie down,' he commanded Elvis.

Elvis obediently dropped to the ground, tongue hanging out and panting furiously. His sharp brown eyes followed every movement of the sheep, alert and ready for just one of them to step out of line.

He had done his job well. There was no panic among the flock and Walter was able to guide them gently into the pen with his shepherd's crook. He shut the gate quickly behind them and in a moment Elvis was at his side.

'And who gave you permission to move, lad?' Walter smiled down at the panting dog.

Elvis's ears flattened out. There had been no command to move and he knew it. Walter stroked his head. 'I'll overlook it this time, lad, but if we want to win *One Man and His Dog*, you'll have to do better than that.'

*One Man and His Dog*! Elvis knew what his master was talking about. He'd seen all those dogs in Walter's house. Elvis puzzled how they got in. He never saw them arrive or leave. They were just suddenly there, in the living room, behind a screen, doing what Elvis loved doing best – chasing sheep.

Elvis grinned happily up at Walter and together they surveyed the sheep contentedly. Now that they were free from Elvis nipping at their heels, they calmly began cropping the grass within the pen.

The September sun was beginning to dip, casting shadows over the patchwork of fields that stretched away to meet the distant hills.

'We'd best get on, lad.' Walter made a move towards the pen of sheep. 'I'd have done this job afore now if that daughter of mine hadn't kept me busy at that café of hers all morning. She thinks I'm retired and can jump to any time she wants. Between her and helping Ellie, I'm amazed I ever get any time for me poor old sheep, let alone me fruit and veg gardens.'

Happily grumbling, Walter let himself into the makeshift pen and began checking the condition of the sheeps' feet. The weather had been cool and wet recently and that could start foot rot in his flock if he didn't keep an eye on them. He was bent over his task, absorbed in trimming the hoof of one of his favourite old ewes, so he didn't see Ellie running down the field. Only when she was near and shouting his name did he look up. He let the ewe go and came out of the pen to meet her.

'What's up, lass?' Walter was concerned to see his usually serene wife so visibly agitated.

'Come quickly, Walter,' she panted, holding her side and trying to catch her breath. 'It's Rose and that chap she took up with. Arthur, I think.'

'Oh heck, what do they want?' A visit from his older sister, Rose, was not high on Walter's wish list.

'They want to stay for a while,' Ellie gasped.

'Whatever for? They've got a perfectly good home of their own.'

'Well, that's just it. They haven't. They've had to leave their smallholding. The owners of the land have sold it to a property company for building on. Come *on*, Walter,' Ellie insisted urgently. 'They've come with two lorries. One's got all their furniture in and one has all their animals. She wants to know where she's to put her alpacas and peacocks. *And* she's got a dog– scraggy-looking thing. It scoffed Elvis's dinner the minute Rose let it out of the van.'

Walter looked grim. This was the worst news possible. He kept Rose at arm's length at the best of times. The idea of her taking up residence with them was appalling. She made everyone's mother-in-law seem like an angel from heaven. This just could not happen.

'Stay here and get your breath, Ellie love,' Walter commanded. 'Take your time. I'll go and deal with Rose and this Arthur fella. They're not staying here with all them animals!'

As Walter approached the house, he saw Rose Breckenridge pacing impatiently around the farmyard. Mentally bracing himself he called out, 'Now then, Rose, what's to do?'

'My, you took your time, our Walter. You've seen Ellie, haven't you? Then you know what's to do. That pension company that owns the land we rent sent in the bailiffs. They turfed us off the holding this morning. I need somewhere quick for my alpacas and my birds, so where else would I go but to my nearest and dearest in my time of dire need? I knew you would help me out.'

Walter winced. Rose always swung a good line in emotional blackmail. They were never 'nearest and dearest', even as children. 'You can't stop here, Rose. I haven't got the room. I've only just got enough space for *my* animals. Where would I put yours? And what about that vanload of furniture Ellie says you've brought?'

'You do fuss on, Walter,' Rose said wonderingly. 'It's simple. I've had a look around and the furniture can be stored in that barn over there. You've a couple of lovely fields for my alpacas and my hens can knock about with your lot. And the peacocks please themselves, anyway. It's not a problem, is it?'

She beamed at him and turned to Arthur, who was waiting

patiently behind her. 'Hop in, Arthur, and we'll offload our girls and boys into that field down there. We need to get them settled before nightfall. Mind out, Walter, we need quite a bit of space to turn this van about. Thanks a lot for having us. I knew you wouldn't fail.'

She jumped up into the van beside Arthur and called down to Walter, 'I hope Ellie's got something nice for supper. We're starving.'

Walter watched them bump down the track, the big van swaying dangerously under its heavy load. Alpacas in his best hayfield all winter, churning up the ground and eating the grass down to its roots... He had plans to convert the barn to expand Ellie's jam and chutney business and planned a small vegbox enterprise. Now Rose wanted it as a furniture warehouse.

Someone please tell him he was having a bad dream, that he would wake up in a moment and find Ellie snuggled up beside him in bed and all would be right with the world.

# CHAPTER 1

B arney Anderson was in a buoyant frame of mind. Against all the odds, Anderson and Cranton had just won a difficult case in court and he was in the mood to celebrate. He made his way to Castlegate, intent on persuading his wife, Jackie, to leave Café Paradise in the safe hands of the staff this evening and come out to dinner with him. After all, it wasn't every day a top barrister heartily congratulated you on sterling work and intended to put your name forward to his London firm to use in the future.

Barney pushed open the door of the café, delighting afresh at its new, elegant interior. Jackie had good taste and the café had been transformed from the greasy spoon of her mother's era to a fresh, clean-lined space people queued to come to. Freshly ground coffee mixed with a faint aroma of garlic and wine assailed his nostrils. He became aware of how hungry he was. It had been a working lunch at court and not much of it.

He frowned when he saw Jackie at the coffee counter. She was expecting twins in a few months and was supposed to attend to the paperwork in her office, not do long stints at the coffee counter.

Jackie looked up as the door swung open and flushed guiltily when she saw who it was. 'I've only been here for ten minutes,' she forestalled him.

'Then it's ten minutes too long.' Barney looked stern. 'Where's Genevieve? I thought she was learning to do this.'

Jackie made a face. 'I don't think it's her forte. There's only so much frothed milk I can afford to waste in one day. Genevieve could go through a whole tankerful. I'm waiting for young Marianne. School's out; she'll be along any minute. Anyway, enough of all that. How did the case go?'

'Guilty as charged, and seven years for his trouble. Jury couldn't believe his track record when it came out afterwards. North Yorkshire will be a lot happier without him for a while.' Barney beamed. 'So here I am, ready to sweep my wife off her feet and take her out to dinner at her favourite restaurant.' He held up his hand. 'Wrong. Café Paradise is her favourite, but this comes a close second.'

'The York Tollbooth?' Jackie said, ecstatic, then her face fell. 'I can't, not tonight.'

'Why not? Henri's here and Genevieve will be helping, so what's the problem?'

'I'm meeting with the man next door.' Jackie smiled up at him.

Meeting with the man next door … was he missing something here? 'About?'

'About buying the property.'

'Excuse me?'

Jackie flushed again. 'Yes. I know you don't know anything about it and I was going to tell you when I got home tonight. I didn't know you were coming in here early before I'd got anything to tell you at all and I still haven't, but I might have later.'

Talk about losing the plot. Barney hung on grimly to Jackie's original statement. 'Buying the property next door? Since when?'

'Since this morning,' she said serenely.

'How come?'

'Obvious. Next door is selling up and the building's up for grabs.' Jackie's face lit up. 'What a golden opportunity, Barney. I can double the size of the café. Think of the covers in the restaurant at night! I can't wait to get started.'

Barney's heart sank. Café Paradise in its present form kept Jackie busy, so what about when the babies came along? The time wasn't so far away; would she be up to her eyes in another renovation project? He was more than willing to shoulder his share of child-rearing, but would Jackie find time for her share?

Barney looked around the bustling café. 'We can't talk about this here. Can't you rearrange your appointment with … what's his name?'

'Michael Roberts, and no I can't. I'm sorry, Barney, but a peach of a building like that is going to have buyers queuing up. He's given me first option.'

Barney shook his head.

'I'm not passing it up, Barney,' Jackie said firmly. 'This chance may never come again. Who knows what I might get next door if I don't? Competition, maybe. Another café or restaurant. No. This is a great chance for us and I'm not walking away from it.'

'So, no celebratory dinner tonight.' Barney sighed and turned away.

'Tomorrow, I promise. And we'll talk about it properly. I'll know far more and I bet you'll see it from my point of view.'

Barney doubted it but he could see that his lovely, headstrong wife was in no mood for reasoned discussion. Maybe after a night's sleep, tomorrow might bring a different perspective to events.

\*\*\*

Even as his car bumped up the lane to Claygate Farm, Barney wondered whether enlisting Walter's help would make things better or worse. Father and daughter loved each other dearly but they were too alike; the sparks could soon fly when they were together.

Turning into the farmyard, Barney braked sharply as a scrawny brown-and-white mongrel dog ran out of the barn and almost under the wheels of the car. It circled round, barking furiously, and then reared up and scrabbled at Barney's door.

A man came out of the barn, calling to the dog. 'Jack, Jack, come away. Get thissen indoors now.'

Jack took no notice and continued to scrape away at the paint on Barney's car door. Barney leant hard on his horn, hoping to scare the dog off, but it made him bark all the more.

Walter appeared at the house door. 'For God's sake, Arthur, get that bloody mutt off and tie it up somewhere. I thought you had done. That's my son-in-law. Look at his car! That'll take some repairing.'

Arthur dragged the dog off and into the barn. 'Bit of T-Cut should do the job,' he threw over his shoulder laconically.

'And you can do it,' Walter shouted after him. 'Right now, whilst the lad's in the house.'

'Aye, all right.'

Walter raised his eyes heavenwards. 'I swear if you said the world was going to end in five minutes he'd still say, "Aye, all right." Come in, lad.' They turned towards the house. 'I'm always pleased to see you, but what brings you out here on a Sunday morning and without my beautiful daughter?'

'A story with Jackie, as ever, Walter.' Barney sat down at the big kitchen table and nodded agreement at the proffered teapot. 'But first of all, what's Arthur and dog doing here? Is Rose here too? I didn't think they did visiting. And why's your yard in such a mess? There's stuff everywhere.'

Walter poured their tea and joined Barney at the table. 'Everywhere,' he echoed Barney flatly. 'They've taken over our barns, our fields and half our house with all their stuff. They expect Ellie to wait on them hand and foot – which, by the by, she is not doing. But it doesn't stop them asking.'

'Well, what's going on?' Barney was confused. As far as he knew Rose and her swain were usually safely tucked away on their smallholding at Allsthwaite.

'Bailiffs.' Walter took a reflective sip of his tea. 'They've been given notice to quit, as the land they were renting was sold some time ago. They've nowhere to go so they came here, along with their worldly goods, herd of alpacas, hens and a bunch of peacocks. And horrible things they are too. Elvis is terrified of 'em. They screech like banshees and he hates it. He only has to see one and he's off. Between them and that dog of theirs… That dog's another story; he's just like Rose. Listens to no one and does as he likes – and he likes to terrorise Elvis. My poor dog's a nervous wreck.'

Barney pursued Walter's first statement. 'Why have they been evicted? Haven't they paid their rent to the landlord? They must have had letters warning them about what action would be taken. Bailiffs don't just swan in out of the blue.'

'That's just it. That's what they do,' Walter replied.

'Yes, but not without a lot of correspondence beforehand,' Barney insisted.

'And that's one Rose and Arthur don't do,' Walter said gloomily. 'They had plenty of letters, plenty of notice to quit. The land's been sold on and they have to find somewhere else. They would have known all about it if they'd only opened the bloody letters. But, feckless pair that they are, what do they do? Just stuff them in a pot, along with all the other letters. They would have got round to them, so they say. They've just been busy lately and it slipped their minds. Slipped their minds!' Walter was bitter. 'It didn't slip their minds to know where to come when it was all too late, did it? And now look at the mess we're in. We can't live like this.'

They were silent for quite some time, lost in contemplation. Barney realised the reason for his visit to Walter paled into insignificance compared to what his old friend was facing.

'I'll look into things, Walter,' he promised. 'We must be able to do something. Surely we can find them some land to rent at a reasonable price. They can't possibly stay here. It's madness.'

'They say they're going to look around, but I know our Rose. She's as tight as a duck's backside and that's *watertight*. She'll not want to pay the fancy rents they ask for land these days but nowt's going to part Rose from her animals. I know what she's up to. She thinks if she parks on me long enough,

I'll do anything to get shut of her, even help with her land rent. She's got more money than I'll ever shake a stick at, lad.

'But enough of my problems, Barney. How's things with you and my lass? She'll be needing to take it a bit easier now, with the twins on the way.'

'Ah,' Barney said slowly. 'There's a bit of a problem with that.'

Walter was instantly alert. Privately he was tickled pink at the prospect of twin grandchildren arriving into his life and couldn't wait to take them about the farm with him. 'What's up?' he demanded.

'You won't believe this one, Walter. As if we haven't got enough going on in our own lives, the building next door is coming on the market and the owner has given Jackie first refusal. She wants to buy it and double the size of the café.'

Walter stared at Barney. 'Is she off her trolley? She's got her hands full as it is. The café's going great guns. She doesn't need to double her workload.'

'That's not how she sees it,' Barney said. 'She says it won't. She thinks she has all the systems in place now. She thinks it's just a question of the renovations, which she has been through already so she knows what she's doing, and then employing some more staff.'

'She's barmy.' Walter shook his head.

'I know that, Walter, but you know how headstrong she is. If you say black, she'll say white. Tell her it's too much and she'll want to prove you wrong.'

'Aye, she's her mother's daughter, all right. Marilyn would never see reason either.'

'She says she needs a new challenge.'

'A challenge!' Walter's incredulous face expressed it all. 'Isn't having a busy city café in the centre of York and twin babies going to be challenge enough?'

'Allegedly not.' Barney shrugged his shoulders. 'I thought maybe if you had a word with her…'

'We've been down that road afore, Barney, and it didn't get

us anywhere. She still got entangled with that Tom Young and his dodgy Trades Council outfit.'

'We've moved a long way from there,' Barney said. 'She trusts your judgement a lot more these days. Please, just try and talk her out of it.'

'What about her sister? Can't she make her see sense?'

'Annabel's busy in London, Walter. She's just got a place studying at an auction house down there and her head's full of fine art and antiques. She tried in her own gentle way to suggest maybe the timing wasn't so good but Jackie was having none of it. You're my only hope, Walter.'

Walter drained his tea and set his mug down on the table. 'I'll talk to Ellie when she gets home from the market. She can mebbe suggest a few pointers to get Jackie to see reason. I'll try lad, but I doubt I'll get me head in me hands just the same.'

# CHAPTER 2

Walter was not feeling sanguine as he made his way through Café Paradise on Monday morning. Ellie had been no help at all and Walter couldn't blame her. She was running a successful business making and marketing her jams and chutneys at markets around the area and now had to contend with Rose and Arthur and all their livestock about the place, getting under her feet and making a mess in the yard in spite of her all her deterrents. Far from supporting Walter in his desire to dissuade Jackie, Ellie was all for Jackie's expansion plans.

'She's young and strong, Walter. Why try and stop her? Women these days manage to keep all the balls in the air. You can't stand still in business these days, I know that. Look at me: I'm loving what I'm doing and thriving on it. Jackie can give me thirty years. I'm sure she'll take it all in her stride and Barney will do his share.'

There was nothing for it. Walter had promised to talk to Jackie and talk he would, but when his daughter got the ball she ran with it. She had inherited all of Marilyn's determination and strong will and in forty years Walter had never been able to get the better of Marilyn. He didn't suppose he'd have much luck with her daughter this morning either.

He was relieved to see Penny at the coffee counter. At least he would be spared a quietly hissed argument with his daughter as he tried to persuade her to leave her post and come into her office to discuss the café development.

'What's the weather forecast today then, Penny?' Walter asked.

'Fair, but could be stormy soon if you've come for what I think you've come for.'

Penny and Walter had developed their own code over the years when Walter was the Café Paradise chef in its greasyspoon days, under Marilyn's reign.

'Aye, it could be,' he agreed.

He drew himself up, as if this would stiffen his resolve, walked through the café and knocked on Jackie's door. When she answered, he opened the door and went in.

Jackie was at her desk, surrounded by paperwork. Her face lit up when she saw her visitor.

'Hello, Dad, lovely to see you. You've just timed it right. I was thinking about a coffee break.'

Walter kissed his daughter. A pang of regret shot through him. How soon would this lovely atmosphere between them be soured? 'Aye, coffee would be nice, lass. No, you sit there. I'll fetch them.'

Jackie had half-risen to her feet and Walter was alarmed at how large she had become with her advancing pregnancy. The babies weren't far off now and weren't twins often early? However would she manage with them and a building site here?

Collecting the coffee from Penny, Walter raised an enquiring eyebrow.

'Flogging a dead horse, Walter,' Penny said, adding Walter's favourite chocolate biscuits to the tray. 'She's agreed it all with that Mr Roberts in principle and the bank's OK about it, and that's all since Friday.'

'What do you think about it, Penny?' Walter was curious. Penny could be ditzy but sometimes she offered remarkable nuggets of common sense.

'I think she should go for it. Like Jackie says, when would she get the chance again? Yes, I know the timing's not the best but that can't be helped. We'll get through.' She patted Walter's arm consolingly. 'You'll help out, I'm sure, and we all will when we can. Don't talk her out of it.'

Walter sighed. Help Jackie out? How was he going to do that with Rose and her menagerie occupying his every waking moment at Claygate Farm? If he turned his back, they'd be up to some mischief or another.

'I promised Barney I'd try,' he said mournfully. He eyed the chocolate biscuits wistfully. 'I only hope I get the chance to get one of those down me neck before she throws me out.'

He took the tray from Penny and returned to Jackie in her office. 'Aslan's den,' Walter thought, and he himself was no lion tamer.

Carefully putting the tray down, he sat opposite his daughter. 'You're looking well, lass,' he began. 'I hear there've been developments.'

Jackie looked down at her swollen stomach. 'We've done that one, Dad. Don't you remember, or is senility setting in?'

Walter controlled his exasperation. She enjoyed baiting him. 'No, I am not senile and I think you know very well what I mean.' He took a chocolate biscuit and bit into it.

Jackie smiled sweetly at him. 'Developments?'

'Yes, developments. As in *buying next door* developments.'

'Ah,' Jackie continued to smile at him.

For some inexplicable reason, this made Walter feel even more exasperated with her. He felt like a fish on a hook. 'Well?'

'Well what?'

'Are you going ahead with it?'

'Classified information, Dad.' Jackie sat back in her chair and sipped her coffee reflectively. 'I suppose Barney sent you.'

'No, he did not,' Walter snapped. 'I can make my own decisions. I don't need yon lad of yours to tell me what to do. I can tell meself. Aye, and you're not too old to take a bit of advice, neither. Pity you haven't listened to me a bit more afore now. So, what about this daft idea of buying next door? Are you going to do it?'

Jackie put her coffee cup down on the desk and leant

towards Walter. 'It's not a daft idea. It's a very sound idea –"a good business expansion plan", to quote the man at the bank. I suppose you'd like to argue black was the new white with him.'

'Good for business, maybe. But what about when them twins arrive? Tell me that.' He nodded vigorously, as if in agreement with the absent Barney. 'What are you going to do with 'em? It's not like leaving a dog for a few hours and popping home at lunchtime. And, if you're at home with them, who's going to look after the café?'

Jackie scowled across the desk at him. 'Life doesn't have to grind to a halt just because you have a baby, Dad. The world goes on. I'm not quite the idiot you try to make me out to be. I have thought about it. Initially they can come here with me—'

'And what about when they're crawling about the place?' Walter interrupted her. 'They can be nippy, you know. They'll be out of here and into that building site next door before you can say "knife" and then what? Cos you'll be in the middle of it all by then.'

'*Will you listen for once!*' Jackie was getting as exasperated as Walter. 'They can go to day nursery or we'll hire a nanny. One way or another they'll be cared for, and Barney and I will be with them a lot of the time.'

Walter hadn't bargained for the nanny idea. 'My grandchildren palmed off onto a nanny … whilst you… What's the point of having them?'

'Oh, for God's sake, Dad.' Jackie got up and paced about the office, rubbing her back. 'The days of staying at home as a full-time mum went out the window long ago. What about Marilyn?' she challenged him. 'She didn't stay at home with me either, did she? This place was her life, far more than I ever was.'

'Exactly.' Walter was triumphant. 'Is that what you want for your children?'

'No, of course it isn't.' Jackie rolled her eyes heavenwards. 'Times changed, Dad. We have to move on with them. Modern childcare can be a huge asset to a child, give them a great start, in conjunction with a happy home life. If I stay at home engulfed in nappies and childcare I'll be climbing the walls in a very short time. And I notice you're not suggesting Barney stays at home with them.'

'He's just nicely building his business up. He can't—'

'Oh, but I can, can I? And let Café Paradise go to hell in a handcart. No, Dad. I've worked too hard for all this, in Mum's time and in this last couple of years on my own account.' She stopped pacing the office floor.

'I am buying next door and doubling the size of the café. On Fridays and Saturdays we will be offering an evening restaurant menu – and yes, I hope shortly to be having twins and managing them *and* the new project. And *I hope* my family will support me in this, cos it's going to happen.'

Scooping up a couple of biscuits from the plate, Walter rose to leave. 'Do you remember building them playing-card towers with me when you were a kid?'

Jackie gave him a guarded smile.

'Yes, I do … happy times.'

'Not when the bloody lot comes tumbling down, lass. There were tears before bedtime then and I've no doubt there'll be a few more yet, afore we're through.' He swiftly made for the door before an empty coffee cup could be thrown his way.

'And you'll have double the trouble with twins. I hope it is just twins. Did I ever tell you my Auntie Jane had triplets? You never know…'

Walter slammed the door behind him and heard the cup smash against it on the other side.

# CHAPTER 3

'Hello, 539780.'
'It's me, Penny, love.' On the other end of the line George, Penny's husband, sounded excited.

Penny wasn't sure she was speaking to George. Their anniversary weekend was coming up and they usually did something special but Penny suspected George had forgotten all about it.

'Well, George, what do you want?' she asked, a frosty note in her voice.

'I bet you thought I'd forgotten our anniversary but I haven't.' George sounded triumphant. 'Get the bags out. We're off on a mystery tour tomorrow.'

'A mystery tour?' Penny echoed. 'How do I know what to pack if I don't know where I'm going? You'd better tell me.'

'Not a word,' George said firmly. 'It's an anniversary surprise. All I will say is take some warm clothes, aye, and your warmest coat and furry boots. See you tonight.'

The line cut off and Penny had to be satisfied with that. Warm clothes! Visions of snowy Alps, glühwein or maybe even a short cruise up the fjords. She'd always wanted to visit the ice cathedral at Tromsø. No wonder George sounded excited.

Penny happily set about packing their bags. George had to work late into the evening on a big building project and would have no time to pack anything for himself. She would pack all the warm clothes she could find and they would be ready for an early start the next day.

\*\*\*

Turning off the A1 at Scotch Corner and heading up to Penrith, Penny swallowed her disappointment. Notions of sipping glühwein beneath twinkling fairy lights on snowy slopes, or enjoying a romantic dinner by moonlight on board ship as they sailed the fjords, faded fast from Penny's imagination. The grey tarmac road ribboned out before them. It was looking like a bed and breakfast in Keswick after all.

But no, they didn't take the road for Keswick. George turned on to the slip road to join the M6 north. Penny was mystified. 'Are you going to give me a clue?'

George chuckled. 'You'll never guess in a million years and I'm not telling you,' he said. 'It's a surprise.'

A long time later, after they had passed Carlisle and Gretna Green, they turned onto the A75, signposted for Dumfries and Stranraer.

Stranraer! There was the clue! The ferries went to Ireland from Stranraer. Penny's mood lightened. She might not be having dinner sailing down a fjord, but dinner on a ferry headed for a weekend in Belfast was not so bad. Had she mentioned to George her desire to visit the Harland and Wolff shipyard and the *Titanic Belfast* She must have. Penny happily closed her eyes and let the miles slip by. Belfast was renowned as an excellent shopping centre too.

\*\*\*

Penny awoke from her nap just as George switched the car engine off. She sat up and looked about her. 'Where are we?'

'Port William.' George smiled down at her. 'Kings Green caravan and camping site, to be precise. Look out there.'

Beyond the grassy field dotted with a few caravans and tents, white-foamed waves rolled up a stony beach, crashing against the huge boulders that formed the break between the land and sea.

A field … caravans… They were not at Stranraer and the ferry, then. Penny was puzzled. 'Why are we here, George? I thought we were going on the ferry to Belfast.'

'I never said anything about a ferry,' George protested.

'But the road signs said *Stranraer* and that's just around the coast from the new ferry port to Belfast.'

'Stranraer's just the end point. If you'd been awake, you'd have seen all the signposts along the way: Newton Stewart, Wigtown, Whauphill and Port William. You might have guessed by then we were going somewhere a bit different.'

Penny gazed across the field and out to sea. The wind was whipping up the waves and a light drizzle began to fall. 'So why are we here?' she repeated the question.

'Because, my lovely wife, I want to show you somewhere different – the wild Scottish coast in all its glory. And what better place than this?'

'Where are we going to stay?'

George pointed to a white caravan parked on its own overlooking the sea. 'Right there,' he said proudly.

'In a caravan!' Penny felt faint. This couldn't be happening to her. She'd been dreaming of Nordic fjords and alpine slopes and here they were in a muddy field in the rain.

'I knew you'd love it,' George said enthusiastically. 'It belongs to a mate of mine. Do you remember Frank Johnson? He keeps it here for all the season and lets friends use it sometimes. We've been lucky to get it. He has quite a waiting list.'

'Lucky! My wedding anniversary in a caravan in the pouring rain, a force nine gale that might sweep us into the sea at any moment, and you call that lucky?'

George sighed. 'You do exaggerate, Penny. It's only a light breeze and the caravan's well secured for this weather. Come on.' He switched the car engine back on, slowly bumped across the field and stopped, facing out to sea beside the caravan. He jumped out and went around to Penny's side and opened her door.

'You'll love it once you're inside, Penny. It's great. It's got a good bed and a table to eat off: everything. Well, not quite everything. It doesn't have any central heating like the newer vans do, but it has a good electric heater, Frank says.'

'Camping,' Penny said flatly.

'No, it's a caravan, you can see that. It's not a tent.'

'Glorified camping, that's what it is. That's what they call it. I've heard the customers at the café talk about it. Whatever made you think I'd like to spend my anniversary here?'

'Er, well … the sea, fresh air, the outdoors… There's a fantastic restaurant in the square. Frank's recommended it. I've booked us a table for tonight. If you like it we can go back tomorrow for our anniversary and if you don't, there's other places he's told me about.'

'After nearly forty years of marriage, George, God help me, I think you know I like the indoors, away from the freezing seaside and preferably near to some art galleries, theatres and shops. Port William would appear to have none of the above.'

'You'll still love it,' George said confidently and went to open up the caravan.

Penny did not. It was all right as caravans went, if somewhat cold and damp. George bustled about cheerily, rigging up the heater and putting on the kettle for tea. No wonder he'd said to bring warm clothes and furry boots. She thought she might have to sleep in them.

After a brisk walk along the coast Penny felt a bit better. She was bitterly disappointed at not being treated to a nice warm hotel somewhere, but at least George had tried to think of something different. Next year she would do the thinking, and well in advance.

George had been right about one thing: the restaurant *was* fantastic. A handsome, three-storeyed stone building set in the middle of the village square, it served beautifully cooked food and fine wines in a mellow dining room draped with Scottish plaids. The dining room was full and Penny hoped George would be able to reserve a table for the next evening. She would like to sample some of the other delightful-sounding dishes on the menu.

Warm and satisfied, they went out into the cold night. Fortunately, it was only a short walk along the coast to the caravan site as the rain had resumed and the wind had got up. They hurried back to their van, listening to the sea slapping hard against the huge stones along the shoreline.

All Penny's forebodings were fulfilled. It was the worst night of her life. Heavy rain lashed at the windows and, in spite of its extra securing ropes, the caravan rocked alarmingly all night as the wind blew at gale force. Penny, huddled in her coat and boots under a heavy quilt, shivered with cold and fear as she listened to the elements outside. In the opposite bunk George snored noisily, but even he could not drown out the howling wind. Penny listened resentfully. Wild horses would not drag her back to this bed tomorrow night. She would insist on proper accommodation when morning came.

\*\*\*

In spite of the weather, Penny must have dropped off to sleep towards the morning. When she awoke, Port William was a very different place from the night before. The sun shone over a calm sea and the beach looked washed clean, clumps of samphire nodding in the light morning breeze.

George was up already and making tea in the tiny galley kitchen. Penny sat up, stiff and sore after her night tossing and turning on the narrow bunk bed.

'What a fantastic day,' George enthused.

'What a terrible night.' Penny rubbed her neck and shoulders.

'Was it?'

'Hmph. You snored your way through it, although I don't know how you managed it. I thought we were going to be hurled into the sea at any moment. The wind was gale-force.'

'Oh, that was last night,' George said cheerily. 'Anyway, you should have been asleep, not lying awake listening to all that.'

'Could he get any more annoying?' Penny wondered. Why had she not killed him years ago?

'So, apart from finding somewhere a lot more suitable to stay tonight, George, have you planned anything for us today?'

'You've read my mind, Penny. As it happens I have, and I think you're going to love it!'

Penny smiled. At long last the weekend was taking a turn for the better.

After a light breakfast George suggested she put on her warm coat and boots. They were going for a walk.

'So where *are* we going?' Penny enquired.

'This is my anniversary surprise.' George grinned happily.

'What kind of a surprise could it be in a small coastal village like Port William?' Penny wondered. Had he bought them a weekend cottage here? If he had, she would kill him. But if it was a boat … a cabin cruiser, maybe? That would be wonderful.

Sure enough, they headed to the harbour. Penny's excitement mounted. This was worth a bad night in a freezing caravan. She could see several boats bobbing on their moorings in the harbour. Which one was theirs? They all looked great.

They walked along the quayside, but George did not stop at any of the boats. He must have something bigger and better in mind around the corner. Lobster pots and fish crates were piled all along the quayside, where it widened out to accommodate boat trailers, vans and a sea tractor.

'Shut your eyes,' George commanded. 'I want to keep the surprise until the very last moment.' Penny could hardly contain herself. What had he bought? A yacht? Holding on tightly to George's arm, she obediently closed her eyes and warily made her way forward. George came to an abrupt halt.

'You can open your eyes now, Penny love. Ta-da! What do you think to that?'

Penny opened her eyes. To what? She looked down at the harbour but couldn't see anything. No cabin cruiser, no yacht. 'There's nothing there, George.' She looked up at him.

'Not down there, Penny. Here, right in front of you.' George gestured to an old ambulance parked on the quay. It had a *Sold* sign on the back.

'That's an ambulance, George.' Penny was more puzzled than ever.

'It was,' George said happily. 'But it isn't any more. It's been taken out of service and now it's ours. Our new camper. I'm going to fit it out and we'll travel the world in it. Think of it, Penny. No more motorbikes. I promised you that. We'll travel in style and luxury from now on.' George's face was split from ear to ear with a huge grin.

Sick disappointment and outrage fought for the upper hand in Penny's breast. Had he entirely taken leave of his senses? Travel about in that old heap with its bright yellow go-faster stripes? Not only that, since when was George the master of DIY? He could just about knock a nail in the wall to hang a picture but even then she often did it herself, not trusting him to get it centred on the wall or even straight. 'No!' she shouted at him. 'No, no and definitely no. We are not buying it.'

'I already have. I thought you'd love it. Don't you like it?' George looked surprised.

'What in God's name made you think I would ever like a junkheap like this, George Montague? This … this *thing* is my surprise? I don't think so. I am not going home in that.'

George had the grace to look discomfited. 'No, you've got the car. I thought you could take that and I could drive this back to York. I've got it all arranged, the insurance and everything.'

Light began to dawn on Penny. It wasn't an anniversary treat at all. Now she saw why they had come to a grotty caravan in the middle of nowhere. It was nothing to do with their anniversary, but was just a ruse to collect this rusting heap of metal.

She turned on her heel and ran back along the quayside, tears pouring down her face.

'Penny!' George shouted after her. 'Come back. Let's at least talk about it.'

Too upset and hurt to heed his words, Penny stumbled her way back along the road and over the field to the caravan at Kings Green.

She had the keys in her bag. Letting herself in, she feverishly emptied George's things out of their weekend bag and flung her clothes and toiletries in. She was still trembling with anger but dried her eyes and searched for the keys. As she was getting into the car, George arrived.

'Penny! Where are you going?'

'That's for me to know, George. Don't worry about me – not that I suppose you would, anyway. If I were you, I'd be more worried about that precious ambulance of yours. If you think it will get you home to York, good luck to the both of you. I'm off anywhere but here. I've a wedding anniversary to celebrate, remember? And I'm going to find somewhere to do it in style. I might even plan my divorce whilst I'm there.'

Penny put the car into gear and roared away across the field. George groaned. The springs on the car…She'd ruin them.

\*\*\*

After he broke down at Gretna Green, George's pal, Jimmy, came to his rescue. They found a small hotel to stay at whilst Jimmy scoured the local garages to find the parts to repair the ambulance sufficiently for George to limp back to York, with Jimmy following, just to be on the safe side.

On his arrival in York, George didn't feel up to facing Penny. She wasn't taking any of his calls and ignoring his texts. He needed help. He decided to visit Walter Breckenridge at his Claygate farm. Walter had worked with Penny for many years and knew her almost as well as George did. Perhaps he could advise him what to do to get Penny back onside again. He had run out of ideas.

George tooted goodbye to Jimmy and turned off for Walter's farm. He left the ambulance at the bottom of the lane and walked up to make his visit. As he got to the top of the lane, the farmhouse and yard came into view. George stopped, taken aback at what he saw. What had gone wrong?

Usually Walter's yard was spotless and very tidy. Ellie saw to that. When Walter lived there alone and worked at Café Paradise, he had not had the time to keep the place tidy but now that he had retired he put all his efforts into Claygate and their business projects there.

Today Claygate appeared to have reverted to how it was in Walter's bachelor days, only a great deal worse. An old mud-spattered lorry was parked in the yard and a short woman dressed in an old raincoat, with muddy boots on her feet, was struggling to let down the tailgate of the lorry. An assortment of old furniture was stacked behind the lorry – awaiting loading, George surmised.

He hastened up the lane. 'Can I give you a hand with that, love?'

The woman turned at his voice and surveyed him critically. 'Aye, happen as how you've come at just the right time. I don't know where Arthur's got to. I said I was coming to clear the barn a bit. Made hisself scarce. Don't think he's overfond of lifting heavy stuff. Likes his peacocks and alpacas, does Arthur.'

She sighed and turned back to the lorry. 'You're a big, strapping lad and come just at the right time, too,' she repeated. 'I'd be glad of a hand with this lot. Walter says he needs the space in his barn. He's planning a veg box scheme, he says. I reckon he could plan it next year when we're gone, I hope, but no, he wants to do it now and so we have to put stuff back in the lorry and then it'll get damp.'

George had no idea what any of this meant but he lifted the tailgate down to the ground. Who was this woman and who was her 'Arthur'?

As if she'd read his mind, the woman paused and held out her hand. 'I'm Rose, by the way. Walter's sister.'

George gaped at her in surprise. *Walter's sister*. Would there be no end to this man's relatives? First, he had no one, then he had a daughter, then another daughter and now here was a sister. What next? Was Yorkshire dotted with a whole tribe of Breckenridges?

Rose looked down at her outstretched hand and repeated, 'Yes. I'm Walter's sister. Aye, I don't doubt he's kept quiet about me. We were never close. Probably a bit too alike, if the truth be told, and we used to strike sparks off each other even when we were young... Still do, really, but there it is. I'm stopping for a while, with Arthur. Between homes, so to speak. It isn't easy, but we're putting up with it.'

George remembered his manners and shook hands with Rose. 'I'm George Montague. Pleased to meet you, Rose. Is Walter in? Only I wanted a word.'

'Aye, he's in. That daft dog of his – Elvis. *Elvis*,' she said in disgust. 'What a name for a dog. We have a dog, me 'n' Arthur. Proper dog, too. With a proper name: Jack. *Elvis*... Any road, yon Elvis got a thorn in his paw and Walter's doctoring him inside.'

When he'd finished helping Rose load the lorry, George went inside to find Walter. When Walter heard what George had just been doing, he was cross. 'Bloody cheek of her. She's got that great hulk of hers swanning about the place, mooning over his alpacas all day, fussing over 'em. If he ain't brushing their coats, he's cleaning their feet. I tell you what, George, he damned near brushes every blade of grass in that field for 'em. And as for them peacocks...'

George didn't want to cause trouble between Walter and Rose. 'I didn't mind helping her, Walter, honestly. It didn't take long and I'm none the worse for it.'

'Hmph,' Walter grunted. 'Just as well. It's good to see you, lad. Take a seat. There's tea on the go if you'd like a cup and Ellie's made a chocolate cake. I'm sure we can tempt you to a bit.'

George sat down at the kitchen table. 'I'd love a cup of tea. How's Elvis, by the way? Rose said he'd picked up a thorn in his paw.'

'Daft dog,' Walter said fondly. 'There's not a thorn bush for miles – I'm all drystone walls here – and he comes home with a thorn. He's all right now. Feeling a bit sorry for himself in his basket in the back porch. I daresay the sight of a good dinner later will make him forget all about it.'

George sighed longingly. 'Ooh, a good dinner. What wouldn't I give for one of those.'

Walter looked at him. 'Since when? Penny's a good cook, as I recall, lad. She helped me out many a time at Café Paradise. Her liver and onions…'

Both men were silent for a few moments, contemplating happy memories.

'Pork chops and crispy roast potatoes,' George said dreamily.

'Does she still make fantastic fish and chips?' asked Walter. 'Nobody ever made 'em like your Penny.'

'She does. She *did*,' amended George.

'What do you mean, "did"?'

'She's not speaking to me, Walter, that's what I mean. I took her to Scotland for an anniversary treat and now she's not speaking, never mind cooking. I haven't seen her for quite a few days but I can bet my last five-pound note there'll be no dinner for me when I get home tonight. That's why I'm here, really.'

'Well, we're feeding Rose and Arthur, so what's one more tonight? I'm sure we can make it stretch, George.'

'No, no,' protested George. 'I didn't mean that I wanted dinner. I've come for advice, Walter. You know Penny really well. I thought you might have some fresh ideas as to how to handle the situation.'

Walter brought the tea to the table and cut them wedges of Ellie's chocolate cake. 'I haven't a clue what you're on about, lad. Get that down you and then tell me all about it. You haven't been putting them frocks on again, have you?'

With a mouthful of cake, George indicated that this was not the problem.

\*\*\*

The teapot was emptied and George had eaten most of Ellie's cake. He sat back in his chair, looking a lot brighter. Walter sat quietly, considering the story George had just related to him.

'If I never see another plastic sandwich or mug of watery coffee it won't be too soon,' said George.

'By my reckoning, lad, you should be on bread and water for the next month at least,' Walter said tartly. 'And you probably will be.'

George gaped at him. 'Is it that bad?'

'Aye. Even for you, George Montague, a carry-on like that takes the biscuit. I know I can't talk; I'm not the world's expert on women. Let's face it, who is? There can't be a man born who understands what goes on in a woman's head, but we have to try, lad. And that applies to you too.'

'It wasn't a carry-on,' George protested. 'I planned it specially for our anniversary. I thought she'd love it. No more motorbikes, just like I promised. A camper van! What could be better? I thought she'd be thrilled.'

Walter shook his head pityingly. 'I can't believe I'm hearing this from you, George. Don't you ever learn? What woman on her anniversary wants to be dragged to the middle of nowhere, offered accommodation in an old caravan and then shown a beat-up ambulance that you hope might one day pass as a camper van as her present? As they say in Yorkshire, lad, tha's lost the plot.'

George looked miserable. 'Maybe I got the timing wrong, I'll grant you that. But I bet when I've done it up she'll see things differently.'

'Maybe,' Walter agreed. 'But in the meantime, you have to go home and get her talking again and hopefully cooking, or you'll be doing the rounds of the local takeaways for some time to come.'

'What can I do to put things right between us, Walter?'

'First of all, grovel a lot. You've debt to pay off. And then, if she didn't like the ambulance as her anniversary present, George, you have to get her a proper present, one that will really impress her and get you back in her good books.'

George could see the wisdom of this idea. 'What kind of present? Women are so difficult to buy for. Whatever I get it's going to be wrong.'

Walter shook his head. 'Piece of good jewellery, George. It never fails. Aye, it might cost you a bit, but think of it as an investment in your future if you want to stay married to Penny. Better still, think of her fish and chips and them scones of hers… Then you'll have to fork out for something special. A peace offering, and an impressive one at that.' He sat back in his chair.

'She'll be thinking you're going to slink in the door with a bunch of supermarket flowers in your hand and she'll be ready to tell you just where you can put them. Show her you're made of something better, lad. A right good piece of jewellery … a brooch, a ring, or expensive earrings – them dangly ones she likes. That'll win the day.'

George smacked the table hard. 'Walter, you're a genius. You're right. It'll cost me an arm and a leg but she's worth every pound of it. A woman who can make toad-in-the-hole like she does…'

He got up, eager now to be off and to find something before the shops closed. He shook Walter firmly by the hand, making him wince. 'I knew you'd know what to do. Thanks, Walter. I owe you. Next time that sister of yours wants a hand with her stuff, just call on me.'

'I will, George.' Walter saw him to the door. 'Next time, I hope it's to send them back to Allsthwaite.'

He shut the door on George and turned back into the kitchen. Elvis padded through from the back porch. It was getting near to his dinnertime and he didn't want Walter to forget about him. Walter stroked the dog absently. 'A man can dream, I suppose.'

\*\*\*

George had found an exquisite pair of diamond earrings in a York jeweller's shop. Carrying the beautifully wrapped present in its presentation box along with a bunch of flowers he had found at the market, he opened the house door and called out cheerily,

'Penny … Penny, darling, I'm home.'

Cautiously he walked through the hall and opened the kitchen door. A delicious smell of Penny's signature beef casserole wafted out to him. His mouth watered. The kitchen was empty. There was no sign of his wife. Leaving his gifts on the table he went back out to the hallway and called up the stairs, 'Penny … Penny darling, I'm home. Are you up there?'

Penny appeared at the top of the stairs. 'Oh, it's you.'

She stood looking down at him. George looked up at her. This was not a promising start. 'Please, Penny, come downstairs. I know we've had our problems and I want to make things up to you. Please come down,' he repeated. 'I've brought you a present.'

'Huh.' Penny tossed her head. 'A present… I know what that will be, George Montague. A bunch of supermarket flowers, if I know you. Well, I'm not coming down for them.'

She was about to turn away.

'No, listen, Penny. It's not flowers. Well, it is, but they're just by the by. I've got you a proper present. Come and at least see it, love. I think you'll like it,' he added coaxingly.

'Oh yeah,' Penny said drily. 'Like you thought I'd like your ambulance as an anniversary present. That kind of like, is it?'

'No. This time, you really will like it. Please come down.'

With a reluctant air, Penny descended the stairs and followed George into the kitchen. She saw the bunch of flowers on the table and raised her eyebrows, but made no comment.

George picked up the gift box and solemnly presented Penny with it.

'Happy anniversary, Penny, love. I'm an idiot. This is what I should have got for you last week. Please forgive me and accept this gift. I hope it reflects more truly your real worth to me.'

Walter would be proud of him.

He watched as Penny slowly opened the little parcel. Her eyes widened in astonishment as she took out the lovely diamond earrings. 'They're beautiful,' she breathed. 'However did you think to get them…?'

She brushed past him and out to the mirror in the hall to try them on. She sighed with pleasure as she contemplated her reflection. 'Fabulous. George, you're forgiven.'

George breathed a sigh of relief. Maybe he'd get to share that beef casserole tonight. And making up could be fun too … He made to take her in his arms but she took a step back. 'You're forgiven, but… That ambulance thing … I take it you've still got it?

'What about it?'

'It's not living on the drive, George. If you insist on keeping it, you'll have to find a garage for it. I'm not trying to get past that thing every day. It's too big. And anyway, I've told you, it'll never make a camper. And, even if it did, I'm too old for all that carry-on. What's wrong with a nice hotel?'

Dangerous ground when he'd only just got home. George decided to give in gracefully for tonight. 'I'll find a garage for it, love, and work on it. You'll see; you'll feel quite differently by the time you see it again.'

'No, I won't.' Penny turned to admire herself in the mirror again. 'It's casserole for dinner, George. Perhaps you'd like some.'

George shook his head. Walter was right. There was no fathoming women.

# CHAPTER 4

Kate Peterson moved restlessly on the sofa. 'I need a hot drink,' she said to Stan.

'Hot chocolate and…' She thought for a moment. 'Yes, a banana.'

Stan sighed. Not again. He'd heard of women developing odd fancies during pregnancy and his lovely wife had certainly found some strange ones. He got up and made them both a drink and brought the tray into the sitting room, along with a banana.

'One won't do. I need two, at least,' Kate said, dunking the banana into the chocolate. 'You should have one, Stan. They're very good for you. Full of minerals and potassium, or something like that.'

'Not just now, thank you,' Stan said. 'The chocolate will do me.'

He used to quite like bananas but once Kate had got over her morning sickness, she'd gone overboard for bananas in a big way. Many more of them and he wouldn't need to drive to work anymore; he could swing there through the trees.

'Have you any houses lined up to look at tomorrow?' Kate unzipped another banana and began dunking it in her drink.

Stan watched her and wondered if they were having a baby or if a little chimp would come out, probably clutching a banana.

'Actually, I've some houses to view in the morning. So don't worry, my love. We shall soon have a lovely new roof over our heads in time for the baby's arrival.'

'You're not thinking of buying anything?' she asked cautiously.

'You know I'm at the Historical Trust tomorrow; it's the big meeting about the new Ebacorum site. The funding's in place now and the trust's going ahead with the purchase of the land. And Friday I'm at Café Paradise. Jackie wants to steam ahead with the purchase of the building next door and needs time to go through the paperwork and do some planning.'

Stan yawned.

'I think I'm ready for bed. No, I'm not going to buy anything. As I said, I just want to have a preliminary look at some places and if they look promising I'll take you to see them. You'll always have the last word on our new home, Kate, so don't worry. Looking costs nothing, as my old mother used to say.'

'Your "old mother" says a lot of things, Stanley darling, and they mostly centre around that fat old poodle of hers. I find it hard to believe she ever said anything as sensible as that,' Kate retorted. 'All the same, can't you delay it until another day when I can come with you?'

'And when is that going to be?' demanded Stan. 'Between the Historical Trust, Café Paradise and antenatal classes, your time is pretty much accounted for. I don't know where you get the energy from.'

Kate smiled serenely and stroked her bump. 'Must be all those bananas.'

'Bah,' said Stan in disgust. 'One way or another I'll find us a house and I guarantee you'll love it.'

Kate loved her husband dearly but he was known for his reckless streak. Still, she comforted herself, he wouldn't buy anything without her.

\*\*\*

Stan spent a busy morning viewing three properties in the York area, none of which he deemed suitable – and he was quite sure Kate wouldn't like them either. Feeling a little glum, he headed back home for lunch and a further study of the properties on the Internet. Time was going by too quickly. They loved their little house in Park Street but needed more space now a baby was on the way.

He found an old house registered with a local agent that stirred his interest. It was in the village of Dunnington, just outside of York, and near enough to their work at the Historical Trust and family and friends. They didn't want to move away from their support network at this time in their lives.

Stan had been appointed Education Officer at the York Historical Trust, which was building a new Roman model site in the city. He had at least three months before taking up his duties and was meant to be working from home, constructing educational packages for school visits and adult tours of the new site. But the pressing need for a new home took his attention away from his work.

He rang the estate agents advertising the property and made an appointment to view it that afternoon.

\*\*\*

Stan drove into the wide driveway of Beech Cottage and stopped the car. He got out and crunched over the fine gravel as he moved back towards the gateway to survey the property properly.

It was an old, two-storeyed stone house that had once been very handsome but was now in need of a lot of renovation. Stan could see why the guide price was quite low. Blistered paint was peeling off rotting window frames and sills and old iron pipes and guttering hung off the walls, their ties long ago rusted away. In its favour, the roof looked in good condition. The red pantiles were well secured in close rows, with new cement down the roof ridges.

Another car swung into the driveway and parked beside

Stan. A lady got out and smiled at him.

'Mr Peterson? Hello, I'm Julie Smeaton from Brammell and Simons. How do you do?'

Stan shook her outstretched hand.

'Very well thank you, Miss Smeaton.' He looked towards Beech Cottage. 'This looks an interesting place.'

Julie Smeaton nodded in agreement.

'It is. It's a beautiful old house and just needs someone to give it some loving care to bring it back to life as a family home. I'll fill you in on the background before we go in and meet Mrs Simpson. It's rather sad. She's a very elderly lady and quite frail now. She was widowed some years ago but had her son here to look after her and then, out of the blue, he was killed in a car crash. She has been living here on her own for the last few years but, as you can see, it's all got beyond her now. She would like to go into residential care, have some company and be looked after.'

Stan's soft heart was touched at this sad tale. 'Life can be cruel sometimes,' he said. 'I can see why she would like to move. Probably far too many memories here for her now.'

'Yes,' Julie agreed. 'The sooner we sell her property, the better. Well now,' she smiled up at Stan, 'shall we go in? Mrs Simpson likes us to conduct the viewings as she's not up to doing them herself. We can start on the ground floor and work our way round and then out into the back garden.'

Leading the way, Julie took them through the wooden front door into a large hallway. Rooms led off to right and left and there was a door at the end of the hall, leading to the kitchen, pantry and downstairs lavatory, if Stan remembered from his study of the floor plan on the Internet.

Stan fell in love with Beech Cottage from the moment he entered the front door. The large sitting room led off one side of the hall and a separate dining room off the other. He felt there was space to breathe in this house – for children to play, to have their own space and pursue their interests.

The upstairs did not disappoint. Four large airy bedrooms

and an old-fashioned bathroom delighted him. To his surprise, Mrs Simpson was sitting in a deep armchair beside her bed, rugs wrapped around her shoulders and legs. Seeing Stan and Julie, she struggled to get up out of her chair.

'No, please.' Stan rushed forward to take her hands. 'Please don't get up for us, Mrs Simpson. He helped her back into her chair and sat on the bed beside her.

'You have a truly beautiful home here,' he said. 'I absolutely love it.'

A smile lit Mrs Simpson's lined face.

'I'm so glad you've come. I knew the right person would come along and love it as much as we did. You would be very happy here, young man. I can tell just by looking at you … you're the one we've been waiting for.'

Stan flushed with pleasure.

'May I bring my wife to meet you soon?' he asked.

'As soon as you like.' She gestured around the room. 'The house is yours and I will be glad to give up responsibility for it now and move to The Elms.' She sat back in her chair, looking tired.

'I think we'll leave Mrs Simpson in peace, Mr Peterson,' Julie said and headed for the door.

Outside they explored the large overgrown garden and found a lovely old summerhouse almost hidden by ivy.

'It's like that film, *The Secret Garden*,' said Stan, gazing at what had once been herbaceous borders, now grown wild and filled with weeds. 'I bet it's a real haven for wildlife. I'd like to keep that going, you know. Log piles for the hedgehogs and beeboxes; that kind of thing. It would be a fantastic garden for kids.'

Julie looked at him speculatively. 'Are you really interested in the property then, Mr Peterson?'

'Yes, 100 percent. I told Mrs Simpson, didn't I, sort of?'

'I certainly got that impression; I just wanted to make sure. Of course, you'll need a second viewing with your wife.'

'She'll love it as much as I do,' Stan said confidently. 'I'll bring her as soon as I can. I'll let you know tomorrow.'

Stan drove home in buoyant mood. He couldn't wait to tell Kate about Beech Cottage and to take her there. Their dream home at last.

\*\*\*

'You told her what? That we'd have it – and I haven't even seen it yet? Stan, you promised. "You'll always have the last word … looking costs nothing."' Kate repeated Stan's words back to him.

She glared at the computer screen. 'This place will cost us the shirts off our backs if the pictures here are anything to go by. Look at the windows – the gutterings and downpipes are hanging off, not to mention the state of the front door. The wood is so rotten you can see daylight through the planks. And you told her we'd have it?' She shook her head in disbelief.

'Look beyond that, Kate,' Stan insisted. 'Take a tour of the rooms. They're beautiful, well-proportioned, full of light, and there are cupboards everywhere. You don't get those in modern houses.'

'What do I want a lot of cupboards for? They just accumulate junk.'

Stan sighed. 'We're having children. They'll have toys, hobbies, stuff. There's space to put everything without tripping over toys at every turn.'

As Stan suggested, Kate had been taking a tour of the rooms. She came to the kitchen and let out a shriek.

'Look at the state of that. That's an Aga, isn't it? Well, I think it is. I can hardly tell for all the rust. What would we do with that?'

'Clean it up, get the Aga man out to service it and use it again,' Stan said promptly.

'There're no cupboards. There's no proper kitchen at all. Is that it? That table?'

'That is an amazing table, Kate,' Stan defended it. 'Seven feet long … the heart of the kitchen. Imagine the meals prepared on that and all the fun and chat we could have around it.'

'As long as you're preparing them,' Kate snapped. 'It's like a time capsule. Nothing's been changed since the last century.'

'That's not a bad thing.' Stan was still upbeat. 'It's a really solid house. Yes, it needs some TLC … but come and see it, Kate. You'll fall in love with it, just like I did.'

Kate continued to study the pictures on the screen.

'Even the estate agents admit it's a "project", and for them to say that is like drawing teeth from a crocodile so it must be in a bad state.'

'It's not a bad state,' Stan insisted. 'It's a wonderful opportunity for us. I can do a lot of the work myself. We don't need professionals for most of it – in fact, maybe not for any of it. I'm very handy on the DIY front.'

Kate stared at him long and hard.

'Oh yeah? Since when? I remember your last efforts at DIY and then I called the plumber in.'

Stan ignored this jibe. 'I've promised her, Kate,' he went on. 'Mrs Simpson, the little old lady who's selling the place. I kind of told her we'd buy it and then she can go into the old folks' home that she's got her eye on. She's lost her husband *and* her son. We can't let her down now.'

'Oh, *we* can't! It's *we* now, is it? I haven't even clapped eyes on the place and I'm going to be the villain if I turn it down.'

'I know you, my beautiful Kate. You won't turn it down,' Stan said confidently. 'It just requires a little imagination and vision and you'll see how it can be. In a year's time, you'll thank me for this.'

'It's a money pit, Stan. If we take that place on, in a year's time we could be in the bankruptcy courts, probably camping out there with a leaking roof over our heads and cooking on the barbecue.'

\*\*\*

'*Imbécile, imbécile!*' Henri Beauparient swept Genevieve out of the Café Paradise kitchen and slammed the door behind her.

Jackie looked up from the coffee counter and rolled her eyes. 'What have you done now?'

Genevieve bit her lip. 'I spoilt the béchamel sauce and now it's burnt. I should have kept stirring it, but — I only turned my back on it for a few seconds…'

Jackie shook her head. Most of the time Henri and Genevieve got on well. After much patient teaching, the ditzy Genevieve was beginning to settle down and show signs of becoming a proficient cook but occasionally her concentration slipped and these mini disasters occurred in the kitchen. To a Frenchman such as Henri, spoiling good food was sacrilegious.

'The day hasn't got going yet, Genevieve. Henri will calm down. Go and check the tables and the big dresser for cutlery and supplies.'

Eight-thirty in the morning and all the day to go at. Jackie sighed and hoped Genevieve got a grip on things soon.

Kate came into the café, tying her apron. She drifted past Jackie and gazed silently out of the window facing onto the street.

Jackie looked at her. 'Morning, Kate.'

'Mm? What?' Kate looked around. 'Oh. Yes. Good morning, Jackie. Oh, Café Paradise,' she said in surprise.

'And where did you think you were? Barbados? St Lucia? How about Florida?'

'Florida?' Kate repeated blankly.

What on earth was going on this morning? Kate was in a daze. For once, Genevieve seemed the normal one among them. They couldn't start the working day like this.

'Genevieve,' Jackie summoned her from checking the tables. 'It's time to open the café and I'm going to leave you in charge of this counter for a while. I need to talk with Kate in the staffroom. Now I want you to really concentrate and get the orders right, or Monsieur Henri won't be the only one shouting "Imbecile" at you.'

Genevieve stared at her. 'I always concentrate. You can leave it to me,' she said confidently. 'I'm really good at this now.'

In spite of her misgivings, Jackie left Genevieve to it and swept Kate off to the staffroom. She made them mugs of strong tea and set the tray down on the table.

'Help yourself,' she said. 'Now, I can see we have certain problems before us and if Café Paradise is going to function at all today then you need to get things off your chest. I've already had Henri throwing a wobbly in the kitchen, so what now Kate? What's up? Spill the beans.'

As she sipped the hot tea, Kate slowly came out of her daze. 'Stan's gone and bought us a house that's a wreck and he thinks he's good at DIY and can do it up himself. But he's not, so I don't know what we'll end up with. What kind of a home is our baby going to end up with?'

Jackie's jaw dropped and silence filled the room. Quickly she recovered herself. 'How has he bought a house? Weren't you with him at the time?' she demanded.

'I was at a meeting with the Historical Trust,' Kate said miserably. 'He went on his own and it's a little frail old lady and he promised her he'd buy it. He took me to see it yesterday and I met her and she was so happy we were buying it and it would be a family home again. How could I say no? And Stan is so full of plans and dreams…' The tears flowed.

Jackie passed her a handful of tissues and sighed to herself. 'Another fine day at Café Paradise. I thought I had problems with Barney over my expansion plans. A piece of cake compared with this.' She hugged her friend.

'Barney and Walter are cross with me and you are cross with Stan and Dad's cross with his sister, Rose, and all the mess she's got herself into, so everyone's cross with everyone else. Maybe we're over the worst and it can only get better from here on in. Believe me. Dry your eyes and come into the café when you're ready. I'd better get back. I've left Genevieve alone for long enough.'

And so she had. At the coffee counter, a red-faced Genevieve was engulfed by a cloud of steam and hot milk as it overflowed from the drip trays on the machine.

'It's got stuck,' she shouted above the hiss of the steam as Jackie raced to hit the switch to turn the whole thing off.

'Then you turn it off!'

God help us all. Did this girl never think? Any more of this and Jackie would be lucky not to drop the twins then and there.

# CHAPTER 5

'There's a gentleman on line one for you, Mr Young. He says he's a friend of yours and it's personal. Shall I put him through?'

Tom Young kept his personal life well away from the office these days, although that little beauty out in reception was proving a sore temptation. As he reached to take the call, he wondered for how long he could keep his hands off her. True, she was a bit on the young side, but if he wasn't much mistaken he'd picked up the vibes. Maybe after a slow, seductive dinner she wouldn't be calling him Mr Young again.

Reluctantly, he let the image go and took the call. Only one person called him on the prearranged 'personal' call.

'Hello?'

A deep voice came over the phone. 'Tom … I thought it would be good to meet up sometime soon.'

There was no need to ask questions. If this man requested a meeting, he must have news that would interest Tom.

'Yes, all right. When and where? I know you're a busy man. You name it.'

'Come up to town tomorrow.' He didn't elaborate. Tom knew 'town' meant London, and he knew where they would meet.

'See you then.' They terminated the call.

Tom leant back in his black leather chair and put his feet up on the desk. The call intrigued him. There must be some new project afoot, or some new information had come to light that would be of interest to him. Whatever it was, Tom was ready for it. Life had been a little dull in the last few months. Since the debacle of letting Annabel Lewis-Langley slip through his fingers, no rich pickings had presented themselves.

His jaw tightened and a deep scowl furrowed his forehead as he recalled the deeply unpleasant scene that had taken place in his office some months previously. Walter Breckenridge and that mangy sheepdog of his, along with the detestable Barney Anderson, had forced him to give up his precious file on Annabel…

Tom could feel his rage rising afresh at the memory. Annabel could have been a very nice blackmail earner for him if they hadn't stuck their outsize noses into his affairs. But he could wait, he could wait. He was used to playing the long game. They would slip up one day, those holier-than-thou Andersons and their precious Café Paradise and, when they did, he would be there to grind them into the dust.

Tom smiled with pleasure. His feet jiggled on his desk as he imagined grinding first Barney and then Walter under his feet. After some minutes of this indulgence, he withdrew his feet from his desk and sat up to consult his diary for the rest of the day. It would be better to leave for London tonight. He could not afford to be late for his meeting in the morning.

Glancing down at his book, he pursed his lips regretfully. He's forgotten about his date with the lovely Jennifer. Now that was a shame. She was a ripe beauty and any man would be proud to be seen with her on his arm. True, she would never win *Mastermind*, but her long, long legs went all the way up, and talk about sensational between the sheets. Where did she learn…?

\*\*\*

Coming out of Oxford Circus Tube station, Tom Young made his way through the rushhour crowds. London was cold and grey in the watery September light. He pulled the brim of his hat well down to deflect the rain that was beginning to fall and wrapped his coat tightly round him. He considered hailing a cab but immediately rejected the idea. There must be no record of his visit today.

After twenty minutes' brisk walking, he turned into a side street and stopped at a plain wooden door. Speaking his name into the entryphone, he gained admittance to what looked like an artisan's workshop.

Long wooden tables lined three sides of the room, stacked with picture frames of all sizes. Completed canvases were propped against the tables and a half-finished oil painting stood on an easel by the large window that took up most of the fourth wall.

Three well-dressed men sat around an ancient butcher's block, the deep indents made by years of razor-sharp meat cleavers thrown into sharp relief by the multitude of paint splatters embedded in the cuts.

Tom removed his coat and hat and took his place on the chair that was ready for him, facing the men. It was reminiscent of all the most difficult school exam interviews he had ever had.

'Good morning, gentlemen.' He was startled by the nervous tremor in his voice. He tweaked his tie and sat up straight. This was no time for nerves to get in the way; he was dealing with the big boys. Creaming off a little 'commission' from the Trades Council was one thing, but these men dealt only with big league stuff. These three men, through a labyrinth of companies, controlled most of the building and civil engineering projects in the world. Tom had swum into their sphere of influence by accident some years ago and knew how far their reach stretched.

The tall man in the middle of the group leant forward, resting his hands on the butcher's block. 'We have a job for you.' His clear grey eyes stared intently into Tom's face. 'Bookwood Developments bought some land just outside Allsthwaite village a few years ago and the time is now right to think about building on it. We have plans for three hundred starter homes.

Naturally there will be objections, and our policy is to cut the ringleaders off at source.'

'Allsthwaite.' Tom swallowed hard. Three hundred starter homes would double the size of the village. The residents would certainly mount a campaign.

The man with grey eyes continued to stare at Tom, quietly assessing him. Under his scrutiny, Tom felt like a specimen under the microscope. He kept his nerve and waited.

'We need the leader of the council onside and the leading objectors *persuaded* to withdraw from the fight.'

Tom saw their drift. 'In my experience carrots are more productive than sticks where councils are concerned.'

'Exactly.' Grey Eyes looked around the room for a few moments. 'City mayors are the big thing nowadays,' he mused. 'I'm sure your council leader wouldn't say no to funding for his mayoral campaign in the future. Think of the power he'd have. And how they all love to think they have power, poor things. And were he to support our planning application and persuade his colleagues on the council to do likewise… Well … the sky's the limit.'

Tom nodded. This would be his task, but what about the objectors to the scheme?

'It's a village, Tom. There's always far more going on in them than you'll ever find in the towns. The objectors will have a past. They didn't just land up in Allsthwaite all squeaky-clean. Scrape the surface and you'll turn up the dirt on them.'

He pointed directly at Tom. 'This application must be granted, Tom. That land cost us a lot of money and we want a good return on our investment. We're relying on you. You've done good work for us in the past and you're perfectly placed for this project. Don't let us down. Don't be a weak link in the chain.'

'And if I succeed?'

'We...ll,' Grey Eyes drawled, sitting back in his chair and idly fingering the deep cuts in the butcher's block. 'Put it this way: I don't think you would need to worry about earning your living from the Trades Council anymore.'

Out in the cold street again, Tom made his way thoughtfully back to the tube station. He had a lot to think about. If he got this one right, he could kiss goodbye to the Trades Council and claustrophobic York city forever. He fancied the Cayman Islands or Barbados … and the girls there…

He had to get to work as soon as he got back to York. He decided to make contact with Matt Carstairs. Matt was a private detective working to a hair's breadth of the right side of the law. If there was dirt to be dished on anyone in Allsthwaite, Matt was the man to find it.

# CHAPTER 6

Samson, the black cat Jackie had inherited from her mother, had an ambivalent relationship with the log fire. The world would be a quiet, warm place, a cat's delight to stretch out and snooze in front of, then suddenly that hot thing in the wall would erupt and flames and sparks shoot out of it, sending him flying.

Jackie was sitting by the fire, the sale documents for the new half of the café on her lap. She wanted to go through the details tonight, even though Barney's firm would be handling the transaction. The print blurred on the page and her head nodded as sleep beckoned.

The log fire crackled fiercely in the grate, sending hot orange sparks showering against the fireguard. Samson yowled and leapt from his place in front of the fire, landing in one bound on Jackie's lap, hissing in fright, his fur standing on end.

Jackie yelped as Samson's claws dug hard into her swollen stomach. 'Bloody cat! Mind the twins. They don't need you bashing them on the head.'

Barney jumped up and grabbed Samson. 'He's going to have to learn to behave when the twins arrive, or he'll be finding a new home.'

Samson stalked out of the sitting room. Twins, indeed. He didn't know what they were but he wasn't leaving home for them. He was here first. In the good old times, it had been just him and Marilyn: fresh chicken, salmon, trout and all sorts of fishy delights came his way. These days he had to share with Jackie and Barney. He was lucky if he got a dish of Kattibix and the occasional leftover morsel of chicken.

Recently there had been talk of these twin things. It didn't sound good to Samson. He would have to go and visit his friend Fergus down the road; maybe he knew something about twins.

Jackie put the sale documents down on the coffee table. 'I had a visit from Dad a few days ago.'

'Nice for you,' Barney said shortly. He was still smarting over Jackie's decision to extend the café and take on major renovations so near the end of her pregnancy.

'Well, it wasn't. He only came to harangue me about my expansion plans. I suppose you sent him?'

Barney's blue eyes widened. 'I don't think anyone *sends* Walter anywhere. He's his own man. I expect he was glad to have an hour away from Claygate with all that's going on there now that Rose and Arthur have invaded them. No doubt he's as concerned about your plans as the rest of us, not that you'll take any notice. You've always been very *independent*.'

Picking up the mild displeasure in his voice, Jackie glanced over at him. Barney presented a bland face. Jackie sighed. 'Look, can we park this argument? As I pointed out to my dear father, no one is expecting you to curtail your business activities when these babies arrive. As we are now in the twenty-first century, although between you two sometimes I wonder if I have landed there, then fair shares all round. I'm going to work at what I love just as much as you are and we'll raise the children between us.'

She was so exasperating, so stubborn. Strong-willed, opinionated. From the moment they had met, Barney had fallen in love with her in spite of these qualities, or maybe because of them. He looked across at her, her fair hair framing her heart-shaped face, violet eyes holding his blue ones challengingly, and fell in love with her all over again.

Pulling her up from the chair, he folded her in his arms and kissed her gently.

'Anything you say, Mrs Anderson, anything you say. We're quite a team already and no doubt we'll manage somehow.' He pushed her away. 'Come on, it's time we went to bed. You're exhausted. Leave the café stuff for me to go through tomorrow. You need your rest.'

Jackie smiled up at him, relieved they were back on good terms. She was indeed very tired but her mind was still preoccupied with the new project. Ever since she had decided to purchase the next-door property, finding a builder to undertake the work had loomed large in her mind. As they made their way upstairs to bed, Jackie voiced her worries to Barney.

'I know Old Mother Stampwick did a good job of renovating Café Paradise in the end, but he drove me up the wall. "It is as it is, Miss Dalrymple-Jones." If he said it once a day, he said it ninety-nine times. He had such a gift for stating the totally obvious that was staring us all in the face. And, as I recall, if it hadn't have been for Dad keeping tabs on him, he would have put the coffee counter in the wrong place, even though we had discussed siting it well away from the doorway.'

She paused at the top of the stairs. 'What do you think, Barney? Is it "better the devil we know"?'

Barney took her hand and led her into their bedroom, pulling her down onto the bed beside him. Putting his arm around her, he held her close.

'I think I can go a lot better than Old Mother Stampwick for you, my darling.'

Jackie turned in his arms and looked at him in surprise.

'You can? And who would you have up your sleeve? Not one of your lame-duck bods looking to earn a bob or two? I'm not having them foisted on to me.'

Barney shook his head. Why did she always have to jump to the wrong conclusions? It had blighted the start of their relationship and here she was, off on one again.

'Nothing to do with lame ducks,' he insisted. 'I have a friend, Brian, who's a builder, engineer, electrician, plumber … you name it and he can do it. He would be perfect for you.'

'How come I haven't heard of this Brian before?' Jackie asked suspiciously.

'You have, you've just forgotten. Brian Box. He's a pal of mine. He came to our wedding.'

Jackie looked askance at Barney.

'He did,' Barney protested. He grinned at Jackie. 'I expect you were so loved-up that day it's all a blur and you just don't remember meeting Brian. He's a quiet bloke, doesn't put himself forward, but you were introduced.'

'Where do you know him from? We've been married for quite a while and I've never even heard you mention him before now.'

'Not needed to.' Barney shrugged. 'Good friends are like that, aren't they? You don't see them for a year or two and then you meet up and take up where you left off. Brian's been working in France for the last year, virtually rebuilding a house for an English couple out there. Now it's finished and he's come home.'

'And where's home?'

'Cumbria mainly, but he goes where the work is. When my father kept a boat on Lake Windermere, Brian was working up there and we met up in the pub and became friends. Brian's a properly trained engineer and often made parts for old boats that weren't easily obtained any more. Honestly Jackie, he's a whizz. What a craftsman. Whatever he turns his hand to is always a first-class job. You'd never get better.'

Barney kissed Jackie lightly and got up to head off for the bathroom.

'Brian's your man, Jackie,' he said confidently. 'Just for once, take my advice and let me get in touch with him.'

Jackie lay on the bed, stroking her restless babies thoughtfully. Barney was a very good judge of character, she knew that. But taking on an unknown for such a big project? She wasn't sure.

After a while Barney reappeared, scrubbed and smelling deliciously fresh.

'Why don't I invite him down and you can meet him and see for yourself?' he suggested.

It sounded like a plan. She wasn't committing to anything and it would be good to meet the mysterious Brian from Cumbria. If he was half as good as Barney built him up to be, Café Paradise would be winning renovation awards all over the place.

# CHAPTER 7

The weather favoured Ellie and Walter at Easingwold market. Crowds of people browsed the stalls in the autumn sunshine, some starting a weekend break by leisurely visiting a Friday market – others taking a longer holiday, taking advantage of the unusually fine weather.

Ellie's stall of cheeses, homemade jams and chutneys proved popular and she and Walter were kept busy all day. It was pleasant work. Ellie had built up a regular group of customers who were fast becoming friends and enjoyed chatting with her as they made their purchases. She was getting to know all about their families, the ups and downs of relationships, health problems and all the minutiae that made up the threads of their lives.

Alongside her regular customers, the holidaymakers crowded around the stall, eager to take home some produce made in Yorkshire. As the other stallholders began to pack up at the end of the trading day, Ellie stood back and looked at her empty stall with satisfaction.

'I think that's been the best day ever,' she said, smiling at Walter.

'Couldn't be any better, could it?' agreed Walter. 'You've nowt left on the stall.'

Ellie laughed. 'Long may it last. It's a long winter but at least we've always got the Shambles Market in the centre of York. My customers there are fantastic. I can rely on them coming every week and I know whatever I take there will fly off the stall in no time.'

Walter nodded agreement and went to open the van doors. 'Aye, we'll make hay while the sun shines, lass. In the meantime, we'd best get packed up and get back to Claygate. See what those two beauties have been up to today.'

'Nothing, I hope.' Ellie said anxiously. 'I'm hoping Rose and Arthur might have tidied up in the barn a bit. I did ask her to, as I'm having difficulty getting to the freezer in there. There's that much furniture in the way.'

Walter looked grim. 'My sister was never organised, Ellie. She makes me look like Mr Tidy on a good day, so I wouldn't get your hopes up. If she hasn't done anything about it when we get back, I'll have words with her.'

Ellie sighed. That's what she was afraid of. Walter and Rose had 'words' all the time. In a lot of ways, they were very alike and the sparks very quickly flew between them, each convinced they were in the right. All the 'words' achieved were a lot of hot air and anger, as far as she could see.

'Don't bother, Walter. I'll speak to her later if things are just the same.'

'Hmph.' Walter began loading the van with Ellie's snowy-white cloths and the used sample dishes from the stall. 'I know one thing, Ellie,' he paused, holding a box to his chest. 'We can't go on like this. Something has to be done and I'm going to do that something. I know just the man to help me do it.'

'And what and who would that be?'

Walter tapped the side of his nose. 'Least said, and all that. You just keep your powder dry and wait and see.'

Ellie had to be satisfied with that.

\*\*\*

Left behind at Claygate Farm, Rose and Arthur were also enjoying the autumn sunshine. Sitting on the bench outside the kitchen door, they drank the strong, sweet coffee they favoured, their dog, Jack, at their feet.

'What about them peacocks, then, Arthur?' Rose watched as the handsome male herded his plain, brown peahens down Walter's hay meadow. 'Do you know, they have a funny name for peacocks,' she mused.

Arthur looked at her. He never knew what Rose would come out with next.

'Go on, then.'

'They're a "muster", or "ostentation" of peacocks. I like the idea of an ostentation of peacocks. Cos they are, aren't they? Ostentatious. Don't know why we have 'em. *We're* anything but…'

'So, what about them?' Arthur tried to follow Rose's train of thought.

'Walter hates them; all that shrieking. It scares the hell out of Elvis. Don't know why. Our Jack's all right with them.'

'Our Jack's never known owt different.' Arthur turned his face up to the sunshine and ruminated for a few minutes. 'What they need is a home of their own, like they had at Allsthwaite.'

Rose looked at him in disbelief. 'Peacocks needing a home of their own…? Well, I'll be… Don't you think *we* need somewhere, Arthur? We can't stop with Ellie and Walter forever. My alpacas need more space and he's going to want his hayfield back in the spring. Besides which, there's no shelter for them there and if we get a bad winter, I'd have to bring them into the barn and then what would we do with our furniture? We can't take it into the farmhouse; there isn't room. We'll have to look about us and see if there's any other land we could rent, else it will be the end of everything,' she finished glumly.

'I could make them a large pen.'

'Not in Walter's best hayfield, you couldn't.'

'No, not the alpacas. The peacocks.'

Arthur looked down at Walter's fields sloping down towards the hills. 'Mebbe that one down there.' He nodded towards an empty field some distance away. 'They wouldn't disturb anyone down there; they can shriek to their heart's content. Well away from Elvis and the house. If that doesn't please Walter, then I don't know what will.'

Rose leant across and planted a kiss on his cheek. 'Genius, Arthur. Why didn't I think of that?' Taking his coffee cup, she stood up. 'Come on,' she said happily. 'You've got work to do.'

'Now?' said Arthur in dismay. 'I was enjoying a sit out here.'

'No time to sit. *We* might be homeless but our birds needn't be. You've a peacock shed to build.'

'What are you going to be doing? Aren't you going to help me?'

'You're a big lad, Arthur. I think I can leave it to you. I'm going indoors.'

'To do what?'

'I'm going to get a meal ready for Ellie and Walter coming home tonight. I haven't done any cooking since we've been here.'

'You can't cook, Rose,' Arthur pointed out. 'You hate cooking. Whatever you do, it always tastes the same. Like shoe leather, not that I've ever eaten it, but your dinners always tastes like shoe leather smells. Beats me how you do it.'

'I could be very hurt by those comments, Arthur Lightowler, but I'm not going to be. I will consider them unheard.'

Rose stomped off into the farmhouse.

'It'll be unheard, all right, lass,' he sighed to himself. 'Unheard *of* if you ever come up with a plate of recognisable food a man can enjoy. I wish Claygate was a bit nearer the chippy. It was a godsend in Allsthwaite. And what Ellie and Walter will make of it, I don't know.'

He got up from the seat and wandered off to see what Walter had around the farm to make peacock housing with. He found Walter's large shed, full of wood and netting, and fell on it with delight. Just what he needed, and he was sure Walter wouldn't mind if he helped himself to some of it. After all, it was in a good cause. If he could build the peacocks and peahens a home well away from the farmhouse, think how pleased Ellie and Walter would be – not to mention their precious Elvis.

Rooting around in another shed, he found tools and nails. Piling everything into a wheelbarrow, he set off for the field he had chosen. Once he got started, Arthur enjoyed working in the afternoon sunshine. He hummed happily as he put up the framework for the peacocks' new home. It was just as well Walter had plenty of wood, as they needed a very large run if they were going to be kept in for some time to come.

Arthur wasn't the only one humming along to their afternoon's work. Indoors, Rose was enjoying herself in Ellie's kitchen. Yesterday Ellie had brought home some fresh fish from the market and put it in the fridge for their Friday evening meal. Rose had taken note and decided to put on a surprise for them. Fish, chips and mushy peas, followed by apple tart and custard. What could be better?

It was just a question of getting everything together. Making a batter to fry the fish in was easy enough. She found Ellie's mixer and plundered her larder for a bottle of beer, flour and cornflour. She whizzed the ingredients around in a large mixing bowl a bit too enthusiastically; slivers of batter spun out of the bowl and splattered all over the countertops and up the kitchen windows.

Rose swiped at them with a cloth then got on with preparing the mushy peas. Fish and chips needed peas on the side. She found tins of marrowfat peas in the larder and popped them into a saucepan with some butter, salt and vinegar and left them to warm through whilst she went to fetch some apples from Ellie's freezer out in the barn. Coming out with a box under her arm, she saw Arthur working on the peacock house down in Walter's field. 'Cooee,' she called and waved.

Arthur looked up and grinned. 'Come and see it, Rose, it's coming on a treat.'

Rose laid the apples on the garden bench and made her way down to Arthur. She was amazed at how quickly he had got the framework up. It could be finished by the end of the day.

'Walter'll be right pleased when he sees this job, I reckon,' she commented. 'He can't complain now. No peacocks, no peahens and no mess about the farmyard. Everything's out of his way.'

She looked up at Arthur. 'What with you doing this and my meal tonight, he might consider letting us stay longer term. How about that for an idea, then?'

She considered her own suggestion for a moment. 'We all get along pretty well, don't we? And we're an extra pair of hands about the place. We could be a real help to them. I could do a lot of the cooking. If they think about it, it's win–win for all of us.'

Arthur looked down at Rose fondly. He loved her dearly, but the things she could talk herself into… Two women in a kitchen would never work for a start-off…

Rose cuts across his thoughts. 'Our hens are great layers. Ellie would have extra eggs to take to her markets, and think about our alpaca wool every year. With the money from that we can pay our way here…'

'Hold on, Rose.' Arthur temporised. 'Let's just see how we go in the next week or two, eh? It takes people time to get used to each other. Let's just see,' he repeated.

In his mind's eye, he conjured up images of some of the meals Rose had cooked at their smallholding at Allsthwaite and shuddered. Even the hens rejected the leftovers.

'Aye, mebbe. I'd best get on, anyway,' Rose said, turning away from him. 'That apple pie won't make itself.'

Arthur watched her walk back up the fields towards the farmhouse. God help us all if she was inflicting her apple pie on them. Last time she made one, he used the leftovers to fill some of the gaps in their drystone walls.

The smell of burning reached Rose as she entered the farmhouse. She rushed to pull the burnt-out saucepan off the stove. The handle was hot. She yelped in pain, dropped the pan and it fell to the floor, spilling the last of the burnt mush over Ellie's clean, scrubbed flagstones.

Dismayed at all the mess and this new delay, Rose set to and cleaned the floor and then pressed on with her dinner plans.

Somehow the pastry was made and potatoes peeled and cut for chips. By the time Ellie and Walter returned from Easingwold Market, she was ready for them.

Walter was first into the house. Taking his boots off in the back porch, he sniffed the air. What was that horrible smell? He spotted the burnt saucepan by the back door. He put his slippers on and walked through to the kitchen, carrying the saucepan. Rose was busy at the stove, wreathed in steam and smoke from the frying pan.

'Hey up, Rose, now what's to do?' he demanded.

'A nice fish and chip supper for us all, that's what, Walter.'

Walter surveyed the carnage in Ellie's kitchen. Every surface was strewn with dirty bowls and dishes. He held out the saucepan. 'What happened to this?'

'Well, they were going to be mushy peas to go with the fish and chips. Ellie had some marrowfats in the larder and I was mashing them up in the pan. I got a bit distracted by Arthur when he called me down to see his peacock run and I was out …'

Walter cut her short. 'Peacock run! And where is he making this peacock run?'

Rose bridled. He needn't take that attitude. They were doing their best to get their birds out from under his feet, weren't they? 'He's down in that old field that runs down to the hills. There's nowt there so he's not doing any harm – and then the birds will be away from here, like you wanted.' Rose smiled sunnily at him. 'All's well then, our Walter. Now you just wash your hands and fetch Ellie in and tea will be on the table in a jiffy.'

Walter thought he was going to explode. 'I'm not bringing Ellie in here, Rose. You've made her lovely kitchen into a tip. You get it cleaned up quick, or you'll be down that road before you can say *bloody peacocks*. You ruined her favourite pan that was her mother's and just chucked it out the door, and I've yet to see what the hell Arthur thinks he's doing in my fields. But if he's doing it where I think he's doing it, then he can jolly well undo it. And what's he done it with, I'd like to know?'

Rose was undaunted by this tirade. She began to gather some of the bowls from the worktop and dumped them in the sink. 'He went in your shed, lad. You've rakes of wood. He didn't think you'd mind lending him a bit of wood.'

'*Lending!*'

Rose's insouciant assumptions enraged him further. Speechless, he turned on his heels and walked out, still carrying the burnt saucepan.

He couldn't stand much more of this. Every time he turned his back something else happened. If it wasn't their bloody alpacas escaping…They were like furry Houdinis. Every time he thought they had them secured, they found some other way of getting out. They should be entered in the Grand National, they were that good at jumping the walls. Peacocks everywhere screeching their heads off and mad hens that would lay anywhere but in a henhouse. Now Rose had invaded the kitchen, and look at the results of that. He doubted the food would be edible and Ellie would be furious.

Something had to be done, and fast. He'd go and see Barney in the morning. Surely he could talk the talk with York Council and find Rose somewhere to go. If they didn't, he might not be responsible for his actions.

# CHAPTER 8

Tom Young pulled into the car park of the Bull and Bear in Settle, just after 8 p.m. Checking the cars, he spotted Matt's discreetly parked at the far end, nose in towards the bushes, only the yellow number plate dimly visible in the inky dark. He smiled. Trust Matt. No one would see them. There would be no witnesses to whatever conversation they would have.

He parked some distance away and walked up the car park. Quietly opening the passenger door, he slid in beside Matt.

'You made good time,' Matt commented.

'The roads were quiet for a change.' Tom peered out through the misted-up windscreen. 'I take it you've heard the rumours about Allsthwaite.'

'Been waiting for it. Those developers weren't going to sit on that land forever. So, have they applied for planning now?'

'Not yet. When they put the application in, everything already has to be in place. Too much opposition from the Allsthwaite residents and it could go to Inquiry.'

Matt sighed. 'Mm …Been here before, haven't we, on other schemes?'

'Nothing like this one, Matt. It's big and there's a lot of money to be made if we can deliver on it.'

Matt smiled into the darkness. 'I like the sound of that. So, what do we have to "put in place" to get this sorted?'

'Go on a digging expedition, Matt, discreetly as ever, of

course. With all the rumours flying about, Allsthwaite Parish Council will be looking into the proposed application and be planning a campaign to oppose it. If we can, er, let's just say, *dissuade* the ringleaders from getting underway in the first place, we can probably stop the whole thing in its tracks.'

'Allsthwaite Parish Council…' Matt's head sunk into his chest as he thought about this.

Tom waited patiently. He knew Matt kept his ear closely to the ground where all matters concerning York and the surrounding areas were concerned and he would consider all angles before he made a move.

'They're a rum lot at Allsthwaite,' he said at last. 'The parish council leader is a right eco-warrior. Used to be quite a hippy in his youth and now he's turned Mr Family Man and settled down. But he would be at the forefront of the fight against any large-scale development at Allsthwaite.'

He shuffled about on the car seat and continued. 'His sidekick, the parish council clerk, he's a right dry old stick. Born and bred in Allsthwaite. Even people who've lived there for thirty years or more he considers incomers. He'd be right behind our eco-warrior friend in fighting against this development. They would make a formidable team and know how to mobilise their troops for a big campaign.'

'Then they have to be dealt with,' Tom said calmly. 'There will be something in their backgrounds we can use. No one leads a blameless life. There is always a past and you will have to go and find out about theirs. This application is going to be passed.'

'We might be able to do something about Allsthwaite,' Matt said after thinking it over. 'But what about the council and the planning committee?'

It was Tom's turn to smile into the darkness. 'Leave it to me, Matt. It's power, isn't it? All about power, who has it and how they can use it. And I've got the biggest carrot ever to waft under the donkey's nose. He won't be able to resist it, because it will bring him more power than he ever dreamt of.'

Matt decided not to pursue these statements. He would have enough on his plate out at Allsthwaite. 'OK. I'll get digging and get back to you as soon as I can.'

It was getting cold sitting in the car with no heater going. The windows were all misted over now and moisture ran down the windscreen in long rivulets.

Tom opened the car door. 'Be very careful and update me when you can. I'll take it from there. Just remember, we're dealing with the London boys on this and if we get it right you can kiss goodbye to York forever.' Then he was gone, walking briskly through the darkness to his car.

Matt started his engine and switched the heater to high. It wouldn't do to get into a collision. He was meant to be a long way from here tonight.

# CHAPTER 9

The purchase of Beech Cottage was quickly completed. Mrs Simpson was very keen to move into The Elms Home for Elderly Persons and, within a couple of weeks, Kate and Stan moved into their new home.

As so much needed doing to the house, they decided to camp out in the main bedroom with as many of their possessions around them as they could cram in. They had some difficulty getting into bed on their first night, as there was very little space left.

'If this baby gets much bigger, Stan, I'll never make it into bed. There just isn't room.'

Stan was upbeat. 'Never fear, my lovely Kate. I'll be setting to work in the morning, and very soon Beech Cottage will be transformed.'

'I just hope your magic wand's in good working order, then.' Kate heaved herself into bed and pulled the covers up. 'Where are you thinking of starting?'

'The bathroom.' Stan got in beside her and pulled her close to him. 'We need a beautiful space for my beautiful wife and child to bathe in. Not only that,' he added practically, 'there's no shower and I don't have time to mess about bathing in the morning. I want a quick in and out before I go to the Historical Trust.'

Kate snuggled into him. 'Quick in and out, eh? I hope that's only showers you're talking about.'

Stan tightened his hold on her. 'Mrs Peterson! Would you like a demonstration?'

\*\*\*

Kate went off to a meeting at the Historical Trust the next morning, leaving Stan to survey the bathroom. He felt confident he could do the work himself in this room. It was just a question of knocking the old cracked tiles off the walls and the bath; once they were off, he could put in a shower and screen and then retile. All Kate would need to do was choose the tiles. Simple. He rubbed his hands and went to fetch some tools.

But it wasn't so simple. No matter how careful he was, chunks of plaster came away with every tile. By lunchtime he had filled several sacks with the old tiles and rubble and the bathroom walls were pockmarked with holes dug into the old plaster.

Ruefully Stan stood back and surveyed his handiwork. We...ll, yes, it would be a bit of a delay, but it would have to be done. He was up for a bit of replastering. After all, the new tiles would cover any mistakes. He could get some bags of plaster from the DIY store, slap it on and the room would look shipshape by the time Kate got home. No worries. But first of all, a man needed his lunch.

\*\*\*

After lunch, Stan nipped down to the DIY store and collected a few bags of plaster for the bathroom. He was anxious to get the work done before Kate returned from the Historical Trust. If she saw all the holes in the walls, she might not understand all the progress he had made.

There was a lot of work to do. After he had carried all the bags of plaster upstairs, Stan looked around for a suitable container to mix it in. He appeared to only have small buckets. They wouldn't be any good; he would spend more time mixing the stuff than slapping it on the wall. An idea came to him. He looked at the bath consideringly. It was ideal. He could mix the whole lot in one go and the room would be done in no time.

He set to work emptying the powdery plaster into the bath and measuring out the correct amount of water. He was a little alarmed at the large quantity it made – it almost filled the bath – but he consoled himself with the thought that there were a lot of potholes to fill in the walls. It wouldn't take long to get down that lot.

The work went well. He soon got into a rhythm of ladling a quantity of plaster into his bucket and then patiently filling in the holes. He was surprised at how much plaster it took to fill some of them. At this rate, he would empty the bath in no time and have to go and buy some more.

Downstairs the telephone was ringing. Stan put down his trowel. He'd better answer it; it might be Kate needing something. It wasn't Kate, but it was a member of the board of the Historical Trust enquiring about Stan's progress with his education programme for the launch of the new Ebacorum site.

Stan owed his job to Mr Marbury and could not fob him off with glib answers. He fetched his precious notes from his briefcase and pulled up a kitchen chair. Patiently he went through the details with his senior and answered his searching questions. After quite a long time Mr Marbury seemed satisfied with what he heard and rang off. Stan heaved a sigh of relief and made his way back upstairs to the bathroom.

Picking up his ladle, he went to refill his bucket with fresh plaster from the bath. The ladle bounced over the surface of the plaster. Stan put the ladle down and prodded the plaster with his fingers. It had set into a solid mass.

For a moment he stood there, scratching his head in disbelief. This could not possibly have happened. He snatched up an empty bag and read the guidelines again. No … it couldn't be; it just could not possibly be. He had picked up the wrong bag. He had a bath full of quick-setting plaster, not the slow-setting he had intended to buy.

He slapped his forehead in disgust. How could he have been such a mutt? Now he had a half-plastered bathroom and a bath full of plaster he couldn't use and, worst of all, he'd never chisel that lot out in a million years. Even if he did, he would ruin the bath in the process.

He would have to get a new bath and Kate would kill him. Yes, she would, he knew she would. Well, maybe not kill him but not be the sunny, smiling wife he was used to. How was he going to get a bath full of plaster out of the room and out of the house anyway?

This was a time, if ever there was one, to find out who his friends were. He needed George, Barney and Walter and maybe even Rose's Arthur, even if he did look like a yard of pumpwater. Every little helped, or Stan was going to be toast.

# CHAPTER 10

Walter paid a visit to Barney Anderson at his new offices in Little Stonegate in the centre of York. Joanna, Barney's Australian secretary, showed him the way to Barney's den. Walking into the new office, Walter looked around. Barney's large solid desk stood on a sage-green carpet. Files were stacked everywhere, on top of filing cabinets and spilling over onto the floor.

'By, lad, I'm more impressed every time I see it. It's a smashing set-up. You look like you've plenty to do.' He looked closely at Barney; he looked tired. 'Are you working too hard, lad?'

Barney smiled at his father-in-law. 'Well, Jake and I certainly have a lot of work on, which is good. It's not that that's making me tired, Walter. It's Jackie. She never stops. I don't know if being pregnant causes the release of some megahormone, but she's definitely on something. Pregnant with twins, running a busy café and now planning major works for next door. She's up half the night with papers and still looks fresh as a daisy the next day, whilst I feel wrecked. There's no stopping her. I'd go and stay at my mother's for a couple of nights just to get some sleep, but I daren't. What if anything happened whilst I was away? And for sure it would.'

Walter shook his head in sympathy. 'She's just like her mother,' he said fondly. 'Marilyn was a real worker, too. She never stopped. But when you came from nowt it was the only way we knew to get anywhere. And you must admit, lad, it paid off for both of us. She had Café Paradise and I have Claygate. Forty years' hard graft and she never really got to enjoy it.' His face was sad for a moment at the memory of those days.

'I don't want that to happen to us,' Barney said with determination. 'We both enjoy our work, but surely we need to make time to enjoy life outside of all that. Make time for each other and, just as importantly, the new babies when they come along.'

'We've had this conversation before, I seem to think,' Walter said drily. 'I tried to have a word and you know how that ended.'

'I think we'll have to make a joint attack on this one. Jackie's a hard nut to crack.'

'Barney, I spent forty years trying with her mother and *I* never got anywhere. But as you say, maybe if the two of us together…' Walter stopped and chuckled. 'Listen to the pair of us. It's Jackie, for goodness' sake. We sound like we're going to war.'

'We are and, what's more, we'll go today. You're here and I'm free…' Barney paused. 'It's always lovely to see you, Walter, and I don't mean to be rude, but shouldn't you be at Claygate keeping an eye on your own affairs? Rose and Arthur?'

As if Walter needed reminding. 'That's why I'm here.' He pulled up a chair and sat down, facing Barney across the desk. 'They are driving me up the wall, Barney, and not only me; Ellie and Elvis too. Not to mention my sheep and hens. We're all at our wits' end.'

Barney sat back in his chair. Walter obviously needed to get a lot off his chest.

'Go on.'

'I know Rose is my sister and I have a duty towards her, but living in the same house with her and Arthur is too much. Lad, if you saw the outside of the farm this morning, you'd hardly recognise it.'

Walter leant forward, anxious to impress the gravity of the situation on Barney.

'They're like travellers. There's stuff everywhere. They never put anything away. They get stuff out, bags of feed that never go away again; they raid my sheds for tools and netting and just leave things at the end of the job and walk away. I've started making the rounds at the end of the day, as I never know what they've been up to and where things will be.'

He paused for breath then continued. 'It's got to stop. They've got to go. It's like they're in a first-class hotel. They never do a hand's tap to help. Jack, their mangy dog, terrorises Elvis and if it isn't him, it's them bloody peacocks of theirs. Even them alpacas sing a bit, and Elvis doesn't like that either. And they eat like horses. Fact is, it's probably cheaper to keep some horses – at least you'd get some work out of them. Rose and Arthur are having a great holiday at our expense.'

Walter drummed his fingers on Barney's desk and eyeballed him. 'How about this one? Me and Ellie had been to Easingwold Market. Meanwhile Rose had the bright idea of getting herself into Ellie's kitchen and cooking dinner for us to come home to. Fair enough; sounds like a good idea, for once. Trouble is, Rose can't cook. She is the world's worst. And she nearly wrecked the kitchen whilst she was in it and ruined Ellie's favourite pan into the bargain.'

He wasn't finished yet. 'Whilst she was doing that, Arthur raided my sheds and took some of my best wood, loads of netting and all the paraphernalia to fix it with, and built a ruddy great shelter with a run for his peacocks and peahens, *in my best field*. And that's only one fr'instance. I cannot stand any more, Barney; neither can Ellie or Elvis. They have to go. That's why I'm here. I want you to find out from York Council what can be done with them. Whilst ever they're with me they're not homeless, but I can't make them homeless now, can I? I can't turn them out on the streets. And what about their animals? What would happen to them? Rose lives for her animals.'

Now it was all out Walter sat back in the chair, looking expectantly at Barney.

'I don't know what I can do, Walter,' Barney said slowly.

'From what you've said, everything is in order. The land was legitimately sold by the owners, and if Rose had gone through the proper channels in the first place...'

'If she ever read her letters in the first place.' Walter was scornful. 'She's useless in that department and that Arthur's no better. He just follows her lead. Please, Barney, please, help us out here. We're desperate. If something isn't done soon, it'll be me and Ellie that'll be leaving home and setting up our tent on *your* lawn. Tell you what, I'll come to Café Paradise with you today and we'll knock some sense into that daughter of mine's head. I won't leave until I've done it, that's a promise – if you'll have a go with York Council.'

Barney was moved by Walter's pleas. The poor man really was desperate and what were his own troubles compared with Walter's? He got up from his desk. 'Come on, Walter. Let's go and have lunch at Café Paradise and then we'll put the world to rights.'

Walter grinned at his son-in-law with relief. With Barney on the job, surely something would happen now.

\*\*\*

Jackie was at the coffee counter when they entered the café. Barney frowned. Couldn't she ever rest? Seeing his scowl, Jackie smiled her sweetest smile at him.

'Well, hello, dosser boy. It's just like old times. Coming to lunch at Café Paradise, are you?'

'As it happens I am,' Barney said tightly. 'Your dad needs a break from Claygate before he strangles his sister or leaves home altogether, along with Ellie and Elvis.'

Jackie raised her eyebrows but made no comment. She finished serving the lady in front of them with her take-out coffee and cake and then gave them her full attention. 'Well, Dad, what're the latest goings-on at Claygate?'

'You don't want to know,' Walter said darkly. 'Your Aunt Rose is a law to herself. Any road, what are you doing standing about here? Shouldn't you be in your office with your feet up?'

Jackie finished wiping down the counter and put the cloth down. 'I'm going there now,' she beamed. 'I was covering for half an hour whilst Penny went for a hairdo. She's back now and just getting changed in the staffroom. She'll be here in a tick.'

Before they could admonish her further, Jackie slid off to her office. 'Enjoy your lunch,' she called over her shoulder. 'I'll see you later.'

'Too right you will, lass,' Walter muttered to her retreating back.

They sat down at a table and perused the menu. These days it was extensive: everything from snacks to main meals and delicious-sounding desserts. Café Paradise was building quite a reputation as a smart city venue, thanks to Monsieur Henri's creativity in the kitchen.

'Not a fry-up and bowl of chips in sight,' Walter mourned, 'let alone a bacon buttie or sausage bap.'

Barney laughed out loud. 'Don't let Jackie hear you say that, Walter. She might flay you alive. All the work she's put into this place and you still want a bacon buttie.'

Walter grinned. 'I know I'll never change. And…' he nodded across the table to Barney, 'I seem to remember a blonde-haired young man who not so long ago, in Marilyn's day, came in here regularly for his big breakfast.'

Barney smiled at the memory. 'Your breakfasts, Walter. Unsurpassable. We eat healthily these days,' he said wistfully.

'Me, too,' said Walter. 'Rabbit food and soya milk.' He brightened. 'I sneak a bag of chips sometimes, though, when I'm out with the van.'

Barney laughed again. 'You're incorrigible, Walter. Now, what are we going to have?'

They turned their attention to the menu. Unable to decide, they enlisted Penny's advice. 'Well, if it was me, I would go for the *soupe à l'oignon gratinée*,' she said.

'How's that?' asked Walter. 'Do you mean onion soup?

That's not much of a lunch. I was expecting better than that.'

'Oh, this is not just any old onion soup,' Penny insisted. 'Emmental cheese melted with butter, and baguettes, onions and tomato puree. It's like a dish of the most divine cheese casserole with a crusty top. Try it, Walter, it's amazing.'

They both agreed to her choice and she smiled broadly at them.

'You're cheery today, Penny,' Walter commented. 'How's things with you and George, then? I haven't seen him for a week or two.'

Penny pursed her lips thoughtfully. 'We're sort of all right, thanks, Walter. You heard about our anniversary débâcle, I suppose?'

Walter nodded. 'Is he still in the doghouse?'

Penny beamed. 'No, he's made up for it. He's still got that wretched old ambulance and says he's going to do it up as a camper van. I mean, is that better than that Harley-Davidson motorbike he bought last year? That was bad enough. And then in Scotland we had a night in a caravan. *A caravan.* That was even worse. I can't see the attraction – a space you can hardly swing a cat in, even supposing you wanted to, and a "kitchen area".' Penny made finger-quotes in the air. 'Kitchen area my foot; space for a kettle and one mug and that's your lot. There would be even less space in a camper and he thinks I'm going to go away in one of those? Well, that'll be the day, that's all I can say. But he bought me the *most* beautiful pair of diamond earrings to make up for that awful weekend and to celebrate our anniversary properly.'

Walter was beginning to wish he'd never asked the question in the first place. Penny in full flood could be very wearing, but he was glad to know George had taken his advice and it had worked.

'And how's Kate getting on?' asked Barney. 'Is she in today, or at the Historical Trust?'

Penny raised her eyes to the ceiling. 'Ooh, don't even go there, Barney. You know they've just moved into a new house in Dunnington?'

Barney nodded. Jackie had told him about Beech Cottage.

'Stan's filled the bath with plaster and they haven't got a shower, so now they've only got the handbasin to wash in.'

Barney exchanged glances with Walter. Who was going to ask the question? Walter was there first. 'Why did he do a daft thing like that?' he demanded.

'It's a long story,' Penny said. 'I haven't got time to go into it now. I must go and place your order. I think you might be getting a phone call from Stan to get the bath out of there. He's spoken to George already and your names were mentioned.'

She whisked herself off, leaving Barney and Walter to make what they could of it.

For once, in the kitchen all was going well. The dishwashers hummed away in the washing-up room off the main kitchen and Genevieve seemed to be keeping pace with the orders. Monsieur Henri felt she had made such good progress these last few weeks that today he had left her in charge of making the French apple cake.

Genevieve had watched him make it many times before. She approached the task a little apprehensively but soon began to enjoy herself under Monsieur Henri's approving gaze. The apple cake turned out spectacularly well. Monsieur Henri was beside himself with joy at the sight of it. He hugged his protégée and gave her a smacking kiss on the cheek.

'Ah, *ma petite* Genevieve, you have done well. We are a team now, eh? Henri teaches you well. One day we will have Restaurant Henri, you and I, *hein*?'

Genevieve giggled. 'Monsieur Henri…'

Penny, delivering Barney and Walter's lunch order, watched the little scene with some alarm. Genevieve was extremely beautiful and effortlessly left a trail of men in her wake. Now that she was really beginning to develop her cooking skills and winning Henri's approval, Penny hoped he was not developing too much of a fondness for her. He was a great deal older and somehow she didn't think Genevieve's parents would be too pleased with a development in that direction.

\*\*\*

Penny was so right: the *soupe à l'oignon gratinée* was superb, and the *crème caramel* that followed it was perfect. Walter and Barney sat back in satisfaction.

'I suppose yon Frenchman knows a thing or two,' Walter admitted. 'I'll have to bring Ellie to try it and get the recipe from him, if he'll part with it.'

'I'm sure he will for you, Walter. After all, you're old work colleagues.'

'That's a pretty way of saying I was his skivvy,' Walter said tartly. 'Which I was.' He grinned at Barney. 'I'm sure he will, though.' He heaved a satisfied sigh and looked about him. Jackie was nowhere to be seen. 'Well, time to beard the lioness in her den, I suppose. And I'm not taking no for an answer this time.'

He got up and Barney made to go with him. 'No, lad, leave me to it. This is a father-and-daughter row. I don't want you falling out with her as well. She needs you at home tonight, all calm and peaceful-like, ready to rub her back and run her a lovely bath and be Mr Romantic. She can get it all off her chest to me and no bones broken. You get back to your office, Barney, and thank you for that lunch.' He shook his head wonderingly. 'How does Henri come up with dishes like that? Must be something in being a Frenchie after all.'

Barney laughed and clapped Walter on the back. 'Never thought I'd hear you say that. Well, good luck, Walter. I hope she's had lunch already and you're not the dessert.'

Walter grinned. 'Never fear. Lion taming's my speciality.'

He went towards the back of the café and walked along the short corridor leading to Jackie's office. He had worked in this café for forty years alongside Jackie's mother, Marilyn Dalrymple-Jones. They had grown up together in the backstreets and fought and loved all their lives until Marilyn died. Jackie was their daughter, although Marilyn denied this fact throughout her life.

Pausing outside what had been Marilyn's office, Walter gathered his thoughts on how best to get through to his strong-willed daughter. If she didn't ease up, she could lose not only her babies but her husband too. Barney adored Jackie, there was no question about that, but a wife who was never going to be at home… Cautiously he opened Jackie's door and put his head round.

'Hi Dad.' Jackie had her feet up on the desk, a sheaf of papers in her hand. Hmph. Walter was not fooled. She was obviously expecting him and this performance was laid on to impress him.

'Resting, are you?' he asked casually.

Jackie looked about her. 'As you see.'

'Not enough, though.'

'And you'd know, would you?'

Exasperation rose in Walter's breast. She always had that effect on him. They were too alike, only she was even more pig-headed than he was. He wasn't going to play her games.

'Aye, I would.'

He pulled up one of the chairs as close to her desk as he could and leant across it, staring straight at her. 'Have you got a death wish?'

It wasn't the question Jackie had been expecting. 'What do you mean?'

Walter chose his words carefully. 'I mean you are carrying twins, soon to be born, and you're carrying on as if nothing's happening.'

Jackie was about to protest but Walter held up his hand. 'No, hear me out before you go off on one. Do you know that saying, "The onlooker sees most of the game"? Well, I can see it, good and proper. Carrying twins isn't just as straightforward as a single…'

'You make me sound like one of your sheep,' Jackie retorted.

'You know I mean nowt of the sort.' Bloody daughters.

'You're not taking care of yourself and you're putting yourself and the lives of the twins at risk.'

Jackie abruptly jumped up and took a turn about the room. 'How dare you—'

''Course I dare. I'm your dad and I'm not going to stand by and see you throw away everything me and your mother worked for, for forty years and more.'

Jackie stopped short. 'And how do you work that one out?' she snapped, angry at Walter's words. 'I'm a successful businesswoman. I'm happily married and now happily expecting the birth of our babies. In anyone's language that's hardly throwing my life away.' She glared at him.

Walter eyeballed her, his brown eyes looking straight into her violet ones. 'And if you lose the babies due to overwork and lose your husband because you're never at home, what have you got then? A café that couldn't care less about you, that won't keep you warm at night, won't be in the least bit bothered whether you go home at night or not. Is that what you want?'

In the silence between them, Walter held her gaze. He was not going to let this one go.

'Your mother did that, Jackie, and well you know it. How many nights were you home alone? Remember? How many nights was she at home, let alone spending time with Barry Dalrymple-Jones? What kind of a life was that? Is that what you want for you and Barney? For by God, lass, I can tell you he won't stand for it for long. Have you seen that secretary of his? Long-legged blonde Aussie girl? She'd snap him up tomorrow if he was free. You need to guard your own, girl, or you'll end up with nowt.'

The stood glaring at each other, neither ready to give an inch. For Jackie, it seemed as if time was standing still as Walter's words reverberated in her head. Walter knew this was no time to weaken. He made himself hold her gaze. After a long while, she broke away and sat down heavily in her chair. 'Joanna Starling…?'

Inwardly Walter heaved a sigh of relief. Maybe now they

could get somewhere. He pulled a chair and sat down, putting his arms around her.

'She's not making a play for him, not that I can see, but…' He turned Jackie to face him. 'An extremely handsome man with a heavily pregnant wife who's always busy… What's going to happen?'

'Barney's not like that,' Jackie protested.

Walter saw there were tears starting in her eyes. Women were bad enough for the waterworks at the best of times. Add in pregnancy and hormones and now look what he'd got on his hands. But he had to press his point home.

'No man's like that till a woman puts it under his nose.' Walter shrugged. 'Not that I would know. Women weren't exactly falling over themselves for me. But we're not talking about me; we're talking about you and that handsome husband of yours. You're just not seeing the wood for the trees, lass, and there's a bloody great forest out there.'

Tears spilt down Jackie's face. She wiped them away and gave a shaky laugh. Walter held her gently and Jackie rested in his arms.

'Oh, Dad, there's nobody quite like you, thank God. I hope he broke the mould after you, that's all I can say.'

Walter laughed out loud at this, partly from relief. The lion taming hadn't been too bad after all, and not even a coffee cup thrown at him today. He became serious again. 'Promise me this, lass. Pace yourself better and give you and that husband of yours some time together. It takes two to tango, you know.'

Jackie wiped tears away from her eyes and managed a watery smile. 'Yeah, I'll tango. I'm not letting that Joanna Starling anywhere near him. We had enough misunderstandings getting together in the first place. I'll be damned if anyone's going to take him away from me … and live,' she added darkly.

Walter patted her approvingly. 'That's my girl. Guard your own. I always made sure of you and now you have to do the same for yourself.'

Leaving Jackie's office, Walter decided to say hello to

Monsieur Henri before he went home. Approaching the doors, he heard a commotion going on within.

"Ow can you forget zee baking powder, my Genevieve? 'Ow could you be so stupeed? I told you. Look at zeeze things. What are they? Paving slabs? Rocks for your garden? Get out of my kitchen, you stupeed girl. I might as well do it all myself.'

Genevieve came drifting out to the back kitchen. Walter eyed her with sympathy. 'I remember a lot of that.'

Genevieve shrugged. 'He throws me out at least six times a day and then forgets and is shouting all over the place for me.'

'What did you do this time?'

'Forgot to put the baking powder in his precious blueberry madeleines.' She dissolved into giggles. 'He said they're like paving slabs, and you know what? *They are.*'

Walter shook his head wonderingly. How Henri put up with her in the first place was a mystery to him. She was certainly very beautiful, with her flowing red hair and luminous green eyes, but a dafter lass he'd yet to meet. Having said that, Penny on one of her good days could beat her hands down.

# CHAPTER 11

Jackie turned into the Café Paradise car park at the rear of the building and nearly collided with a large silver van parked there. She jammed on her brakes, stopping just short of the van's bumper.

'Who the hell is that and what are they doing here at this time of day?' she wondered in exasperation. After Walter's pep talk yesterday, she had gone home early and made a special effort, cooking Barney's favourite meal. One thing led to another and it had been a very late night indeed. She didn't need hawkers to deal with this morning. Jumping out of her car, she approached the van.

'I don't know who you are or what you're selling, but not today, thank you. I'll back up and let you out.'

All hell seemed to be let loose in the van. What seemed like dozens of dogs lunged at her through the windows, barking furiously.

'Pack it in,' commanded the man inside. 'Buddy, Zak … that's enough.'

The dogs subsided and the man got out of the van to introduce himself. He held out his hand.

'I'm Brian. Brian Box. Weren't you expecting me this morning? I thought Barney had let you know.' Inwardly Jackie blushed. Barney had had other things on his mind last night and Brian had not featured as one of them. She took his outstretched hand, slightly flustered.

'Oh, Brian…yes, hello. I'm so sorry, I'm sure Barney did mention it. I think I just forgot. There's been such a lot going on lately I'm meeting myself coming back. Come on in and we'll have some coffee. Have you been here long?'

'I came down late last night. It was quieter for travelling.'

Jackie stared in surprise. 'Did you sleep in the van, then?'

'Oh yes.' Brian seemed quite comfortable with this. 'Me 'n'the dogs. We're used to it. It's very cosy in the van; they keep me nice and warm.'

Jackie had never owned a dog. She cast a wary glance at the van.

'They looked rather big and fierce from where I was standing.'

Brian smiled. 'No, they're big softies. You can meet them later. Buddy's part Lurcher and part Labrador and Zak's a Border collie. Don't worry, they're lively, but they wouldn't hurt you; roll over for their bellies tickling, more like.'

For now, Jackie thought she would take Brian's word for that. She led the way into the back of the café and switched on the coffee machine. She was glad of some company this morning. Although she was looking forward to her new venture, it was another big step away from the days when her mother Marilyn owned the café and Walter held sway in the kitchen. Jackie didn't wish for those days back but, with hindsight, how comforting it was to come into the café every morning to find Walter there with his mop and bucket, making the place ready for the day and putting the world to rights with Kate and Penny.

Jackie shook herself and made coffee for them both. As they sipped their drinks, Jackie studied Brian. She liked what she saw. He was of medium height with glossy black hair and gentle brown eyes, deep-set in a square-jawed face. She noted approvingly that firm muscles rippled beneath his T-shirt. He was no stranger to hard work: just the kind of man she needed for the café renovations.

She produced the plans from her desk drawer and rolled them out.

'If you'd want to know what would be involved, Brian, have a look at these and then we can go next door. Originally the two halves were all one building, so it might just be a question of knocking through to our café side again.'

Brian cocked a quizzical eyebrow but said nothing. In his experience, no building project was ever that simple, but he would wait and see.

Outside Jackie's office the café was coming to life. Henri's rumbling, heavily accented voice could be heard calling orders to Genevieve; plates and cutlery rattled as Penny stocked the dresser for the morning. Soon the hiss of the coffee machine sounded and enticing smells of coffee and freshly baking croissants drifted around the door.

Brian's mouth watered. A cup of coffee was all very well but was he going to get the chance of some breakfast before he started on the Grand Tour?

Jackie must have read his mind. Suddenly she jumped up from her seat.

'What am I thinking of? You won't have had any breakfast, will you? And all these lovely smells wafting under our noses. Come on, let's see what's on offer and then we can get down to business.'

She paused in the doorway. 'What about your dogs? Are they all right in there?'

'Oh, aye,' Brian said comfortably. 'They'll be all right for an hour or so and then I'll take 'em a walk and they can run some energy off.'

Jackie led the way towards the café and introduced him to Penny and Kate. As they shook hands, Penny said,

'This is the man you need to talk to, Kate. He might be able to give Stan a few tips.' Brian looked at Penny, waiting to be enlightened.

'He filled their bath with plaster and it set,' Penny explained.

Brian glanced from Kate to Penny and back again, trying to pick up a thread of the tale. None came.

'It would.' He didn't know what else to say. Why would

you do that? Not knowing this Stan, he felt he had better not comment for now.

Jackie stared at Penny. She was obviously out of the loop on current developments in her friends' lives.

'I'm sorry, but we're going to have to catch up on this later. Could you just get Brian something to eat and then we can go and look at next door?'

Behind them from the kitchen came Monsieur Henri's voice, increasing in volume with every rolled French syllable.

'Genevieve Anderrrson … 'ow is zat a crrroissant? You are making ze English roll of ze sausage, no? When did you see a croissant like that? En France? Nevair. *Vous êtes stupide.* Take it away, take it to Madame Anderson. I will not have you *dans ma cuisine.*'

Genevieve drifted into the café, holding a squashed-looking croissant, smiling ruefully. She held it out to Jackie.

'Mr Henri…'

'I know,' Jackie sighed.

'It *is* the first time I've tried to make them.' Genevieve was apologetic. 'He showed me how to shape them, but somehow…' She shrugged her shoulders helplessly. 'I'll just give him five minutes. He'll be OK by then.'

Jackie took the proffered croissant and fetched a plate from the dresser.

'Here's a start to breakfast, Brian.' She offered him the croissant and pointed to the butter and jams on the dresser.

'I'm sure Genevieve can rustle up a bacon and egg roll for you.' She cocked an enquiring look at Genevieve.

'No problem,' Genevieve said promptly. 'Even *I* can't ruin that.'

She turned and made her way back to the kitchen. Brian stared after her, open-mouthed.

'Who is *that*?' he asked.

'Genevieve, and for my sins she's my sister-in-law. Did you never meet her up in the Lakes?'

'Oh … Genevieve! No, they never bought her there. Always

left her at home, after her first outing with her father in his boat.' Brian smiled to himself.

'Well, go on,' Jackie said impatiently. 'What happened that was so bad they never took her again?'

'Her dad forgot which daughter he had on board. He was thinking it was Juliet and told her to put the sail up. She did all right, but hoisted the sail upside down.'

Jackie rolled her eyes. It fitted; only Genevieve could do that. Was there a right side up to a sail? She supposed there must be. 'Go on.'

'Barney's dad nearly died when he saw what she'd done and sent her to put it up the right way. Only she got halfway up the mast and made the mistake of looking down and froze, so then she couldn't get up or down. Her father had to get her down one foot at a time, which took forever. The boat was all over the place and he ended up coming into his moorings still with the sail upside down. You can imagine the stick he got for that in the pub, not only that night but for years to come. So, as you can imagine, she was never allowed to set foot on his boat again.'

Brian shook his head wonderingly. 'So, that's Genevieve, is it? No one told me she was beautiful. They only ever spoke of her as their numbskull kid sister.'

Jackie tutted, 'She *was* very accident-prone at one time but I truly believe she's a lot better now. She lives in her own flat and manages very well and, although it may not look like it this morning, she gets on very well with Monsieur Henri. She's in a fair way to becoming quite a good little cook.'

Jackie could have said Genevieve had two heads and had just sailed backwards around the world and it would not have registered with Brian. He was smitten. The most beautiful girl in the world had just walked into his life and spoken in the tones of an angel. He knew his life would never be the same again.

\*\*\*

Jackie and Brian spent most of the morning looking at the

next-door building in great detail. Only the ground floor was to be utilised as the new part of the café; the flat upstairs would be let off to a tenant in the future.

As they walked around and discussed the alterations, Jackie's liking for Brian grew. Barney was right; he was a man to be trusted and had all the crafts and skills at his fingertips. She felt he could be trusted to occupy the flat upstairs whilst he did the café renovations. But would his dogs settle there?

Brian was delighted with the offer. 'Them dogs'll settle anywhere,' he said, smiling happily. 'Long as they get a good meal and a few walks, they're happy.'

Jackie was relieved. Brian could start straight away, which was wonderful. Better still, she wouldn't have to endure her previous builder, Old Mother Stampwick, for the next few weeks. That was a major bonus in her life. Barney might not be too happy about her expanding the business at this time, but at least she was using his friend for the work.

They returned to her office and she gave Brian the key to the upstairs flat.

'Get yourself settled in and we can talk about ordering materials tomorrow, if you'll be ready.'

'It won't take me long to shake down, Jackie. We can start this afternoon if you like.'

It got better and better. When Brian had gone Jackie sat back in her chair and looked up at the ceiling.

'Well, Mother, what do you think? A bit of a chip off the old block, after all. I wonder what you'd make of Café Paradise these days. Would you approve of what I've done with my inheritance from you?'

Outside in the yard, Brian let Buddy and Zak out of the van to take them for a run by the river. As he passed the front of the café he paused on the pavement and looked at it. 'Genevieve,' he breathed softly to himself. Why had he never known…? It was indeed Café Paradise. He turned away and strode towards the river with the dogs at his heels. Life was going to be grand from now on.

# CHAPTER 12

It was Saturday morning. Kate had gone off to her parent's home with their laundry.

'And whilst it's whizzing around in the machine, I'm going to have a lovely soak in their bath, seeing as how we *don't* have one.' She kissed Stan goodbye. 'But we will have one in place by the time I get back tonight, won't we, Stan darling?' she said sweetly.

Stan detected the note of steel behind the tight smile. He nodded.

'Oh yes, it's all lined up. The guys are coming over in about an hour and it will all be sorted, I promise. After today, you can bathe to your heart's content, in asses' milk if you want.'

'Hmph. Asses'…' Kate suppressed a smile and kissed the tip of his chin. 'See you tonight.'

After she had gone, Stan turned the stop tap off under the kitchen sink and turned the cold tap on to run off the water. Leaving it running, he went to the garage to fetch his toolkit. He might have had to fork out for a new bath but at least he could recycle the taps from the old one. He thought he could get them off fairly easily. Kate would be pleased on two counts: saving money, and also because they were handsome, old-fashioned taps that fitted the Beech Cottage style.

By the time he had assembled his tools, the water had stopped running and he went up to the bathroom to make a start. Having removed the panel, Stan squeezed himself into the small space behind the bath and manoeuvred the wrench around the nut at the top of the nearest pipe connecting the stalk of the bath tap. It had been in place a long time and resisted all Stan's efforts to unscrew it.

Wriggling back out, Stan found a hammer and squeezed his way back in. This time, with the wrench tightly clamped around the nut, he managed to bang the handle of the wrench with the hammer and force the nut to loosen its grip on the pipe. Success. He was able to unscrew it fully. One tap saved.

The other tap proved just as intractable and Stan grew hot and uncomfortable in the small space. Would the thing never loosen? Had some past benighted plumber glued the thing in place? There was nothing for it – somehow, he was going to have to saw it off.

Another trip to the garage and he found a small hacksaw that might just do the job. Back underneath the bath once more, he hauled himself as near as he could to the intransigent pipe and began to saw at it. He was at an awkward angle for the job, but slowly made progress. A little residual water trickled down his arm as he opened up the pipe and suddenly he was through. Then the pipe gave way altogether.

And with it came a deluge of hot water from the tank in the loft. With no tap to hold things back, the water flowed freely out of the pipe and straight onto the floorboards, finding its way through the cracks and into the ceiling void of the kitchen below.

Stan yelped and backed out of the space, vainly looking around for something to catch the water in. It was such a small space that there was no room to fit a container. He grabbed an old towel and frantically dabbed at the flowing pool gathering around his feet. To no avail. The towel was instantly sodden and the water continued to flow.

He charged downstairs looking for more towels, anything that would absorb the water. Kate had taken them all for the laundry; all that was left was a small kitchen towel. Even as he grabbed it, Stan knew it would be useless. As he searched around for something else, he was aware of the sound of water dripping, dripping, relentlessly dripping.

He looked around the kitchen, searching for it, but could see nothing. Still the dripping continued. Then he looked up and stood back in horror. The ceiling had developed a large bulge and water from the bathroom above was slowly running down the wall above the old pine dresser.

As he stood watching helplessly, the doorbell rang. Stan backed out of the kitchen and ran across the hall to greet Walter and George standing on the doorstep.

'Morning, lad,' Walter said breezily. 'Barney's just coming. He thought he'd better park his car well out of the way if we're getting this here bath out.'

For a moment Stan stood on the doorstep, wordlessly opening his mouth. 'The bath…'

'Aye, lad, the bath. Had you forgotten we were coming?'

'*No*, only… Come quick, come and see. I think the ceiling's going to come down.'

He grabbed Walter and dragged him towards the kitchen. George followed, with Barney now close behind. Standing in the doorway, Stan pointed to the bulging ceiling.

'Bloody hell,' exclaimed Walter. 'How the heck did that happen?'

'I took the taps off the bath and that lot came down.'

'Didn't you know about the hot water tank in the loft?' asked George.

'Never thought about it.' Stan's blue eyes were huge in his head.

'What on earth can we do? We still need to get this bath out. The ceiling's about to come down and Kate will be back tonight. At this rate I'll have no bath and no kitchen either.'

'That about sums it up,' said George lugubriously.

The four men stood watching with awful fascination as the bubble in the ceiling spread. Barney shook himself. This wouldn't do. Standing watching a disaster unfold wasn't going to help Stan.

'Come on, let's get the table and chairs out of the way and see if we can move that cupboard.'

The big pine table was very heavy and it took all four of them to move it. They managed to turn it around and park it against the far wall. The dresser tested all their strength; they didn't have the time to see if it would come apart and, with all their muscles straining they heaved it away from the wall and the increasing flow of water. Red-faced and panting, they collapsed onto the kitchen chairs to catch their breath.

'Eh, lad,' Walter gasped.

'Just promise me this: next time there's a plumbing job needs doing, you'll fetch a plumber in to do it. We're none of us twenty-one anymore.'

'I was trying to save us some money,' Stan said mournfully. 'I thought I could recycle the taps onto the new bath.'

Barney grinned across the table at his friend. 'I should stick to Roman villas if I were you, Stan. I think their plumbing might have been a bit simpler.'

'Well, as a matter of fact, it wasn't—'

'Never mind Roman plumbing right now,' George interrupted, before Stan really got going on his favourite subject.

'We've still got a bath full of plaster to get down the stairs, haven't we? And then do something about this here ceiling.'

'We'll have to take all that area down,' Walter said, studying the bulging plaster.

'Then it will need time to dry out before it can be replastered. Sorry, Stan, you'll just have to live with a big hole up there for a little while.'

Stan covered his face with his hands. 'You know what this means, don't you?'

Walter, George and Barney looked at him sympathetically and nodded as one.

'She'll likely have your guts for garters,' Walter said sagely. 'Women ... they don't understand. Never did, in my experience. But there it is, lad. All we can do is get the old bath out and put the new one in place, *with the old taps*, and hope for the best.'

'Buy her a nice present,' said George. 'I did for Penny and it worked a treat.'

'I was supposed to be saving money by doing this. I think I know where she would put any present I bought her and it's somewhere the sun don't shine.'

Barney winced. 'We'll have a really good clean-up and take all the rubbish away in Walter's van. She'll hardly notice the ceiling then.'

Stan looked pityingly at Barney. 'Like Jackie wouldn't notice? You know Kate'll kill me,' Stan said miserably.

'She will,' they chorused.

\*\*\*

It was early evening when Kate arrived back to Beech Cottage. She felt a lot better, having had a long soak in the bath at her parent's house, and had come home with clean laundry for them both. At least they would have a new bath installed by now and maybe, in the kitchen, even the washing machine plumbed in.

Stan heard her car crunch on the gravel drive and went out nervously to meet her. He swept her up in a fond embrace.

'Darling Kate…Here, give me that basket.' He took the laundry basket from her and carried it in, making for the stairs.

'No, Stan.' Kate checked his progress. 'Take it through to the kitchen, will you? I want to sort it out on the table. Not all of it's for ironing.'

'Ah ... the kitchen.' Stan hesitated. 'Can't you sort it out upstairs?'

'No, it's easier on the kitchen table at the moment. All the other rooms are crammed with our stuff and still need sorting out.'

'We…ll—' Kate stiffened.

'We...ll?' Just what was going on here?

'Well, it's just not quite as you left it this morning, that's all.'

That was enough for Kate. She marched through the hall and into the kitchen. She saw the dresser and table and chairs piled up against one wall and looked about her in puzzlement. What *was* going on here? She turned to Stan.

'Why the seismic shift?'

'The what?'

'The seismic shift in the kitchen furniture. It seemed perfectly all right where it was when I left here this morning.'

'Ah,' Stan temporised. 'That was before…'

Kate raised an eyebrow. 'Before…?'

'Be…fore…' He couldn't bring himself to say it.

Kate swept her corn-coloured hair back from her face and looked about her. Looking up, she saw the large hole left in the ceiling after George and Barney had taken down the sodden plaster.

Her green eyes grew round in her face. Wordlessly she pointed upwards and looked at Stan.

'Ah, mm, a slight accident getting the bath out,' he offered by way of explanation.

'Slight accident?'

'Yes.'

'Having taken a bath out, do we have a bath *in*?'

'Ah, no.'

'No?'

'No.'

'Why not?'

Stan squirmed uncomfortably. 'The floorboards are soaked. They're too soft at the moment to take the weight of the new bath. They'll have to dry out and then I'll have to see what can be salvaged from them.'

'So, where's the bath now?'

'In the garage.'

'I can't take a bath out there, can I?'

'No, not really.'

'And I've no kitchen now…'

'Ah, it looks like that.' Stan waited for the eruption. You could only push Kate so far.

Much to his surprise, she turned on her heels and walked

back down the hallway, picking up the laundry basket as she went. She opened the front door and stepped outside. 'I'll leave you to it, then,' she said evenly.

'What?' This was not what Stan had expected. Kate couldn't just abandon him. Give him fireworks, yes, but just walk out…

Kate turned back to face him, her green eyes serious. 'I can't live here, Stan. I'm pregnant. There is no bath, no kitchen and no proper heating. What do you expect me to do? I need to look after myself and our baby and I'm still working. I'm going back to my parents.'

'You're leaving me?' Stan took a step towards her.

Kate warded him off. 'No, I'm not leaving you in that sense, Stan. I just can't live here. You've still got another couple of months before you start at the Historical Trust full-time. You'll have to make this house habitable for us all before then.'

She broke off, unable to bear the stricken look on Stan's face. She took a step towards him and he rushed forward, enveloping her in a bear hug.

'I love you, Stan, but I can't live like this.' She hugged him, tears flowing down her cheeks. 'Just do something about it all and we can be a family again.'

She turned away, got swiftly into her car and drove away from Beech Cottage.

# CHAPTER 13

George withdrew his head from under the bonnet of his beloved ambulance and straightened up. His wiped his dirty hands on an old towel and surveyed the engine lovingly. Now that she was fixed up, the lady should go like a bird for a long time to come.

Luckily for George, his friend Jimmy had his own transport business with a large yard at the rear of the premises. George had been able to park his old ambulance there, checking over all the engine parts until he was satisfied everything was in working order.

Jimmy joined him and they both looked admiringly at George's handiwork. 'First-class job, that, George,' he commented.

'Thanks, Jimmy. Coming from you, that means a lot.'

'Never mind me, our lad. What about Penny? Now you've got this old lady running right, do you think you can talk her into keeping it?' George lowered the bonnet of the ambulance and patted it proudly.

'I reckon so, Jimmy. You just listen to this.' He got into the driver's seat and started up the engine. It idled quietly. 'Sounds like a Rolls-Royce, doesn't it?'

Jimmy raised his eyebrows. 'Not quite, George, but it sounds to be running well. You'll just have to use all your charms on her.'

George grinned. 'Who? My old lady here, or Penny?'

'I think you'll have to work on Penny to get her to ride in this girl, George. She might sound like a Roller, but she definitely isn't.'

'Oh, Penny will come round,' George said breezily. 'When she hears this purring away like a little old pussycat on the driveway, she'll love it. Just think of the holidays and weekends away we can have in it.'

'You're asking the wrong person, George. I spend a lot of my life in sleeping in lorries. I wouldn't thank you for one on holiday. Give me a nice hotel every time.'

'Well, Penny doesn't, so I've great hopes of convincing her of this. Let's face it, Jimmy, she spent last summer on the back of a Harley-Davidson and managed that all right. This has to be an improvement, doesn't it?' Jimmy laughed and clapped George on the back.

'I'll say this for you, George, you're ever the optimist.'

***

Penny was washing up at the kitchen sink when George arrived home with the ambulance. She looked out of the window and frowned when she saw it pull onto the drive.

'Oh God,' she thought. 'What's he bought that thing home for? It can't stay there. It blocks all the light out.'

She wiped her hands on a towel and went to the back door. She watched George alight from the cab and gently shut the door. He stood back with arms folded, smiling admiringly at it.

'Oh, for goodness' sake,' Penny sighed to herself. 'It's like he's fallen in love with it. And should I be jealous?' She opened the door and went out onto the drive.

George turned at her approach.

'Isn't she beautiful? I've called her Esmeralda. Don't you think it suits her? Sort of … stately and dignified.' He continued to smile at the ambulance.

Penny was nonplussed. He really had fallen in love with it, a heap of metal and four wheels. He was gazing at it like it was Elizabeth Taylor in her prime. She felt she had to do something before things got any worse.

'George…' she began uncertainly.

George smiled encouragingly at her. 'I know,' he said. 'She's lovely, isn't she? I knew you'd come round. She's a grand lady. She's really going to take us places.'

Worse and worse. Penny didn't want to be taken to any 'places' in that old heap. She'd better put her foot down and keep it down. 'I told you before, George, I am *not* going anywhere in that thing.' George looked at her in surprise.

'But I've fixed it. It won't break down again. It's got a new radiator, spark plugs, battery, fan belt … the works. Jimmy's given it the once-over and he's happy with it. And you know how fussy he is.'

Penny shook her head. 'It's an old heap and there's no way I'm going to spend my holidays in it, George Montague. How many times do I have to say it? You can replace all the spark plugs in the world and it will still be an old heap.'

'No, you don't understand, Penny love.' George grasped her arm as she made to go back to the house. 'I've got the engine running perfectly. Now that I've fixed that I can start on the inside, fix it up like a real camper. I'm good at woodwork. You can have all the cupboards you want, a wardrobe, tables. I can make us a bed…'

Penny looked at him in surprise. What planet was he living on? He might manage a double glazing and conservatory business and heft heavy doors and windows about every day, but the joiners and tradesmen did the fitting and building work. What did *he* know about making cupboards and beds?

Before she could voice these thoughts, George pulled her towards the van.

'Look, just come out with me for a ride in her. Esmeralda's so quiet, she runs like a Rolls-Royce.'

Before she knew it, Penny found herself installed in the passenger seat of the ambulance. This had seen better days too: the plastic was worn and cracked in places and the seat was hard.

George saw her disapproval. 'I can get new foam rubber for these seats and cover them to look as good as new.' He started up the engine and slowly backed out of the drive.

Penny closed her eyes and prayed for their safe return home.

'Just a short ride, George,' she pleaded. 'You might have fixed up the engine, but the springs aren't up to much.'

Esmeralda responded to every bump in the road. George smiled ecstatically.

'Isn't she grand? What a girl. She goes like a bird. I can't wait to get her back on the open road. She'll fly!'

Penny felt she might fly out of her seat altogether as they bounced along, her head hitting the cab roof when George took the speed bumps too quickly. At her cry, he slowed down and made his way sedately down the street. As they came to a parade of shops, they saw a crowd had gathered a little way ahead. George sounded the horn to make them aware of his approach. As they drew near, Penny saw they were bending over a figure prostrate in the road.

Looking up and seeing the ambulance approach, a man jumped up and waved George down. George braked sharply, nearly sending Penny through the windscreen.

'What the…?' he exclaimed. 'I could have killed him.'

'Oh, never mind me,' cried Penny, nursing a cricked neck.

Ignoring her, George wound his window down and leant his head out. 'You want to be careful, mate. I could have killed you there. You shouldn't go jumping out in front of cars like that.'

'You're an ambulance, that's why I jumped out! Quick, come and help us. There's a young lad here just collapsed in the road. Think he might be on drugs, by the look of him. You'll have to get him to the hospital quickly. Might be an overdose. He's got needle marks all up his arms.'

As he was speaking the man opened the cab door and, in his agitation, almost dragged George out of it.

'Hang on a minute,' George protested. 'I'm not an

ambulance. It's retired. It's a private vehicle now. I can't really help you.'

The man glared at George. 'You're an ambulance,' he insisted.

Other people joined him.

'Come on, let's get him aboard,' said a formidable-looking lady. 'I'm a retired nurse. This man needs the hospital, now. If it's an overdose of heroin it will slow his heart and breathing, and he must get immediate treatment.'

'But I'm not…'

No one took any notice of George. Penny jumped out of the cab and came to the back of the ambulance as the retired nurse opened the doors.

'We're not an ambulance,' she insisted. 'You can't put him in there.'

Although the ambulance had been stripped of its equipment, the main bed was still in place, with two seats on the other side.

The former nurse turned to Penny and said fiercely, 'There's no time to call another ambulance. It's coming onto rush hour. By the time they get through this man could be dead. Do you want to let that happen?'

'No, of course not, but…'

'No buts,' the nurse said firmly. 'We can lie him down on the bed and your husband can drive to the hospital. Pronto!' she shouted towards George, 'Get in and let's get going. I'll stay in the back with him. You can come in too,' she said to Penny.

'Good idea,' said George and made for his driver's door.

'What's a good idea?' Penny demanded.

'You can help stop him from falling off the bed,' called George over his shoulder. 'It's going to need two of you. I'll be driving fast. There're no straps on that bed, and, as you noticed, the springs aren't the best in these seats. But I *will* be rectifying that, Penny. It'll be a smooth ride in Esmeralda when I've finished with her.'

Without more ado, the unconscious man was lifted into the ambulance and the nurse hauled Penny in after her. In a moment they were off, George hitting the accelerator and shouting 'Nee-naw, nee-naw,' with his head stuck halfway out of the window.

'I knew I should never let you talk me into this.' Penny held on tightly to the young man on the bed, as much for her own benefit as his.

'"Just come for a little ride," you said. "She runs like a Rolls-Royce," you said. Well, I know one thing, George Montague… Just remind me never to invest in a Rolls-Royce, that's all I can say.'

Penny threw herself across the body of the young man as George took the roundabout at speed. The nurse, at the chest end of the man, did likewise. Whether it was having two women throwing themselves at him that stirred the young man, no one knew.

He moaned and opened his eyes. They were glassy and vacant. Red-faced and sweating profusely, he tried to sit up. Finding himself forcibly restrained, he began fighting with the nurse, his fists flailing randomly in the air and kicking out with his feet, throwing Penny across the ambulance clutching her stomach and groaning in pain. A lucky punch gave the nurse a black eye. Momentarily she eased her hold on him. It was all he needed. He sat up, holding his head, staring at her in horror.

'Get away, get away from me! I know you're the devil! You're a monster. You're red, red, red, red! See your black heart. No, you're not taking me with you. Get off, get off.'

He jumped up from the bed, making for the doors, rattling frantically at the handles and shouting incoherently, 'Never… Leave me… Door…door.'

'Help me,' ordered the nurse to Penny, who was still doubled up on the chair.

Penny staggered up and between them they dragged the screaming man back to the bed, shouting to George to hurry up.

'Doing me best,' he shouted back and put his foot to the floor. 'Mind, this won't do my engine any good you know.'

Holding on grimly, Penny mouthed, '*His engine!*' Wait until she got her hands on him; he might never walk again.

*** 

'Impersonating an ambulance, speeding fines enough to bankrupt us, a fractured rib and I'm lucky to still have all the bits I started out with.'

'I'm sorry about your rib, love.' George had the grace to look sheepish, even though Penny had vented every ounce of anger she possessed. 'It wasn't my fault we got stopped. That retired nurse hijacked us.'

'I wish you'd get hijacked,' Penny said bitterly. 'I know one thing: I wouldn't pay the ransom for you. I wouldn't even haggle. They could keep you. I might even advertise.' Slowly she limped out of the room, one arm to her back, one to her stomach.

Sadly, George watched her go. He might never get her out in his ambulance again, even if it didn't look like one. Yes, that's what he had to do even before he fitted it out. A few coats of paint and you would never know what it had been in a previous life.

He brightened up at the thought. Things weren't so bad after all. He grinned to himself. In spite of being 'hijacked', as Penny put it, he'd actually enjoyed that drive to the hospital, foot to the floor, riding the bus lanes, straight through the lights. Not a bad job, that, just a pity about the lad in the back.

He wouldn't mind having a go in a real ambulance. Maybe best not say that to Penny, though.

# CHAPTER 14

It was a busy Monday morning. Andrew Markingham, leader of York Council, was riffling through the papers on his desk prior to attending a meeting with the social services department. His private mobile phone rang. He looked at it and frowned when he saw it was Tom Young, head of the York Trades Council. No doubt Tom was at a loose end this morning and fancied a chat, but Andrew just didn't have the time.

He answered the call. 'Hello, Tom, I'm sorry I can't talk now. I'm just heading off for a meeting.'

'That's OK, Andrew. I was just wondering when you were next going to be in London. Perhaps we could meet up?'

'London? Well, as it happens, I'm there on Thursday, seeing our MP in the morning.'

'Splendid,' Tom said smoothly. 'I'm in London then too. Can I treat you to lunch, in a very special restaurant?'

'Mm, lunch? Well, I wouldn't say no to that, Tom. Is it a special occasion I don't know about, or just my lucky day?'

'It just could be your lucky day, Andrew. Hold that thought and I'll see you in Hammersmith. Shall we say one o'clock?'

'One o'clock it is.'

In his office in Swinegate, Tom Young ended the call and smiled to himself. The line was baited; he just had to bide his time for the fish to bite. If he knew his prey, the prospect of wielding so much power in the future would lure him in, as surely as an artificial fly would a salmon.

On his way to the meeting with social services, Andrew pondered his conversation with Tom Young. If ever there was a slippery customer … and there had been rumours last year, of course. His lucky day? He would have to be careful. A London lunch in an exclusive restaurant might come with a price tag.

\*\*\*

Tom had booked a table by one of the full-length windows that overlooked the restaurant's terrace and gardens. He was looking at the winter set menu when Andrew Markingham arrived. He greeted him warmly and settled him into the chair facing the terrace.

Andrew looked about appreciatively. 'How on earth did you manage to get a lunch booking at such short notice?' he demanded. 'I thought you had to book weeks in advance.'

Tom smiled and shook his head. 'I can't give away all my secrets.' He offered the winter menu to Andrew. 'I rather like the look of this, but if you would like the à la carte…?'

Glancing down the winter menu, Andrew smiled happily. 'Oh, that looks good to me. The *antipasti prosciutto di Parma* and *crostini* is making my mouth water already.'

The two men kept the conversation general over the *antipasti* and *primi* courses, the light Italian wine gradually mellowing the mood between them. Andrew had had a very successful meeting that morning with the sitting MP and could afford to relax over a long lunch before catching the evening train back to York.

As they waited for the *secondi* course of *branzino al forno*, a roasted sea bass dish, Tom felt the time was right to test out where Andrew stood on the forthcoming planning application by Bookwood Developments.

Fortuitously Andrew enquired how the members of the Trades Council were faring during the ongoing difficult cutbacks.

Tom admitted things had not been easy for a lot of the

registered members.

'However,' he said, taking a sip of his wine and looking quizzically at Andrew over the rim, 'I hear there could be some good news for the people of Allsthwaite in the near future. A large housing development would require a lot of local tradespeople … just the boost that York needs, in terms of housing and employment.' He set his glass down carefully and looked across the table at Andrew.

'So,' Andrew said slowly, 'the rumour mill has swung into action already, has it? I shouldn't be surprised, should I? York's a small place, really. Word was bound to get out.'

Tom was silent, waiting for Andrew to expand on this.

Andrew glanced around the room, checking no one was within hearing. He leant forward towards Tom and said carefully, 'I believe Bookwood Developments have some proposals in mind but no formal application has been lodged as yet. Let's just say there have been some discussions.'

'And does the council, and its leader, have a view about the proposed development?'

'It might have. Are you asking on behalf of the Trades Council?'

They were at the nub of things now. Tom took a breath and stared out at the garden. He looked back at Andrew. 'No, I'm asking for you.'

Andrew was taken aback. What did Tom mean?

'Were the council to look kindly on the Allsthwaite scheme, certain advantages could accrue to the city and yourself in the future.'

Andrew's eyes narrowed. 'I hope we're not talking bribery or backhanders, Tom. I've never gone in for any of that. If you are, we'll stop it right there.'

Tom shook his head. 'No, no, no, Andrew, you've got it all wrong. Sit down, relax.'

Andrew had half-risen from his seat but at Tom's words he sat down again, twisting his wineglass in his hand.

'Besides,' Tom smiled gently at him, 'there's the sea bass and the lemon tart to come. Let's not waste a good lunch by being at crosspurposes, my friend. There is no bribery in my proposal. Just hear me out and I think you may be interested in what I have to say.'

Over their main course, Tom outlined the brief from Bookwood Developments. Andrew was still a young man and, even if the proposals for regional mayors took a few years to come to fruition, he would be in prime position to put himself forward for the post. Think of the huge region he would have command over: all of Yorkshire and Humberside, possibly. What power and influence he would have at his fingertips.

As Tom painted the rosy picture of York as the command centre of this powerhouse, as it had been in previous centuries, he could see Andrew drinking it in and turning the idea over in his mind.

A campaign fighting fund would be needed. Very large sums would be made available to Andrew for this purpose, were he to look kindly on Bookwood's plans.

Grey Eyes at Bookwood Developments had been right. The appeal of being in a position of huge power was almost irresistible. Tom watched in amusement as Andrew struggled with himself, half-wanting to dismiss the idea out of hand but not being able to do so. Finally, the vision of the mayoralty of several metropolitan councils, huge cities and towns – as far as the eye could see – won out.

'I think I can carry the council with me on this one,' he said at last. 'Allsthwaite always was the first on the list for possible expansion. It's long overdue and can easily carry this new development.'

'Good man.' Tom raised his glass in a toast to Andrew. 'Here's to Allsthwaite.'

Later that afternoon, Tom texted Bookwood Developments:

*A good day's fishing. Caught a big one.* Grey Eyes would be pleased with that.

He went on his way, deciding there was time for some shopping before returning to York. That hot little blonde

Jennifer deserved a present from London. Mm, lacy underwear maybe, then he could have the pleasure... He turned his steps briskly towards Oxford Street.

# CHAPTER 15

'Ee, the feed prices round here,' Rose commented to Arthur. 'I think we're going to have to take a ride out to our old supplier at Allsthwaite for new supplies. Price of pellets at that feed shop Walter uses! He must think we're made of money. And as for his hay suppliers! We'll have to have a chat with our old neighbour, Mervyn … see if he has any he can spare us to see the alpacas through the winter. I was hoping Walter might have let us have a bit of his – he's got plenty – but he's not biting, for all my hinting. Them horses belonging to his neighbour gets it all.'

She sighed. 'Aye, let's have a day out, lad. I miss Allsthwaite. It'll be nice to see Mervyn again. Maybe he can do us a bit of a deal.'

Arthur nodded. 'Aye, and his wife does a nice steak pie,'n' all. It's Monday. She always does pie on a Monday.'

Rose brightened. 'So she does.' She got up from the garden seat and called the dog. 'Come on, Jack, let's go and see your Uncle Mervyn. Bet *he'll* have a treat for you.'

Her loud calls were intended to reach Walter's ears, as he worked in his nearby barn. He came to the door.

'What you shouting the odds about now, our Rose?' he demanded.

'We're off out for the day, Walter. Going to see our old neighbour for some hay and get some feedstuffs for the girls. Too pricey round here,' she sniffed.

'It isn't,' Walter snorted. 'You're just too tight to pay the proper price for stuff. Who you going to try and do a deal with this time, that poor old sod of a neighbour of yours? If I know you, you'll be skewering him into the ground, never mind do a deal.'

'Think what you like, Walter Breckenridge. I won't be taken advantage of, not like you.' She stalked off towards her lorry. 'At least *he'll* let me have some hay so my poor girls don't starve.'

'Tcha,' Walter exclaimed in disgust. '*Starve*. They're bloody pampered pets, that's what those woolly-backs are. They don't need a load of best hay throwing at them morning, noon and night. They're in my best hayfield; they won't get better grass anywhere. You've only to look at 'em. If they get any fatter they'll hardly be able to waddle up and down that field.'

'Nonsense. You're talking out the back of your—'

Walter never did find out the end of the sentence. It was lost as Rose slammed the lorry door and revved up the engine. Arthur jumped in beside her and they were ready.

Rose leant out of the window as they passed Walter. 'Tell Ellie we'll get our dinner at Allsthwaite. It's steak pie today. We're not going to pass that up.'

Walter watched the lorry bump down the lane. '"*Tell Ellie…*" She's leaving instructions for the staff now, is she? We'll have to do summat about you, madam. I can't stand much more of this, and neither can Ellie.'

He stomped back into his barn, consoling himself with the thought that every cloud has a silver lining. He was going to enjoy telling Ellie that they'd got shot of them for the day.

\*\*\*

Without Rose and Arthur, lunch was a peaceful affair. Rose liked the news on at lunchtime. Walter thought it was just so that she could shout back at the reporters when she disagreed with them, which was most of the time. Even Elvis seemed to appreciate the peace and stretched out on his back in his basket, sighing contentedly.

Walter looked at him and smiled. 'I wouldn't mind coming back as a dog. Good food, warm bed and a little work now and again. Other than that, snooze in the sunshine when you like.'

'Always provided you have a good owner,' Ellie said practically. 'Would you like to be Rose's dog and sleep in a cold lorry and get the scraps?'

'Not bloody likely,' Walter grimaced. 'But, thinking of snoozing, I might just take advantage of a quiet house and have forty winks in the chair.' He grinned at Ellie. 'Unless…?'

'I'm potting up jams in the byre.' Ellie moved towards the back door. Seeing Walter's disappointment, she smiled and added,

'But not all afternoon, Walter. You get your snooze whilst you can.'

Walter settled down in the deep armchair and smiled happily. Life wasn't all bad.

Half an hour later, the jangling phone brought him out of his sleep. He'd been fishing by a beautiful lake, the cool greeny-blue mountains behind him, with cows grazing right down to the water's edge. He'd just caught this enormous fish…

The phone continued to ring, bringing Walter to full consciousness. 'Wha … what the…?'

The wisps of his dreams dispersing, Walter heaved himself out of the armchair and went into the hall to answer the phone. It was Will, a nearby farmer.

'Now then, Walter,' he began. 'Hast tha started keeping alpacas?'

'No.' Walter was instantly alert. What now?

'Well, I seen some in your field last week and now there's a whole rake o' them up and down the road outside here. Are you sure they're not yours?'

Walter heaved a sigh of exasperation. He might have known the minute Rose sloped off there would be trouble of some kind coming his way. 'They're not mine, Will, they're me sister's. Our Rose and that loopy Arthur, her partner. They're daft about them.'

'Well, them alpacas ain't so daft,' said Will. 'They're making short work of the grass verges down here. You'll have to come and get them, Walter. They're blocking the road and I'm expecting a feed delivery any time.'

'I'm on my way.'

Walter put the phone down and cursed his sister roundly. Instead of a wonderful afternoon stretching ahead of him, he was going to spend half of it rounding up them bloody alpacas. He wondered if Elvis would be of any use; after all, he managed the sheep a treat now. All Elvis had to do was get the alpacas off the road, turn them up the lane and back into the hayfield. Shouldn't be too difficult. With luck, he'd be back in half an hour, tops, and by then Ellie would have finished them ruddy jams…

Calling Elvis, Walter made his way down the lane and into his hayfield, where the alpacas had been grazing since they arrived at Claygate Farm. He shook his head, surveying the broken fencing. Arthur had assured him the alpacas would not jump the fencing. It was too high for them.

Mournfully, Walter could see his afternoon disappearing before his eyes. He might be able to get them bloody animals back in here, but he was going to have to repair a whole lot of fencing as well and *that* didn't take five minutes.

He shook his fist at the skies. 'Thank you, God, thanks a bundle. One afternoon after weeks of those two and you send me this. Just one afternoon, that's all we wanted…' Words failed him. 'You're a real pal.'

Climbing over the broken fencing, he made his way down to the road. He could see the alpacas strung out along the roadside, happily pulling at the grass on the steep banks either side. 'Come on, Elvis,' he called to the dog. 'We've got work to do. Just pretend they're sheep – a bit bigger, that's all. We'll get them rounded up in no time.'

When they reached the road and Elvis saw the alpacas, he stopped dead. It had taken him a long time to get used to the sheep but these weird hairy things that sang and squeaked at him… No, he wasn't going anywhere near them. They could let fly with those hooves of theirs, too. He remembered that one all too well.

'Come on, you daft bugger,' Walter shouted at him. 'It's just a bloody big sheep, that's all. Same difference. Just get to the back of them and send them this way. I'll stand in the road and turn 'em up the lane. Come bye, Elvis, come bye.'

Elvis was having none of it. No amount of Walter shouting, swearing or jumping up and down would make him move. Finally, Walter lost his temper and got hold of him, throwing him up the road towards the alpacas.

'Git away bye and do your job, Elvis,' he shouted after him. 'Or it won't be *steak* pie on our menu tonight, lad. It might be *you*.'

But Elvis was sure of one thing: he was not going to tangle with those creatures at any price, no matter how much Walter shouted at him. Regaining his balance, he scrambled up and over a drystone wall into a field and raced at top speed, away from the yelling Walter.

Walter watched him go, calling to him at the top of his voice. It was to no avail. Elvis did not come back.

Now what to do? Walter knew he couldn't round the alpacas up on his own. He'd have to go for Will and see if he would help. 'If he wanted his feed delivery, he would have to,' Walter thought grimly.

'I thought you had a dog,' Will said, when Walter had asked for his help.

'I have,' Walter said shortly. 'For all the good he is. I thought I was in a fair way to training him. He was getting good with me sheep but he won't entertain them alpacas. I told him they were just bloody big sheep but he wouldn't have it. He's run off,' he ended gloomily.

''Spect he'll make his way home when his belly's empty,' Will said consolingly.

'Not so sure.' Walter surveyed the grazing alpacas in the

lane. 'I told him he might be tonight's dinner if he didn't get on with the job.'

Will chuckled. Walter was known to be a big softy around his animals. He even used to have an old house hen, Sarah, in his bachelor days. She ruled his life.

'He'll come back. Now then, let's get these beasts back where they belong.'

***

Walter sank wearily onto the kitchen chair. Ellie poured him a cup of tea, which he drank down thirstily, regardless of it nearly burning its way down his throat.

'I wondered if they might be a bit skittish.' Ellie refilled his cup.

'*Skittish!*' Walter exclaimed. 'They were a bloody sight more than skittish. They're wild. I might have known it. Nothing belonging to our Rose is ever going to be docile, is it? I'd sooner round up a bunch of them bounding gazelles you see on the telly. That lot aren't far off.'

'Thomson's,' Ellie said thoughtfully.

'Thomson's?' Walter was thrown off his stride for a moment. 'What's Thomson's got to do with anything?'

'Gazelles, Walter. I think they're called Thomson's gazelles.'

'Well, bloody Thomson can keep 'em, and the alpacas too.'

'It's called pronking,' said Ellie.

'What is?'

'That bounding about that the young gazelles do. I think I've heard it called pronking.'

'Oh God. Women,' he thought. 'How did we get here?' He'd been talking about alpacas.

'Well, them alpacas could pronk for Britain,' Walter said tiredly. 'They had me and Will all over the place before we got 'em up the lane and into the field. And he's older than me! He won't want to do that again any time soon, I do know. I owe him big time now.'

Walter rubbed his back. 'That big 'un, by heck, it was a bit feisty, that one. I got a hold of it to get it to go up the lane. It didn't want to go and we had a bit of a set-to. Will said it was as good as watching a rodeo.

'Wait till our Rose gets back. They can fix that fence properly. I've put some temporary shuttering up for now to keep 'em in, but they'll have to make a job of it –no doubt with *my* fence posts and netting. Be too much to expect her to go and buy any,' he ended bitterly.

'And where's Elvis?'

'You might well ask.'

'I am asking.' Ellie adored Elvis. She'd got him as a pup and it had been love at first sight. 'So, where is he?'

'I don't know. He ran off. I took him with me to round up them alpacas but the daft bugger, he doesn't like 'em, and he legged it up and over a drystone wall of Will's and away he went.'

'And you didn't go after him? You'll have to find him. It's his teatime and the butcher gave me a lovely bone for him.'

Walter was outraged. 'I've just spent the last two hours chasing the most brainless four-legged creatures God ever made up hill and down bloody dale, run miles, hurt me back and me knees are knackered. I'm filthy dirty and starving hungry and all you can worry about is Elvis's tea.'

Ellie was unmoved. 'Drink your tea and have a wedge of fruitcake and some cheese. It'll fill you up and then you can go and look for Elvis. There'll be no dinner or *anything*,' she said with emphasis, 'until that dog is home.'

Walter knew when he was beaten. Where Elvis was concerned, Ellie was immovable. He knew his place in the pecking order: well below Elvis, the sheep and possibly even her hens and goats.

After he had demolished the cake and tea he made for the door. 'What if I don't find him before dinner?'

'Don't come home until you do,' Ellie said tranquilly. 'I'll keep something for you.'

Marvellous. Rose and Arthur got to dine out on juicy steak pie at Allsthwaite, whilst he might be lucky if he got beans on toast at this rate.

*\*\*\**

It was dark and the night was cold as Walter made his way back up the lane to Claygate with Elvis in the back of the car. He had found him miles away, limping down the centre of the main road of a village. Walter recognised him immediately and called out of the window to him. Elvis ran to the side of the road and cowered under a hedge.

Cursing himself, Elvis and the whole bloody world, Walter jumped out of the car and walked slowly over to the dog, holding his hands out. 'Come on, Elvis,' he called softly. 'What're you doing out here? Come on, let's go home.'

To his dismay, Elvis shrank away from him. He tried to get up and hobble away but his injured leg slowed his progress. Walter made a dive and grabbed him. Elvis yelped in pain.

'Sorry, old lad.' Walter bit his lip anxiously and carried the dog to the car. He laid him gently on the back seat and put the interior lights on to check Elvis over properly. From what he could see, he had no injuries other than the injured leg. It didn't appear to be broken; probably a strained muscle from jumping over walls.

Heaving a sigh of relief, Walter set off home for Claygate. At least he would be out of the doghouse with Ellie now and maybe they would all get a decent supper.

Far from being out of the doghouse, Walter was further in it. He might just as well have locked it up and thrown away the key. Ellie was far from pleased to find her precious Elvis had come home with a severe limp. Walter was sent to the barn for quantities of ice cubes to fill up a bowl. Elvis's leg was tenderly lowered into it, with much loving murmuring from Ellie.

Elvis loved all the attention and, in between fondly licking Ellie's face, he managed to swallow down the choice morsels of chicken and gravy she had saved for him.

Walter hovered, hoping his supper would soon be forthcoming, but Ellie was too occupied with Elvis to worry about him. 'Mm, supper? There's beans on toast if you can manage it, Walter. As you can see, I've got my hands full right now.'

Walter wandered off in disgust. Beans on toast... He might have to seek out the local pub and see what they had on the menu. Having said that, it had changed hands recently and the reports of the new landlord weren't that good.

He sat down in his armchair, undecided about what to do. Then he heard the voices in the hallway. Rose and Arthur were back. In a moment they were in the sitting room, bringing the tang of the cold night air with them. 'What a grand day, our Walter,' Rose said, a wide grin splitting her face.

'Aye, it *was* grand,' Arthur echoed, smiling happily at the memory. 'I don't know what Mervyn's wife does to a steak pie, but it was grand.'

Walter was ready to explode. Alpacas, Elvis, no dinner, steak pies... 'Grand! Well, I'm bloody pleased to hear it. Let me tell you two, I have *not*, repeat, *not* had a good day and the sooner you two and them bloody alpacas of yours are out of here, the better I'll like it. Now, if you'll excuse me, I'm off to the pub. At least I'll get a bit of peace down there and even maybe *a bit of dinner.*'

# CHAPTER 16

It was a bright October day and at the Café Paradise the morning rush of customers was over. In the café, the two new waitresses were kept busy – Louise at the coffee counter and Mandy waiting on the customers who were sitting in. Genevieve was lodged safely in the kitchen under Monsieur Henri's eagle eye, aiming for the perfect tomato, melted leek and blue cheese galette.

Jackie, Penny and Kate retired to the staffroom with their morning coffee. Penny smiled as she looked at her friends, both heavily pregnant, lowering themselves gently down into their chairs.

'Brings back memories,' she commented. 'I was as big as a house with our first one. George thought I must be having triplets. Glad it was only one – that was enough to take care of. Come to think about it, I think I did have two babies. George needed as much looking after in those days. I'm not sure much has changed,' she ended reflectively.

'Has he still got the ambulance?' asked Kate.

Penny's lips tightened and a scowl darkened her attractive face. She said through tight lips, 'Yes, unfortunately. Nothing will persuade him to part with it, even though I have ricked my back and fractured a rib.'

'He hasn't had you working on the thing?'

Penny tossed her head. 'Certainly not! That is never going to happen. I foolishly allowed him to talk me into going for a short ride in it, as he assured me everything's working properly. We ended up at Wigginton Accident and Emergency with a drug addict having a bad trip.'

Penny enjoyed the silence that followed these remarks and watched incredulous expressions creep over her friend's faces. Jackie and Kate settled themselves more comfortably in their chairs and demanded the story.

'George said we'd been hijacked,' Penny ended bitterly. 'I've told him I hope he does get hijacked in it again for real. And, believe me, I wouldn't pay the ransom. They could keep him. I've had enough. He's lucky he's still walking about as it is.'

Jackie shook her head. 'Only George could get into such a scrape. Wasn't the Harley enough last year?'

'It seems not. Now we have a big white elephant with go-faster stripes down the sides. I never wanted a camper in the first place. I don't know where he got the idea from but wherever he did, he can take it back again. We've no space for an elephant.'

Kate giggled as the vision of a large white elephant parked in Penny's sitting room floated across her eyes.

Penny turned to her indignantly. 'It's not funny, Kate. You try restraining a young man in the back of an ambulance who doesn't want to be restrained. I'm lucky I've only got one fractured rib.'

'I'm sorry.' Kate reached out and hugged her friend affectionately. Penny winced. 'Sorry,' she repeated.

'At least you've got a home to go to.' Kate sipped her coffee and looked at her friends sadly. 'Stan is busy destroying ours, bit by bit. We now have no bathroom and no kitchen. We would have a bed to sleep in, but we can't get at it because we're not gymnasts.'

Kate looked down at her swollen stomach and sighed. 'Not at the moment, anyway. So I've moved back to my parents for now. I just hope we'll have something resembling a home before the baby arrives. The joke is that Stan is trying to save money by doing things himself, but they are things he's no experience of.'

'Since when did that stop a man from having a go?' asked Jackie. 'Barney wants to make the nursery at our house, but I have other plans.'

'Does he know?' asked Penny.

There was a mischievous gleam in Jackie's eye. 'Let's just say I have a cunning plan.'

Kate and Penny nodded at each other. They knew that spelt bad news for Barney.

Jackie patted Kate's hand. 'Don't worry too much, Kate. I'm sure our boys will help Stan out. Beech Cottage has to be ready for its new arrival. We'll put our heads together.'

She pushed back her chair and got up slowly. 'In the meantime, come and look at what Brian's up to. Barney thinks I'm crazy and so does Dad – well, he would, wouldn't he? But I think you'll love it.'

\*\*\*

Brian had made good progress in taking out the fixtures and fittings belonging to the old shop and the whole place was filled with dust. But now the old cupboards were gone, the space was opened up and Jackie could see how light and airy the new part of the café would be. There were lots of holes to fill up in the walls before a final screed of new plaster could be applied and then the whole place would have to be thoroughly cleaned.

Gingerly, the girls picked their way around the room, discussing the positioning of new tables and chairs and possibly another cutlery and condiments station. Brian waited patiently whilst they made their tour. He was wondering about taking an early lunch break and giving Buddy and Zak a walk by the river, but once these women got their heads together and started planning, they could be here until teatime.

He was proved wrong. Penny felt she had left the new girls alone in the café for long enough and Kate was needed at the Historical Trust. They went off, leaving Jackie to survey her new domain with Brian. She smiled happily, looking at the swift progress he had made.

'I can't believe you've got this far already. We'll be up and running for the Christmas rush at this rate. I'll have to get my skates on and start ordering the new café furniture.'

'Aye.' Brian brushed down his dusty jeans. 'I've to chase in the electrics yet. I'll make a lot of dust with that. I might do that on a Sunday, when you're closed. Same for concreting the strip between the old and new parts…Messy job, that. It's coming on, though,' he mused in his quiet way.

Jackie beamed. 'It's fantastic, Brian. I'm delighted. I know, how about lunch in the café today, on me? You deserve it and I think the food will be particularly good. For once, harmony is reigning in the kitchen. Monsieur Henri actually seems pleased with Genevieve. There is going to be a wonderful French savoury galette on offer, so I'm told. How about it?'

Brian didn't need to be asked twice. Genevieve *and* a good lunch. No man could refuse that. He glanced down at his dirty clothes. 'Thank you. I'll take the dogs for a run and tidy myself up and I'll be in. Tell Genevieve to save me some. I wouldn't miss this for the world.'

\*\*\*

Half an hour later, Brian made himself ready in the flat above the café. Buddy and Zak had had a good run and lay panting in their beds, watching a newly showered Brian carefully comb his hair and splash on some aftershave.

Walking into the café, he made his way to a vacant table for two and sat down, looking about him. The lunchtime rush was on and Penny and the other waitresses were flying about, taking orders and delivering food at top speed. Brian watched them admiringly as they wove their way around the tables and the hungry customers. There was no doubt about it: delivering armfuls of food was a real skill. All that balancing of plates up their arms. One wrong move and… No, he wouldn't like to try it.

Jackie was busy at the coffee counter, deftly dispatching a queue of customers with coffee, scones and cakes. How she managed in that small space Brian would never know. As he watched, he worked out how she had placed everything within her reach so that it was more a question of turning left to right or reaching behind her to access most foods and drinks.

Penny interrupted his thoughts, order book in hand. 'Now, young man, I hear a large slice of Genevieve's galette is reserved for you. Good choice. It looks gorgeous.'

If it's half as gorgeous as her… 'Yes, please,' he said aloud. 'But only if I get to thank her afterwards.'

Another one smitten, Penny thought. The way they all fall for her, it's amazing. She's not at all vain; she doesn't seem to be conscious of her own beauty. Wish I had half of it. A little wistfully, she gave the order to the kitchen and delivered Brian's message.

Genevieve smiled her wide smile, green eyes glowing. 'He hasn't eaten it yet but I'm sure he'll like it. It looks yummy. Even Monsieur Henri is pleased. Let me know when he's finished it, then we'll see,' she ended a little shyly.

But Monsieur Henri was having none of it. There was no time for Genevieve to be sloping off into the café in the middle of a busy lunchtime. 'Madame Pennee can accept his thanks for you. I need you 'ere right now. Ere is my special chicken roulade to cut and make the *salade* for and we have orders for three more smoked salmon croque norvégien There is work for us, Genevieve. There is no time for this Brrrrian.'

Lunch lived up to its promise but Brian was very disappointed not to get even a glimpse of Genevieve. Every time the kitchen door opened he looked up hopefully, but sadly it was only the waitresses in and out with the dishes.

He could not sit there all afternoon; he had his work to get on with. He went to the coffee counter and thanked Jackie for his lunch and made his way sadly out of the café and back up to the flat to change his clothes. He was determined to see

Genevieve before the day was out, Monsieur Henri or not.

He plied his drill vigorously, cutting out a channel for new wiring. Brian Box was not going to be deterred by a bossy Frenchman, however good his cooking was. He was going to ask Genevieve out and that was that.

\*\*\*

Genevieve worked hard in the kitchen, all through the busy lunch period and on into the afternoon, when demand was high for afternoon tea and Monsieur Henri's special patisseries. Tiny individual cakes had to be filled with cream and fruits: millefeuilles, chocolate *framboisiers*, eclairs and tiny meringues assembled into perfect works of art on a plate.

Genevieve had a particular talent for this work. Painting was her great love in her spare time and, in assembling the tiny component parts of the patisserie, she could see the finished work she needed to create to satisfy Monsieur Henri.

It seemed only moments before the afternoon rush subsided and she had time to draw breath. She had been thinking about Brian as she worked and was determined to see him before she left that day. If he finished before her – which was quite likely, the way things were going today, he would be up in his flat with his dogs. Genevieve didn't feel bold enough to go and knock on his door. What on earth would she say if he answered it? 'Hello, I've come so you can thank me for my galette.' Hmm, dumb and dumber.

It was almost the end of the afternoon. As luck would have it, Monsieur Henri decided to go and talk to Jackie in her office about a supplier he was not happy with. As soon as he was safely out of the way, Genevieve prepared a tray of tea and small cakes and hurried through the back of the café where Brian was clearing up after his day's work.

She peeped cautiously round the dustsheets and boards that separated the café from the new building. The back door was open and she could see Brian taking old bits of cupboards outside to the skip in the yard. Carefully negotiating her way, she stepped around the boards and placed the tea tray on an old table. She straightened up as Brian came back for more of the old broken-up wood.

He smiled broadly when he saw her. 'Hello, I'm so pleased to see you. Penny said that old Monsieur Henri wouldn't let you come into the café. Bit of a slave driver, isn't he?'

Genevieve blushed at the warm welcome. 'He's all right really. He's just dedicated and wants everyone else to be the same. And we were really busy today. I think people have started their Christmas shopping already and must be having lunch and tea out too.' She indicated the tea tray. 'I brought you these…Thought you might like some afternoon tea. I can't stay. Monsieur Henri won't be long with Jackie and he'll go bonkers if he finds me gone.' She smiled shyly.

Brian eyed the delicious-looking cakes ravenously but this was not the time to tuck in. They faced each other across the tea tray. Now was his moment. 'Thank you, it was very thoughtful. I think Monsieur Henri has a real treasure in you and he doesn't realise it. Lunch was wonderful and those cakes look fantastic. Did you make them?'

Genevieve demurred hurriedly. 'Oh no, Monsieur made the meringues and sponges. I just put the fruits and bits and pieces together. It's his work really.'

'Mm, I don't agree but we shan't argue over it.'

Genevieve turned. 'I've got to go, Brian. Enjoy your tea.'

'Come on, lad,' he told himself in exasperation. 'Never mind prattling on about bloody cakes. Get her asked.

'Hang on a minute.' He moved round the table to her side. 'Will you come out with me? There's a great show on locally at the weekend. I wondered if you'd like to come.'

Genevieve's lips parted in surprise and her green eyes glowed. 'I'd love to,' she said.

Brian heaved a sigh of relief. She hadn't said no. She was so beautiful, it took his breath away and she was going to go out with him. Result. The same joy washed over him as when he got Buddy and then Zak, only this time even better.

Genevieve broke into his thoughts. 'What kind of a show?' she asked.

Brian wasn't sure he should tell her it was a car show; women could be funny about them. 'I'll keep it for a surprise,' he said. 'But I will tell you it's outside, so wrap up warm and wear sensible shoes …no tottering about in high heels. It's not that kind of show.'

Genevieve nodded and smiled. 'OK. Is Sunday all right? Only I think I'll have to work on Saturday.'

'Perfect.' Brian smiled back at her.

They could have remained like that indefinitely but for the roar of Monsieur Henri calling for her. 'Genevieve! Genevieve! Where is my Genevieve got to now?'

'I've got to go. See you Sunday.' Genevieve dived back through the dustsheets and ran off into the café.

Smiling after her, Brian addressed himself to the plate of tiny cakes.

'Someone's got to do the decent thing and I'm the only one here…' He sat down on a box and popped a little cake into his mouth. 'Life can be tough, working in a café,' he thought, 'but on the other hand…'

# CHAPTER 17

Brian was up early on Sunday morning to give Buddy and Zak a good run before his day out with Genevieve. The weather was bright and sunny and looked set fair to stay that way. After an hour of running, the dogs tired and were ready for home. A good breakfast awaited them and a long snooze. They would not miss him until teatime now.

After he had seen to the dogs, Brian showered and dressed carefully. Genevieve was a lot to live up to and he knew heads would turn admiringly as they made their way about at the car rally.

They were travelling to Castle Howard in Genevieve's car, a small Fiat, as Brian only had his works van, which he didn't feel was really suitable. Trundling up the majestic driveway to Castle Howard in his white van didn't fit in with his idea of escorting the most beautiful girl in the world to a fairy-tale castle. The Fiat it would have to be.

Genevieve was on time and Brian ran down the stairs to meet her. He didn't want the dogs jumping all over her. That would not get the day off to a good start. She was already out of the car and about to lock her door. She looked up at Brian's approach and he caught his breath in wonder. Out of her chef's whites she was stunning, dressed simply in well-cut trousers and a cashmere sweater, with a jaunty felt hat completing her outfit.

Brian counted his many blessings as he got into the car. He

had this lovely girl all to himself for the day. She was not only beautiful but funny and kind. It was going to be amazing.

Genevieve strapped herself in and started the car. She turned to Brian.

'Well, unless it's a mystery tour, you'll have to tell me where we're going.'

'Oh yes, I didn't tell you, did I?' Brian feigned surprise. He rubbed his hands together with glee. 'Castle Howard, young lady, to a car rally. Let's get going.'

Genevieve's eyes widened. 'Castle Howard …one of my favourite places. And there's a car rally there today?'

'Yup, veteran cars, classic cars, steam traction engines…You name it and they'll be there. You do like cars, don't you?' he added anxiously, suddenly worried in case it might be the worst day out in the world for her.

'Love them,' she answered happily. 'Dad used to have an old Morris Minor, split screen with a side-valve engine. I think it was 1951 or 1952. He never let me near it, though.'

As they drove along the A64 out of York and towards Castle Howard, Brian could see why. Genevieve drove as she lived life, with great gusto and a sense of adventure. Many times, Brian found himself applying his foot to an imaginary brake on his passenger side and it began to dawn on him what the phrase 'white-knuckle ride' really meant.

Genevieve was a fast driver, speeding up the dual carriageways and only pulling in at the very last moment as she ran out of road. Once, when Brian glanced across at her, she had her eyes shut as she pulled in after overtaking. 'Genevieve!' he exclaimed. 'Open your eyes, will you?'

She looked across at him and smiled guiltily. 'I know. I shouldn't do it really, but if I shut my eyes I know it will be all right. I don't like bends either,' she confided. 'I'm never too sure I'll make it round them, so I shut my eyes and hope for the best. It's worked so far.'

Brian covered his eyes and groaned.

'I'm not sure I actually like driving.' She negotiated a

roundabout and continued. 'I know I have to do it, in a necessary evil kind of way, whereas a lot of people really enjoy it. I have a friend, Margaret, and she loves driving. The minute she passed her test she went off all round Manchester and Leeds and had a whale of a time, just driving. Mm … not for me, I think.'

'Definitely not,' Brian agreed silently. For his own peace of mind, he offered to drive them home. 'I'm insured to drive any vehicle with the owner's permission and I do like driving. You could enjoy the scenery on the return trip.'

They left the Fiat in one of the car parks sited away from the castle and crunched their way along the gravelled paths which led to the archway that opened out to a courtyard, where there were shops and a restaurant. At the ticket office, Brian asked Genevieve whether she would like to visit the inside of the castle as well.

'I would,' she answered hesitantly, 'but it might be a bit expensive along with the rally fees. I could pay for us to visit the house.'

'No, you won't. It's my treat today.'

Passing through the ticket office, they made their way to the front of the castle. It was like stepping back to the *Brideshead Revisited* film set. Vintage cars from the early twentieth century were drawn up in front of the imposing entrance, their drivers dressed in leather coats and hats, wearing goggles that protected their eyes from the road dust. The ladies wore long driving coats with picture hats held on by long diaphanous scarves.

To Brian's amusement Genevieve was immediately entranced by the period clothing and made a beeline to talk to the ladies, leaving him free to wander around the vehicles and marvel at their pristine condition a century after they were built.

Genevieve soon fell into conversation with the ladies. Seeing her admiration for their clothes, one of the ladies let her try on her full-length driving coat with a deep fur collar that could be turned up against the cold. A wide-brimmed black hat accompanied the outfit, held on by a black silk scarf. Set against Genevieve's long copper-coloured hair, the whole effect was stunning.

The ladies oohed and aahed and took pictures of her with their phones. Genevieve was beginning to feel a little embarrassed by all the attention and went to remove the hat. Before she could do so, the owner of the 1928 Bentley motioned her to stop. 'Don't take it off yet, miss. I'd like to get a photo of you. In fact, would you mind sitting in the car, as if you're driving it?'

He opened the car door and Genevieve stepped in. She gripped the steering wheel with glee. 'Oh, wow, this is amazing. Does this thing work?'

'Of course she does,' the owner of the Bentley said indignantly. He switched on the ignition and the car sprang into life. 'She's a racing car; won them all in her day. Listen to that engine.' He stepped back and surveyed the car proudly.

Genevieve tentatively touched the accelerator pedal and the engine roared satisfactorily. Oh, she would love one of these: so much more fun than her Fiat. She might even enjoy driving if it was in one of these.

What was the lever on the side here for? The boot, by the look of it. As she fingered it, her foot was still on the accelerator. As the Bentley owner stepped forward to reach in and stop the engine, the lever gave way and Genevieve shot forward at speed, careering away in front of the castle.

Brian had his head deep inside the engine of a 1926 Austin 7 Box saloon, discussing the new arrangement of the gearing mechanisms, when loud shouts were heard coming from the around the castle entrance. One of the cars, a 1928 racing Bentley, was being driven erratically around the neatly kept paths. Brian withdrew his head from the Austin and looked around. No, it could not be… Genevieve was at the wheel of the Bentley, looking alarmed as she steered the car away from the people and on to the front lawn. The owner of the car was running behind her, frantically shouting and waving to get her to stop.

'I don't know how!' she shouted back.

'Stand on the bloody brakes!' he yelled at her. 'The brakes, girl, use the bloody brakes!'

For a few seconds, everything seemed to slow down as Brian watched Genevieve careering around the lawns. He stood paralysed with shock at the sight of an irreplaceable piece of history madly circling the grounds. Then he shook himself as a rush of adrenalin coursed through his body, bringing him fully alive to the awful situation developing in front of his eyes.

He sprinted at full tilt across the paths and the manicured castle lawn. He was younger and faster than the Bentley owner and made it to Genevieve first. Genevieve's hat had blown away and her long red hair was flying wildly behind her. Her green eyes were wide and a scared expression fixed her lips in a rictus smile.

Brian didn't waste his breath in shouting after her. With one flying leap, he made it over the passenger door and into the seat, grabbing the steering wheel with one hand and the handbrake with the other. The brakes squealed, digging a path through the turf as the Bentley slewed to a stop.

In a moment the owner of the car was upon them. 'You stupid girl, what did you do that for? If you've harmed my car in any way, you'll pay for it! And restoration costs don't come cheap, young lady.'

'Hold on, hold on.' Brian raised his hand. 'There's no damage done. I'm sure it was just an accident, wasn't it, Genevieve?' He looked at Genevieve. She was shaking her head in disbelief at the situation that had just occurred.

'I don't know what I did,' she said at last. 'They asked me to sit in the car. They wanted me to put on the driving clothes so they could take photographs for a magazine.'

'And that's all,' spluttered the enraged owner. 'Not run off with the bloody thing.'

'I didn't mean to. I didn't know that lever was the handbrake. I thought it opened the boot.'

'Shouldn't have touched it at all, then you wouldn't have

gone charging all over the place. Lucky you didn't kill anyone.'

'Come on,' Brian said decisively. 'This is getting us nowhere. Come on out of there, Genevieve.'

He helped her out of the car and turned to the owner. 'The car isn't harmed in any way, I'm sure of that. You drive it back onto the path and I'm sure you'll find it's fine. After all, it is a racing car – it will have done far worse than this in its day.'

A crowd had gathered and cheered as the Bentley slowly made its way back up to the castle entrance. Brian put his arm around Genevieve. 'It's going to be all right, you know. There's no harm done.'

Genevieve tried to smile through the threatening tears. 'I hope so. I never meant anything to happen. Are you all right? I've never seen anyone jump like that before.'

Brian rubbed his leg. 'I may have a sore muscle in the morning but that's about it, apart from a few grey hairs I didn't wake up with this morning.' He grinned and kissed her lightly on the forehead. 'Come on, let's go and see if Mr Bentley Owner has calmed down a bit.'

Finding his beloved Bentley was perfectly OK, the owner did indeed calm down and advised Genevieve to keep well away from all the other cars if she was intent on staying at the rally for the day. 'He made it sound as if I deliberately spend my time stealing rides in other people's cars,' Genevieve said indignantly.

Brian chuckled as they walked away towards the classic cars display. 'Can't blame him. You did steal his car and nearly ran half the visitors over whilst you were at it.'

'I never…' she began and then saw his huge grin.

'Come on, let's go and have some lunch. I'm starving. You can't do any damage around a beefburger and a glass of rosé, surely. Unless you squirt me in the eye with the ketchup or throw your wine over me.'

'Brian Box … you could regret that…'

\*\*\*

Lunch in the Courtyard Café passed pleasantly. Brian and Genevieve found they had a great deal in common and spent a happy hour discovering more about each other. Genevieve was a huge animal lover and was envious of Brian being able to have his dogs with him. 'I couldn't have one. It would be left alone all day whilst I was at the café and I couldn't do that.'

Brian agreed. 'I know a lot of people do it but to me it's self-indulgent. You can only leave a dog for a few hours at a time.' He smiled at her tentatively. 'You could share Buddy and Zak with me, if you like. They're always up for a run. Or if you just want to go in and sit with them for a while, they would love it and,' he hoped he wasn't pushing his luck too soon here, 'I would too.'

Genevieve looked steadily at him, searching his face for he knew not what. He returned her gaze unflinchingly. She must know he was sincere. 'I'd like that,' she said at last and smiled.

In some indefinable way they had crossed the Rubicon. Brian let out a long, slow breath and smiled back.

'Good.'

Emerging into the autumn afternoon, they decided there was still time to see around the castle and view the other vehicles displayed around the grounds before the light faded. They walked hand in hand up to the castle and waited with a group in the entrance for the next guided tour of the house.

They did not have long to wait. An official guide gathered them up and swept them off. She introduced herself as Cynthia and took them up the impressive grand staircase that led into the castle interior. It had stone steps with carved wooden balustrades either side. Antique sculptures and family portraits were everywhere.

Genevieve was very interested in the portraits of past members of the Howard family and would have liked to linger, but Cynthia moved them inexorably onwards. Brian dragged her away and they moved through the China Landing and on to several bedrooms with four-posters hung with luxurious old silk hangings. Then they went through the dressing rooms and the Antique Passage and on to the grander rooms: the Crimson Dining Room, the Turquoise Drawing Room and the Music Room. From there they walked through the Long Gallery into the Great Hall with its high, frescoed dome.

They were allowed to linger here for a while. Brian was fascinated by the dome's construction and listened carefully as Cynthia explained how Pellegrini's masterpiece was destroyed by fire in 1940 and rebuilt in the 1960s. Genevieve was not so interested in the massive and highly decorated columns that drew the eye up to the impressive dome above and wandered off to explore on her own.

The Long Gallery appealed to her sense of history and she wanted to look at it in more detail. Quantities of leather-bound books were carefully housed in antique bookcases and there was barely a space on the walls, they were so filled with huge paintings of ancestors and landscapes.

Pausing at the entrance to the Long Gallery, Genevieve could feel centuries of history surround her like a familiar old cloak. She gazed down the length of the room, the dim light of the high chandeliers bringing a glow to the polished oak flooring.

Slowly she wandered down the gallery, imagining herself in eighteenth-century dress, obliged to exercise indoors during the cold Yorkshire winters. Maybe a green silk costume trimmed with lace with wide petticoats beneath. And Brian accompanying her, dressed in silk pantaloons and frilled shirt, diamond-buckled shoes on his feet. Smiling to herself, she stopped to examine the first picture, a large landscape presumably painted when the castle was first built.

''Twas very different in those days.'

Genevieve had seen no one else when she entered the Long Gallery and jumped at the deep male voice. She turned and found a tall man smiling down at her, dressed in eighteenth-century clothes, just as she had been imagining Brian. He was very handsome, with deep blue eyes set in his fine-drawn face.

'Oh, hello,' Genevieve replied. She forced her gaze away

from him and looked back at the painting. 'Yes, it must have been. The fountains and temple hadn't even been thought of then and the grounds wouldn't have been landscaped for a long time afterwards, I don't suppose.'

'You suppose rightly, young lady.'

He offered her his arm. 'Come and see a later view of the castle. My son, the fourth earl, had it painted in 1771 and you can see the building is nearly finished.'

Genevieve stared at the man. 'In 1771? Your son?'

The man laughed gently. 'Yes, dear Henry. He worked so hard here. I'm very proud of him. Of course, the lion's share of the castle was built during my lifetime.' He paused for a moment, contemplating the painting.

'I started it in 1700, you know. Ten years of continual building, but we almost did it. John Vanbrugh designed it. Yes, we were both members of the Kit-Kat Club in London in those days.' He shook his head wonderingly.

'How we achieved what we did I'll never know. He was a dramatist; didn't know much about architecture. What were we thinking of? But there you are.'

He smiled at Genevieve, his blue eyes crinkling at the corners. 'And here *we* are.'

Again he offered her his arm. He was charming, whoever he was. She could hardly resist him. She slipped her arm through his and found the silk sleeve of his jacket was cold to the touch.

They began a slow walk down the Long Gallery, pausing to look at the later painting of Castle Howard. Genevieve stole a look at her companion.

'If your son was the fourth earl,' she said slowly, 'does that mean…'

'It does, indeed,' the third earl replied, twinkling at her. He made his bow. 'Charles, third Earl of Carlisle. May I have the pleasure of knowing your name, miss?'

'Genevieve,' she stammered, 'Genevieve Anderson.' She tugged lightly at his sleeve and asked, trying not to show her confusion and embarrassment, 'I don't want to sound stupid, but does the castle employ actors to give the tours more ... atmosphere? You're just so ... real.'

The earl shook his head sadly. 'No, they don't. I don't think there's the money to spare for that. In fact, I don't approve of half the things they get up to in my castle these days, but what can I do? I'm only a dead earl and no one listens to me.'

Genevieve's lips parted in a round 'Oh'.

'Well, look around you. Here's a case in point. Look how that Tatham artist fellow decorated this Long Gallery. Not my taste at all – all those books mouldering behind glass; no one reading them. What's the good in that? They should be out on tables for my visitors to read, curled up in a chair by a roaring fire here on a winter's afternoon like this. And what do we have instead? No fire, no books. What kind of a house is that?'

Genevieve was bravely trying to hold on to the notion that she seemed to be conversing with a ghost. The third earl had died in 1738, she'd heard Cynthia say so not five minutes ago. 'If you're a *dead earl...*' she said slowly.

'Sadly, yes,' Charles answered cheerily. 'Don't come much deader than me. Please do call me Charles, my friends all do. I can't complain,' he continued. 'I had a good, long life and left a son to carry on the good work. Still...' He stopped, looking wistful. 'I wish I wasn't a ghost here now. All these modern ways. Look at today. Cars everywhere... Such contraptions: deathtraps. Give me a carriage and four any day. You can always rely on your horses.'

*The car rally! Brian!* He'd be wondering where on earth she had got to. And he'd never believe she'd been chatting to the third Earl of Carlisle, Charles to his friends.

She turned to face him and said with real regret, 'I'm sorry, Charles. It's been amazing to meet you, but I have to go. My friend is still in the Great Hall and he'll be missing me by now and I'm not too sure he would understand about ... you.'

'Ah, the Great Hall,' mused the earl, 'now *that is* an achievement.' He sighed. 'I know you have to go. No one can stay, not even me. I visit on Sundays, you know, just in case you're here again. I'm quite shy really, but I couldn't resist escorting such a beautiful young lady as you today. Do come again. I've enjoyed our little chat and I can show you so much more another time. Goodbye, Genevieve, or shall we say *au revoir*?'

In a moment the earl had melted away through the picture of the castle they had been looking at. As she stood there staring at the painting and shaking her head, Brian entered the gallery.

'Here you are … I've been looking all over for you. What are you doing in here on your own?'

'I was talking to the earl,' she replied. 'What a sweetie he is; has charm by the bucketload.'

'Oh.' Brian stopped short, seeing something in her face he could not quite read. 'He wasn't cross about your car escapade earlier, was he?'

'No, he never mentioned it. Probably didn't know about it. He doesn't like cars. He called them contraptions and deathtraps. He prefers a carriage and four. Said he could always rely on his horses.' She turned to walk towards him.

'Well, he would, wouldn't he? What would he know about cars? They weren't invented in the 1700s.'

'Excuse me?' Brian shook his head. Had he missed something or had the rosé gone to her head at lunchtime?

Genevieve smiled and took his arm. 'I was talking to the third Earl of Carlisle. He asked me to call him Charles. He died in 1738.'

'Oh, been chatting to a ghost, then, have you?'

'Mm,' Genevieve answered serenely. 'He asked me to come back again. He visits on Sundays. I think I probably will. He was lovely.'

'Aye, and so is a bottle of rosé, but maybe not so much of it next time.'

She had been right. No one would believe her, but she knew what she had seen. Keeping a tight hold on her arm, Brian led her back down the Grand Staircase and out to the car rally once again. Ghosts …whatever would she come out with next?

# CHAPTER 18

The year was drawing on, bringing in the long November evenings. Barney was acutely aware it was time for them to acquire an estate car that could be used for transporting the twins when they came along and all the paraphernalia they would have to cart about for them. After dinner one evening, he settled Jackie in the armchair by the fire, brought the laptop in and began perusing websites selling cars.

Seeing them settled down, Samson crept quietly into the room and curled up a safe distance from the fire. This was perfect for a winter's night and, if he played his cards right, he might to get to stay in here after those two went to bed. That fire could well last him through the night. It was wet outside and the mice could rest easy in their beds; he was not going out hunting. There would be plenty of time in spring for that.

'There're some great bargains to be had,' Barney commented. 'A lovely Volkswagen Passat here, and a Skoda Octavia.'

'Marilyn used to have a cat called Octavia,' Jackie murmured, mesmerised by the blue and gold flames leaping up the chimney.

'We can't drive a cat,' Barney said. 'Mm ... no. Oh, wow, there's a brilliant Volvo V90 estate for sale here, nearly new but a great price. That would be perfect for us, solid and reliable and plenty of room for everything. Trouble is, it's down in Dorset.' He frowned in concentration, his face lit blue-white by the screen.

'I love Dorset,' Jackie mused. 'Next to Yorkshire, I think it's my favourite county. Marilyn and Barry took me on holiday there when I was a teenager. The weather was gorgeous. So were the boys,' she smiled reminiscently.

Barney looked at her and smiled. 'Are these the secrets of your misspent youth coming out?'

Jackie laughed. 'Not misspent enough; Marilyn made sure of that. She kept an eagle eye on me but I managed to give her the slip sometimes.' She chuckled at the memory.

'I climbed out of my window and jumped into the flowerbed below. It wasn't very far down and it was worth it. Mm, teenage love – a spotty youth with an overlarge Adam's apple.' She shook her head. 'What was I thinking of?'

Barney put the laptop down on the floor and kneeled by her armchair. 'Well you can jolly well stop thinking of him now.' He reached up to take her in his arms. 'Never mind spotty youths. I was one once.'

Jackie ruffled his blonde hair, 'Mm-hmm, and look at you now.' She put him from her and said, 'Tempt me no more. We were talking cars.'

Reluctantly Barney resumed his search on the laptop. Some time later he raised his head. 'That Volvo in Dorset looks a good deal. I think I'll ring up about it. Now, where did I leave my phone?'

'Kitchen, I think. Ow, babies, stop kicking. Snuggle down. It's nearly bedtime for you two and it soon will be for me, so give me a break here, OK?'

Barney returned smiling. 'Yes, it's still for sale. I could go down on Saturday morning and see it.' He looked thoughtful. 'Trouble is, if I buy it I can't drive two cars back and you can't come with me… I could ask Jake, but I have a feeling he's busy this weekend…'

'Stan?'

Barney shook his head, 'Too busy on the house. Kate would kill me.'

'Yeah, me too, probably. What about George?'

'He often works Saturdays, but I could ask.'

'Brian,' exclaimed Jackie. 'He doesn't have to work Saturdays. He could go with you. Boys' day out.'

'I like the sound of that.' Barney grinned at Jackie. 'It would be good to spend some time with Brian. He's a great guy. Ah, but what about his dogs?'

'Mm, what about his dogs? I know! Genevieve!'

Barney looked at her askance. 'What do you mean, "Genevieve"?'

'She could look after the dogs. She does already. She and Brian are an item, you know, and she often goes in and collects the dogs and takes them out. I'm sure she'd love to dogsit for the day. In fact … it's a good few hours down to Dorset. Why don't you make a boys' weekend of it? Might be your last chance before fatherhood claims you.'

'Not a bad idea,' Barney said thoughtfully. 'In fact, that could be a plan.'

Jackie smiled to herself. A brilliant plan; she had ideas of her own. When the cat's away … and she didn't mean Samson.

***

'Dad? Are you busy at the weekend?'

'Who wants to know?' Between keeping tabs on Rose and Arthur at Claygate and helping Ellie at the markets, Walter had enough on his hands.

'I do, Daddy dear,' Jackie said sweetly.

Walter was instantly alert. When Jackie used that dulcet tone of voice to him, it usually meant trouble for somebody and more often than not, for him.

'What's up now?' he asked flatly. 'If you've got yourself into some scrape, I'm not getting you out of it. Barney's sure to find out and then I'll be in even more bother.'

Jackie chuckled down the telephone line. 'Oh ye of little faith! There is no scrape, no trouble. I would just like a little help from my dear old dad this weekend.'

'What kind of help?' Walter asked guardedly.

'Well, Barney's abandoning me for the weekend and off on a jolly with Brian Box. You know, his friend from Cumbria who's doing the work at the café for me.'

'Aye, I know him. What do you mean, "a jolly"? This is no time to be going away, with you in your condition.'

'It's all right, Dad, keep your hair on. I told him to go. We need a bigger car to accommodate the twins when they arrive and he's seen just the thing for us, only it's away down in Dorset. So I suggested he take Brian to drive our car home and make a weekend of it.'

'Hmph,' grunted Walter. 'Why can't he go to a garage in York? It'd be easier.'

'Oh, but this was such a good bargain, too good to pass up. A gorgeous almost-new Volvo estate. Anyway, let's not waste time on all that. I just want to know if you could give me a hand this weekend.'

Walter thought for a moment. It might be nice to have his daughter to himself for a while. At least he could keep an eye on her. He didn't like the thought of her being on her own with Barney away overnight. 'I suppose I could,' he said. 'When you say this weekend, do you mean the whole weekend?'

'Yes, I do,' Jackie said. 'I've a project I need a hand with and I think we could manage it between the two of us. You could stay over and then we'd get it all done before Barney gets back.'

'Does he know about it?' Walter asked. He'd been here before with the women in his life. They were all as crafty as a cartload of monkeys.

'Oh, yes,' Jackie said airily, her fingers crossed behind her back.

'All right, then. I'll be round on Saturday morning.'

Jackie put the phone down and rubbed her hands. Operation Nursery was about to swing into action.

\*\*\*

Saturday morning was dry and bright and Barney departed early to collect Brian from the flat above Café Paradise. Brian had been quite happy to accompany Barney to Dorset and was fairly confident that Genevieve would be all right looking after Buddy and Zak. She was going to stay in the flat for the weekend and Brian had no doubt his beloved dogs would be very spoilt the whole time.

As it was a boys' weekend away, he and Barney had decided on a proper full English breakfast enroute. By 9a.m., their rumbling stomachs brought them to a truckers' café where Brian confidently predicted they would get the best breakfast in Yorkshire.

He had not exaggerated. Huge plates filled with sausages, bacon and eggs came their way, followed by thick doorsteps of hot toast dripping with butter and lashings of marmalade. A long time and several mugs of hot, strong tea later, they staggered back to the car and took up their journey again.

'Did you tell Jackie the breakfast plan?' Brian asked as they got underway.

'No,' admitted Barney. 'She's got the healthy eating kick, what with the twins coming and everything. Annabel, her sister, was always into it and so is Walter's wife, Ellie. So what chance do I, a mere male, have?'

'Mm.' Brian ruminated on these remarks for a while. 'Are they all like that?' he asked eventually.

'What do you mean? Like what?'

'Like… Well, Genevieve's not keisty about her food, not that I know of.'

'Keisty?'

'Yeah, keisty: fussy. She eats anything and doesn't worry about what's in it and how much cholesterol it's got.'

'Well, she doesn't need to, does she? She's always eaten like a horse and never put on an ounce. I don't suppose she ever will. My dad's tall and still quite slim, but my mother still fusses over him. He never even sees the chicken skin or the fat on a steak. It's all whipped away long before it gets to the table.'

Brian raised his eyebrows and mournfully contemplated this vision. He had fallen irrevocably in love with Genevieve and found the numerous scrapes and difficulties she created for herself at the café endearing. Her kind and generous nature was far more important to him. He only hoped she never got too keisty with him about their food. Now that *would* be one move too far.

After their enormous breakfast there was no need for a lunch break and they made good time to Bridport. The traffic was not too heavy and Sally satnav brought them to the Ship and Bottle at teatime.

It was a pub with rooms. Trade was quiet in November and Barney had been able to get them two single rooms. Leaving their bags in their rooms, they went down to the bar for a drink. The Ship and Bottle had kept its traditional atmosphere and still retained the old wooden countertop with hand-pulled beer pumps. High bar stools were ranged along the bar.

Barney sat on a stool. 'That was a long drive. I think we've earned a drink now. What will you have?'

Brian looked at the beer pumps ranged along the bar. 'Mm,' he mused. 'There's a lot of Palmers here. Are they a local brewer?'

The landlord nodded. 'Proper beer, brewed just down the road. The brewery's been there for over two hundred years. I can recommend them all to you. What's your fancy? If it's a thirst quencher you're after I would start with the Palmers Copper Ale. That's light and refreshing.'

Brian nodded. 'I like the sound of that. We could try some of the others later.' Barney agreed and they were soon slaking their thirst with two foaming pints.

\*\*\*

As soon as Barney was safely out of the way on Saturday morning, Jackie went to the garage and retrieved the sturdy cardboard boxes she had been storing there. Back in the house, she carefully began to pack the contents of Barney's study.

They had not discussed in detail where the new nursery for the twins would be. Jackie knew Barney had assumed it would be the room at the end of the corridor upstairs but, as far as Jackie was concerned, he had assumed wrongly. His large study, the room next to their bedroom, was perfect for the twins' nursery. With a whole weekend to herself, now was the time to sort it out. That way, faced with a fait accompli, she hoped Barney would give in gracefully and make do with the smaller room for now. In the future, they would have to make other arrangements. If the twins were not the same sex, their family would soon be running out of rooms.

Walter arrived promptly at ten o'clock. Jackie wasted no time and took him upstairs to Barney's study, where she had already stacked some filled boxes.

'Aren't we having a cup of coffee?' Walter asked. 'I didn't have time for one at Claygate. I had to sort Rose out with yet more netting to keep them peacocks of hers penned in.'

'No time for that now, Dad. We can have an early lunch and lots of tea with it,' Jackie suggested brightly. 'Come on. Let me show you what's to do.'

'Aye, all right, then.' If he wasn't getting any coffee he might as well get to work, he thought gloomily. 'So, what's to do?'

At the top of the stairs Jackie turned and grinned at him. 'We're going to make a nursery for the twins over the weekend.'

'*We are?*' Walter looked at her suspiciously. 'Does Barney know about this?'

'And why wouldn't he?' Jackie asked blandly.

'Well, why else would you ask me? I know you too well. You're my daughter, remember. What are you up to?'

'We have to make a nursery sometime, Dad, and Barney's always so busy. So I thought now's as good a time as any. This way, Barney doesn't have to take any time off work and it will all be done when he comes home. Nothing for him to worry about.'

Walter was not convinced but was well aware that when

Jackie got the bit between her teeth she would bolt with it, and there would be no stopping her. And, in her present condition, if he wasn't there she might set about it by herself. And where would that lead?

Luckily there was very little in the smaller room, just Jackie's sewing box and a small chair. She moved them out and Walter began carrying the boxes in from Barney's study. As he was doing this, the doorbell rang, announcing the arrival of George Montague.

Walter was relieved to see George. He had been eyeing up the furniture in Barney's study and wondering how he was going to shift it. It didn't have far to go but it looked heavy.

'I hope you've had a good breakfast,' Walter said.

'Not the best ever,' George said mournfully. 'Penny's watching my weight for me. Toast and marmalade's off at the moment. I'm hungry already.'

'Nonsense,' Jackie said briskly. 'It's all in your mind. Tell you what: get this furniture shifted and it's bacon butties all round. How does that sound?'

George rubbed his hands with glee. 'You're a real star, Mrs Anderson. Show me the way.'

\*\*\*

Unfortunately for Barney and Brian, the Ship and Bottle stocked all of Palmers' beers and they spent the next three hours sampling them. Being a Saturday evening, the pub soon filled up and they found themselves in good company among the Bridport locals. A friendly rivalry broke out between the men from the south and the two from the north. Beers were sampled and solemnly pronounced upon, then a ratings board was set up and marks out of ten awarded for each beer. The Palmers strong 'Tally Ho!' beer topped the night, by which time the north–south rivalries were forgotten and they were all best friends.

When it was discovered that Barney had come to buy a Volvo, everyone poo-pooed the idea. 'No style, man,' Barney's new friend said. 'You're way too young for that. It's for the oldies. No, you want … you want something more sporty.'

'Did I hear sporty?' A girl further along the bar moved nearer to them. 'Are you looking for sporty? I've got a sports car I'm looking to sell. You might be interested in it. Shame to come all this way and go home empty-handed.'

'Sporty!' Brian liked the sound of that. He clapped Barney on the back. 'Sporty,' he said solemnly. 'S's'just what we need. We *are* sporty. Knew we came for something and that was it!'

Barney shook his head. 'No… don't think so. Didn't come for sporty, did we? Volvo…' he managed to enunciate. Somewhere in the dim recesses of his mind, a Volvo had some significance but he couldn't for the life of him recall what it was.

'I've got it parked outside,' said the girl. 'Would you like to come out and see it?'

Brian lurched for the door. A man didn't get an offer like that every day. 'C'mon, Barney, let's see what this young lady has to offer us.'

The car park to the rear of the pub was well lit and the little blue Mazda MX5 soft-top was parked under some lights. 'What do you think?' the girl asked anxiously. 'Would it suit?'

Barney nodded, not able to speak.

'I think he means yes. Yeah, let's have it, Barney boy. Think of all the fun we can have in that.'

Sports cars were fun. Barney remembered having one when he was a youngster. Be nice to have one again. 'Done.' He held out his hand and shook with the girl. ''S a deal. Got some cash somewhere.'

'Back pocket,' Brian prompted.

Returning to the Ship and Bottle, Brian had an idea. 'Never mind all this poncey beer. Let's have a real northern drink. A Percy … a Percy … a Percy Ssspecial,' he got out at last.

'Wassat?' asked Barney.

'Invented by the tenth Duke of Northum … berland,' Brian managed. ''S'for when you go hunting. 'S'cold in north … nor … you know. Anyway, 's'cold, so you drink Percy Special.

Landlord…' Brian raised his hand to attract the landlord's attention. 'Percy Specials all round. Whisky and cherry brandies all round', he repeated. 'Keeps out the … something.'

\*\*\*

Late on Saturday, George left Jackie's house at Acaster Malbis replete and happy. He and Walter had made short work of moving Barney's desk and cupboards down the corridor and into the smaller room. Gradually Jackie filled up the cardboard boxes with books and papers and the men carried them into the new study. By lunchtime, Barney's old room was empty.

Jackie was delighted and rewarded them with two large bacon butties apiece, washed down with mugs of strong tea, and promised there would be no word said to Penny.

After lunch, Walter sat back, ready for a quiet half-hour. Jackie had other ideas. 'We haven't got time for resting, Dad. You can do that when you're in your box. We've still got work to do.'

'By heck, you're a slave driver. You're your mother's daughter.'

Jackie grinned at him. 'I'm my father's daughter, too, don't forget. So come on. Rome might not have been built in a day, but that's only because we weren't there.'

Grumbling to himself, Walter followed her upstairs. 'What's next, then?'

'We put the dustsheets down and paint the walls. I can't have our babies looking at sludge brown. It'll give them a complex for life. I've got some lovely primrose paint in the garage and the brushes. It shouldn't take the two of us long. We can have the first coat on this afternoon and another one in the morning. Whilst the first coat's drying, we can put the cots together and bring up their little bits of furniture. Hey presto: one nursery, nearly done.'

Walter regarded her wonderingly. 'You don't want much, do you? Shall I do a fan dance with a rose between me teeth whilst I'm on it?'

Jackie smiled at him. 'Well, that's up to you, Dad, but I'll be hard put to find you a rose at this time of year.'

\*\*\*

Smells from the kitchen wafted up the stairs of the Ship and Bottle on Sunday morning. Barney woke with a start and sat up. He groaned and held his head. What on earth had happened and where was he?

Gingerly, he looked at his watch. Twelve fifteen. Was that morning or evening? He looked at the curtained window. It must be morning; that looked like daylight out there. Nearly lunchtime. Oh, his poor head.

He looked around the room. It definitely wasn't home. Where on earth was he? As he got up and went into the small bathroom for a glass of water, some memories of the previous evening came back. Something about a car?

There was a knock on the door and Brian appeared, looking pale and drawn and as dishevelled as Barney felt.

'Have you seen what time it is?' asked Brian.

'Yeah.' Barney was still puzzled. 'Brian? What are you doing here? Come to that, where are we and what am I doing here? Something about a car?'

Brian sat down heavily on the bed. 'We shouldn't have had those Percy Specials.'

'When did we have those?' asked Barney.

'Last night. Seemed like a good idea at the time, but not on top of a lot of Palmers Tally Ho! beer.'

'Don't remember that either.'

'Do you remember the Mazda sports car?'

'Nope. Should I?'

'Yeah, you're the proud owner of it. Talking of cars, we're supposed to go and buy that Volvo estate this morning. I hope he's kept it for us. We said we'd be there at ten o'clock.'

In one horrified moment, the events of last night crowded into Barney's sore head. He dimly remembered the sports car and not much after that. Had he paid the girl for it?

'Yep, you had the money in your back pocket.'

Despairingly, Barney cradled his head in his hands. He had no money left for the Volvo, even supposing the man had kept it for him. Maybe he could arrange something. He picked up his wallet from the bedside table and pulled out the telephone number for the man selling the Volvo estate. Dialling, he sent up a silent prayer, but he was too late.

'I let it go an hour ago,' said the seller. 'You said ten o'clock and I kept it for you till then, but when you didn't appear I sold it to the next person on my list. Sorry, mate.'

They would have to take the Mazda sports car home to York. Jackie would kill him.

\*\*\*

Walter worked hard over the weekend but, try as he might, he could not persuade Jackie to take any rest. In spite of telling her at regular intervals that he was quite capable of painting walls without her supervision, she would not leave him to it.

By mid afternoon on Sunday, the second coat of primrose paint was drying nicely on the nursery walls and Walter began bringing in the new cots and nursery furniture. He was studying the cots, trying to decide the best way to put them together, when he heard Jackie shout from downstairs. He put the little piece of cot down and headed downstairs. He was ready for his afternoon tea.

There was to be no tea for Walter that day. Jackie was doubled up over the sink, moaning in pain. Walter rushed to her side. 'What is it, love?' he demanded, scared to see her like that.

'I don't know,' she whispered. 'The pain …the babies. Oh Dad, I hope they're not coming early.'

'Hospital,' Walter announced. 'Come on, get in the car. If they are coming, that's where you need to be.'

For once Jackie did not argue with him and he supported

her very gently out to the car. On the way to Wigginton Hospital, Jackie held her stomach. Walter could see she was trying not to cry out and had to restrain himself from racing all the way there.

When she was safely deposited with the nursing staff at the maternity unit, Walter was dispatched to wait in the reception area. He sat down shakily on a chair and rang Barney, who he knew should be on his way home from Bridport by now. Unsurprisingly, Barney's mobile went straight to his message service. Walter left a message and then left one at their home number as well, just in case.

*\*\*\**

Barney glanced guiltily at his phone as it rang and went to the message service. He should have telephoned Jackie this morning but had not felt equal to it. How could he explain the Mazda MX5 to her over the phone? Instead he had opted to drive his own car home and let Brian bring the sports car.

Seeing some services ahead, Barney signalled for Brian to follow and they pulled in. Walter's message shocked them both. They decided the best thing to do was to leave the Mazda at Acaster Malbis and drop Brian back into York. Barney could go straight on to the hospital. Hopefully, Walter would hold the fort until then.

*\*\*\**

It was almost five o'clock when Barney drew into Wigginton Hospital. He parked the car and hurried into the maternity unit. There was no sign of Walter. After checking with the staff, he was taken to the small room where Jackie had been admitted.

Walter was with her and put his fingers to his lips as Barney entered. 'She's having a little sleep,' he whispered and motioned for them to go outside the room. He looked at Barney's white face and immediately set his mind at rest. 'It's all right, lad, there's no harm done. It was a false alarm. She overdid things a bit, but she's OK and the babies are fine. With a bit of luck, they'll stay put for another month, at least.'

Barney was full of questions. What had happened to bring this about? Walter looked about him uneasily, not meeting Barney's eyes. 'I think she just overdid it,' he repeated.

'Overdid what?' asked Barney.

'Well, you know Jackie: always on the go. Lucky I was there, having a cup of tea. I got her to hospital straight away, lad.'

Barney thanked him warmly, although there was a lurking suspicion he had not got to the bottom of the matter.

Later that evening, after Walter had departed for Claygate, Jackie woke up. She was surprised and, Barney felt, a little dismayed to find herself in the hospital with Barney at her side. What had been going on?

*\*\*\**

After a chat with the doctor, Jackie was allowed home on the strict understanding that she was to rest for the next couple of days and take things very easy after that.

'Shouldn't be a problem,' Barney said. 'You've only a café to run and a new part under renovation. Piece of cake: you can do it standing on your head.' He glanced across at her, ensconced in the car beside him. 'Only don't do it, will you? The standing on the head bit.'

Jackie smiled tiredly at him. 'No, I promise I won't. I've had my scare and I'll be as good as gold from now on.'

Barney had to be satisfied with that.

It was dark when they arrived home to Acaster Malbis. Getting out of the car, Jackie looked across at the Mazda parked in the drive. She stared at it, trying to make out what it was. She turned to Barney. 'What's that?' she asked.

'That?' he queried.

Jackie pointed to the car. 'That,' she said flatly. 'What is that? That is not a Volvo.'

'Oh, that.' The moment of truth had come. What could he

say? 'Ah, no, that *isn't* a Volvo.'

Jackie lost patience. She could not stand there all night, trying to drag information out of Barney. What was going on? 'Well, unless it's a pink elephant, or a flying pig with spots on, *what is it?*'

'It is a car,' Barney offered.

'So help me, I'll swing for you,' she cried in exasperation. 'Don't treat me like an idiot. I can see it's a car. Why is it sitting on our drive, instead of the nice Volvo estate you went to Bridport for?'

'Mm...'

'Mm?'

'Mm...'

'Shall we stand here all night and have this conversation? Only it doesn't seem to be going anywhere.' Barney was silent. Jackie stepped over to inspect the car. 'It's a sports car.'

'A Mazda MX5,' Barney said eagerly. 'You'll love it.'

Light dawned on Jackie. She did not need to be told what had happened in Bridport. Barney, plus Brian, let loose in a pub with rooms. She should have known better. She turned to go into the house. 'I *will* love the car,' she said. 'I'm going to have heaps of fun bombing around York in that. You might be home alone minding the twins because, as you can see, there isn't room for them. But you obviously thought of that when you bought it.'

She stalked inside. It didn't matter what he made of his new study now. They were even-stevens. A sports car versus a nursery? She wasn't sure who had won the day.

# CHAPTER 19

It had taken a few weeks for Matt Carstairs to investigate all the members of Allsthwaite Parish Council, but by late November he had come up with the information Tom Young required.

Meeting well away from York was essential and, over the many years of their association, they had got used to seeking out secluded places to meet up in. This time Matt had arranged a small pub down a backstreet in Sunderland. He was there before Tom and ordered two beers, taking them to a table in a quiet, dimly lit corner of the dingy lounge bar.

Driving up the A19, Tom thought pleasurably about his retirement plans. A yacht moored in the Bahamas and a penthouse overlooking a bay. Reluctantly he put these pictures from his mind as he parked near to the Dog and Gun pub that had been chosen for their meeting.

Tom soon found Matt in the pub and, after the usual greetings, he settled himself back against the elderly, squabbed seat and looked narrowly over the rim of his glass. 'So, Allsthwaite parish councillors are not all whiter than white, I take it? What have you got for me?'

Matt Carstairs smirked into his beer then put the glass down carefully. 'It's even better than I'd anticipated,' he said. 'The leader of the parish council, one Christopher Jones, is our eco-warrior, as I said when we last met. And what a past he has.'

Matt obviously had good information and was going to

spin out his moment of glory. Tom could wait; things were shaping up well. He nodded his approbation.

'Many years ago down in the deep south, our Mr Jones was addicted to various substances: cannabis, heroin, etc. He shared an extremely insalubrious squat with like-minded addicts. And then an event occurred in this squat that caused our Mr Jones not only to flee the area, but to turn his life around, get clean and become the paragon of the community that we see in Allsthwaite today.'

'And this event was…?' Tom was thinking Aids and related deaths, or maybe fights among addicts for their supplies.

'Murder,' Matt said softly and with intense satisfaction.

Tom cocked an eyebrow at this. Murder was serious business. If Christopher Jones had been mixed up in that in his past incarnation… Oh, what couldn't he do with that information? 'Go on,' he said softly.

Matt chuckled. He could see his share of the booty dancing before his eyes already. 'It seems one of his regular dealers got greedy and tried to cut out the supplier higher up the chain. Big mistake, as it turned out. He came to a nasty end one night on the end of a knife down a back alley and it so happens our Mr Jones was in the vicinity and witnessed it.'

'He didn't feel so moved as to report the matter to the police, I take it,' Tom said drily.

'No,' Matt said soberly. 'He was warned what would happen to him: possibly not as nice an end as our dealer friend's. That's when he disappeared from the squat and got clean, appearing some years later in Allsthwaite with a wife and two kids and "greener than green", if you take my meaning. He would certainly lead the villagers in any campaign against Bookwood Developments. Greenbelt land is almost sacred to him.'

Tom smiled gently. 'Well done, Matt. However, sacred though Mr Jones may regard this land, he could be made to see the error of his ways were his wife and children exposed to some … risk, don't you think? Bookwood Developments have fingers in many pies and were it to be known…'

Matt nodded. 'His life would be down the tube and it would leave his wife and children exposed to danger ever after.'

'So, that's our Mr Jones.' Tom sipped his beer reflectively. 'If he were out of the way, so to speak, is there anyone else ready to step up and take over the campaign?'

'Joshua Copeland,' Matt said with great satisfaction.

'And he is...?'

'Clerk to Allsthwaite Parish Council, born and bred there, and he's now in his late fifties.'

Tom was intrigued. What mischief was to be found in Allsthwaite during the last forty or fifty years? 'Surely Mr Copeland hasn't had his fingers in the parish till?'

Matt laughed mirthlessly. 'Probably has, for all I know. Nobody would question what he was about. He's devoted to the village and knows everyone's business. He cross-questions every newcomer relentlessly, really puts them under the microscope, but no one seems to know much about him. He lives with his wife, a mousy little thing, at the top end of the village opposite the fields that Bookwood Developments want to build on.'

'Yeah, that would really spoil his view,' commented Tom. 'He'd be keen as mustard to stop the development.'

'He would,' agreed Matt. 'But if someone were to let slip his sexual proclivities, perhaps at Allsthwaite Church, where he is a regular worshipper, or to one of the many village societies he belongs to or, best of all, to his poor wife, I think his credibility as a campaign leader might be somewhat tarnished. In fact, the press would have a field day.'

'I'm agog.' Tom lazed back against the beer-stained seat. 'Tell me more.'

Matt looked around to make sure they were not being overheard. 'S and M,' he said quietly. 'Every Friday afternoon with "Lady Lucille", a long-legged brunette in a basque and stilettos. His wife thinks he's going to see his aged mother in a nursing home in Leeds. He does go there but only shows his face for half an hour and then pushes off to see this Lucille.'

'Taking a bit of a risk, isn't he?' Tom asked. 'How does he

account for his awayday to his wife?'

'From what I can gather, she never asks. Seems to be glad to see the back of him for the afternoon. She gets to catch up on all her favourite soaps on the TV and he gets to catch up with Lady Lucille. Everyone's happy.'

'Any snaps?'

'When did I let you down?' Matt grinned and reached into his jacket pocket. He passed an envelope to Tom. 'She's dynamite. Can't say I fancy an afternoon with her but, as they say, don't knock it till you try it. Rubber suit, whips, chains, the lot. Old Ma Copeland could never compete with that.'

Tom tucked the envelope safely away in his coat to study later. 'Would she want to, even if she knew?'

'Nah,' said Matt. 'She's got her telly and a load of cats. I should think Lady Lucille's welcome to him. Even so, his wife wouldn't want it to get about the village.'

Tom finished his beer and stood up. 'You've done very well, Matt, as always. I'll let Bookwood know and handle things from here.' He clapped Matt on the shoulder. 'Start buying your suntan oil. You'll be booking that cruise soon.'

Driving back down the A19, Tom thought about the information Matt had supplied. He shook his head in the dark. He should not be surprised at what Matt had turned up. Villages always harboured more interesting characters than the towns, and frequently with colourful pasts, but this time Matt had surpassed himself. The planning application would be in the bag as soon as it was submitted.

Once home, he examined the photographs Matt had supplied and whistled softly to himself. Matt had managed to get clear images of Joshua Copeland spread-eagled on a bed, hands and feet tied firmly with ropes and Lady Lucille wielding her whips upon him. As Matt had said, they were dynamite.

He put them in his safe and texted Grey Eyes in London:
*The hooks are baited. Fish to be reeled in soon.*

# CHAPTER 20

Stan Peterson stood in the bathroom at Beech Cottage and surveyed his handiwork. So far, so good. The new bath was in place, with the recycled taps sitting proudly at its head with the new shower above. Only the tiling to go and the floor to lay, and that would be one room completed. If he got the kitchen ceiling replastered and a new central heating boiler installed, Kate would be home soon. He couldn't wait. He missed her dreadfully and wanted her back.

Undeterred by the list of jobs in front of him, Stan gathered his tools together and opened the first box of tiles. He had picked large white ones so he would have less grouting to do when they were all in place. Kate had chosen a brown and cream dado strip to break up the white. Otherwise they might feel they were bathing in an igloo.

Stan had done his homework and watched the video on YouTube on 'How to Tile a Wall'. He had made careful notes and intended to follow them to the letter. That way he couldn't go wrong. He set to work with a will and marked up the vertical and horizontal lines with his spirit level so that he had his starting point. Soon he was underway, fixing a wooden batten to the wall to keep the large tiles in place and spreading the tile adhesive generously, copying the procedure he had seen in the video. It was very satisfying to start placing the tiles with the spacers in between and he made good progress along the first wall.

By lunchtime he was halfway round the bathroom and decided to take a break before tackling the second half. Tomorrow he would take care of the dado rail and the tiles above it. Kate would be delighted at how good it looked. Stan went happily down the stairs to make himself a sandwich.

Kate arrived soon afterwards. She had taken an early break from the Historical Trust and come to see how work was progressing.

'Wait until you see the bathroom. You won't believe it,' Stan told her enthusiastically. 'Another couple of days and you'll be bathing in asses' milk.'

'Bathing in Yorkshire Water would do for now.' Kate smiled at him. 'It's all very well staying at the beloved parents' but when you've left, you've left. I'm even looking forward to moving back here, whatever state it is in.'

Stan wasn't too sure what to make of this. She did want to come home to him, didn't she?

Kate tried to put her arms around him, but her bump got in the way. 'Of course I do,' she reassured him. 'I can't wait for us to be a family. This little one won't be long now. So you'd better get a wiggle on, or you'll be visiting us at Mama's house.'

Kate's parents were great but Stan was definitely not up for that. 'Come upstairs,' he urged her.

Kate shook her head and grinned at him. 'I would love to but I haven't got the time, Stan. Have to get back to the Trust in half an hour.'

'I wish,' Stan said and held her gently. 'Come upstairs anyway and see the bathroom.'

'Who could resist an invitation like that?'

Kate made her way slowly up the stairs and into the new bathroom. She gazed at Stan's work for a few moments, a slightly puzzled look on her face. She cocked her head from side to side, saying nothing.

Stan could not stand it. 'Well. Do you like it?'

'I think I would … if it was straight,' she said eventually.

'What do you mean? It *is* straight. I've been meticulous

with the spirit level and the bubble was bang in the middle every time. It's not wrong.'

Kate raised her eyebrows. 'It is. You check it again. I'm telling you, those tiles will not meet on the same line when you get round the wall. Trust me. I've got a woman's eye for these things.'

'No, you…' Stan began but Kate wasn't listening.

'I've got to go. I'll pick up a sandwich on my way back to the Trust and I'll see you later.' She gave one more glance at the rows of tiles on the walls and made her way back down the stairs.

Stan shook his head at her departure and picked up his spirit level. He placed it carefully against the row of tiles and noticed with satisfaction that the bubble was exactly centred. 'So much for a woman's-eye view,' he thought to himself with satisfaction. When you applied technology, you couldn't go wrong.

Two hours later, as his rows of tiles neared the point of joining up, Stan stood back and scratched his head. Wonky wasn't in it. He could see they would miss by a mile. He didn't understand it: what on earth had gone wrong? He had done exactly as the video had instructed him to do – the spirit level, the spacers to keep everything in line – and yet he could see the tiles were not going to meet up.

What was he going to do? If he didn't know where he had gone wrong, how could he fix it? Kate would be calling round after work at the Trust. She would mince him when she saw this.

He trailed back downstairs and made himself a cup of tea, mulling things over in the empty kitchen. There must be something he had missed, something they didn't tell you in that video, but how would he know?

He decided to pay Brian Box a visit at Café Paradise. Brian was the original jack-of-all-trades and was master of all of them. Perhaps he would be able to advise Stan.

\*\*\*

Brian was busy in the new part of the café. He had just replastered a wall and was washing out his float when Stan appeared. Stan was relieved to find him there and not away in his van, buying materials for his work.

'Now then, Stan, how are you doing?' Brian greeted him.

'I thought I was doing all right,' Stan said dolefully, 'but now I don't think I am.'

'Oh, that doesn't sound so good. Tell you what, why don't we go into the café and have a cup of tea and see if things can be put right?'

Stan brightened a little at this suggestion. Maybe Brian could suggest something that would put things right. If he couldn't help him, no one could.

Brian took off his overalls to reveal a clean T-shirt and trousers underneath. 'There we are. I'm fit to be seen now.'

In the café, Penny brought them tea and large fruit scones, with butter and jam.

'There you are, lad,' said Brian. 'Get on the outside of that and the world will look a lot better place.'

Stan addressed himself to the tea and scones. Talk of tiles definitely came second to Café Paradise food. When he had finished and mopped up all the crumbs, Brian looked enquiringly across the table at him. 'So, what's "not all right", then?' he asked.

Stan told him the tale of the tiling, watching the video, using the spirit level, putting the batten up to support the tiles and precisely using the spacers. 'And yet, no way on this planet will they meet up when I get to the end of the wall. So, I don't know what on earth I've done wrong. I'm going to have to knock them off and start all over again. Sometimes I think we'll never get moved properly back into this house.'

Brian sipped his tea and thought about the matter. There was only one place Stan might have gone wrong and unfortunately that was right at the beginning of the process. 'Your spirit level,' he asked cautiously. 'Is it a new one?'

'No,' said Stan. 'I've had it for years and it's never let me down. It's spot on. The bubble's bang in the centre.'

'It might well be,' Brian agreed. 'But if it's an old one, it might have been knocked about a bit and that can put it out of true whilst it still shows as accurate.'

Stan stared at him. 'Knocked about a bit?'

'Have you ever dropped it or banged it hard against something? That could have disturbed it.'

'No,' Stan insisted. 'I'm always careful with my tools. I never throw them about. In fact…' He stopped, struck by a memory of a week ago. 'Oh, now you come to mention it, I did drop it. I was up a ladder in the kitchen seeing if the wall was straight and I dropped it. But when I picked it up, it seemed perfectly all right.'

Brian nodded. 'It would. But if you test it against a spirit level that you know to be accurate, it might tell a different story.'

Stan nodded slowly. Maybe that was it. In which case, he could be way off with his calculations.

'I tell you what,' Brian suggested. 'I've to let that wall that I've just plastered dry, so why don't I come back with you and take a look? We'll take my spirit level – which I know is accurate – with us and check yours against it.'

Stan was relieved to hear Brian's suggestion. A professional eye on the job would help a great deal and might go a long way to explaining things to Kate later on.

*** 

Brian was right, of course. Stan's level was inaccurate – hence the less than straight rows of tiles.

'You'll have to develop an eye,' said Brian.

'I've got two already. How many more do you think I need?' Stan answered, not knowing what Brian meant.

'Well, look at things properly, then,' said Brian. 'Stand back and take a critical look at things. Just standing here, I can see that they're not straight.'

'That's what Kate thought,' Stan said glumly. 'I thought she was talking rubbish, until I got towards the end there and I could see she was right. She'll go bonkers when she gets here tonight.'

'No, she won't,' Brian said, 'because she won't be any the wiser.'

Stan laughed shortly. 'Shall I wave my magic wand over it, then?'

'No, but you can roll your sleeves up and start knocking off those tiles. We can have the job done again if we frame up. Kate needn't know anything about it.'

'Brian, you're a real pal.' Stan was delighted and relieved. After the last time, he could do without any more catastrophes in the bathroom.

\*\*\*

As luck would have it, Kate was delayed at the Historical Trust. Brian, his van and tools were parked back at Café Paradise long before she reached Beech Cottage.

'And keep shtum,' he told Stan. 'I was never here, OK? Sometimes women don't need to know everything a man gets up to.' Stan agreed and gratefully went upstairs to admire the gleaming new room.

When Kate arrived he proudly displayed the new bathroom and showed her the tiles with the dado strip in place, all perfectly in line.

Kate shook her head in astonishment. 'I would have laid good money on those never meeting up in a million years,' she said. 'I don't know how you've managed it but it looks fantastic.'

Stan smiled smugly. 'Just a little video I watched on YouTube and there you are. The job is almost done. Just a little matter of the floor tomorrow and I'll order in the asses' milk.'

Kate couldn't quite put her finger on it but she wondered if something had been going on. If Stan was not telling her maybe it was best not to ask.

'Asses' milk it is,' she smiled.

# CHAPTER 21

George Montague gave a final polish to Esmeralda, his beloved old ambulance, and stood back to admire her. What a great old girl; she looked amazing. George conceded that Penny had been right in the first instance: Esmeralda had seen better days when he purchased her. But now... Penny was going to love her, just as much as he did. He had turned her from an old ambulance into a smart, fully fitted camper van.

His friend Jimmy had repainted Esmeralda in mid-blue 'Morning Sky', according to the paint manufacturers. George had worked on the inside, stripping out the old ambulance fittings and installing a small kitchen and bunk seating that could be turned into beds at night.

George was particularly proud of his efforts with the soft furnishings. Penny had been adamant that if George was intent on keeping 'that thing', as she termed Esmeralda, he was not to spend all their money on kitting her out. George had kept to this agreement and scoured the local charity shops for curtains, bedding and cushions. Now it was all finished, he was sure Penny would love it as much as he did and be prepared to give campervanning a try. Maybe he get could her interested in wild camping; they could go to Scotland and be free as birds there.

Full of enthusiasm and rosy pictures of the two of them bowling merrily along the open Highland roads, George took Esmeralda home for Penny to view. He parked her in their driveway and jumped out, hurrying into the house and calling excitedly for Penny.

Penny was upstairs, sorting through her clothes. Her winter wardrobe needed updating and it was time to cull some of the older and shabbier friends. She heard George shouting impatiently downstairs and went to the top of the landing. 'I'm not on the moon, George, or deaf. You don't have to shout like that.'

'Sorry, love,' George apologised. 'I get carried away. I'm just so excited. Come and see Esmeralda. You'll be amazed.'

Mm … 'carried away'. Sometimes Penny almost wished … not really, but that was George all over. He never did things by halves. Always had to dive in with both feet – and not always with the best results. And here he was with Esmeralda again. Mentally, Penny braced herself. This had better be good, really good.

When she went downstairs, George was outside giving Esmeralda another final, loving polish. Seeing Penny at the door, he stood back to show the camper in all her glory.

Penny was surprised to see how well Esmeralda looked. She actually appeared to be a camper now, not the tired old ambulance George had bought back from Scotland. Even the colour was quite chic.

Seeing her pleased surprise, George took advantage of the moment and opened the back doors. 'If you think the outside is good, my love, come and see the inside. It's like Aladdin's cave in here.'

Penny climbed up the steps and into the back of the camper. She winced at the garish mismatch of colours that met her eyes. Esmeralda might be chic on the outside, but inside it was more like Gypsy Rose's van. Every colour assaulted the eyes: red, yellow, green and bright blue jostled together in throws, cushions and curtains. Stripes, dots and zigzags made Penny's eyes dance. She was dumbfounded.

'What do you think, Penny?' George asked enthusiastically. 'She's warm, cosy and all ready to rock and roll away with us on a great adventure.'

Penny knew George had put his heart into this project and didn't want to throw cold water on it, but… 'The furnishings, George,' she said tentatively.

'I know. I got some great deals in the charity shops. You wouldn't believe it. They were nearly giving some of this stuff away.'

Penny looked at the zigzag cushions and nodded. 'I can believe it. You would *have* to give them away. No one in their right minds would buy them.'

George looked hurt. 'I thought you'd like them, Penny.'

Penny wondered how he came by that idea. Maybe that accounted for some of George's more dubious presents in the past and the clothes he'd bought for himself in his cross-dressing days.

'Well, it's not the most important thing at the moment, George,' she temporised. 'Why don't you show me around the van and all the work you've done to it?'

This was more like it. Now was his opportunity to really impress her. She would be packing their bags for Scotland tomorrow. George showed Penny the seating arrangements, and how they could be made into single beds or into a double, and the fitted storage space beneath them. With Jimmy's help, he had made cupboards above the beds and in the cab area too. There was even a small wardrobe with hangers all ready for Penny's clothes.

In spite of herself, Penny was impressed. 'You've done very well, George. There seems to be quite a lot of storage space.'

'Come and see the kitchen,' George urged. 'It's got everything. Jimmy's a magician. There's a little sink and drainer, cupboards for your pans and a bit of worktop space. You'll love it, Penny. It's like playing house when we were kids.'

Penny wasn't so sure she liked the idea of 'playing house' when she was on holiday. Wasn't the essence of a holiday to get away from all that kitchen stuff?

'A bit of toast and marmalade in the mornings, love. That's all,' said George happily. 'I've bought a barbecue. I can do the man thing outside. Imagine it: chair out by the lochside, best steak and a bottle of wine under the stars. I can't wait.'

Penny felt the rug was being pulled from under her. She wasn't at all sold on the idea of this camper lark and the great outdoors. Give her a warm hotel and a fine dining room any day. But George had gone overboard, as usual, with the whole thing. 'Well, now we've seen the living area, the bedroom and the kitchen, what about the bathroom?' she asked brightly.

'Bathroom?' George looked blank. 'We don't have one of those. No room for one, and anyway the campsites have all the facilities – toilets and showers and washbasins. Even laundry facilities.'

Penny slowly digested this information. 'So, we do our own cooking, we bathe communally and do the laundry when we're away, do we?' She turned to look at George. 'I do all these things at home – well, not the communal bathing bit. I can't see the point in going away if it's not much different from being at home.'

'Well, it is,' George insisted. 'You've somewhere different to explore. Somewhere you've never been before. It's exciting and you meet new people.'

'In the showers, or the laundry or over the washing-up,' Penny said flatly.

'It's not like that at all,' George spluttered in exasperation.

'Are you telling me there is no toilet or handbasin on this bus?'

'I've told you. They've got all the facilities on-site.'

'And in the middle of the night, when I want to use the "facilities", I might have to trek half a mile in the dark to find them?'

'You'd have a torch,' George said brightly.

'And I know what I'd use it for,' she said wrathfully. 'And it wouldn't be to find my way in the dark, George. You'd be wearing it.'

George winced.

'You seriously expect me to trek over a damp field in the

pitch-dark, or queue up for a shower in the mornings and get dressed in a tiny cubicle, like you used to do at the swimming baths as a child? And worse, wild camping with no facilities at all! If you do, you have lost the plot big time, George Montague. No bathroom, no camper trips – and that's my final offer.'

Penny turned and clambered down the steps. George looked after her mournfully. It looked like it was back to the drawing board, then.

\*\*\*

Back at Jimmy's yard, George spent another couple of weeks taking a piece off Esmeralda's kitchen and making a small bathroom with a toilet and handbasin and even fitting a mirror above it. He was determined that Penny would like it this time and consent to a trip away.

Although it was now early December, some campsites stayed open all year round. George would have liked to try wild camping but realised he'd better not push his luck on their first trip. Penny would not entertain the idea of trying Scotland in case Esmeralda proved unreliable again, so George found a campsite near Keswick in the Lake District and booked them in for the following weekend.

He was anxious to make a success of the trip and determined that Penny would have every home comfort on board so she would see how enjoyable holidaying in a campervan could be. He loaded the van up with warm bedding and an electric heater. He could leave it on low when they were parked and it would keep them cosy. He stocked the fridge and cupboards with Penny's favourite foods and packed a small barbecue and awning. She would have the best of both worlds: a taste of the great outdoors, and the best food cooked on-site. None of your expensive nouvelle cuisine lark – one bite and it's gone.

It was only for a weekend so he didn't think much clothing was needed. Penny, however, had other ideas. She came marching out of the house with armfuls of clothes that she directed George to house in the wardrobe, then returned to the house for boots, shoes and coats.

George eyed the pile on the sofa with dismay. Really, they were carrying enough weight already. Any more and the van might never get up the hills. What did she think they were going to get up to this weekend? He knew Penny would like to visit Keswick and maybe Ambleside but, as he planned on cooking, why did she think she was going to need frocks? He shrugged and started stuffing them all in the tiny wardrobe.

There was still no sign of Penny when he had finished. If they were going to get to Keswick before dark, they really needed to be getting underway. George went into the house. 'Come on, love, where are you?' he called. 'Time we were going.'

'With you in a minute,' Penny's muted voice called from upstairs. 'Just finishing my make-up.'

Make-up? They were going camping; what did she want to plaster herself in make-up for? They'd be lucky to clap eyes on a farm sheepdog today and he wouldn't need much impressing. He swallowed his impatience and sat down to wait.

Ten minutes later, Penny came downstairs. She looked gorgeous in well-cut trousers, a cashmere jumper and a wrap-around pashmina. George couldn't help admiring her but he wondered uneasily if she had got the drift about campervanning. Did a big open field warrant such high-end style?

'I'm going away for the weekend, George.' Penny answered his unspoken question sweetly, as if she had read his mind. 'I always like to look my best, so why not today? I like to think of it as glamping, not just camping.'

George rolled his eyes, but said nothing. Glamping …who put that idea in her head?

\*\*\*

The weather was kind to them and Esmeralda happily ate up the miles between York and Keswick. Going over the tops of the A66, a wispy mist hovered above the wintry fields. The remains of a recent blizzard still lay on the ground, leaving a patchwork of white among the green. Waterfalls of melted snow tumbled down the hillsides. Small fields edged with drystone walls spread away to the horizon and were dotted with sheep grazing the short, yellowing winter grass.

Turning off the A66, they made their way to the campsite just outside Keswick. It was a small site on a working farm and the owners made them very welcome. They were the only visitors for the weekend so far, so George chose the pitch nearest to the field gate. Although Esmeralda would be on a concrete base, he didn't fancy driving across the field if the ground was soft.

It didn't take them long to make themselves at home, hooking up to the electric supply to make a cup of tea and sample the fruitcake Penny had brought along. There were still a couple of hours left for exploring and Penny was delighted with George's suggestion. 'OH, yes, let's go into Keswick. We haven't been there in a long time.'

Eagerly she rootled in the tiny wardrobe and pulled out her raincoat and a warm hat. 'We can explore the shops and stay on for our evening meal,' she said, happily struggling into to her coat in the confined space of the van.

'I don't know about that,' George began.

'Ooh, I do,' said Penny firmly. 'We're on holiday. I'm not eating at home every night.'

'We're only here three nights.' George was talking to himself. Penny was already out of the back door and ready for the shops. 'Oh, well, I suppose…'

\*\*\*

How could one woman do so much shopping in two short hours? George was mystified. Penny had been like a woman on a mission and had visited most of the major shops in Keswick before closing time. Not only had she visited, she'd made several purchases as well. Whatever happened to the days of window-shopping? George could quite happily browse the windows of any emporium without being drawn inside and relieved of alarming sums of money.

Penny was made of sterner stuff and restocked her winter wardrobe, bought new books from the bookshops and old books from the Oxfam shop. When they emerged from the last shop at 5.30p.m., it was cold and dark, with the promise of frost in the air.

George was laden down with Penny's purchases. 'Thank goodness they're finally closing,' he said. 'I can't carry any more.'

'Nonsense,' Penny said briskly. 'Wait until tomorrow. We could do Bowness and Windermere. There's plenty of shops to explore there.'

'I thought a nice walk up the fells tomorrow...'

'Hiking in December, George? We could be up to our knees in snow before we know it. Besides, I want to take this opportunity to do some Christmas shopping. There are lots of different gift shops here, a complete change from York. We can get up early and hit the towns.'

George groaned. A whole weekend spent shopping. They could be walking by the lakes, taking in the magnificent scenery. He'd wanted to show her a get-away-from-it-all holiday in Esmeralda.

Penny broke into his thoughts. 'Let's take the shopping back to the camper and have a walk down to the lake. It will be so romantic by moonlight and we could have dinner there at the restaurant.'

'Well, if we're going back to Esmeralda, why don't I cook us—?'

'No,' Penny said with finality. 'You can have your turn tomorrow. It will be a whole new experience, George. And be fair to me. I'm giving it all a try.'

George had to be satisfied with that. What with two days shopping and dinner out, he was beginning to wonder if Esmeralda was going to be the bargain-break holiday he had hoped for.

In spite of all his misgivings, Penny was proved right. The evening was cold and clear, with so little cloud that the sky was carpeted with stars. They strolled companionably into the village and along the lakeside to the restaurant, listening to the water lap gently on the shore. The path was lit by old-fashioned wrought-iron lamps, enhancing the romantic atmosphere.

The restaurant proved memorable, serving fine Cumbrian food to delight even George's hearty appetite. Fresh soup, ale-braised beef and roasted vegetables, followed by sticky toffee pudding, put the seal on the evening. George had to admit Esmeralda couldn't match this.

They walked back to the camper arm in arm, enjoying the frosty night. Penny wondered if she could get used to glamping. Maybe now and again, if tonight was anything to go by.

George had high hopes. He would show her how marvellous life could be in a camper. Tomorrow night, they would dine out in the awning with the flaps folded back to see the stars as they sipped their wine. The heater would keep them warm. The best of all worlds.

*****

Penny spent a very happy Saturday around the shops in Windermere town and then in Bowness-on-Windermere. George could only stand so much shopping and by midmorning had retired to a café by the lake after arranging to meet Penny for lunch.

Left to herself, Penny concentrated on her Christmas shopping list. There were so many lovely shops to explore, all stocking unusual gifts. She particularly wanted to find gifts for the new Café Paradise babies, her three sons and the other staff at the café. And there was George, of course. What was she to buy for him? He had shown a lot of interest in cooking lately. Maybe she could get him a mangadget. He always loved a new kitchen toy.

At one o'clock, George strolled back into Windermere town

and met up with Penny. She was already at the café, surrounded by parcels. George raised an eyebrow; more shopping to find a home for in the camper. If she didn't stop buying things soon, she would be riding home on the roof.

'Nonsense,' Penny said crisply to this remark. 'You keep telling me there's plenty of storage space.'

'*There was*,' George answered. 'But we've filled it up with clothes, bedding and shopping. Remember yesterday? We went to Keswick and didn't exactly come away empty-handed.'

Penny made a face. George could be very negative sometimes.

After a pleasant lunch they made their way back to the car park by the lake and loaded up Esmeralda with Penny's latest shopping haul. George's misgivings proved unfounded and he found space for everything. 'Though whether Esmeralda will ever move again is another matter,' he muttered darkly.

Penny ignored him and climbed into the passenger seat, ready for an afternoon in Bowness-on-Windermere. Esmeralda rose to the challenge and very soon they were in the public car park at Rayrigg Road, a few minutes' walk from the village centre. Walking over to the pay-and-display machine, George read the price tariff.

'How much? Three pounds for two hours? By the heck, they know how to charge. I'll get two hours, shall I?'

Penny consulted her watch. 'It's only two o'clock, George. Better get at least three.'

George stomped off muttering under his breath. So much for a quiet weekend away. When he came back with the ticket, Penny was all ready to go. 'Are you staying with me this afternoon, George?' she enquired.

George looked wary. 'More shopping?'

'I've been writing a list,' Penny said happily. 'Teddies for Kate and Jackie's babies, lovely perfume for Genevieve, a hamper for Monsieur Henri and maybe the same for Brian and his dogs.'

George bridled at this. 'Hang on a minute, Penny. Since

when did we buy food hampers for dogs?'

'I don't mean buy *them* a hamper, George. I'm not that daft. But if we buy Brian a hamper, as he lives on his own, I'm sure he'll slip a little something from it to Buddy and Zak.'

'Hmph.' George had to be satisfied with that.

'Well?' Penny repeated. 'Are you coming with me? I could do with you to carry the shopping. I don't think I can manage it all myself.'

It got worse. George resigned himself to visiting every shop in Bowness at least twice before Penny finally made up her mind and then revisited the ones she had gone to in the first instance.

\*\*\*

During the course of the next three hours, George made several trips back to the Rayrigg car park, laden with Penny's shopping. By five o'clock, cold, tired and very hungry, they made their final journey back to Esmeralda, both of them hidden behind a four-foot fluffy teddy bear.

George had never indulged their own three sons with such enormous soft toys. What would a newborn baby make of such a thing in its bedroom? Penny said the bears were perfect; he only hoped Kate and Jackie would think the same. Women were funny creatures.

By now it was dark and the temperature had dropped to almost freezing. George dumped the last of the shopping in the back of the camper, keen to get back to the site before the weather worsened. Even Penny looked twice at the chaos in the van. 'We might have to have a little sort-out when we get back, George,' she said. 'I can't even see where the bunks are now.'

Privately George thought they might end up sleeping with the huge teddies, but judged it best to leave that suggestion until later. Maybe a nice glass of wine or two might make the idea acceptable. Where else was there?

\*\*\*

Once they were back at the campsite, George cheered up. Now Esmeralda would really come into her own and he could show Penny how much fun glamping could be.

A strong moon provided him with enough light to attach the awning to the van. He stood back, admiring his handiwork and rubbing his hands gleefully. She ain't seen nothing yet.

Whilst Penny refreshed herself in the little bathroom, George dragged the barbecue out from under the bunk and assembled his ingredients and pans beneath the awning. He was determined to produce the best steak, chips and salad that Penny had ever tasted. The weather was perfect; even the temperature had gone up. Who said you couldn't eat almost al fresco in December?

Whilst George busied himself in his kitchen, Penny made valiant attempts to find homes for her Christmas shopping. It was very difficult, as every available nook was already taken. Maybe they *would* end up sleeping with the teddies. How would she sell that idea to George?

Eventually Penny gave up trying to cram any more things away. She would have to ride home with lot of items around her feet and on her lap. George bustled in cheerily from the awning with a glass of wine for her.

'Now,' he suggested, 'you sit down and relax. It's been a hard day at the shopping face, hasn't it? Put some music on and your feet up, and a culinary feast will come your way soon.'

Penny was impressed and rather touched. There was something very sweet about George's efforts to make everything special for her. 'Can I help you at all?' she asked.

'It's all under control.' George made a sweeping bow, tangling his apron in his legs as he did so. Penny giggled. 'Mock not, Mrs Montague. Dinner with stargazing thrown in will soon be served.'

Dinner and stars. We...ll, the wine was excellent, to start with. After all these years, maybe George could still surprise her.

Out beneath the awning, George bustled about his new

minikingdom. He carefully set a small dining table with a paper tablecloth, napkins and the camper cutlery. The steak was very tender, so the knives should cope with it. He placed an electric heater near to Penny's seat and fastened back the flaps of the awning so that they could see out. Satisfied with his handiwork, he lit the candles on the table and called Penny in.

Stepping down from the camper, Penny caught her breath at the sight of the candlelit table. Fancy George thinking of all that. Indeed, he *could* still surprise her. She took her seat at the table and fingered the cloth wonderingly. Whatever had got into him? They had motorbiked all over Europe the previous summer and he hadn't displayed an iota of romance on that trip. Something about Esmeralda must have really caught his imagination.

With a flourish, George bought the salad to the table and served up the steak and chips. '*Madame, le steak-frites*,' he announced proudly and pointed to the starry skies outside. 'With a view of the universe thrown in.'

Picking up his glass, he toasted his wife. 'Here's to our night under the stars.'

'To the stars,' Penny agreed and picked up her knife and fork, ready to begin.

But they were only a few mouthfuls in when the weather took a dramatic turn for the worse, as is its way in the Cumbrian hills. Low cloud blotted out their view of the stars and heavy drops of rain began to spatter down. In a few moments it became torrential and thunder echoed around the hills. George rushed to close the awning as the rain was driven in the doorway by the strong wind. But it was not the entranceway that proved to be the problem. The whole awning leaked and water dripped everywhere. It soaked their lovely table, putting out the candles and making a pulp out of the cloth. Penny scooped up their dinners and ran into the van with them.

Behind her, George went to disconnect his extension leads for the oven and barbecue, getting a mild shock for his troubles. Penny squealed when she saw him jump back but he brushed off her panic. 'Don't fuss, woman, it's nothing,' he said.

By now the rain was thundering on the roof of the campervan, which mercifully was proving watertight. Penny sadly contemplated their sodden dinners, now reduced to a mush of soggy chips and cold, waterlogged steak. It had lost its appeal.

George, soaked and cold, joined her in the van. 'I've covered things over for now,' he said. 'Sorry your dinner was spoilt, Penny.'

Penny chivvied him to get out of his wet clothes. As he shrugged out of his sodden shirt, a thought occurred to him. 'It's not all bad news,' he said brightly. 'The bread is still in here. We can have steak sandwiches.'

Penny was lost for words. All his hard work wiped out in an instant and their dinner wasted and he could *still* find a silver lining. She took a sip of her wine and contemplated the rain streaming down the windows. Thunder still rolled around the hills and the wind rocked Esmeralda. She shook her head in wonder. George was still so blooming *happy*.

\*\*\*

Penny was tired after her long day's shopping and, in spite of the bad weather outside, she was soon curled up cosily in her bunk, ready for a good night's sleep. She couldn't resist pointing out the benefits of their on-board bathroom to George. 'At least you don't have to trek across a sodden field tonight to use the bathroom.'

George chuckled. '*I* wouldn't mind, but as this is a working farm and a very small site, their facilities are a bit primitive, to say the least. I only booked it because we had our own facilities. You never would have entertained them.'

Penny didn't even want to think about it. The two large teddies took up all the aisle space between the bunks. She hoped she remembered them if she needed to get up to the bathroom. Treading on something very soft and squidgy might give her a nasty fright.

Tomorrow was Sunday. She needed to take a leaf out of George's book. Maybe when they awoke the December sun would be shining and Keswick would look like a freshly washed world. She snuggled down beneath her thick quilt. Really, George had done remarkably well...

\*\*\*

Someone was shaking her. Penny put her arm out of the quilt to stop them. 'Go away, whoever you are.' She was in the middle of a lovely dream. George Clooney had dropped by for tea.

'Penny!' George was shouting urgently in her ear. 'Wake up, Penny! The awning's about to take off. We need to get it down pronto or it will get shredded in this wind and bring all the other stuff into the van. Get up, quick.'

Something in his voice roused Penny and regretfully she tore herself away from George Clooney and back to the present. The rain was still pouring down, even more heavily than earlier in the evening. As she took in the sense of George's words, she struggled from her quilt and swung her legs out to sit upright. She squealed as they touched something cold and furry.

'It's only the teddies,' George said impatiently. 'Never mind them. Come and rescue this awning and all our stuff before it gets blown away or ruined.'

In a fog of half-sleep, Penny stumbled her way outside. That really woke her up. Out here it was freezing cold and the wind was howling and dragging at the fine fabric of the awning. Where it was attached to Esmeralda, the seams strained to hold on as the wind tugged at it remorselessly.

Working under George's direction, they threw the barbecue equipment, little oven and George's kitchen equipment into the back of the car. When the awning was emptied out, they struggled together to unzip it from the campervan. All the while the icy rain beat down upon them.

Where did one put a sopping awning? Not into the

campervan, where they would have to sleep alongside its dampness for what remained of the night. George came up with the solution: it could drip in the bathroom all night. He just hoped neither of them wanted to get to the toilet.

Sopping wet and freezing cold, they climbed back into Esmeralda in the early hours of the morning and stripped off. They fished out oddments of clothing to sleep in and climbed back under the covers for what remained of the night.

# CHAPTER 22

Ellie was making the most of the Christmas markets in and around the York area. Her 'Claygate Preserves' business was doing very well and between tending his own stock and helping his wife, Walter was kept very busy.

This dark and frosty December morning was no exception. Ellie was going to the Shambles Market in the centre of York. Walter had loaded up the van with the jam, jellies and chutneys and some vegetables from the farm. Ellie's friend, Jane, was coming to help her as Walter was going to see Jackie at Café Paradise. Jackie had been a bit mysterious when she'd phoned him last night and asked him to pop in to see her.

Walter shut the van doors and went to lock up the barn he had converted for Ellie's business. He kept it locked these days when he wasn't going to be around. Rose and Arthur would help themselves to anything they fancied when his back was turned. Thinking of how his sister made free with everything about the Claygate farm as if it were her own, Walter jumped when she appeared in the barn doorway.

'Now then, our Walter, this is a bit of a to-do.' Rose looked very cross.

Walter sighed. He didn't need a head-to-head with her this morning. What was up now? He ushered her outside and locked the doors behind them. He squared his shoulders and turned to face her. 'Well, what's up?'

'That tup of yours, Walter, that's what. He's broken out

of his pen and been in with my alpacas. Upset them all, he has. Chased them all over the place. It's taken me and Arthur half an hour to catch the little bugger and by the heck, he's a strong 'un. He's back in his pen for now but you'll have to do something to keep him in a bit better. I can't have him round my animals again.'

Walter bristled. 'Rose, if *your* animals weren't on *my* farm, eating their heads off in *my* best hayfield, *my tup* wouldn't be troubling them. And as I have to go out this morning, you can get that big lump of an Arthur to see to the tup's pen. He's like your ruddy alpacas, eating his head off all day with nowt to show for it.'

'Now, see here, Walter—' Rose began but Walter wasn't listening. He stomped off into the house for his breakfast, before he started a real set-to with her.

Thankfully, all was tranquil in the kitchen and Walter's temper subsided at the sight of the plate of bacon and eggs Ellie put before him. She smiled at he tackled them with gusto. 'Did I do something right for a change?' he asked, happily buttering a slice of toast.

'I thought you deserved a treat. You've been working so hard lately, loading and unloading the van for me, working around the farm…'

Walter waved his knife in the air, interrupting her. 'Aye, and a sight more than them two lodgers of ours.' He told Ellie about his encounter with Rose.

She pondered this thoughtfully for a few moments. 'Arthur's not even up yet,' she commented.

Walter shook his head wrathfully. 'You see, a more idle pair you couldn't wish to meet. It's only because she dotes on them ruddy alpacas of hers that Rose is out of her bed. And I hope you're not cooking them bacon and egg,' he added.

Ellie shook her head. 'No, they can see to themselves. Jane will be at the bottom of the lane in a minute and then we're off. Getting back to Rose and Arthur, Walter, I've noticed that they are settling in here.'

'Aye, too ruddy much,' Walter agreed.

'Exactly. I know she's your sister and we have to help them out in this emergency, but it strikes me that we've made them too comfortable and they've stopped looking for any alternatives.'

Walter stared at Ellie, much struck by this idea. 'I think you're on to something there, lass. Come to think of it, I haven't seen them looking for anywhere else to live for a couple of weeks at least. Mm, we'll have to gee 'em up a bit.'

Just then Arthur stumbled sleepily into the kitchen. 'I could smell the bacon,' he said hopefully.

'Aye, you could,' Walter replied, looking at Arthur's rumpled pyjamas in disgust. 'And I've eaten it all. I was out *working* for a couple of hours before breakfast. There's none left.' He got up from the table. 'Come on, Ellie, let's get you down the lane to meet Jane. These two beauties can clear up when they've had their own breakfast, although it will be nearly lunchtime by then.'

His pointed remarks were lost on Arthur, who sat down at the table, waiting for Rose to appear.

Walter went whinnying to the door. 'Gee up, lad, gee up.'

Ellie laughed and pushed him out of the door. 'Stop it. He'll think you've lost the plot altogether.'

'I have not,' Walter said firmly. 'I'm just getting in some practice.'

When Ellie had gone, Walter went back into the house. Rose followed him into the kitchen. 'I've got them settled now,' she said to Walter. 'I'll get Arthur to rebuild the wall yon tup knocked down.'

'Can he do walling?' Walter asked. As he remembered Rose's smallholding in Allsthwaite, the drystone walls hadn't looked in very good condition.

'Best waller in Yorkshire,' Rose said proudly.

'Hmph.' Walter would wait to be convinced. 'You haven't found anywhere to stay yet, I gather.'

Rose was taken aback. 'Well, no. But … we're getting on all right, aren't we? Seem to have shaken down very well together all in all, apart from this morning's little hiccup. I *was* wondering…'

'No,' Walter exclaimed loudly, waking a semi-comatose Arthur. 'Not in a million years. You need to find somewhere of your own and take them bloody peacocks with you. I hate the things, screeching away all day and half the night. And find somewhere soon, because after Christmas I want my home and farm back. You've got a month. Surely you can find somewhere by then.'

\*\*\*

Walking through the doors of Café Paradise later that morning, Walter paused on the threshold and watched the scene before him, feeling an unexpected rush of nostalgia for the old days.

The café was very different these days, sleek and modern with an international menu designed to appeal to tourists and locals alike. He watched as Jackie worked briskly at the coffee counter, dispensing food and drinks to go to a line of waiting customers.

The waitresses quietly worked around the tables, delivering the food from Monsieur Henri's kitchen. Walter could hear him faintly in the background, calling as usual, for 'Genevieve, my Genevieve'.

He wondered what Marilyn would have made of all this. She had reigned supreme over the café's greasyspoon days with Walter as her faithful aide for over forty years, when bacon butties and all-day breakfasts with chips were staples of the menu. He thought she would be pleased with the inheritance she had left behind for her two daughters. Jackie now ran the café and Annabel was training in London, ready to set up her own design and interiors shop in York next year.

A quiet pride settled on Walter. It was a fine inheritance. He was glad to be part of it all and looking forward to the next generation when Jackie and Barney's twins came along. And who knew? Annabel and young David Hall might have their own tribe after they tied the knot next year…

Jackie looked up briefly from her work and saw Walter watching her with such love and pride in his face that she paused, her heart softened by this unexpected moment. She called Louise to take over from her and went to greet her father.

'Are you going to have these babies in the café, then?' Walter asked, kissing her.

Jackie grinned. 'There are worse places, only I wouldn't like to upset the customers with my screeching on the day. Come into the office. I want to talk to you.'

'Aye, I gathered when you phoned last night. Bit mysterious.'

'Not really, but I needed to see your reaction. Shall I get us a tray of tea?'

'You go and put your feet up and I'll fetch the tea,' Walter said firmly.

When the tea was poured and Walter had his favourite biscuits in front of him, Jackie put her proposal to him. 'As you know, Dad, the twins are not far off being born and if I'm not careful, I *will* be having them here. I need to be at home. Doctor's orders.'

Walter sat up in alarm. 'No, it's all right. There's nothing wrong, but I don't want to get carted off from here.'

'No, you gave us enough of a fright when we did up the nursery. You did far too much then, but would you be told? Any road,' Walter continued, 'at least you two have made it up over that car fiasco and you nicking his study when his back was turned.'

Jackie grinned, her violet eyes impish with delight. 'I think we're quits now. Barney's still looking for a proper car nearer to home and I certainly won't let Brian Box have any more fingers in that pie. But we're going a bit off-piste here, Dad. I want to talk about something else.'

'Skiing?'

'No,' Jackie said in exasperation. 'Flaming skiing, in my condition?'

'I did wonder.'

'Just shut up for two minutes will you, Dad, and let me get a word in?'

Walter recognised the danger signs and meekly drank his tea.

'As I said, I need to be at home now – which means I need someone here, someone experienced, who I can trust to keep an eye on things for me and also run the coffee counter. From there, you can keep tabs on everything. I want you to be that someone, Dad, if Ellie can spare you for a few weeks.'

Walter was speechless. She actually wanted him back in the café? At that moment she could have knocked him down with a feather.

'Well?'

What would she do if he said no? Walter swelled with pride. He beamed. 'I would be delighted. Imagine me, front of house for a change.' Then his face fell. 'But all those coffee gadgets and things. I haven't got a clue about those.'

'I'll train you, Dad. Don't worry about that. Let me know when you can start and I'll get Penny to organise the waiting staff and take care of the supplies ordering. Genevieve's doing well in the kitchen with Monsieur Henri and Brian's well on in the new part of the café. So, if you can run the coffee counter I think we can cope for a few weeks until I'm back in action.'

'I can start tomorrow,' Walter said decisively. 'That big lump that's eating his head off at Claygate can earn his keep for once. I told them this morning they were getting far too comfortable and gave them a month to find somewhere. In the meantime, Arthur can get up at a sensible time of a morning and help Ellie load up for the day and unload her when she comes back at night. It will be good for him to have something to do instead of mooning over them peacocks of his. He's as bad as Rose with her alpacas.'

'Are you sure about tomorrow?' Jackie said dubiously. 'Better check with Ellie first.'

'She'll be right behind me, I know. She's been saying for weeks you should be putting your feet up. And if I'm needed here, well, that's all that needs to be said.' Walter grinned across the desk at Jackie. 'It will be like old times.'

'No it won't.' She was quick to pounce on that idea. 'Everything's different now. Come smartly dressed in the morning and we'll fit you out with a Café Paradise staff apron, so you look the part behind the counter.'

'I don't need to be told to dress smartly,' Walter said indignantly.

'Oh no? Hmm. And what were you like before we got you the chef's whites? And even then, trying to get you to wear them was a major achievement. You're front of house in a smart city café tomorrow. You've got to be the best.'

Going home to Claygate, Walter pondered his daughter. She was as tough as Marilyn had been and nothing got past her. He was really chuffed that she'd asked for his help but he felt apprehensive about the forthcoming training. Whenever he and Jackie had worked together at the café, it was worse than two cats fighting inside a bag. He only hoped she'd mellowed a bit or it might not be fur that was flying...

\*\*\*

Driving up the lane to Claygate in his old van, Walter saw the vet's car parked at the fieldgate near the house. Surely Rose wasn't fussing over her alpacas again. That woman called the vet at the drop of a hat. He was only glad he wasn't paying the bills.

He parked the van in the yard and walked across to the gate to see what was going on. Jack, Rose's terrier, was shut in the old barn where Rose stored her furniture. He was barking furiously and scrabbling at the door to be let out. Walter ignored him and climbed over the gate and down into the first field.

From this vantage point, Walter could see John the vet was not with the alpacas but in with Walter's sheep. He was on his knees tending to one of Walter's ewes. Swiftly, Walter ran across the fields, anxious to know what had happened. His ewes were due to lamb early in the new year. He didn't want any problems at this stage.

Rose and Arthur were holding a ewe and looked up as Walter approached.

'What's going on?' he demanded, dropping to his knees beside the vet.

'Our Jack got loose, Walter. I'm sorry. He had a go at a couple of your sheep before I got to him.'

'A couple of 'em?' Walter looked round. Another ewe lay on her side, her skin bare of fleece where the vet had stitched her up. He looked down at the ewe the vet was working on, stitching up a small tear. 'They're inlamb,' Walter said shakily.

'I know, Walter,' John said softly. 'I hope they'll keep them, but it's touch-and-go. The shock of the attack might make them abort early. Thank God it was only the two and he didn't go through the whole flock.'

Walter rounded on Rose. 'How did he get out? I told you to keep him under control at all times. I've a good mind to get the vet here to put him down right now. I can't have a killer on my farm. I might lose these two and their lambs and if I do, you'll have to pay for them and John's fees for today.'

Rose and Arthur, still on their knees with the wounded ewe, looked shocked.

'Oh, please, Walter,' Rose pleaded. 'I know you're within your rights but please don't put Jack down. He means the world to us.'

'And my sheep don't, I suppose.'

'I'm really sorry, Walter, and I promise, truly, it won't happen again. We'll pay for everything and we'll keep Jack in the lorry. He can't get out of there. That I do know.'

The vet had finished his work and got to his feet. 'Straw out the shed for a night or two and keep them in there. They might do all right. Only time will tell.'

When the vet had gone, Walter set to work in his shed and made some pens with hurdles for his two injured sheep. He carried the ewes across as tenderly as a loving parent and laid them on the warm straw.

His first instinct had been to tell Rose and Arthur to clear out there and then but, as he worked, he realised he would have to rely on them for the next month to help Ellie whilst he was at the Café Paradise.

But as soon as Jackie was back in action, those two would have to go and they had better start looking for somewhere. Claygate Farm was not going to be turned into an alpaca hotel.

# CHAPTER 23

Walter's sheep made it safely through the night. He was up several times to check on them and was thankful to see them resting in the warmth of the clean straw.

On his return from an early morning visit, Rose and Arthur were up and making tea in the kitchen. They were both very subdued and eager to make amends for the previous day. Rose put a mug of tea on the table for Walter. 'Don't worry about a thing today, Walter. You just get yourself off to the café and help your Jackie out. Arthur and me will see to things here and help Ellie. There'll be no mistakes, I promise you. We'll do everything we can to help out whilst you're away.'

In spite of his anger still seething from the previous day, Walter was slightly mollified. He needed Rose and Arthur just now if he was to help Jackie out. He only hoped they didn't drive Ellie completely round the bend.

'Keep on eye on all the stock and make sure they've plenty of feed and fresh water,' he said, keeping his tone neutral. 'And collect the eggs and clean 'em and keep your eye out for any that's laying away. One or two are showing signs of getting broody and might start making nests anywhere about.'

'I know how to…' Rose subsided before she really began. This was not the time to be fighting.

'Aye, you might know how to with your stock, but these are *my* stock I'm talking about.' He was leaving nothing to chance and gave them detailed instructions on their duties to his sheep, hens, vegetable garden and how to load Ellie's van until their eyes rolled in their heads. He was still talking when Ellie came into the kitchen. 'Make sure the trays are locked on to the runners. Don't want umpteen jars flying off when you brake at a roundabout.'

Ellie could see Rose and Arthur had soaked up as much information as they could for now. 'Go and get ready for the café, Walter. I can manage now with my helpers.'

'And what about Elvis? He's going to need a run. Maybe I should take him out now.'

'And maybe you should not,' Ellie said firmly and steered him towards the door. 'Go and get ready. Jackie won't want to see you with straw sticking out of your hair.'

Grumbling quietly, Walter took him himself off to the bathroom.

***

It was a long time since Walter had been at Café Paradise in the early morning. He remembered the days when he opened up and did the cleaning before the staff arrived. Sometimes just opening the café without incident had been a challenge as he wrestled with the alarm system and its complex code. Many a time the police had arrived to arrest him as a prospective burglar. Walter smiled sadly as the memories flooded back. Now, in contrast, with his amazing wife Ellie to share his life with, he realised how lonely he had been in those days. He had loved and been loyal to Marilyn Dalrymple-Jones for forty years and watched Jackie grow up, never being allowed to acknowledge her as his own daughter. Forty years of working on his farm and in the Café Paradise's rackety kitchen with only old Sarah, his pet hen, and his sheep to go home to…

Walter walked through the back door into the main body of the café and looked around. All traces of the old days were dead and gone. Jackie had breathed new life into the place and made it her own. It was clean and bright and fragrant with

188 head in satisfaction. Most of all, it spoke of welcome.

fresh flowers dotted about the large room. Walter nodded his head in satisfaction. Most of all, it spoke of welcome.

In a few moments, the café came alive as Penny and the other waitresses arrived and Monsieur Henri and Genevieve bustled about the kitchen.

Penny kissed him affectionately. 'Welcome back, Walter. It will be just like old times, only without the bacon butties and chips.'

Walter grinned. 'Didn't do me any harm, did they?' He looked anxiously at Penny. 'I hope I can get the hang of that coffee machine, though. It looks to be all whistles and bells to me.'

'You'll be all right, Walter,' Penny said confidently. 'If Jackie could let Genevieve loose on it, I think you'll be pretty safe.'

'Could be something in that.' Walter felt a bit better. Everyone thought twice before they let Genevieve near any piece of equipment. He went behind the coffee counter and began practising on Penny. 'Well, Madam, how can I help you today?'

Penny thought for a moment. 'I'd like a small single-shot skinny latte, extra hot, please.'

Walter looked at her blankly. 'Single shot? Are we in the Wild West? I thought you wanted a coffee.'

'Wait until they ask for a hot chocolate with cream and marshmallows, or double-shot espresso, or a chai latte. Ooh, or a nice crème brûlée latte.'

'Shall we just start with a nice flat white, Penny?'

Penny jumped at Jackie's voice behind her. 'Stop giving him the habdabs.'

'Aye,' Walter protested. 'It's bad enough having to learn all this from the maestro without you adding to the mumbo jumbo.'

'Just saying…' Penny smiled encouragingly at Walter and took herself off to the staffroom to get ready.

Jackie and Walter faced each other across the coffee counter. 'Eee, lass, I never thought I'd see this day. Me, front of house. Marilyn was only happy when I was up to my armpits in fry-ups round the back.'

Jackie smiled fondly at him. 'I'm relying on you, Dad.' She produced a green and brown Café Paradise apron. 'Put that on, then at least you'll look the part.'

Walter took the apron without a murmur and put it on. Jackie smiled and silently blessed Ellie. It wasn't so long ago, when Walter was still helping out at the café, that they used to fight like cat and dog to get him to wear anything but his old farm clothes with a dirty apron over them.

'You're going to have to pay close attention to everything I do, Dad,' Jackie began. 'I can't go too slowly because the customers come thick and fast at this time of day. Just watch and try and take it in. There'll be a slack period about nine thirtyish and we can go over a few things then.'

Over the course of the next hour it seemed to Walter that Jackie must have at least ten hands. She seemed to be everywhere and at lightning speed, in spite of her pregnancy bulk.

Occasionally Walter tried to be of help but this only seemed to break Jackie's concentration. After the fourth 'No, not that one – that one', and he still hadn't a clue which 'that one' she meant, he retired to watch her from the other side of the counter.

Penny, flying by with plates of teacakes and hot croissants, sympathised with his plight. 'Clear as mud, Walter? Don't worry, in a day or two you'll be like an old hand.'

An old hand. That was a very good description, Walter thought ruefully. That was the trouble. He was an old hand. Would he ever be able to master all these new tricks? Well, he would have to, he told himself. Café Paradise was depending on him and he wasn't going to let them down.

He ventured back behind the counter. There was only a small queue now. He would be able to have a go himself in a minute. Without breaking off, Jackie called out, 'More milk from the stores, Dad, and bring a new sack of beans whilst you're there. Tell Henri we need more croissants over here. I hope he's made plenty.'

Croissants, baguettes, wraps. What was wrong with a slice of good old-fashioned white bread with a lovely chunk of bacon on it and maybe a fresh egg on top of that, the yellow yolk soft and runny, soaking into the bread?

Walter dismissed this image as rapidly as it came to him. The world was full of Americanos, lattes and infusions these days, with croque-monsieurs, tartesTatin and the like. Oh, for a Yorkshire fat rascal and a pot of strong tea. Crumpets and pikelets, dripping with butter and raspberry jam. He sighed and went to deliver the message to Monsieur Henri and get the supplies for the coffee counter. He knew one thing: if he didn't get his act together soon, Jackie would be eating *him* for breakfast, never mind one of them croissant things.

\*\*\*

As Jackie had predicted, there was a lull at the coffee counter and she was able to take Walter through the basics of preparing coffee for the customers. It was fiddly and time-consuming as there were so many variations on a basic coffee, but slowly Walter began to get the hang of things.

Penny, watching from the sidelines, could not believe how well they were getting on together. She wondered if some pregnancy hormone had kicked in to mellow Jackie. She was patience itself with Walter's slow fumblings with the milk and varied coffees. However, passing by half an hour later with a tray of eggs Benedict, Penny could tell Jackie's patient mood had evaporated.

'Oh God, Dad, how many more times? Are you working at losing me customers? Stretch the milk like this. It has to be really hot. No good sending the customers out with lukewarm coffee. They won't come back.'

'Stretched milk,' Walter echoed in disgust. 'Since when did you stretch milk? It's a flippin' liquid. I suppose you stretch the cow an' all before you get it.'

'It's the technical term, Dad, that's all. Just accept it and we'll get on a lot faster. Now have another go and *please* don't get so much over yourself this time.'

It was all too good to last, Penny said to herself. They were too alike. Throw in Marilyn's genes and it was an explosive mix.

But, by lunchtime, the fog had cleared for Walter and he was beginning to move more confidently about the coffee counter. Jackie felt she could leave him in the care of Louise, an experienced barista, for an hour whilst she spent some time with Brian Box in the new part of the café to finalise the position of the power points before she took herself off on maternity leave.

Jackie knew she was tired and felt guilty at biting Walter's head off during the morning. Poor man, he had mostly borne it very well, considering he had come to help her out. She made her way through the café and into the new part by way of a temporary door Brian had fitted to allow access.

It was like stepping into another world. After the noise and bustle of the busy café, here all was quiet and peaceful. Brian had completed the noisy and dirty work and now the new ground-floor interior was a completely different space. The old fittings were out and walls replastered. The wiring was in place for the new lights, emergency lighting and sprinklers. All that was needed were a few power points for the cleaning equipment to plug into.

Jackie paused by the doorway for a few moments, letting her mind adjust to the quiet. She watched unnoticed as Brian quietly made his way in and out of the back doors, taking unwanted tools back to his van.

The new Café Paradise was going to be quite a place, a 'destination' for York city visitors. She wondered what her mother, Marilyn, would have made of it all. In fairness, Marilyn had left both her and Jackie's sister, Annabel, a very sound inheritance. When Annabel set up her interior design business in the centre of York next year, they would both have extremely good businesses. Of course, they owed a lot to Walter as well. Without him, Marilyn would never have made such a success of Café Paradise. He had kept them all grounded.

She moved into the main body of the large, airy room and greeted Brian.

'I can't believe how much you've achieved in such a short time. Truly, you've worked miracles.'

'I don't know about miracles,' Brian replied, looking embarrassed. 'I've kept working steadily and it's all coming together now… Just the last few power points, and when they are done I can finish the floor between the two rooms and get this decorated and Bob's your uncle.'

'We'll be ready to open just about the time the twins come along,' Jackie mused. 'Then we'll need more staff. I'll have to get on to it. First things first, though. Let's decide on these power points.'

As usual, Brian gave Jackie sensible advice. As he was talking to her, Jackie wondered why he had never married. He was such a lovely man. Maybe he didn't put himself forward enough, or maybe he was a natural loner. She knew he had taken Genevieve out a few times and they seemed to be on very good terms. Genevieve often took Buddy and Zak out for a run when Brian needed to get work finished off in the café. They were such opposites: beautiful, scatty Genevieve, full of chatter and charm and able to drive the sanest people to distraction within five minutes of knowing her, and Brian, so quiet and dependable. Maybe that was it: nothing flapped or fazed him, not even Genevieve at her best.

'So, shall we put a double one there and a double over the other side? I think that'll be enough.'

Brian's suggestions cut across her thoughts. 'What? Oh, yes. That will be fine.'

As they were talking, the back door banged fully open and Buddy and Zak galloped in, making a beeline for Brian and Jackie. They jumped up excitedly, their wet tails swishing water everywhere.

'Hey,' Brian exclaimed, looking towards the open door. 'Where have you two sprung from? How have you got out?

Calm down, the pair of you.'

He batted them away from Jackie and dived to get hold of them. But the excited dogs were having none of it and dodged away from him, running towards the open café door. 'Oh God, don't let them in there,' Jackie shrieked. 'The place is full. They'll cause havoc.'

Brian chased after them just as a breathless Genevieve ran in the back door. 'Are they here?' she panted.

'No,' Jackie shrieked. 'They've got into the café. Brian's gone after them.'

'Oh, no,' Genevieve wailed. 'I'd just got them up the stairs and they did an about-turn on me and ran off. I didn't know where they had gone.'

'Get after them, Gen, quick,' Jackie ordered. 'They're soaking wet and Lord alone knows what damage they'll do in my café. Hurry up,' she urged, as Genevieve seemed rooted to the spot with shock. '*Go on.*'

The final shout seemed to do the trick and Genevieve raced to the café door. On the other side, mayhem reigned. Unfettered by leads, they made the most of all that was around them, turning deaf ears to Brian's calls.

Café Paradise was doggie heaven, with tables full of delicious-smelling food. Buddy and Zak wasted no time in jumping up and hoovering everything within their reach, splattering sauces and cakes indiscriminately all over the crisp white table linen, along with muddy paw marks and a trail of smashing crockery as their tails swished wetly in their wake.

Brian made a dive for Buddy but the dog was too quick and his long legs soon covered the distance between the café and Monsieur Henri's kitchen. He was followed slavishly by Zak. They left a trail of devastated tables and shrieking customers behind.

Monsieur Henri was busy in the kitchen, meeting the lunchtime demands of the hungry customers. It was Genevieve's half-day and Sandie, one of the part-time ladies, was standing in.

Buddy made it first to the kitchen and jumped up to see what was on offer. A hot leek tart with bacon and Gruyère was out on the counter, ready for slicing. Buddy downed it in two gulps. Zak, as usual, followed his big brother's example and jumped up. He found a smoked croque-madame and wolfed it down with enthusiasm. Brian entered the kitchen in time to see a whole tureen of fresh vichyssoise soup crash to the floor and Buddy and Zak slurping it up with glee.

Monsieur Henri was afraid of dogs and made no attempt to stop them. He backed into the corner of his kitchen, waving them away with his teatowel. '*Oh là là, mon Dieu. Ces chiens-là, qu'ils sortent dema cuisine. Vite, vite,*' he shrieked.

'Keep your hair on, I'm getting them.' Brian grabbed both dogs firmly by their collars and turned them round to get them out of the kitchen.

'It is not my hair that needs the keeping on,' Monsieur Henri screamed at him. '*Ma cuisine*, it is full of the hair now from these beasts. Yes, I say these beasts that you have let loose in my kitchen. Everything will have to be cleaned. I cannot cook here now. Take them away.'

Genevieve had followed the trail and came to help Brian haul the dogs out of the way. 'I'm so sorry,' she cried. 'We were right at the top of the stairs to the flat and they streaked off. They've never done that before. I think they must have heard your voice through that open door.'

Monsieur Henri waved his hands in the air. 'Genevieve … I might have known. The beautiful girl with no brains. I spend months teaching you to cook and you still burn my food. There is no working with you, and now this. You must ruin *ma cuisine* also. You are too stupeed. I will have no more of you.'

Hot tears stood in Genevieve's eyes at this unexpected onslaught. She turned to leave the kitchen, holding tightly to Zak.

'I'm not having that,' Brian said sternly. 'Don't you dare speak to Genevieve like that. She is not stupid and probably has more brains and humanity in her little finger than you'll ever know. You can apologise to her right now.'

'Apologise? Nevair.' Monsieur Henri was on the short side and rounded, but he drew himself up grandly. 'I say it again. She is so stupeed, I will not have her here any more.'

This was too much for Brian. Letting go of Buddy's collar, he stepped towards Monsieur Henri and grabbed his chef's lapels. 'Apologise to the lady, or else.'

'What is ziss "or else"? I am a Frenchman, I nevair apologise. I tell the truth.'

Genevieve squealed as Brian's hands curled into fists, ready to take on Monsieur Henri.

Hearing the commotion continuing in the kitchen, Walter left the coffee counter and ran to see what was going on. Immediately seeing that a fight was about to break out, he leapt on Brian and dragged him away from Monsieur Henri.

'Come on now, lad, that'll solve nowt. Get away and take them ruddy dogs with you. I'll deal with Henri here.'

'He was rude and insulted Genevieve. I can't have that. He has to apologise.'

The fury in Brian's voice told Walter all he needed to know. So that how it was between them, eh? It was never a good idea to antagonise a man when he was violently in love.

'He'll apologise, all in good time,' Walter soothed. 'There's been enough damage done for one day. Let's not make any more. You and your lass take them dogs home and we'll think about things when everyone's calmed down. I don't suppose Henri meant the half of it, really. He's frightened of dogs and I expect that accounts for his reaction.'

Brian paused in the doorway at this information. 'Frightened of dogs? He's not worth bothering about then, is he?'

By the time Walter had soothed Monsieur Henri's ruffled ego and organised some of the staff to help clean up the kitchen, Jackie and her staff had brought some kind of order back to the café. Spoilt food was swiftly removed and fresh linen put on the tables. Replacement meals had to be ordered and alarmed customers calmed down and apologised to. By some miracle, no one had walked out in disgust and the situation seemed to be saved.

Much later that afternoon, when Jackie wearily sipped a much-needed cup of tea in her office, leaving Walter and Louise manning the coffee counter, she thanked her lucky stars that Walter was still in her life. But for him, today could have turned very ugly. He had turned a very bad situation around. She, Barney and her children, Ellie, Annabel and Café Paradise looked set to need him for a long time to come.

# CHAPTER 24

Bookwood Developments were keen to move events forward. Grey Eyes instructed Tom to take the heat out of the parish council campaign before it got underway.

On Monday morning Tom telephoned Chris Jones in his role as head of York Trades Council and requested an appointment with him, mentioning promoting employment in the area. As leader of Allsthwaite Parish Council, Chris had heard of the Trades Council but had not had direct dealings with Tom Young. He welcomed anyone with new ideas and readily agreed to meet with Tom at his office in Swinegate the next day.

As usual, Matt Carstairs had been thorough in his investigations and provided Tom with names, addresses and dates of the events that took place in London when Chris Jones lived in very different circumstances. When his secretary ushered Chris in, Tom closed the folder on his desk and told her they were not to be disturbed.

Chris Jones sat down in the chair facing Tom's desk. Tom eyed him speculatively and found him an interesting specimen. He had all the hallmarks of the eco-warrior, with his long hair and clothes that had seen better days, long-ago better days.

Chris looked at him expectantly. 'It's good to know someone is doing their job properly, Mr Young. I've been trying to get some employment training for our youngsters in Allsthwaite, but the council says it hasn't got the funds to spare. Nor has central government, so any help from the Trades Council would be very welcome.'

'Ah, well now, Mr Jones,' Tom shuffled the papers on his desk. 'I can see you're very diligent in your duties as leader of the parish council and that is very laudable, very laudable indeed.'

Chris Jones was gratified by these opening remarks and smiled. 'I do my best. We all have a duty to look out for the best interests of our villages.'

'Indeed we do,' Tom replied smoothly. 'Ah, but sometimes ... one person's interests can stifle another's.'

A puzzled looked descended on Chris's face. 'I'm sorry? I don't follow you. Are we talking employment skills here?'

'Well, not quite,' Tom said blandly and sat back in his chair.

Chris Jones looked at him narrowly. 'Well then, why have you asked me to come here and what *are* we talking about?'

'Development, Mr Jones. Development. More specifically, Bookwood Developments.'

There was silence in the room as Chris Jones tried to make the connection between Bookwood and employment training opportunities.

'I know about Bookwood Developments buying the land on the edge of Allsthwaite village and I've picked up the rumour that they are going to apply for planning permission to build on it, but if you think it will generate employment in Allsthwaite you couldn't be more wrong. We intend to fight the application all the way. Bookwood will never build in Allsthwaite.'

'Mm...' Tom Young linked his hands behind his head and gazed across at Chris Jones. 'That is not music to my ears, Mr Jones. I was rather hoping you might see your way to supporting the application.'

'What world is this guy living in?' wondered Chris. 'Why on earth would we do that?'

As if he had read his thoughts, Tom abandoned his relaxed pose and leant across the desk to Chris. 'Because it is in the best interests of a great many people that this application is approved without any fuss and the project goes ahead.'

Chris laughed in Tom's face. This man was not living on the same planet as everyone else. 'Are you mad? You invite me here to talk about developing employment skills in the area and now you're banging on about Bookwood Developments. I tell you again: the two are not connected, as Bookwood will not happen. I have already convened an extraordinary meeting of the parish council to discuss mounting our campaign against it.'

'You will not be leading it, Mr Jones. Not if you want you and your family to stay safe.'

'Come again?' Chris's anger was mounting. He rose from his seat and paced around it. 'Is this some kind of threat, Mr Young? Because if it is…'

'Sit down, Mr Jones. I don't deal in threats. I deal in certainties. Sit down.'

Reluctantly Chris Jones resumed his seat and glared at Tom. Tom picked up the Manila folder on his desk and waved it. 'You might be leader of Allsthwaite Parish Council and a pillar of the community now, Mr Jones, but that was not always the case, was it?'

Chris eyed the folder and licked his lips nervously. He stayed silent, wondering what was coming.

'According to my sources, back in 1993 you were addicted to heroin and living in a squat in the East End of London.'

Chris shrugged. 'So? So were a lot of other people.'

'Indeed they were,' Tom agreed. 'But other people didn't have a dealer called Si Mapperly who got greedy and got himself murdered.' Tom was gratified to see he had Chris Jones's full attention now. 'It precipitated your desire to "get clean", I believe is the phrase, and ultimately your departure for the north of the country to your parents in Allsthwaite.'

Chris sat stiffly on his chair, his arms folded tightly across his chest.

'Pity if that particular drugs cartel got to know you spilt the beans on them—'

Chris exploded into life. He could not contain himself in the chair but leapt up and paced about Tom's office. 'I never did!' he half-shouted at Tom. 'I was warned, if I ever … I would be a dead man. How did you find out? And I don't understand, why now?'

'I have many connections, Mr Jones,' Tom answered quietly. 'Bookwood is one of them and they too have interests in many, shall we say …*industries*. As a witness to this event, you have been long known to them and they have kept track of your whereabouts, just in case … should they need to know. And it so happens, now they do need to know.'

'You mean they'd finger me?'

'Interesting terminology, but yes.' Tom consulted the Manila folder. 'A certain individual, Clarence Maczynski, may not be too pleased to find out you have been putting certain information into the public domain.'

Chris Jones froze. He could see again the flash of the blade in the clear evening light and hear the stifled groans of Si Mapperly as he lay dying in the filthy alley that led to the squat. Shakily he resumed his seat once more. 'My wife … my children…'

'Quite.' Tom paused for a few moments whilst the full implications of his words sank in. 'You might find a way to step down as leader of the parish council and thus not be in the position to lead the campaign against Bookwood.'

'Step down,' Chris said dully. 'Step away. Go away, perhaps.'

'Pointless,' said Tom. 'These people have a very long reach, so why uproot your children when they are so happy in Allsthwaite and your wife's parents are there too?'

'You know everything about us, don't you?'

'Pretty much,' Tom agreed.

'Didn't someone once say the past is another country? Obviously not true, is it?'

'No,' Tom said in a matter-of-fact voice. He was getting bored with this man. It was time to bring the meeting to a close. 'You will resign as leader?'

Chris Jones nodded, unable to speak. 'Today. I'll think of something.'

He stumbled to the door. Tom went to open it for him. 'Make it convincing, Mr Jones. We don't want any slip-ups.'

When he had gone, Tom returned the Manila folder to his wall safe and sat back down at his desk, a small smile playing around his lips. Two down, one to go. He loved what fear did to people. You could smell it, that rank, sour, sweaty smell – and then you knew you had them.

***

Joshua Copeland was having a good day. Matron from his mother's nursing home had telephoned and asked him to call in as soon as he could, as there were aspects of his mother's care she wanted to discuss with him. Joshua had promised to go in the morning and, if he could arrange things with Lady Lucille, he might make a day of it. Tuesday *and* Friday: how lucky could a man get? He only hoped his mother would survive for a long time to come. If not, he might have to cook up another reason to go to Leeds on a Friday and he didn't know if Mavis would swallow it.

When the phone rang again, he answered it cheerily. 'Allsthwaite 75980.'

'Mr Copeland?'

'Yes.'

'My name is Tom Young. I believe you are the clerk to Allsthwaite Parish Council.'

'Yes, that's right. How can I help you?'

At the other end of the line Tom smiled. He would not need any help from Joshua Copeland. 'I wonder if I could arrange to meet up with you, Mr Copeland. I have some information, pertinent to Allsthwaite, that you might be interested in.'

'Oh?' Joshua Copeland did not quite know what to make of this.

'It's a delicate matter. I don't think we should discuss it on the telephone. It would be better if we could meet. Perhaps you remember *Lucille Ball* on the television some years ago?'

Joshua nearly dropped the telephone.

'Are you still there, Mr Copeland?'

'Y ...yes,' he replied cautiously.

'There's a big lay-by just outside Mortimer's Corner, off the A64. Do you know it? It's well sheltered by a belt of trees.'

'I know it.'

'We could meet there this afternoon. Say two o'clock, if you're free?'

'I'm free,' Joshua replied. 'Can't you tell me what this is about?'

'As I said, Mr Copeland, not on the telephone. I'll see you at two, then.'

'Wait a minute. How will I know you?'

He could hear the smirk in Tom's voice as he replied. 'I'll know you, Mr Copeland. I'll certainly know you.'

The line went dead. Joshua sat down heavily on the sofa.

\*\*\*

Tom was already at Mortimer's Corner when Joshua Copeland drew in. Joshua passed him and drove halfway into where the tall leylandii trees were at their thickest and screened the car completely from the road. He switched off the engine and looked cautiously around. In his rear-view mirror he could see a tall, dark-haired man walking slowly towards the car. He got out and waited for Tom to speak.

'Shall we sit in?' suggested Tom. 'It's not the best of days to be standing about.'

Tom went round to the passenger door and got in. When they were settled, Joshua stared through the windscreen and waited, terrified of what might be coming. This man had mentioned Lucille. What did he know – and *how* did he know? Was he after money?

'I'm so glad you could make our little date this afternoon, Mr Copeland,' Tom began.

'I wouldn't have missed it for the world,' Joshua said drily.

'I think you'll find you most certainly wouldn't have.'

Joshua gripped the steering wheel tightly, steeling himself

for whatever might be coming. 'So? Why are we here?'

Tom laughed lightly. 'I think you know the answer to that one, Mr Copeland. Lucille. I know all about her and you … your Friday afternoons in Leeds. Pity if your wife were to find out.'

Acid bile rose in Joshua's throat. He swallowed it down. His worst fears were being confirmed. 'That's blackmail, Mr Young, and you know it. I don't know where you got your information from, but it's wrong. I go to see my mother on a Friday afternoon. Her nursing home can confirm that.'

'I know you do, Mr Copeland. What a good son you are, and so assiduous in your visits.' Tom reached into his jacket pocket and pulled out an envelope. 'Only you don't *just* visit your old mother, do you? You visit another lady, and a very interesting afternoon it looks, too.'

Joshua stared aghast at the pictures Tom spread out in front of him. He made to grab them, but Tom was too quick and held his arm in a strong grip. 'Oh no, these are mine, my friend, and just to be on the safe side there are more copies in the safe at my office. My colleague knows all about them.'

Joshua slumped over the steering wheel. There he was in the pictures, naked, with Lady Lucille standing over him, whip grasped firmly in her hand. 'How much?' he mumbled, his head still buried in the steering wheel.

'I beg your pardon?' Tom asked sweetly.

'I said, "How much?"' He raised his head, red-faced and furious. 'That's what you've come for, isn't it? Filthy blackmail. Well, come on, how much are you going to bleed me for before I get my hands on those pictures? I'm not rich, you know, and it's no good thinking you can keep coming back for more. I haven't got it.'

'Calm down, Mr Copeland. It isn't a question of money.'

'I tell you, I haven't—What? Not money?' Joshua Copeland sat up and looked at Tom properly for the first time. 'You don't want money?' Now he was completely confused. 'Well, what do you want?'

Tom replaced the photographs in his pocket. 'I want you to support the Bookwood Developments planning application when it comes before the planning committee.'

This time Joshua almost choked on the bile that rose in his throat. 'Bookwood Developments... Are you out of your mind? It would ruin Allsthwaite and ruin the view from my house too. How am I going to explain that to the parish council?'

'I'm sure you could think of something,' Tom said blandly. 'Better that than Lady Lucille splashed all over the papers, don't you think?'

Joshua Copeland blenched. 'The p ... pa ... papers?' He hadn't thought of that one.

'Mm,' Tom said thoughtfully. 'The nationals and the local press love a good story like yours. Upright pillar of the community, church treasurer, clerk to the parish council involved with Miss Whiplash on a Friday afternoon. Meat and drink to them. I can see the headlines now...'

'All right, all right.' Joshua Copeland wrung his hands. 'I'll think of something. Just give me some time. There's an extraordinary meeting of the parish council coming up to discuss this. I'll have to be ready for them.'

'You will,' Tom said gently. 'And I think you'll find your Mr Jones may be amenable to the project too.'

Joshua stared at Tom. 'Chris Jones?' he said incredulously. 'Not in a million years.'

'Mm, I think you will find...'

'What have you got on him?'

'Best that you don't know, Joshua. Let's just say he's come round to our way of thinking.'

'Our way?'

'Bookwood Developments. They have a long reach. Be assured of that.'

Walking back to his car, Tom took out his mobile phone. Grey Eyes needed to know right away how well he had done.

*It's been a good day*, he texted. *The fish are all in the net.*

# CHAPTER 25

Life had settled down again at Café Paradise and an uneasy truce had broken out between Monsieur Henri Beauparient and Brian Box. When his kitchen was gleaming again, Monsieur Henri calmed down and apologised to Genevieve, eager to have her back as his right hand again.

In the following days, Brian noticed that Genevieve was more subdued than usual and she had taken Buddy and Zak out again in her spare time. The intimacy that had been growing between them seemed strained. Brian wondered if she was avoiding him, as no tea tray or delicate little cakes found their way to him during his working day. Had he overstepped the mark? Presumed too much from their relationship when he stepped in to knock down Monsieur Henri? He knew he loved Genevieve and wanted to spend the rest of his life with her but sometimes she was so ditzy he was not sure how she really felt about him.

He needed to find out the cause of this new distance between them and decided to request some late afternoon tea from the café, priming Penny to send Genevieve with it.

'Special occasion, is it?' Penny asked, her curiosity getting the better of her.

'I don't know,' Brian answered honestly. 'Things haven't been the same since the dogs got into the kitchens. I think she's avoiding me.'

Penny nodded. 'She has been very quiet since then. We've

all noticed it. I know she has her moments and can drive us all up the wall but we really miss her smiles and lovely giggles. She was always so cheerful and positive. I don't know...It's like someone's put the lights out.'

'Well, get her to bring that tea over before she goes home and I'll try and get to the bottom of it.'

'I wish you luck,' said Penny.

Brian felt he might need it. The new room was almost ready for decorating. He had fitted the power points and all that was left to do was to take down the temporary doorway and partition he had put in place and cement the hole in the floor, prior to laying the new wood floors on top.

As the day's business wound down and the customers thinned to a trickle, Brian dismantled the old doorway and mixed some concrete to fill in the hole between the two rooms. That was the last dirty job and, when it was finished, he carried his bucket and float outside to clean them off.

Time was getting on and, when there was no sign of Genevieve, he began to worry that she was not coming at all. But when he returned to the new room, Genevieve was just putting the tray down on his old table. To his dismay she had left a trail of telltale footprints leading from his new concrete to the table.

He couldn't help himself. 'Oh, no, not my concrete.'

Genevieve looked blankly round. 'What concrete?'

'That you've just stepped in. Didn't you see it? That wet, grey patch in the middle of the floor.'

Genevieve looked behind her and realised what she had done. 'Oh, you see. Isn't that typical of me? If it can be done, I do it. I'm just no good, no good at anything. Monsieur Henri was right. I am so stupid.'

'Don't move,' Brian ordered and ran to get his float and a cloth.

So, that was it. Monsieur Henri had cut her to the quick and shattered her confidence with his thoughtless Gallic burst of temper. And now, *he* hadn't helped things either. He cursed himself for being such an ass. He had to save the situation.

Genevieve was a picture of dejection and sadness when he returned to her. To hell with the floor, Brian thought. That was easily repaired, but the love of his life might take a lot more restoring to her old self. He threw down his tools and took Genevieve firmly in his arms, kissing her gently.

'You *are not stupid*,' he said and kissed her again. 'You are beautiful and intelligent and funny and everyone in the café, including me, wants our lovely bright girl back again. Monsieur Henri is the donkey in this case and, if he was really honest, he would say so himself.'

He looked tenderly down at her and was relieved to see a glimmer of the old Genevieve return as she smiled back up at him.

'What about your concrete? Have I ruined it? I didn't see it. I think I was trying to be so careful with the tray and was taking small steps.'

Brian kept his face straight. A hole big enough to put a baby elephant in and his darling didn't see it. 'It's easily fixed. Let's clean up your shoes and then I can worry about that old concrete. To make it up to me properly, how about we go bowling tonight? We could give the dogs a run together and then take ourselves off. If you're not doing anything, that is,' he ended, looking down at her anxiously.

Genevieve smiled her old smile and the world lit up for Brian. 'I'd love to,' she said. 'Dogs and bowling.' For a moment she looked anxious again. 'I haven't been bowling before. I always thought it looked fun...'

'It is,' Brian assured her. 'You will love it and we'll have a great time. We can have a bite to eat afterwards. I'll get changed and we can go from here.'

Genevieve nodded. 'I won't be long. I have to finish in the kitchen and I'll tidy myself up and come up to the flat.' She turned away and headed off for the café, carefully avoiding the new concrete this time.

She could have danced all over for it for all Brian cared.

What was a bit of concrete compared with having her back in his life? Ditzy, crazy, Genevieve. He hoped she never changed.

\*\*\*

The Ritz Bowling was already very busy when they arrived, so they had a drink in the bar whilst waiting for a lane to become available. Brian, enjoying watching Genevieve, was quite happy with this. Their walk with Buddy and Zak in the frosty December air had bought a rosy flush to her pale cheeks, enhancing the beauty of her green eyes and flowing red hair. She drew admiring glances as she quietly sipped her gin and tonic and took in her surroundings.

Suddenly she turned to him, catching him offguard watching her. She flushed lightly and said, 'Have you nearly finished the work at the café, Brian?'

'Yeah,' he said slowly. 'There's just the walls to paint and the wood flooring to put down and then it's all done, ready for the new café furniture and any pictures and what have you. Jackie could be open in time for the Christmas rush.'

'Will you be in York for Christmas?' asked Genevieve. 'Or have you got another job lined up somewhere else?'

Brian's happy mood bubbled over. This line of questioning was very interesting. Genevieve really wanted to know about the 'what next'. Hopefully, she was wondering if it would include her.

He turned to face her and took her hands in his. 'I'm definitely going to be here for Christmas because you're here and I'm going to stay here beyond that. And set up my own business because you're here and I'm not going away from you, if that's all right with you. I'm hoping to rent the flat from Jackie and … and … be with you.'

Before she could reply, they were called for their bowling lane. Brian wasn't sure if he was glad or sorry for the interruption, as Genevieve gave no indication of how she might have responded to his speech.

The main body of the bowling alley was very busy and every lane was in use, many of them with teams lined up to compete with each other. Bowls were continually being thrown down the lanes, striking the skittles at the end, scattering them noisily before they were mechanically set up again.

As Genevieve was new to the sport, Brian had to shout instructions in her ear. They found the right weight of ball for her to manage and she tried an experimental throw down the alley, narrowly missing Brian's foot, dropping the ball as she drew her arm backwards in preparation for a throw.

'Flipping heck, look out,' he shouted, hopping swiftly out of the way of the heavy ball.

'Oops, I'm sorry,' she exclaimed. 'It's a lot harder than it looks.'

'Be careful,' he shouted. 'You nearly had my foot off then. Have another go, like this.' Brian swung his arm to demonstrate the technique.

Genevieve tried again and managed to get the ball into the side gutter this time, before it rolled away to the collecting area. She looked disappointed.

Brian decided to have a go. 'Watch me, Genevieve, and then have another try. Don't worry about it going into the gutter. It takes time to get the hang of it.' Expertly he threw the ball down the lane and hit the skittles at the end. Six went down.

Genevieve clapped her hands. 'Bravo. That was so good. If I can get it to stay in the lane, I'll be happy.'

But no matter how hard she tried, Genevieve could not master the bowls. They consistently went into the gutter – and once right across into the lane next to them.

The cry went up, 'Oi, what are you doing?' Three brawny men turned wrathfully towards Genevieve. Quickly she apologised.

'I'm so sorry. I've never played bowls before. It's hard to keep the ball straight and they're quite heavy. I won't do that again, honestly. I'm so sorry.'

Brian, standing protectively behind her, was quietly amused

to see how quickly their anger was dispersed by Genevieve's innocent charm. She could probably bowl into their lane all night and they'd lap it up, he thought.

Things calmed down and they began to enjoy themselves, taking turns to dispatch the skittles. Brian began to think Genevieve was getting the hang of things until, on her next turn, her fingers got stuck in the holes and she could not let go of the ball. She almost went her length down the bowling lane as she flung the ball with vigour at the skittles, much to the amusement of the other players in the alley.

The surface of the lane was slippery and she struggled like a landed fish to get up. Brian rushed to help her. Pink with embarrassment, Genevieve dusted herself down, looking upset.'Oh, Brian. You see? I'm so hopeless. I never did have any coordination. No wonder Monsieur Henri gets so cross with me. He multitasks all the time and I plod in his wake, just managing to concentrate on one thing at a time. I'll never be any good at anything. I can't even throw a ball at a skittle without make a hash of it.'

Brian held her close and smoothed her hair. 'Don't ever say that,' he said firmly. 'You're good at lots of things. You just don't realise it. All you're seeing at the moment is things that are taking you longer to learn. But you'll get there. Do you think for one moment Monsieur Henri would have you in his kitchen if you weren't good? He's a perfectionist and if you can please him – and you *do* – you must be good. And,' he went on, 'Jackie wouldn't keep you for a minute if you weren't up to it. She doesn't carry passengers and she's delighted at how much you have come on these last few months. So no more talk like that, please.'

Genevieve smiled shakily at him. 'You're very kind, Brian.'

'Kindness doesn't come into it.' He was tempted to say more but the middle of a bowling alley was not the place. Besides, he wanted to make certain of her feelings for him, to see that she too saw a life with him beyond his time at the café and beyond Christmas too. They still had a lot of talking to do.

He made a decision. 'To hell with the bowling. Come on, let's go and reclaim our shoes, head off, go and get ourselves something to eat in town. The world will look a lot better place when we're by a nice fire with lovely food in front of us.'

Genevieve readily agreed. She'd wanted to try the bowling and was disappointed to find out it was a lot harder than it looked. Maybe she should stick to dog walking in future.

# CHAPTER 26

On her way to work at the York Historical Trust, Kate decided to call in to Beech Cottage. Staying with her parents for several weeks was all very well and they had indeed made her welcome and comfortable, but Kate missed Stan and her own home. This morning the need to be held in his arms and be together, even for a few precious moments, was almost unbearable.

Stan was sitting at the table in what would be the new kitchen, finishing off his breakfast. He beamed with pleasure when Kate appeared and jumped up to enfold her in his arms. 'Well, this is a lovely surprise. I wasn't expecting you this morning.'

Surfacing from his long embrace, Kate sighed with pleasure. 'I missed you,' she said simply. 'Will I be able to come home soon? We need to be a family again. I don't want to be taking our new baby home to my parents' house. We want to be home in Beech Cottage.'

'You will be,' Stan said firmly. 'George is coming over to help me. I've got lots planned for him.'

'Ooh, that sounds good. Tell me.'

'Nope.' Stan steered Kate towards the front door. 'It's a surprise. You'll have to be patient. Now, be off with you, beautiful lady, or I won't be responsible for my actions – and George will be here soon.'

'I'll call back on my way home later.'

'Yeah, that's fine. We should be ready for you by then.'

'Mysterious. I like it.'

Stan saw Kate safely to her car and went back to the house to get ready for George. He had hoped to have everything in place without mentioning anything to Kate, but she'd caught him on the hop this morning. Never mind. She would get a wonderful surprise when she returned this afternoon.

When George arrived half an hour later he found Stan out in the garage. He wandered in to see what he was doing. After exchanging greetings Stan pointed to a large box stacked in the corner.

'Just in time, George. There's the beast. She's heavy and I think it will take two of us to get her into the house and up into the loft.'

George went over and peered inside the box. He whistled softly in admiration. 'By heck, Stan, that *is* a beast. Where did you say you got it?'

'I didn't get it. Kate did. She bid for it at a country house auction she went to years ago, before we met. She was waiting to have the house to put it into and this is the house. I thought that, with all the things that have gone wrong lately, it would be nice to give her a lovely surprise. She can come home today and see her beautiful antique chandelier gracing that lovely stairwell drop. It was made for it.'

Stan could see it all in his mind's eye. 'The best thing is, George, I don't think she's given it a thought lately, what with work and the baby coming. Last thing to think about, isn't it? But she'll be over the moon when she sees it. With luck, we'll be done and dusted by this afternoon.'

Between them, they lugged the heavy box into the house and heaved it up the stairs. The plan was to get up into the loft, cut out the hole, fit the ceiling rose and lower the chandelier through it. Stan would then screw the decorative securing plates in place.

'And Bob's your uncle,' said George, rubbing his hands in anticipation. 'Let's get going, then. We don't want to keep the lady waiting.'

Stan put the ladders up to the loft hatch and hauled himself up. Once he was in, he turned round and reached down to help George get the chandelier up through the hatch. After ten minutes of delicate manoeuvring, George backed down the ladders, still carrying it.

'Trouble is, Stan,' he said, 'this chandelier is round and that there hole is a rectangle. We can't take this thing to bits. Those crystal drops look to have been fastened on for centuries and, in any case, we'd never get it back together again.'

Stan made his way back down the ladders. 'So, what are we going to do? I promised her a surprise. She's waited years to put this thing up.'

'We make the loft hatch bigger, that's what we do.' George beamed at Stan. 'Not rocket science, is it? You, me, a tape measure and a good saw, and "a" will go through "b".'

'George, you're a genius. I don't say I wouldn't have got there eventually, but … good man.'

Stan clapped George on the back and, in great heart, they went back out to the garage to find the 'good saw'.

\*\*\*

An hour later and the loft hatch was made larger. George measured up and Stan sawed out the necessary pieces of floorboards to be able to get the chandelier through in one piece. The hallway below was full of sawdust but there would be time to clear that lot up before Kate came home. They made even more mess cutting a hole from the loft through to the hall ceiling for the chandelier to pass through and then be fixed to the joists with its heavy decorative plates.

Looking through the hole in the ceiling, George surveyed the sawdust and plaster coating the hall floor. 'We mebbe should have put a dustsheet down there, Stan,' he mused.

Stan shook his head. 'Don't worry. I'll get it with the hoover when we're finished. That old carpet's coming up anyway. The floorboards underneath are beautiful. Let's get this job done and we'll worry about that later.'

This time they managed to haul up the chandelier through the new loft hatch. George, being the stronger of the two men, was entrusted with lowering it very gently through the new hole in the ceiling. Stan would be ready to receive it and hold it, whilst George screwed the first of the securing plates to the joists in the loft.

In the hallway, Stan put his ladders in place underneath the hole in the ceiling and climbed up.

'Ready?' George gathered up the chandelier and gently manoeuvred it to the edge of the opening.

Stan steadied himself on the ladder and looked up towards George. 'All ready. Slowly does it, and then it won't swing about.'

George moved the whole chandelier out in line with the hole in the ceiling. Holding it on his own took all his strength. His arm muscles strained as he heaved it out and down to Stan waiting on the ladders below. The rope securing the chandelier tightened around George's hands. Gritting his teeth, he held on tight as the chandelier swayed just out of Stan's reach.

'A few more inches and I'll have it,' Stan shouted up.

George let it go a bit more. A bit too much. The rope slipped out of his hands and, like a wrecking ball demolishing a wall, the chandelier swung inwards in an arc and took Stan off the ladders and on to the hall floor below. He landed on his back, all the breath knocked out of him.

George rushed down from the loft to find Stan struggling to his feet and covered in tiny shards of glass. 'Oh my God, Stan! Are you all right?'

Stan hung on the wall and fought for his breath, his chest heaving with the effort. After a few moments he was able to stand upright and look about him. He groaned loudly at the sight that met his eyes. 'Oh, no! She'll kill me. She's waited years for this chandelier to go up somewhere and now look at it. We could set up our own glass recycling centre with this lot.'

'Calm down, Stan. Let's think about this.' George had faced

many a worse crisis in his years of marriage to Penny. He wasn't going to let something like a busted chandelier get in the way of Stan's marital bliss. He sat down at the bottom of the stairs.

Stan joined him and gloomily contemplated the wreckage around him. 'I'm thinking,' he said. 'And all I can see is Kate's face when she walks in the door and sees this lot. Some surprise, huh?'

'That's it!' George jumped up excitedly. 'She won't see it, any of it. She'll have to see something else, something entirely different.'

Stan looked pityingly at George and then at his watch. 'We have, ooh, approximately four and a half hours, maybe five at a pinch, before she walks through that door again. Got your magic wand about you, have you?'

George clapped Stan on the back and a shower of glass tinkled down the stairs from his clothes. 'I think I have, my friend. Here's the plan. You go into York, to that antique lighting centre place, and purchase a chandelier as near as you can get to the late, great one here. Meanwhile, I go to the DIY shop and hire a sander.'

Stan looked at George blankly. 'We're hanging a sander in the hall, right?'

George grinned and went to get his coat from the kitchen. 'We sand the floorboards in this hall as you wanted to. We make a mess. Kate comes in, sees the mess. She's delighted with the boards – that's her surprise and she can get cross about the mess. Win–win for us. She'll be so busy ticking us off about that, she won't look up and see a different chandelier where hers should be. With a bit of luck, by the time she moves back in and *does* notice it, you can be all righteous and wonder why it's taken her so long to notice all your labours.'

Who would have thought George was capable of such duplicity? Stan couldn't care less. He loved the idea.

\*\*\*

Two hours later, Beech Cottage hummed with activity. Stan's fervent prayers on the way into York had been answered. The antique lighting centre had a beautiful chandelier in stock that was not too far away from the one that Kate had treasured. Stan made up his mind to stick to his guns that this was the original, if Kate ever queried it.

Whilst Stan was busy in the city, George had hired a sander and got busy in the hallway of Beech Cottage. When Stan arrived home with his antique treasure, the air was thick with dust that was settling in every corner and on every surface of the house.

George was wearing a tight-fitting facemask and could not speak, but his broad smile and thumbs up filled Stan with hope and encouragement. He only hoped that George would still be around to help him with the big clean-up in the days after Kate's visit.

The new chandelier, in spite of a strong resemblance to the one Kate had found, was not as heavy or as difficult to manoeuvre. Second time around, George and Stan managed to fit it without any more mishaps. Standing in the dusty hallway, they looked up at their handiwork and studied it carefully.

'Blind man on a galloping horse…?' George ventured.

'Very drunk, very blind man on a very fast galloping horse.' Stan was far from convinced that sharp-eyed Kate wouldn't see that something was different.

'Best we can do,' George said. He gathered up his tools and coat and made for the door. 'I hope it all goes well, Stan. I'll be back tomorrow to give you a hand to clean up and then I'll be away for a few days. I'm taking Penny away in the camper for a few days' rest. She's been working very hard at Café Paradise since Jackie went on maternity leave and we'd both like a break. I'm not telling her where we're going or she wouldn't go, but she'll enjoy it when she gets there. You're not the only one who can surprise their wife. I've got some surprises lined up for Penny this weekend.'

Stan was too tired to pursue this with George. He still had

Kate to face – and very shortly.

*** 

'Did we decide on an indoor beach when I wasn't listening?'

Stan winced. His beautiful Kate might have corn-coloured hair but there several strands of red in it. If ever there was a time she might live up to the notion of redheads and temper, this was the moment. He braced himself but, to his surprise, she took an entirely different tack.

'I appreciate all your hard work today, Stan, my darling, and I'm sure the hall floor will look magnificent –*when the beach is removed.*'

She walked back to the front door. 'I tell you what, I'll go away and pretend I haven't seen this. When I come back, I'm sure the cleaning fairies will have been and it will all look wonderful and then after that, with a bit of luck, you might make a start on the kitchen. Something really *useful.*'

Stan winced again.

Kate smiled sunnily up at him. 'There would be the possibility of me moving back in then. We would have a workable kitchen and bathroom.' At the front door, she turned and kissed him lightly on the cheek. 'You, me and a soon-to-arrive new baby. Get a wiggle on.'

She left Stan at the door, still dazed by her calm response. Women were strange creatures.

# CHAPTER 27

Penny had been putting in a lot of extra hours at Café Paradise since Jackie had gone on leave. Christmas shoppers crowded into the café from the moment it opened in the mornings until closing time at night. Even with the extra staff Jackie had laid on everyone was rushed off their feet, and Penny arrived home at night exhausted.

Business was very busy for George too. The demand for new windows and finished conservatories always rose before Christmas and he had a very special place in mind for a quiet weekend.

He decided to keep things simple this time. He told Penny to pack a bag for a relaxing weekend away in Esmeralda. They would not be taking the awning, so she didn't have to worry about that blowing away in the night. He wouldn't tell her where they were going, only that he knew she would like it and he was going to spoil her a bit.

Penny was none too sure about another weekend in Esmeralda in December, but she was too tired to argue. Hopefully, after their Cumbrian weekend, George would make this one a bit special. She certainly liked the idea of being spoilt.

'Just a few warm clothes,' George said airily. 'It's December, after all, but I think you'll enjoy where we're going and we can both have a good rest. Oh, and maybe one smart outfit.'

A smart outfit… Penny was intrigued, but George would not be drawn on the subject. 'You've got hundreds, Penny. Just bring one.'

Saturday morning dawned bright and clear. Esmeralda was sitting on the driveway, loaded and ready. George had wanted to drive to their destination on the Friday evening after they finished work but Penny was so tired she just wanted to fall into her own bed for a good night's sleep. Two days away in the camper would be fine for her.

They were underway by eight o'clock, heading up the A1. Penny could see they were going north again and looked anxiously at George. 'Tell me it's not Cumbria again.'

George smiled at her. 'No, it's not. It's somewhere even better and I'm not telling you any more than that, so don't ask. Enjoy the scenery and relax. It's your weekend off.'

Penny resigned herself to the mystery tour and hoped George hadn't chosen somewhere that was too wacky. She never knew what he might think of next.

Passing Scotch Corner and soon after joining the A66, George turned into the entrance and car park that led to a beautiful stone building housing a huge farm shop with a busy, light and airy tearoom leading off it. George switched off the engine. 'Come on, Penny. Time for breakfast. I think you will like it here.'

So this was why George had insisted they were not having a bit of toast before leaving home. Even at a little past nine o'clock, the café was busy. Waitresses were flying in all directions with plates of bacon and eggs and trays of coffee.

George rubbed his hands in anticipation. 'You order whatever you want, Penny. You won't be disappointed. The food here is really good, and plenty of it. Me and the lads have stopped here a few times when we've been on jobs out this way.'

Penny was impressed. Being treated to a lovely breakfast and this fabulous shop at the start of the trip was wonderful. Walking through the shop, she saw it was packed full of interesting Christmas food and gifts and there was a very promising-looking upstairs with gifts and clothing. If George wasn't careful, she might spend half the day in here.

\*\*\*

Two hours later, after a hearty English breakfast and, for Penny, some very enjoyable shopping, George managed to prise Penny away and back into the campervan. 'We want to get to where we are going today, Penny love,' he said, heading off up the A66 again.

'Well, if I don't know where we are going, I don't know how long it's going to take to get there, so I don't know if we're late or not. Will we get there today?'

George grinned. 'We better had. There's something a bit special there.'

Wherever *there* was. Alarm bells began ringing in Penny's brain as they turned off the A66 and passed the signs for Carlisle and kept heading north. Not Port William again, please. He couldn't do that to her again. 'Tell me it's not Port William, George,' she said quietly. Because if it was – well, it jolly well wasn't going to be.

'No, it's not Port William, although that is a lovely place.'

'The Borders? Scotland? Ireland?'

'We haven't got time to get to Ireland today. We've only got the weekend, love. Another time perhaps, for a proper holiday. Esmeralda would like that. We'll settle for Scotland for the next couple of days.'

Scotland. It was a big place. Where on earth did George have in mind? 'Edinburgh? Glasgow?'

'No,' George said firmly. 'You've had your fix of retail therapy this morning. What we both need now is a bit of R & R, so don't ask again. I'll get you there and you'll love it, I guarantee.'

Penny had to be content with that. There were obviously some miles to cover, so she settled down for a snooze. Maybe they would get there for bedtime. When she awoke, the dusk of the afternoon was drawing in. Esmeralda seemed to be bumping over a rough track. Penny held on tightly to the arms of her seat.

'Have I woken you up?' George asked.

'Where on earth are we?' Penny asked. Looking out of the window, she could only make out the outline of some bushes and trees.

'We're here,' George announced proudly. 'One of the lovely places in south-west Scotland: Sandhead, overlooking Luce Bay. We can't do it justice tonight because it's dark now, but we can have a lovely walk on the beach in the morning. You can go for miles along the sands.'

'I thought we'd come for a rest, not a hike,' Penny protested.

'I said you *can* go for miles. I didn't say we would.'

What on earth were they going to do here, in the middle of nowhere by the look of it, for the rest of the evening? Fish and chips and a good book, she supposed. It was all a bit dismal to her way of thinking, but she knew George meant well and had bought her away for a complete rest.

George smiled to himself as he made them a cup of tea. He could see by Penny's face what was going on in her head but he wasn't going to play his trump card yet.

After the cup of tea, he suggested they have a walk along the beach. Having got warm and cosy in the camper, Penny was dubious.

'It's a lovely night, Penny,' George encouraged her. 'It's a really bright moon. Look out there. You can see the sea from here.'

Penny looked out of the window and saw that George was right. A big moon was shining over the sea, casting silver rays across the water. The tide was coming in and white waves were rolling up the beach. It looked an inviting scene. Quite romantic, really.

'A romantic walk along the beach by moonlight,' George suggested.

'And then what? Do they do fish and chips in the village?'

George chuckled. He had been expecting this. 'A romantic walk by moonlight,' he repeated, '*and then* dinner at an amazing restaurant along the road there.'

Penny stared at him. 'An amazing restaurant? Here? In this

little quiet village?'

George nodded. 'We're booked in for this evening. That's why you've bought your gladrags. So, come on, let's get that walk. You'll need to sharpen your appetite for dinner.'

Penny didn't really enjoy holidaying in Esmeralda. The suspension wasn't all that great, and she had jolted over every bump in the road. She tried not to imagine a large, warm hotel room with ensuite facilities. She knew George had really tried, and she had to admit that this time he had got it right.

The restaurant did not disappoint. It was full and the pre-Christmas diners were in happy mood. Penny was amazed that a tiny village by the sea attracted such a crowd. But afterwards, relaxing in the lounge with coffee and liqueurs, she appreciated all that the place had to offer. The food and service had been superb: three courses, beautifully cooked and presented, had rivalled anything Monsieur Henri had ever cooked for them. The soft lighting and discreet service made the whole evening special.

Penny felt she had really had a memorable day. 'And we only have to cross the road to get home to Esmeralda,' she marvelled.

'Aye, and then there's always tomorrow,' George promised mysteriously.

Penny looked across at him as he sipped his liqueur. 'Have you got plans for that?

'I might have … and I might not. And if I did have, I wouldn't be telling you.'

George was at his most frustrating. Penny knew there was no point in pressing him and decided to enjoy what was left of their evening. Tomorrow would take care of itself. She only hoped the night would stay calm and no sudden winter storm would whip up to upset their night's slumber.

The weather had changed by the time they left the hotel and made their way back to the campervan. A light drizzle had started, accompanied by a stiff wind. They hurried across the road and climbed into Esmeralda, thankful she was so near at hand.

Climbing into her narrow bed, Penny wondered if she would sleep a wink. The van was rocking with the wind. It could be rock-a-bye, baby all night. Having had quite a lot of wine, followed by those liqueurs, she wondered if they would stay down.

George, as usual, was out like a light. Penny lay awake, listening to the rain battering the windows and feeling her bed rock with the strong winds outside. She dropped off into a fitful sleep eventually, dreaming of floating on the sea in Esmeralda. At the peak of the dream, Penny woke up, struggling to get out of the van as it sunk beneath the waves. Gasping for air, she shot up out of her little bed, banging her head on the side of the van.

'Oww,' she yelped, coming abruptly awake and rubbing her head.

George was already up and making tea. 'That was some dream you were having, love,' he commented.

Penny looked out of the window. 'Thank goodness we're still on dry land. I dreamt we were out at sea and sinking. I was trying to get out of the van.'

'Ah, that would account for all that fighting with your quilt, then.'

Very relieved to find they were safe, Penny drank the tea and took in the bright morning outside. 'I can't believe it's so calm now. All that wind and rain through the night and now look at it, bright and sparkling, as if it's always like this.'

'Speaking of bright and sparkling,' George squeezed himself on to his bed, 'get your clothes on and we'll go and have a mega breakfast up the village at the tea room before we set off for home. That'll set us up for the day.'

'A mega breakfast! If I eat any more this weekend, I won't fit back into this van to go home.'

'Well, you have a small breakfast, then. I'll manage the mega one. We can't leave Sandhead without a visit to the tea room. All home-cooked food and lovely coffee. They do take-outs for the beach if you want, but it's mebbe a bit nippy for that. We'll have a walk along the beach and that'll set us up for a bacon buttie or two.'

Penny was grateful for small mercies. It was surprising that George *didn't* want to sit on the beach with his breakfast.

It was turning out to be a surprising weekend and Penny had to admit George had been right to come away and rest. She felt a lot better and enjoyed the walk along the sands of Luce Bay. It was too early on Sunday morning for many other people to be about. There were only a few dedicated walkers, throwing sticks into the surf for their dogs.

They had a lovely home-cooked breakfast. George made short work of his full English and Penny managed a bacon buttie accompanied by delicious coffee. Reluctantly they made their way back to Esmeralda to pack up for home. Quite a few more cars and campers had joined them in the parking area overlooking the sea and the beach was busy with families and walkers.

Heading back down the A75, Penny watched the green and varied landscape pass by her window and reflected on the very different experience she had enjoyed this weekend compared with their wedding anniversary one. Would she do it again? Maybe occasionally, but she didn't want to get too enthusiastic about it in case George got the idea that she never wanted to darken the doors of a hotel again, which definitely was not the case. They had been lucky with the weather this time, although there was a distinct change in the temperature now they were away from the sea.

Breaking into her thoughts, George commented on the weather as they passed through Springholm village, on their way to Dumfries. 'It's a bit different down here, Penny. Looks like it might be getting icy. I'll have to be careful. Esmeralda doesn't like ice.'

George was right: Esmeralda did not do well on the ice. Several times they felt her wheels slipping on the freezing road and, two miles on, they hit a bad patch and skidded right off the road, landing nose inwards to a drystone wall. Penny screamed as the lights smashed against the stone and the metal bonnet scrunched up.

George kept his head. 'Are you all right?' Penny nodded. 'Then get out quickly,' he shouted, 'I'll try and push her off the road. I can't leave it stuck out like this. She might cause another accident.'

'But George…'

'Don't argue, get out.'

Penny jumped out and waited, shivering, at the roadside whilst George extricated himself from the caved-in driver's side. He managed to rock Esmeralda out of the drystone wall and together they pushed and steered her to the grass verge. It was obvious that she was wrecked. Her front end was squashed and the chassis looked out of kilter.

George shook his head in disbelief. 'She'll never go again,' he said sadly. 'Only to the scrapyard on a low-loader. All that work and we've hardly had any fun out of her.'

'Well, at least we're alive,' Penny pointed out. 'And speaking of low-loaders, are you going to phone the RAC before we die of hypothermia?'

*\*\*\**

They arrived home in very different frames of mind. The journey on the low-loader had been long and tedious, giving them both time to explore their thoughts.

George was despondent that his beloved Esmeralda, which he had spent many happy hours restoring to glory, was now a wreck. She'd never tour the open road with them again. What was he to do now? Would he ever be able to find such a little treasure again?

In spite of the long delays and the uncomfortable journey home, Penny's spirits lifted as the import of what had happened slowly sunk in. Esmeralda would be no more and if Penny had anything to do with it, she would not be replaced. Mentally, she was already down at the travel agents, booking them into Lanzarote for a Christmas break. She would not take no for an answer from George – and if he did say no, she would go by herself.

In future, they would stay in nice hotels or a good bed and breakfast when they needed a break and that was her last word about it. George would have to find another hobby, one that did not involve dragging her around the world in or on unsuitable vehicles.

\*\*\*

The whole of York could have heard George's howls the next day when he broached the subject of a replacement for Esmeralda and was turned down flat. 'You can't mean it!' he roared. 'No more Esmeraldas?'

'I do mean it,' Penny said firmly, setting her jaw firmly, the determined angle and gritted teeth telling George all he needed to know. When Penny looked like that, the battle was lost before it had even begun.

'Lanzarote? For Christmas?'

'Why not? The boys are going to be away doing their own thing, so let's go and get some winter sun and set ourselves up for the new year. I know we had some lovely walks at Sandhead but it was cold. Even you must admit that. Think of Lanzarote in a couple of weeks' time. We can sunbathe and swim in a lovely warm sea. Doesn't that tempt you just a little bit?'

George went away grumbling quietly to himself. He knew Penny was right and the thought of sunshine and warm seas was attractive, but he almost felt bereaved by Esmeralda's demise. He'd lost a friend. Now what would he do?

# CHAPTER 28

Chris Jones approached the offices of Anderson & Cranton, solicitors and commissioners for oaths in Stonegate. He was in a sombre mood. After his meeting with Tom Young he had given a great deal of thought to his situation. He knew that the information Bookwood Developments had gathered on him was too dangerous to ignore. He would have to withdraw from the parish council to safeguard his wife and family and, to this end, he was going to lay the whole matter before Barney Anderson. If anything happened to him, at least his story was safely lodged and some action might be taken.

Barney was pleased to see Chris. He had great respect and admiration for the time Chris devoted to Allsthwaite village. Under his leadership, the village had become a thriving community where no one was forgotten.

Chris was usually a cheery person and Barney was surprised to see the very serious look on his face as they shook hands. Chris took the seat opposite Barney and settled himself for a few moments before beginning his story.

Barney listened carefully, making notes as Chris told his tale of living in the London squat and the subsequent murder of Si Mapperley. Barney was a good listener and allowed Chris to bring events up to date: his election as leader of the parish council and the proposed planning application by Bookwood Developments to build a housing estate on the fields at the edge of the village, doubling it in size and putting a huge strain on already stretched resources.

Barney looked up at this statement. 'You'll be fighting the application, of course,' he said.

Chris looked serious. 'I sincerely hope the village will but I cannot, which is why I've come to see you.'

'Go on,' Barney said quietly. He knew Chris must have very good reasons not to take on this fight and wondered if the story he had just heard had bearing on it.

Chris Jones poured out the tale of his visit to Tom Young's offices in Swinegate and Bookwood's threats against him. 'I know in a perfect world I should go straight to the police about all this, Barney. But believe me, I know these people and they don't take any prisoners. You only cross them once. Look at Si Mapperley. He wasn't a big-time dealer but they crushed him as a warning to anyone else who might think about doing the same thing. I *have* to keep my wife and family safe. You must understand that.'

Barney nodded. He understood. He thought of Jackie and their expected twins. He would do anything to protect them, whatever it took. But Tom Young was, as ever, at the bottom of every nauseously stinking event. What handsome sum was Bookwood paying him for his part in all this?

He shook his head. 'If you won't go to the police, Chris, how can I help you?'

'I want to leave a written account of all these events, including Tom Young's and Bookwood Developments' involvement, just in case.'

Barney agreed and drew his legal pad towards him. As they assembled all the details of Chris's story, Barney was aware of his own mounting anger. What a loss Allsthwaite village would suffer when Chris Jones stepped down. He would have been an outstanding campaigner against the planning application. Now Tom Young and Bookwood Developments might well be successful.

'No they won't,' he said aloud, as he wrote the final words of Chris's statement.

'What?' Chris looked at Barney in confusion.

'Tom Young and Bookwood are not going to have it all their own way. Not without a fight, Chris. And if you're not there to lead it, well … I'll lead it myself.' Barney was grim. 'It's time Tom Young got his comeuppance. He's ruined a lot of lives over the years and got away with it, but not this time.'

Chris Jones jumped up and leant across the desk to shake Barney warmly by the hand. 'That's my man. I knew you wouldn't let me down.'

Barney had made his promise in a rush of anger and meant it, but after Chris had left he sat back in his chair and reflected ruefully. What would Jackie have to say about this latest turn in their lives?

There was one good aspect to it: he had promised Walter he would try and get Rose and Arthur away from Claygate. If Bookwood Developments didn't build at Allsthwaite, they might be able to go back there.

# CHAPTER 29

Beech Cottage was beginning to look like a home now. Stan and George had had to work very hard to clean up their diversionary mess in the hall and the rest of the house. Their plan had worked and Kate had not noticed the new chandelier high up in the hall ceiling, but the price had been dust in every corner of the house.

On her way to work, Kate called in to see her husband. He was out in the garage sorting out tools for the day. Surprised and delighted by her visit, he folded her in a bearhug of an embrace. Sometime later Kate put him from her. 'Steady on, let's not get the baby too excited. I don't want it to come just yet. Anyway, I've got to run and I don't want to be late. I'm giving my report to the Historical Trust today.'

Stan smiled fondly at his heavily pregnant wife. 'Run?' he said quizzically. 'Walk, I hope. I don't want Junior coming early either. I'm not quite ready.'

'What's on today?' asked Kate.

'The kitchen. Our end-of-line kitchen is about to be fitted. The dining room is full of flat-packs and George is coming to help out. Penny wants him out from under her feet. She's getting ready for Lanzarote.'

'Lanzarote!'

'Long story. You haven't got time. But don't worry. With a bit of luck you will soon have a kitchen.'

'I'm not worrying,' Kate said, a mischievous smile playing

around her mouth. 'I'm sure you have it all worked out – a cunning plan. As long as my Belfast sink goes under the window and I can look out at the garden, I don't mind the rest.'

As she sped out of the drive, Stan closed the front door and leant against it. A cunning plan…That's just what he didn't have. He had a sink, some taps, an awful lot of flat-packs and a big bag of assorted fittings that the kitchen shop had thrown in. It could be a case of trial and error to make the whole lot fit.

\*\*\*

George had enjoyed his weekend away in Scotland with Penny until his beloved Esmeralda had skidded into the drystone wall. Now he was back at Beech Cottage to help Stan whilst Penny organised her clothes for her holiday in Lanzarote.

'I like Christmas at home,' he said wistfully to Stan. 'Turkey and Christmas pudding, but she's having none of that this year. The boys are all away, so she's gone and booked it.'

'Cheer up,' said Stan. 'Sunshine, nice wine, blue sea… It can't be all bad.'

'I suppose not.' George sighed, unconvinced. 'Anyway, lad. What about this new kitchen of yours? I see you've been shopping.' When he'd arrived that morning, George had seen all the flat-packs lined up in the dining room.

'I got a real bargain there, George,' Stan said proudly. 'They were selling it off at half price. There is just one thing, though. There aren't any instructions with it. You know – which bit goes where and fits with what.'

George shook his head. 'Not a problem, Stan. Two brains like ours on the job, we'll have it done in no time.'

They unpacked the first two boxes and examined the contents. The first appeared to be all cupboard doors. 'Well, at least they can be put to one side for later.' Stan lugged the box over to the window.

George looked inside the second box. 'Mm … I think these are the sides of the cupboards but, there again, they might be the base units. We might have to unpack quite a few more before we know which is which.'

'Are you good at doing jigsaws, George?'

'No,' said George cheerfully. 'I could do the edges with the sky and the grass and that was about it.'

\*\*\*

An hour and much unpacking later, the dining room was strewn with empty boxes, shelves, cupboards and base-unit sides, countertops, coving, kick boards and dozens of packets of screws and pieces of dowelling.

Stan scratched his head. 'I think we need a cup of coffee before we tackle any of this lot.'

They drank their coffee and studied the variety of boards around the room. George pointed to some boards propped up in the corner. 'Base units. Got to be.'

'Looks like a cupboard to me.'

'Never. It's too big. You can't hang that off the wall.'

'There's only one way to find out.' Stan finished his coffee and stood up. 'Let's try it out.'

Stan carried what looked like the base units through to the kitchen and George carried what he thought were wall cupboards. They tried putting them together and they didn't fit.

'Maybe we've got a mixture of the two,' Stan suggested. 'We're going to have to bring the rest of these through and see what we might get to go together.'

George shook his head. 'You know, Stan, this might not end up such a money-saving idea after all.'

'Has to be,' Stan said with determination. 'I can't go out and buy another one. I've blown the budget on this.'

Another couple of hours passed as Stan and George tried to fix the boards together, arguing over every base-unit back or side, or top-cupboard side. The only thing they could agree on was the cupboard doors. The kitchen looked like a war zone, with random bits of cupboard strewn everywhere.

Stan was running out of patience. Half the day was gone and they were still no further on. 'Look, it's obvious. That's a cupboard side and that's a cupboard side. Find the back of it and we can get it up on the wall. It would be a start. We have to start somewhere.'

George disagreed. 'And if it's not right and we're trying to screw pieces together that shouldn't be, we'll have holes all over the place in units and cupboards and holes in the wall and generally be making a right old mess. Kate would be really pleased with that.'

'Well, we can't stand and look at them all day, playing "Guess the Kitchen Pieces". What are we going to do with them all?'

They looked long and hard at the jumble around them and then at each other.

'Get Brian Box,' they said in chorus.

\*\*\*

Luckily for Stan and George, Brian was able to come over and help them. His work at Café Paradise was finished and he was looking for new projects.

'I can't afford a lot,' Stan said anxiously over the telephone.

'Consider it a house-warming present,' Brian said calmly. 'I've got some spare time. I'll get over this afternoon. Don't worry, Stan. I've had this problem before. There's a knack to it and you need to know the tricks of the trade to put them all together. But, with luck, we might get them put together today and can start fitting them tomorrow.'

Stan and George sat down to lunch in a much more cheerful frame of mind. The cavalry was coming and Beech Cottage would get its kitchen.

\*\*\*

It was like watching a well-rehearsed dance performance. Brian moved confidently among the various kitchen pieces. Stan and George were on hand to receive cupboards and doors from him and take them to their allotted place as instructed.

Apart from a few quiet mutterings Brian said very little, concentrating intently as he moved around the litter of kitchenalia. The right screws and hinges were found and, as the afternoon passed, the cupboards were assembled. The base units were butted up to the newly plastered walls and judged ready for fitting in the morning.

Stan and George could only look on open-mouthed. It reminded Stan of watching a magician producing the impossible from thin air by sleight of hand. 'Rabbits out of hats,' he said.

'As long as he doesn't ask me to step inside that cupboard and want to saw me in half,' said George.

By five o'clock, Brian had sorted out the mess that Stan and George had unsuccessfully wrestled with in the morning. The three men stood back to survey their work. Stan shook his head wonderingly. 'Amazing. It looks like a kitchen.'

Brian looked at him in surprise. 'What did you think it was going to look like?'

'No, that wasn't what I meant. I knew I had a kitchen. Well, I *thought* I had a kitchen, or maybe some pieces of a kitchen, bearing in mind it was the last one in an end-of-line sale. I never thought it would look as good as this.' He shook Brian's hand vigorously. 'And I would never have been able to fathom all those pieces out. I owe you big time.'

Brian chuckled. 'Let's get it all fixed up tomorrow and see if it really does look like a kitchen.'

\*\*\*

Brian and George arrived at Beech Cottage early on Sunday morning to find Stan had the bacon sizzling in the frying pan and the coffee pot on. 'We need to keep our strength up,' he said. 'Can't be heaving cupboards about on a bowl of muesli.'

'I tried that one with Penny,' George said gloomily. 'It didn't make any difference. And to cap it all, she's gone in for that fat-free milk an' all. It's like gnat's pee, that stuff. Nothing to it at all. Might as well have water,' he ended in disgust.

Stan slapped a large bacon sandwich down in front of him. 'Never mind gnat's pee. Get that down you, lad. The world will seem a much better place.'

George beamed in delight. 'Have you buttered the bread?'

'Of course,' said Stan.

'Fantastic.' George took a large bite of his sandwich and sat back in his chair, his eyes closed in ecstasy.

Brian looked on, his mouth watering. 'Is there one coming my way?' he asked hopefully.

'Of course, coming right up.'

Another large sandwich was placed on the table. Brian eyed it appreciatively. 'Now if Monsieur Henri cooked like this I'd eat at Café Paradise every day.'

'I don't think bacon sarnies are in his repertoire,' said George. 'Mind you, I reckon Genevieve could knock 'em out for you, Brian. She had a bit of tuition in Walter's day.'

Stan and George had heard about Brian's friendship with Genevieve, but if they hoped for any information, they were disappointed.

'I can produce a pretty good bacon buttie myself,' Brian said laconically and quietly demolished his sandwich.

Happy and satisfied with their breakfast, the three men set to work with drills and screwdrivers. As the day progressed, the kitchen took shape. The cupboards went up on the walls with the base units beneath. The cream worktops were fitted and glued into place. Brian was pleased with the finished result. 'We'll leave it to dry overnight and then I can come back and tile tomorrow.'

He looked down at the black flagstone floor. It was covered with sawdust from their day's work. 'They'll need a bit of scrubbing now, Stan,' he said. 'We've made a mess and ground it in a bit.'

'Don't worry about that,' Stan reassured him. 'That's a small price to pay for such magnificent work. We've got a kitchen! And it looks fantastic.' He clapped Brian on the back. 'Thanks,

Brian, you've been a real pal. Thank you too, George. What would I have done without you?'

'You'd have figured something,' George said modestly.

'Well, we can't do any more today. Come on, lads, let's head off to the Dog and Gun and have a pint. You've earned it and I think I have too. I could drink the pub dry right now.'

\*\*\*

Stan's relief at having an almost-finished kitchen lent an air of recklessness to the evening. Several pints of Black Sheep were quickly dispatched to slake the dust of the weekend's work.

Brian had intended to only have one pint and make his way home in his white van but, in the merry company in the Dog and Gun, one pint led to another as Stan urged him to try the other ales. Two hours later, he realised he would not be able to drive home. Perhaps he could ring Genevieve and ask her to look after the dogs for the night. He could doss down at Stan's for the night and nip home in the morning.

Genevieve did not answer her phone. Brian thought perhaps she had gone to visit her parents. He texted her in the hope she would pick it up soon, only he didn't realise he really had had more than one over the eight.

Switching the hoover off in her little flat, Genevieve heard the ping of Brian's text on her phone. Her brow wrinkled as she tried to puzzle it out:

*The Black Sheep and the Dog and Gun are way too good. Can't drive the van. Could you look after the dogs and I'll tomorrow.*

She knew Brian had gone to Stan's for the day to help him with the kitchen. What was this about a Black Sheep and a Dog and Gun? Ah. Light dawned. She knew Brian enjoyed a pub. The Dog and Gun – was that the Dunnington local? Had they called at the Black Sheep first? It sounded like it could be turning into a pub crawl and he wouldn't make it home. What if Stan and George were in the same state? Anything could happen. Look what had happened when he went to Dorset with Barney.

Genevieve knew how she got into scrapes easily. She couldn't just sit at home and wait for one to unfold around the three men.

***

An hour later, she drew up at the Dog and Gun in Dunnington. She had enquired from several people for 'The Black Sheep' and been met with blank looks. The Dog and Gun was a small pub tucked away at the back of the high street. Entering the cosy lounge bar, Genevieve was immediately spotted by Brian.

'Genevieve,' he called out. 'My beautiful Genevieve. Am I dreaming? What more can life hold? A foaming pint of Black Sheep and my heart's delight, all in one room.' He made his way unsteadily towards her.

Genevieve flushed with embarrassment. This was not the normally quiet, reserved Brian she knew.

Stan and George joined in. 'Genevieve, Genevieve,' they chorused. 'Come on, have a drink. We've finished the kisshen and Kate's coming home soon. Lots to celer … celer … brate,' Stan said cheerily.

Brian put his arm around her. Black Sheep bitter wafted from his breath. 'Hello, my love. How did you know where to find me? I'm really pleased to see you.'

Genevieve backed away. 'You sent me a text, if you remember. All about black sheep and dogs and guns.'

'Ah, Black Sheep. The best bitter ever. You must try some.'

Genevieve dodged away from his embrace. 'No thank you, I need to be getting home. Buddy and Zak need their dinners and a run.'

'Mm, dogs … love 'em.' Brian mused for a moment. 'Not as much as I love you, though,' he slurred. 'Love yooou, Genevieve.'

George and Stan cheered and waved their pints in the air.

'Genevieve! Brian loves Genevieve. Hurray. Kiss her, man. She's gorgeous. I know, let's all kiss her.' George approached enthusiastically.

Genevieve flushed red. She was angry, with a fury she had never felt before in her life. How dare they make such sport of her – and in public too? She would not stand here and take it from anyone, least of all these three.

'Right,' she called out in a loud, clear voice that startled her. 'Enough's enough. Outside. Now. I've got my car and I'm taking you all home. You're a disgrace. Stan – how is Kate ever going to move back to Beech Cottage if you carry on like this? George – you have a job to go to in the morning. And as for you, Brian Box…'

Whatever Genevieve thought about Brian would never be known. She turned on her heels. 'Come on,' she shouted angrily.

This completely unknown Genevieve stunned them all. The merry atmosphere in the lounge bar quietened down considerably in the face of her anger. The landlord, polishing glasses, jerked his head towards the door. 'Best do as the lady says, lads. She's in no mood for an argument tonight. Get home to your wives. You may have some explaining to do and I wouldn't want to be a fly on the wall. I might get flattened.'

Outside the Dog and Gun, Genevieve bundled the three men into the car. After several unsuccessful attempts at securing their seat belts Genevieve lost patience and strapped them in herself. Stan was in the front, as he would be dropped off first. He giggled helplessly as she leant over to strap him in. To her annoyance, the crosser she got the more they loved it.

'Magnificent woman,' George grinned to himself in the dark of the car.

'Mag … ficent,' echoed Brian. 'Mag…'

Genevieve ignored them. Jumping into her seat and snapping on her seat belt, she started the car and drove away from the pub.

'Mind now,' Stan cautioned from his vantage point in the front. 'Nasty junction coming up here, Gen … Gen …vieve. Drive carefully.'

'I can see it perfectly well, Stan, thank you,' she said crossly.

'Jus' saying.' Stan managed to get out and then subsided as the motion of the car produced a queasiness in his stomach.

'Don't feel very well,' he mumbled. 'Feel sick.'

Genevieve glanced across at him in alarm. 'Don't be sick in my car, Stan, please. We're nearly at Beech Cottage. Just hang on for one minute.'

Genevieve put her foot down and swerved into the driveway of Stan's house. She rushed round to release him and pull him out of the car, not a minute too soon. Hitting the cold night air tipped the balance for Stan and he heaved all his Black Sheep bitter into the bushes.

The house lights went on and Kate was at the door. Peering out into the night, she recognised Genevieve's car. 'Genevieve?'

'It's all right, Kate. I've got Stan here. He's a bit the worse for wear, but OK other than that.'

Kate shivered on the doorstep, listening to the unlovely sounds of Stan being sick. 'Now what's he been up to? I came to see how they'd got on with the kitchen today and no one was here. It looks wonderful. They've worked really hard all weekend and now it looks finished.'

A pang of remorse smote Genevieve. Her initial anger had subsided and she realised that after all their hard work they deserved a drink. Then she had come along and spoilt it all for them. 'I think they had a few pints at the Dog and Gun, so I'm taking them home. I've got Brian and George in the back. They're so tired, I think they've gone to sleep.'

Not strictly true but, now that she had calmed down, she didn't want to get them into trouble. 'Stan's tired too. I think he just needs to go to bed for a good rest. I'm sure he'll be fine in the morning.' She led a half-dazed Stan to the front door and handed him over to Kate. 'I think he'll make it up the stairs all right,' she said.

'Well, if he doesn't, he'll have to sleep in the hall.' Kate smiled and thanked Genevieve for bringing him home. 'They didn't have to get drunk – a pint or two would have done them.'

Genevieve quietly admired Kate's stance. Maybe she should

toughen up like that. After all, hadn't she just rounded up three drunken men from the pub? Maybe she wasn't a redhead for nothing.

Penny took much the same attitude as Kate when Genevieve hauled George out of the car. She was very grateful to Genevieve for bringing him home safely, but wasted little sympathy on him. 'I think I'll put him out in the conservatory,' she said, as if he were a vase of flowers to keep cool overnight. 'He'll be comfortable enough in there. But I wouldn't like to be inside his head in the morning.'

Genevieve agreed and got back in her car for the last time that night to take Brian home to the flat above Café Paradise. She would have to get him up the stairs and see to Buddy and Zak. They would be hungry and very lively after a day indoors.

Brian woke up as she helped him up the stairs to the flat. He was delighted to find Genevieve with her arms around him and was inclined to be amorous all over again. Genevieve was having none of it. Her temper flared again. Telling her he loved her in front of everyone in the pub? What kind of love was that? Drunken love. No, she did not want that. If that was what he had to offer, he could keep it. She wanted a lot more than that from the man in her life.

Up in the flat, Genevieve manoeuvred Brian on to the sofa. Looking down at him her heart almost broke. For the first time she admitted to herself how intensely she loved him. It had grown steadily over the weeks they had been seeing each other, but she was not sure that he loved her in the same way. Perhaps she had been mistaken – he saw her through rose-coloured glasses when he was drunk. But when he was sober...

Wearily she moved away and turned her attention to Buddy and Zak. Maybe the unconditional love of the dogs was her lot in life.

# CHAPTER 30

Barney drove home in a thoughtful mood. In the short time since his meeting with Chris Jones, he'd grown more and more excited about taking on Bookwood Developments and spiking Tom Young's guns. What a bully that man was with his threats and blackmail plans. Barney pursed his lips grimly. If he had anything to do with it, Bookwood Developments would be sent packing.

From his working life in London, Barney had seen at first hand how to mobilise the media around a cause. He could put the experience to good use now in leading the campaign at Allsthwaite against the proposed housing scheme. He couldn't wait to get home to Acaster Malbis to share his news with Jackie.

But, to his amazement, Jackie was dead against him having anything to do with the Allsthwaite scheme. 'Are you mad, having anything to do with a project with Tom Young at the back of it?' she demanded. 'Haven't we had enough problems with him in these last few years? And you want to go looking for another fight with him?'

'It isn't with him, my darling,' Barney insisted. 'It's Bookwood Developments. *They* are making the planning application. To all intents and purposes, I have no knowledge of Tom's hand in this, or that of his sidekick, Matt Carstairs. And I'll bet my last penny that he's been digging up the dirt for Tom.'

'If Tom Young's involved,' persisted Jackie, 'I don't want us to have anything to do with it.'

'You're not involved,' Barney countered mildly.

Jackie stared at him incredulously. 'Not involved? Oh no – only my husband's now the ringleader of the campaign against the development, a development Tom Young's very keen to see through. Now I wonder why? Out of the goodness of his heart, no doubt.' Barney flinched at the sarcastic note in her voice. 'And I'm not involved,' she continued. 'Somehow, I don't think Tom Young will see it like that.'

Barney stepped forward to take her in his arms but Jackie was too angry. She pushed him away, her violet eyes blazing. 'It's not only me. It's you. What about you? You know he'll stop at nothing to get what he wants. Think what he could do to hurt you – and we have our babies on the way.'

'Like sending in the heavy mob to work me over.' Barney laughed lightly. 'He wouldn't dare. Not with our history.'

'You're living in cloud cuckoo la—Oh my God, what's that?'

Jackie stopped suddenly, staring down at the floor as Samson came through the cat flap and stalked across the kitchen floor. He carried a limp and terrified mouse in his mouth.

Barney reacted quickly and bent down to catch Samson but he was not quick enough. Samson streaked across the hall and into the sitting room with his prize He dropped the half-dead mouse on the carpet, patting it gently between his paws. As Barney caught up with them Samson, delighted with his latest toy, gave the mouse a heavy clout and sent him scuttling underneath a bookcase. Even though he couldn't see him, Barney knew by Samson's continued interest that their visitor was alive and well.

Jackie stood in the doorway of the sitting room and would not venture further. 'You'll have to catch it. I'm not coming in here with you until you do. Set a trap or something.' She moved back into the hall. 'I'm going up to bed. What with that mouse and your news, it's really set the babies off and I need to lie down. I'll try and do some paperwork to take my mind off things.'

As she turned to go she made one last plea. 'Please think about what I said, Barney. Let Allsthwaite sort its own problems out.'

Barney lifted his head. 'As long as it's not in my back yard, eh? Well it might not be, but somebody has to stand and fight for the green fields of Allsthwaite. They need a leader and I'm not backing out now. I made a promise to Chris Jones and I'm standing by it. Ow, Samson, you little bugger, get off.'

Samson, tired of his sport being disturbed, clawed sharply at Barney's leg to send him on his way. In the ensuing distraction, the mouse shot out of his bolthole, across the carpet and disappeared down a tiny hole by the radiator pipe.

Samson meowed in disgust and stalked off. He knew from experience that once his prey disappeared down that particular hole, he would never be seen again. Playtime was over. He would have to go out hunting all over again.

\*\*\*

It was late when Barney eventually went to bed. After Samson's departure, he had set a humane mousetrap and sat quietly in the kitchen to wait for the emergence of the mouse into the dark and deserted sitting room. Three hours later, he gave up. He would have like to have released the little creature before Jackie saw it again, but he feared it was going to be a one-way trip for his furry friend.

A night's rest and reflection had not changed either of their opinions and a frosty atmosphere prevailed at the breakfast table. Before Barney left for the office Jackie tried one last time to change his mind. 'It's not your fight, Barney. You don't even live there. They have enough people of their own to make a real case against Bookwood.'

'It's everyone's fight,' Barney said stubbornly. 'We all have to stand up against these juggernaut companies. They try to steamroller us into lying down in their path, so they can flatten us – as they will.'

Juggernauts, steamrollers … Jackie wasn't sure where he would go with all this. 'You don't have to get involved,' she insisted.

'I'm already involved. Chris Jones is my client. He's a little man trying to do the right thing and the likes of Tom Young comes along – and not only to him, but to Joshua Copeland as well, from what I gather. All right, they haven't led blameless lives but, hand on heart, who has? And blackmail and intimidation should not be the way forward. It has to stop.'

Jackie realised she would get nowhere. Part of her admired Barney for taking this stand. In other circumstances she would have backed him all the way, but against Tom Young? There was too much history between them.

She was going into Café Paradise that morning and contemplated enlisting her father's help. Maybe she could get Walter onside. She knew he could be powerfully persuasive if her interests and those of his forthcoming grandchildren were affected.

But Jackie found the world was a surprising place these days. On her arrival at Café Paradise, not only did she find everything running smoothly, but also her father seemed to have acquired a new dignity in his new role as paterfamilias. Jackie noted how the young waitresses looked to him for direction. Even Monsieur Henri, once the bane of Walter's life in the kitchen, now greeted him as an equal.

When the morning rush was over, Jackie and Walter retired to her office with a tray of tea and biscuits. Jackie noticed Walter did not help himself to the biscuits like he usually did. 'What's up, Dad?' she asked. 'Ellie got you on a diet again?'

Walter sighed across the desk at her. 'No, she hasn't. Fact is, lass, when you're among 'em all day, you go right off 'em. Funny thing, that. I never went off chips and bacon butties in the forty years I worked in the kitchen for your mother but a few short weeks in that there coffee bar of yours …if I never see a biscuit, scone or cake for some long time, it won't be too soon. People scoff 'em morning, noon and night.' He shook his head in wonderment. 'Fancy wanting a caramel latte and cake at five o'clock. I'm thinking about my dinner then.'

Jackie laughed affectionately. He might give out all the fatherly airs in the world, but he was still Walter underneath it all. When they had finished discussing the affairs of the café, she turned the conversation to domestic matters. Here Walter was on home ground and delivered a fierce diatribe against his sister and her partner.

'A right pair of numpties if ever there was,' he fumed. 'You give them the simplest instructions and they still make a hash of things. Can't trust them with anything. And they're driving Ellie quietly round the bend. I hope your Barney sorts something out for them soon. I asked him to see what he could do.'

This was her moment. Swiftly she pounced on it. 'He's doing something about it all right, but I'm not so sure you'll approve of it.'

Walter cocked an eyebrow. 'Aye? How's that, then? What's he been up to now?'

Jackie related the story of Barney's involvement with the Allsthwaite campaign against Bookwood Development's planning application and Tom Young's intimidating part in the proceedings.

'Well I never.' Walter whistled when she came to the end of her story. 'That Tom Young. I knew he had a finger in a lot of pies locally, but this big international conglomerate … that fair takes the biscuit.'

There was a hint of admiration in Walter's tone that irritated Jackie. 'You're missing the point, Dad,' she admonished him. 'Barney is about to tangle with Tom Young again. And if Barney gets in his way – and worse, in Bookwood's way – they won't think twice about removing him to get what they want. What can Barney and a few Allsthwaite villagers do against the big boys?'

Walter didn't need to think about it. 'A great deal,' he said energetically. 'And I admire the lad for having a go.' He grinned at Jackie. 'I always knew you'd married a good 'un and this just proves it. I hope he gets a real good campaign going. I might join in meself. We'll see them London lads off, or I'll eat hay with the donkey.'

'I'll order a bale especially for you,' Jackie said drily. 'Dad, you don't realise what you're getting into—' she began.

Walter interrupted her. ''Course I do. I've known Tom Young a sight more years than you and I know we can beat him. We always have before,' he said challengingly.

'This is different.'

'It is not,' Walter said firmly. 'Barney's right. Young's not going to walk all over us without a fight.'

Driving away from Café Paradise, Jackie contemplated the immediate future. She had never imagined her father or her husband as eco-warriors but it looked like they were becoming just that. She wondered where it would all end.

# CHAPTER 31

The morning after Genevieve rescued Brian from the Dog and Gun, he woke up on the sofa in his flat with a very sore head and wondered why he wasn't in his bed. Slowly, fleeting memories came back to him – something to do with sampling all the liqueurs ranged on the shelf above the bar and the Black Sheep beer and … and… Oh yes, Genevieve. Genevieve being extremely cross. He'd never seen Genevieve get cross before. Why was she cross? Brian couldn't puzzle it out.

He looked at his watch and started up in amazement. It was ten o'clock. He should have been at Stan's house an hour ago. Perhaps *he* would remember why Genevieve was cross. Had they parted on good terms?

A quick phone call reassured Brian that Stan had not been waiting for him. He was in the same poor state as Brian and had endured a telling-off from Kate into the bargain. Brian mentioned Genevieve and Stan groaned.

'Yeah, not the best day of your life, Brian,' he said.

'What did I do?'

'Look, why don't you and the dogs come on over? We'll have some strong coffee and I'll remind you.'

Mystified, Brian loaded his tools and the dogs into the van and made his way to Beech Cottage.

\*\*\*

'Told her I loved her, I really loved her?' Brian was horrified. Drunk, and in front of everyone. No wonder she was cross. She probably thought it was the drink talking and he didn't mean a word of it. But he did, he reflected soberly. He meant every word of it, only it might be more difficult to convince her of that now.

And so it proved to be. Genevieve was extremely elusive during the following week. She did not answer his phone calls, so he tried texting his apologies and asking to meet up. A terse *I'm busy*, was the reply.

When he called at Café Paradise Penny, looking embarrassed, told him Genevieve could not see him. Monsieur Henri was busy teaching her some new dishes in the kitchen and she could not leave her work for anyone.

In a despondent mood, Brian made his way up to the flat to an ecstatic welcome from Buddy and Zak that intensified his sense of loss. In former times, he would have been eagerly anticipating Genevieve's arrival and they would have gone out together with the dogs.

As he walked through the dark city streets that evening, passing the happy throngs of night-time Christmas revellers, Brian thought about the love of his life. What was his sweet, beautiful Genevieve doing now? What was she thinking? How did she feel? Had she ever cared for him if she could cut him off like this?

He could bear it no more and turned back to the flat. A man was allowed one mistake. He would woo her again, and this time…

\*\*\*

Brian was very busy at Beech Cottage the next morning, helping Stan to finish his new kitchen. The tiles were cleaned after grouting and they scrubbed the flagstone floor and left it to dry. At lunchtime Brian excused himself, promising to be back the next day to help George start fitting the new windows.

He had a few urgent errands to carry out.

York city centre was crowded with Christmas shoppers. Brian joined the throng and spent the afternoon making his purchases and arrangements for the following day. Later that evening he rang the doorbell of Genevieve's flat at Clifton Moor holding a large bouquet of flowers as a peace offering. When Genevieve came to the door he held the flowers out to her. 'I'm sorry,' he said. 'I behaved like an idiot and you were quite right to be cross. I miss you. Please forgive me and can we start again?'

At his words Genevieve's face softened. He missed her. But was that all? She had missed him terribly, burying herself in work at Café Paradise. Could she start again? Was he saying he'd been an idiot to say he loved her? It was all very confusing. She was unsure about letting her guard down again.

'I missed Buddy and Zak,' she said and took the flowers, stepping back to let Brian in.

He had to make do with that. At least she hadn't dismissed him out of hand and had accepted the flowers. Encouraged, he moved on. 'I wondered if you might come out with me tomorrow night,' he ventured. 'I'll make it somewhere special.'

'It's my half-day tomorrow,' Genevieve said non-committally.

'Even better,' Brian enthused. 'You could bring your smart clothes in the morning and leave them at my place and we could go for a walk in the afternoon. The forecast is good. And then we could go out in the evening.'

He stopped, unable to read the expression in her vivid green eyes. 'Please say yes,' he asked quietly.

'All right,' Genevieve said slowly. 'I enjoy walking the dogs.'

She had agreed. That was enough for now. He would have to try very hard tomorrow to make her understand his real feelings for her and that they weren't just the result of the rosy glow from the Dog and Gun beer.

\*\*\*

Brian was up very early the next morning. He took the dogs for a good walk and was at Beech Cottage by eight o'clock to give George a hand with Stan and Kate's new windows. He explained apologetically that he could only give them half a day but would be back tomorrow to help again. When he explained he was meeting Genevieve, Stan and George grinned.

'Has she forgiven you?' asked Stan.

'I *think* so,' Brian said a little dubiously. 'She missed Buddy and Zak.'

'You'd best develop a good bark and walk on all fours, then,' laughed George. 'You might get a biscuit and a pat on the head.'

Brian hoped it would work out a lot better than that.

They worked hard all morning and replaced the upstairs front windows, leaving the downstairs for the next day, when Brian would be back. After a hasty lunch, Brian jumped into his van and waved goodbye to Stan and George, standing on the doorstep grinning like a pair of naughty boys.

'Good luck,' they called as he crunched out of the gravel driveway. 'Stay sober and mind your tongue this time.'

As he drove towards Castlegate and Café Paradise, their words echoed in his mind. They were right. Keeping to the shandy and careful words might put things right. Although a stiff whisky for Dutch courage might do the job better.

\*\*\*

Luckily, Genevieve still had the key to his flat and had been in to leave her clothes in the spare bedroom. Brian washed and changed ready for their walk, relieved she had not changed her mind overnight.

Genevieve arrived late, hot and a little flustered from a difficult morning at Café Paradise. 'Monsieur Henri was not in a good mood this morning,' she explained, sinking gratefully into a chair and accepting a cup of tea. 'His mother proposes to come over for Christmas and he's none too pleased. Apparently she does nothing but criticise his cooking!'

Genevieve's gurgle of laughter lifted Brian's spirits. How he had missed that giggle and her lovely sense of fun. He wanted to sweep her up in his arms there and then and tell her so, but stopped himself. He had a lot of ground to make up yet.

'Well, he needn't have given you a hard time about it.'

'I let most of it wash over me these days.' Genevieve smiled at him.

Was he mistaken, or was there more warmth in her eyes than yesterday? He hoped so. She looked so right there, with Buddy and Zak at her feet.

They decided on a circular walk out of the city and along the riverbank to bring them back to the Museum Gardens and up on to Castlegate.

The path along the riverbank was hard with frost. Old muddy footprints were frozen in deep ridges. Grasses and gorse bushes were powdered with a light snowfall that had fallen and frozen on to every blade and stem. Spiders' webs, delicately outlined with frost, were strung out like tiny hammocks among the bushes.

Buddy and Zak slithered in delight along the banks, chasing each other and the unsuspecting rabbits they found among the gorse. To and fro they ran, circling Brian and Genevieve and racing off again, their energy never flagging.

Brian took Genevieve's hand. 'This is how it should be,' he said.

She did not withdraw her hand but she wondered what he meant. She wasn't sure she wanted to ask. Did he just mean a walk with the dogs on a frosty December day? Was that how the world should be?

Brian was grateful for her warm hand in his, even if she made no reply to his comment. He decided just to enjoy the walk with her and see how the day developed. There was always this evening. He cleared his throat nervously at the thought of it.

'Are you all right?' Genevieve looked concerned.

'I'm fine.' Brian coughed again. 'Just the cold air caught me for a moment.'

They both enjoyed the afternoon, watching the birds on the river as they dived for food or sat quietly on the riverbank cleaning and oiling their feathers ready for the cold night to come. Buddy and Zak eventually tired, their pink tongues lolling out of their mouths, and stayed to heel.

Genevieve was entertaining Brian with an anecdote from Café Paradise. A customer had sent back one of Monsieur Henri's dishes, a French opera cake, wanting to know if he had forgotten to put the coffee in it because she couldn't taste any. Monsieur Henri nearly blew a gasket and had to be restrained from marching into the café and exploding at her.

Before Genevieve could finish, Buddy spotted a large cat across the water and launched himself into the river. Zak followed immediately. At the splash of the water, the cat streaked away, leaving Buddy and Zak paddling about in the muddy shallows. Just beyond, on Joseph Rowntree Walk, were steps leading up from the water. Brian and Genevieve ran back to them, calling to the dogs all the while.

'Come on out,' ordered Brian. 'Come on, we're going home.'

He was exasperated. Two wet and soggy dogs were not in his plans. They wouldn't dry off before they reached Castlegate. He would have to put them on the lead and walk them a bit more. Maybe Genevieve had had enough by now.

'Buddy, Zak, come here,' Genevieve called, almost tipping over into the dark water in her attempts to coax the reluctant dogs to the steps.

Brian grabbed hold of her and pulled her back. 'Steady, Genevieve. I don't want to be going in after you as well.'

Genevieve giggled. 'I often wondered what it would be like in winter.'

Brian shuddered. 'I don't want to find out. Not today anyway. Buddy, Zak, come on.'

Finally the dogs took some notice and paddled to the steps. In her relief at having them safely ashore, Genevieve didn't step back quickly enough and received the full blast of dirty river water as the dogs shook themselves. She shrieked as the icy cascade hit her. Brian stepped in to pull them away but it was too late. Genevieve was soaked and splattered with river mud.

Brian's heart sank. What a way to end their afternoon. She would be really chilled by the time they reached Café Paradise. Would she just want to go home? Oh, please God, not that.

Fortunately Genevieve had been in worse scrapes in her life and took her soaking with good humour. 'Dogs always do that,' she said in response to Brian's apologies on his dogs' behalf. 'I should have jumped out of the way.'

Seeing the worried look on his face, she kissed Brian's cheek lightly. 'I'll have a hot shower when we get home. I'll be fine.'

There, maybe that would encourage him. All afternoon she had been hoping for an explanation of the Dog and Gun, but he had never mentioned it. Only last night, and that was to say he'd been an idiot. If he regretted it, why ask her out again? Was it only ever going to be a friendship?

Brian took heart from her gentle kiss. Was that a sign he was on the way to being fully forgiven? Maybe this evening would tell.

\*\*\*

By the time they reached the flat above the new part of Café Paradise it was getting dark and beginning to freeze again. Gratefully, a shivering Genevieve headed off for the shower and to change for their evening out.

'Take as much time as you like,' Brian called after her. 'I've booked the table for half past seven.'

'Where are we going?' she asked.

'Somewhere special,' was all he would say. 'For someone special.'

Genevieve's spirits lifted. Someone special. Was she, after all?

Brian gave the exhausted dogs their dinners and settled them down in their beds. After all the miles they had run that afternoon, they would not stir now until the morning.

Genevieve called when she was out of the shower and Brian took his turn in the bathroom. He shaved carefully, not wanting to present himself all cuts and cotton wool on their evening out. Best grey suit hung on the wardrobe door with a new white shirt and a grey and silver tie. Gleaming black shoes waited beneath them.

When he was dressed, he inspected himself nervously in the mirror. Mm, not bad. But, more importantly, would Genevieve like what she saw? He pocketed his wallet and bits and pieces and took a deep breath. It was nearly time to go. The car would be here soon.

It was very quiet down the corridor. He'd better see if Genevieve was ready. Gently he knocked on her door.

'Is it time?' she called. 'I'm nearly ready, just getting my shoes on.'

Brian waited in the little sitting room. When Genevieve came in, he caught his breath. She had looked beautiful in jeans and thick jumper that afternoon. Now, in a long emerald-green dress and with a fur cape around her shoulders, she looked stunning. Her red wavy hair flowed around her shoulders and down her back. Brian was speechless.

'Will I do?' Genevieve asked anxiously. 'You wouldn't tell me where we're going, but if it's special, I…'

Brian hastened across to her, smiling in admiration and took her in his arms. 'You are beautiful,' he said huskily. He wanted to pour it all out, his deep love and endless devotion to her, but stopped himself. Their car would be at the door. He could wait a little longer.

Genevieve was surprised and touched to find Brian had ordered a cab for the night.

'That is not a frock for a van, my love,' he said firmly. 'And we'll not be turning up at this venue as White Van Man and Co.'

'Am I allowed to know the venue yet?' Genevieve ventured.

'You'll see in a minute,' Brian assured her.

Only when the cab drew up outside the gates of the hotel did the penny drop. Genevieve breathed a silent 'Oh', her green eyes large in her head. 'Are we eating here?'

'We are.' Brian answered. 'I said somewhere special for someone special.'

'I came to a wedding here last year,' said Genevieve excitedly. It was amazing, and the food...' She fell silent. This more than made up for the Dog and Gun. Had he meant what he said?

Brian felt a surge of relief. At least his choice had met with approval.

The hotel dining room had a stately elegance that echoed its past history as a private home, combined with an understated twenty-first century look with polished wooden tables and leather dining chairs. Heavy crystal glasses twinkled on the tables, reflecting the light from the spotless white napery.

Brian was delighted with Genevieve's response to his choice. He patted his pocket. The evening *had* to go well from now. Soft lighting, a lovely meal in a lovely setting. Her heart must soften towards him.

The evening flew by. The food was faultless. Brian was aware that Genevieve had developed an experienced and critical palate under Monsieur Henri's tutelage, but she was not a lady to go looking for faults and she enjoyed every course and the wines that accompanied them.

As dinner progressed, Brian's nervousness rose. He wanted to broach the subject of the Dog and Gun and take things from there, but he couldn't find the right moment. Genevieve, sitting across the table from him looking so dazzlingly beautiful, did not help. He felt even more tongue-tied and helpless than ever. How dare he, an ordinary engineer and craftsman usually working with industrial machinery, hope for the love of this amazing woman?

At the pudding stage his appetite deserted him. When he refused all the waiter's suggestions, Genevieve looked concerned. She knew how much Brian enjoyed a pudding. Was he all right? Did he need to go home?

Brian waved the waiter away. He needed a little more time. He wasn't quite ready. Genevieve inspected him closely. Beads of perspiration stood on his brow. He could not be well. How selfish she was to keep him out when he should be at home, possibly in bed, not out on a freezing night like this.

'There's nothing wrong with me, Genevieve,' Brian said a little desperately. 'Nothing physical, at any rate.'

Genevieve was nonplussed. 'What is it, then? Are you sure you're not ill?'

Brian took a deep breath. It was now or never. The ghost of the Dog and Gun had to be laid to rest forever. He had intended to wait until after their coffee and then maybe with a warming liqueur in front of them... He just couldn't wait any longer or he *would* be ill.

Taking a velvet-covered box from his pocket, he opened it and put it on the table between them. He had chosen a beautifully cut diamond, the facets sparkling up at them in the lamplight.

Genevieve caught her breath and looked questioningly at him.

'If ever a man was sorry about visiting the Dog and Gun, Genevieve, it's me,' he began. 'I know I was a complete idiot and I've kicked myself a thousand times for it since. But,' he held her gaze steadily, 'I meant every word I said. I do love you, madly, deeply and forever, and I hope you love me in the same way. Will you marry me and spend the rest of your life with me and Buddy and Zak? Because they love you as much as I do.'

He took the diamond ring from its case and held it out to her. Genevieve, usually so pale, had flushed a delicate pink. Slowly she held out her hand and Brian slipped the ring on her finger.

So engrossed were they in their own affairs, they had not noticed the other diners watching the proceedings with interest. Spontaneous applause and hearty cheers broke out. Genevieve blushed a deeper pink.

The waiter appeared with champagne and glasses.

'Compliments of the hotel, sir,' he said. 'And our congratulations to you both.'

Brian finally breathed out. It must be true, then. She had said yes.

The rest of the evening passed in a blur. They were installed on a cosy sofa by a roaring fire and coffee and liqueurs arrived as if by magic. Genevieve was still stunned at the sudden turn of events. She asked shyly. 'When did you first realise you … liked me a little?'

'I fell in love with you the moment I set eyes on you,' Brian said simply. 'I know it's a bit old hat but it truly felt like I had found my other half. I couldn't frighten the life out of you there and then. Sometimes, I wish I had. All these wasted weeks and misunderstandings.'

'Not wasted,' Genevieve said seriously. 'Café Paradise is finished and Beech Cottage would never have been renovated but for you. And I've had the opportunity to watch it all from the sidelines – and fall in love without even realising it. And of course, there's Buddy and Zak. Who could resist them?' she added mischievously.

Brian held her close. A wonderful new life unfurled before his eyes. Beautiful York city, beautiful and wonderful Genevieve – and their two naughty dogs.

At a late hour, the staff called a cab to take them home. It was the same driver who had taken them to the hotel. 'I take it she said yes, then,' he said laconically as he saw them into their seats.

Brian looked up, startled by this remark. 'She did. How did you know?'

'Seen that look on a man's face a thousand times,' he chuckled. 'Like they're up before the beak, only worse.'

Brian settled himself into his seat and took Genevieve in his arms. If this was 'worse', he could stand an awful lot of it.

As they were passing the Minster, Genevieve called out 'Stop.' Obediently the cab driver applied the brakes and coasted to the side of the road. 'Just wait a few minutes, please,' she requested. 'This is the best night of my life. I've got to share it with the beating heart of York. Come on, Brian, just for a few minutes.' She opened the door and tugged a bemused Brian out of the cab.

'It's freezing, Genevieve. You'll catch your death.'

'No, I won't,' she answered, and wrapped her fur cape tightly round her.

Silently they walked around the perimeter of the Minster, enjoying the peace and tranquillity that emanated from its thousand-year history.

'How many lovers have walked this way?' Brian wondered.

'We are two of thousands,' Genevieve surmised, 'and none happier than us now. As it should be.'

Brian, guessing her thoughts, squeezed her hand. 'Come on, let's go. The Minster will watch over us for the rest of our lives. Let's go home.'

# CHAPTER 32

The remaining new windows were stacked in the garage at Beech Cottage, ready for fitting. Two more days and everything would be ready for Kate. Stan had been working hard and was really looking forward to having his beloved wife home with him again and getting the nursery ready for the new baby.

The plan this morning was for Brian to finish painting the bedroom upstairs and for Stan to fit the window in the downstairs toilet.

Brian arrived early and went off to collect his brushes and paint from the garage where he had left them the previous day whilst Stan began to remove the old wooden window in the cloakroom. He worked happily, applying all the new knowledge and skills that George had taught him when fitting the windows upstairs. Two more days, he told himself, as the old window finally came out, and Beech Cottage would be almost finished.

It was now ten thirty and Brian, having finished the bedroom walls, wandered down to see how Stan was getting on. 'It's a dry house,' he remarked.

'Yeah, very dry,' Stan agreed. 'Mrs Simpson renewed the roof recently. We were glad we didn't have to do that. In fact, we couldn't have afforded to.'

Brian smiled. 'A *dry* house, Stan. I'm not talking about the roof. It's coffee time. A man could die of thirst here.'

After coffee they returned to their respective tasks. Stan

began preparing the window frame to take the new window and Brian cleaned his brushes outside. Whilst he was there, he noticed a wide crack running down the frame of the manhole cover in the driveway. Maybe the recent frosts had done the damage. He had not noticed it previously. He decided to check the inner framework whilst he was there.

When he lifted the manhole cover, he discovered the inside was cracked and some of the old concrete frame had fallen away. He shook his head. He couldn't leave it like that. The cover needed to be a good fit, especially as it was in the driveway with the cars running over it.

Luckily, there was sand and cement in the garage and Brian was soon cementing in the frame of the manhole. When he had finished, he put a board over it to protect it in case the temperature dropped in the afternoon. Satisfied with his handiwork, he went back indoors to get the next bedroom ready for decorating.

For Stan, the best bit was now to come: fitting the new window and sealing it in place. He smiled happily as he collected the window from the garage. It was small enough to manage by himself. Carrying the window in front of him and peering through the blue protective plastic it was wrapped in, he made his way carefully towards the house. The breeze rocked the window like a sail and Stan concentrated on holding it steady. He wondered if he should have asked Brian for a hand.

He did not see the board covering the newly repaired manhole and trod directly on it. The board gave way. Stan slipped and fell as his right leg gave way and snapped as it hit the brickwork inside the manhole. The new window flew across the drive as Stan tried to save himself. Intense pain shot up his leg. Yelling loudly for Brian, he attempted to haul himself up.

Upstairs through the open window, Brian heard Stan's shouts and rushed outside. By this time, Stan was sitting on the edge of the manhole holding on to his injured leg. 'What are you doing there?' asked Brian, running over to him.

'What do you think I'm doing? Passing a December

afternoon sitting down a manhole? Have you had this cover off?'

Brian grimaced guiltily. 'Yeah. I was having a look at it earlier and it was broken at the top, so that the cover didn't fit properly. I thought it needs to be firm and secure with the cars driving over it, so I've been repairing it. I left a board over the top to protect the cement until it dried.'

'Pity you didn't tell me about it.' Stan pointed to his leg. 'I think it's broken. I took a right tumble down there.'

'Why didn't you look where you were going?'

'I was carrying the window. I couldn't see much, but if I'd have known what you'd been up to…'

'Aye, all right. I'm sorry.' Brian got hold of Stan and helped him up. 'We'll have to go to the hospital. Are you sure it's broken?'

'I am. I did the other one when I was a lad. I know what a broken leg feels like.'

On the way to the hospital he tried to phone Kate, but it went to her voicemail service. He left a message and sent her a text in case she didn't see the message:

*I've hurt my leg and Brian's taking me to the hospital. Nothing serious, so don't worry. I'll ring you later.*

***

At the Historical Trust, Kate was getting ready to go home. Her waters had broken and she realised the baby was not going to wait until its due date next week. She cleared her desk calmly and tried to ring Stan. His phone was switched off and her message went to his voicemail.

She had left a hospital bag ready at Dunnington and decided to collect it and ring the hospital from there. When she got to Beech Cottage, there was no one there. Where were Stan and Brian? They were supposed to be doing the final jobs today and tomorrow. She saw the open manhole cover in the drive, now safely marked with a fluorescent bollard. Inside the house, Stan's gaping window opening was letting in cold air. Upstairs, Brian's open paint pot and brushes stood on the floor, just as he had left them.

Kate had no idea where they could have got to. The hospital had advised her to come in to the maternity unit, so all she could do was leave them a note and phone her mother to meet her at the hospital. She wanted someone with her if this baby was so intent on coming today.

***

The doctor at Accident and Emergency studied Stan's leg X-ray carefully and stroked his chin. 'Mm, a nice clean break. We can soon have you plastered up and on your way.'

Stan was lucky; A&E was quiet that morning and he had not had long to wait. The nurses were efficient, and amused at how Stan came by his broken leg. 'Fell down a manhole carrying a window? You want to take more water with it, lad. Christmas is coming. We don't want you breaking the other one.'

Stan gave up trying to explain. How a window behaving like a ship in full sail in the breeze had taken him down a manhole obviously didn't cut the mustard with these battle-hardened ladies.

By early afternoon, he was sporting a brand-new plaster cast and was wheeled out of the hospital and into Brian's van at the entrance. Luckily the cab was roomy and, with help, Stan was hoisted up into the passenger seat.

As they made their way out of the hospital grounds, Stan switched his phone back on. He had a voicemail. Listening to it, he shouted, 'Stop! Kate's having the baby. She's here, at the maternity unit. Come on, why have you stopped? We have to go there.'

Making allowances for one very overexcited man, Brian calmly turned the van around and followed the signs for the maternity unit. If Stan had had his way, they would have mown down everyone in their path. It was just as well he wasn't driving; all his road sense had gone right out the window with Kate's message.

'Oh God, I hope she's all right. The baby's early.' He looked stricken and clutched Brian's arm. 'Why is the baby early? Oh, don't say it's in trouble. I knew Kate was doing too much, but can you stop her? No, you can't! Women, they're all the same. They do as they like. You wait until you're married to Genevieve, you'll find out…'

On and on, Stan gabbled. Brian let it all go over his head, and thankfully the maternity unit was not far away. He drew up at the entrance and made Stan sit tight whilst he went to fetch a porter who could take him to Kate.

Kate was already installed in the labour ward when Stan reached her. He was relieved to find out that everything was normal and that it wasn't a problem that the baby had decided to arrive a few days early.

Now that Stan was there, Kate felt a great deal better. Looking at his leg, she said, 'Any excuse to get out of fitting windows, I see.'

'No,' Stan protested. 'I was doing really well, just going to fit the first one, in fact, and then I fell down the manhole in the driveway.'

'Where you go to fit a window,' Kate replied, raising an eyebrow.

'Where you fall down, if certain people take the top off and only cover it with a piece of board that you can't see because you're hanging on for dear life to a large window that's determined to take off in the wind.'

'Oh, I see. It's Brian's fault, then, I take it. I shall have to have words with him.'

'No, don't do that,' Stan said, alarmed. 'He's been really good and he's said he'll finish off for me today and tomorrow. It wasn't his fault – I should have looked where I was going.'

All thoughts of windows and Beech Cottage were forgotten as a wave of contractions started and Kate gasped in pain. The labour nurse came in to check on her and saw Stan holding her hand. Looking at his plaster cast, she grinned. 'I know they say "Break a leg" for good luck, but did you really have to?'

***

It was a long afternoon and night before Marcus James weighed in at 8lbs 9oz. An exhausted Kate dozed fitfully, with Stan fast asleep in the chair beside her. In his cot baby Marcus snuffled softly, the first baby to be welcomed to Beech Cottage for three generations.

# CHAPTER 33

Stepping out of the shower, Tom Young hummed softly to himself. Life didn't really get much better. When the Allsthwaite planning application was approved, he would be rich beyond his wildest dreams. He had found the perfect apartment in the Bahamas and the contract was ready to sign. Towelling himself dry, he wondered whether to take the lovely Jennifer with him. He was seeing her tonight. He hoped she would be on good form. He'd never known anyone like her for sexual athletics. No other girl came close.

Tom moved into the lounge and poured himself a drink. Checking his watch he saw it was six thirty, time for the *Look North* news. Tom always made a point of watching it. Sometimes they had juicy morsels that his own spies had not yet picked up on.

A smiling presenter was introducing the headlines. A boy had gone missing last week but had now turned up safe and well some forty miles away. Tom smiled wryly. The boy didn't go that far, then. The usual politician touring a factory in Barnsley. A conveyor belt full of bottles whizzed across the screen. Jaw jaw, yaw yaw, as usual.

Tom lay back in his chair and idly sipped his drink as a large crowd of protesters with banners filled the screen:

*Say No to Bookwood, Save Our Green Fields* and *Allsthwaite Says No.*

Tom shot forward to stare more closely at the screen, his

whisky spilling unheeded on the carpet. Allsthwaite. Who was this bunch of idiots? All the protests were supposed to have been closed down.

The TV cameras panned the crowd of demonstrators and came to rest on one man standing on a roughly erected stage at the entrance to the site of the proposed development. It was Barney Anderson.

Tom ground his teeth in rage. However did that bastard get mixed up in this? Would he never be free of him? What was he saying? Tom turned the sound up.

'Bookwood Developments, an international corporation, are about to submit a planning application to build three hundred new homes in Allsthwaite, right here in these very fields. Yes, three hundred. But it isn't just three hundred houses, is it? No, it's three hundred extra cars whizzing about our village and country lanes. And it won't be just three hundred. How many homes have just one car in their drive these days? We can safely double that and say there'll be another *six* hundred cars up and down this village every day. Another three hundred families needing a new sewage system, schools, doctors, nursery places. Allsthwaite is operating at capacity as it is. Will the government provide extra funding for these facilities? No, it won't, because I've already asked and there's no money in the kitty. Bookwood Developments will take our fields to build their houses, take their vast profits and move to another village – who knows where around York could be next? We will not stand by and let this happen.'

Cheers and roars of approval greeted Barney's speech. The crowds jiggled their placards to catch the lens of the roving cameras.

A spokesman for York Council came on the screen, reading a prepared statement. 'York Council has not, as yet, received any planning application from Bookwood Developments in regard to Allsthwaite village. If in the future any such application is received, it will subject to the due processes and reviews by the planning committee.'

Back in the *Look North* studio, the presenter rounded off the item. 'And, of course, we'll bring you any further news on that item when we have it. Now, turning to the sports news…'

Tom Young turned off the TV and sprang up from his armchair. He paced the lounge, hardly able to contain his fury. How had Barney Anderson learnt about the Allsthwaite plans? Tom had been so discreet. He'd told no one. Had Chris Jones or Joshua Copeland ratted? If so, he'd have their hides. As he paced rapidly to and fro Tom turned the ideas over in his mind. No, Chris Jones knew he would be a dead man if he didn't withdraw and Joshua Copeland certainly wouldn't have wanted his sexual exploits splashed across the Sunday newspapers. The leader of the council? No, again. Who would believe their London lunch was not just an innocent social meeting of friends?

The cat was out of the bag. The question now was: could it ever be stuffed back in again?

\*\*\*

Over the next two weeks Barney Anderson mobilised his team in Allsthwaite to bombard local and national press and TV with articles, adverts and interviews with local residents to make their case against Bookwood Developments. The campaign made the national news, even though no actual application had materialised at the planning department offices.

No one from Bookwood Developments was available for comment but Grey Eyes, in his discreet London office, watched the developments with mounting dismay. Terse phone calls to Tom Young yielded little fruit. Orders to 'Stop the campaign now,' got him nowhere. Tom was helpless in the face of Allsthwaite's opposition. Matt Carstairs had made extensive enquiries and could not turn up any involvement by Chris Jones or Joshua Copeland. Barney Anderson appeared to be the ringleader.

The final straw came on a Thursday morning when, during a breakfast programme interview, a spokesman for York Council more or less admitted that the idea of building on the greenfield site out at Allsthwaite was all but dead in the water. There were still brownfield sites available and the council would be looking at these in the future.

In his rage Tom Young lashed out at the TV, kicking it over and smashing it into spiky shards on the floor. The telephone rang. It was Andrew Markingham, the leader of York Council. 'Did you see the news just now, Tom?' he asked.

'Yes,' Tom answered tersely.

'Then you know Bookwood don't have a hope in hell for their application. Everything's off the table now, I'm afraid. Thank you for your kind offer to help in the future, but … there it is. Allsthwaite will not be on the development list in the foreseeable future.' He ended the call.

Tom viciously ground splinters of glass under his feet. If only he could crush Barney Anderson so easily.

The phone rang again. It was Grey Eyes, from Bookwood Developments. He was brief and to the point. 'The fishing trip will not now take place. The boat has been sunk and the captain dismissed from service.'

Click. The line went dead and with it went Tom's dreams of a new life in the Bahamas. He wouldn't be signing the contract for his new apartment. The sandy beaches and endless balmy nights with the luscious Jennifer were now closed to him. And all because of Barney Anderson. That man had robbed him of everything. Robbed him in the past and now destroyed his life and his dreams. He would pay for this and pay dearly.

There was a mad gleam in Tom's eyes. The shock of everything being taken from him tilted something in his mind. Sane reason went out of the window and revenge, revenge on a grand scale, stepped in.

# CHAPTER 34

Tom poured himself a large whisky and downed it in one gulp. He shuddered as the liquid burnt his tongue and throat, but it made him feel better and stiffened his resolve to get his revenge on the Andersons.

He showered and dressed for the office. Somewhere at the back of his confused mind remained a sense of self-preservation. He needed to hold on to his job at the Trades Council and he had appointments to keep this morning.

\*\*\*

Barney looked with some concern at Jackie across the breakfast table. She was perched awkwardly on the chair, so big now with the imminent arrival of the twins that she could not sit anywhere comfortably. 'I hope you're going to take it easy today, darling,' he said.

Jackie rubbed her back. 'Mm ... not planning on conquering the world today, Barney. Maybe a little light pillaging.'

'That's all right, then.' He smiled. 'Lots of rest: those were the doctor's orders. Just for once in your life, do as you are told.' He tried to look stern but it had no effect.

Jackie raised an eyebrow. 'And break the habits of a lifetime? Yes, Doctor Anderson. I promise I'll be good.'

Barney had to be satisfied with that. 'Ring me if there's anything, anything at all.'

After he had left for the office, Jackie mooched disconsolately about the house. Everything was ready for the babies' arrival now and she had nothing to do. Not naturally a woman of inaction, she was restless and bored. She might just as well sit in her office at Café Paradise and do some paperwork as sit here looking at the wall. A little guiltily, she got in her car and made her way to Castlegate.

***

The morning passed quickly for Tom Young. His visitors found him in an abstracted mood, his usual smooth charm replaced by very terse responses to their questions. In truth, he could not be bothered with anyone this morning and was glad to be rid of them all by lunchtime.

Thankfully, his afternoon was free. Restless and angry, he walked around the city, gazing unseeing into shop windows, plots against the Andersons tumbling chaotically around in his head. Walking down Castlegate, he came to Café Paradise. With some bitterness he noticed the tables were full and people were queuing at the coffee counter. Jackie was doing very well, whilst he had lost everything…

Passing the café car park, he noticed her car was there. So she was still working, just like her mother Marilyn, Tom sneered. Never one to turn her back on earning a bob or two.

He bought a sandwich. Walking back to his office, he passed the shining brass plate screwed on the door saying *Anderson & Cranton, Solicitors & Commissioners for Oaths*. He paused and looked at it with loathing. How dare they be allowed to practise in his city? Those two holier-than-thou merchants, taking on all the dossers and dregs of society the Citizens' Advice sent their way. They were an insult to the city. He aimed a kick at the door and walked quickly away.

Back in his office, he dismissed his secretary for the afternoon and tried to eat his sandwich. It tasted like cardboard. He took a sip of his whisky and sat back in his chair, brooding on how he had been wronged.

As the afternoon advanced and the whisky in the bottle diminished, a plan crept into Tom's fuddled brain. A grim smile played around his lips and his hands clenched tightly around his glass. Barney Anderson had taken his future from him. Well, justice must be done and be seen to be done. What was most precious to Mr Anderson that Tom could take from him? His lovely wife, of course. Now that would repay him, wouldn't it?

Tom sat back in his chair, swallowing the last of his drink. He thinks he's got away with it, does he? Thinks he can walk all over me, and everything in the garden is rosy? Just you wait, Barney Anderson. You might find out differently.

\*\*\*

It was five o'clock and Walter was clearing up the coffee counter at Café Paradise. He took the last of the cloths to the laundry and, taking off his apron, made his way to the staffroom to collect his coat. It was dark and cold outside and the streets were quietening down as the Christmas shoppers made their way homewards.

Walter put his head around Jackie's office door. 'I hope you're ready for the off, lass. If Barney finds out you've been here all day, I'll be for the high jump for letting you.'

Jackie stretched uncomfortably in her padded chair. '*You'd* be for the high jump. Imagine what he'd be saying to me! I'll scoot off now, Dad and he won't be any the wiser. I won't tell if you won't.'

Walter kissed her fondly. 'You're so like your mother, headstrong and daft. Now listen to me. I don't want to see you here tomorrow. I don't care how bored you are at home. Put the telly on, put your feet up and watch whatever rubbish is on. You're supposed to be resting.'

'I have been resting,' Jackie protested. 'I've just been sitting here doing paperwork. That's no worse than sitting at home on my own.'

'Mm,' Walter said dubiously. 'Well, we don't want to see you tomorrow, or I *will* tell Barney. Now get your coat on and go home.'

Jackie made a face but said nothing.

Walter collected his bike from the car park at the back of the café and set off for Claygate. Inside the café, Jackie locked the front door and put the lights out. She collected some papers from her desk and made her way to the back door to set the burglar alarm.

In the dark street outside the café Tom Young watched the staff depart, ending with Walter on his bike. After him, no one else. Jackie was still in there, on her own. He waited for some minutes and then drove into the dark café car park. Switching off his engine, he waited a moment. The café was in darkness except for one small light at the back.

Smiling to himself, Tom gathered up the rope and pieces of tape from the seat beside him and got out of the car. Quietly he walked to the back door and eased it open, listening for any movement inside. He could hear Jackie humming softly as she made her way up the corridor towards him. He hung back in the shadows until she was almost upon him and then he struck.

Seizing her from behind in a strong grip, he put a hand over her mouth and pulled her down the corridor and into the laundry room. Briefly he let go and snapped on the light switch, noting with pleasure the alarm and fear in her eyes when she saw her assailant.

'Don't think of screaming,' he said softly. 'There's no one here, only me … and you.'

He felt for the strip of tape in his pocket and, slapped it over her mouth before she could frame any words. He felt so much better just for doing that. One of the Andersons silenced, at least.

Spinning her round, he tied her hands behind her back. She was trussed up and ready. Tom's mood was rocketing. She was in his power now and there was nothing Barney Anderson could do about it. Wait until he got home from his precious office and found his little wife was not there. Tom paused, savouring the panic he would cause at Acaster Malbis.

But first, he had to get her away from here. He knew just the place where no one would find them. A Second World War pillbox on the edge of woodland and overgrown with seventy years of vigorous brambles and nettles, it was the last place a search party would look.

'We're going for a little ride in my car,' he told Jackie as he pushed her up the corridor. Out in the car park, he bundled her into the back of the car and ordered her to lie down. Terrified, Jackie obeyed. With her hands tied behind her back, she could not have kept her balance sitting up.

Tom had drunk a lot of whisky in the course of the afternoon but all his senses were on high alert. He drove carefully, not wishing to draw attention to himself. Once clear of the city, he picked up speed and was soon out in the quiet lanes of the countryside, heading for Akers Wood. In the darkness, Tom's mouth twisted in an ironic smile. Akers Wood, to the north of Allsthwaite, forgotten and overgrown. Who would remember it? No one had been there for years, only him and a 'nature-loving' lady of the night a few times a year.

\*\*\*

The house was in darkness when Barney arrived home at Acaster Malbis. He let himself in and switched on the hall lights, calling anxiously for Jackie. There was no answer.

Samson came strolling out of the sitting room, meowing plaintively for his dinner. Barney looked down at him. 'Where is your mistress?' he asked. Samson meowed again.

Barney made himself a cup of tea and stood thoughtfully in the kitchen, wondering where his wife could be. There was no note. Surely if anything had happened and the twins had started arriving she would have phoned him? Was she at Café Paradise? No, surely not. He telephoned Walter.

'She was there most of the day,' Walter informed him.

'Couldn't get her to go home. You know how stubborn she is, Barney. I left just after five o'clock and she was going to set the alarm and go home. And you say she's not there?'

'No. No lights on, no Jackie, no note, nothing. I'd better get over to the café and see if she's still there. If she is … I'll be very cross,' Barney ended.

'Go easy,' Walter advised. 'I told her she had to stay at home tomorrow or I'd tell you. Let me know she's all right.'

'I'll ring you later.'

Barney rang off, shaking his head in disbelief. He was more convinced than ever that the twins would be born at the café. They would probably come out fully trained and ready to wait tables, as they had spent most of their unborn lives there already.

He reached the café, to find it in darkness and the back door standing open. Dismayed, he put the lights on and searched the place. It was empty. He tried Brian at the flat above but, although the dogs barked, there was no answer. No doubt he was out with Genevieve somewhere.

Worried now, he phoned Walter. 'No sign of her, Walter. Where on earth can she be?'

Walter tried to keep the alarm out of his voice. 'You'd best try the hospitals, lad, starting with the maternity unit. She's probably tucked up in bed there by now waiting for you to turn up.'

Jackie was not tucked up in any bed at the maternity unit and no one had heard from her. Barney phoned a worried Walter.

'She said she was going straight home,' Walter insisted.

'Well, she isn't there and I've tried everyone I can think of, even Annabel in London. No one's seen or heard from her.'

\*\*\*

In Akers Wood, Tom sat watching Jackie inside the old pillbox. Her face was scratched and bleeding where the sharp barbs of the brambles had caught her as he dragged her through the doorway. He had at least untied her hands and smiled as she rubbed her sore and chafed wrists. 'Yeah, it's not good when it you're on the receiving end of things, is it?'

Her mouth was still taped up so she could not answer him. Her violet eyes, huge and scared, told him what he needed to know. Here was one terrified lady. How good was that? And Barney Anderson was missing a wife. Bet he was worried out of his wits by now. Even better.

Tom took a swig from the whisky bottle beside him. Hey, now that was a good idea. How about telling Barney how much his wife was missing him? Surely he would like to know.

Tom took out his phone and looked up Barney's number. He'd got it from Annabel, the bitch, in the days when they were friends. That hadn't lasted long and she was another reason to get even with the Andersons – and give a bit of grief to that old Walter Breckenridge, too. It was win–win. He hated the lot of 'em and would see 'em in hell before he returned Jackie to them unharmed.

The glow of his phone threw Jackie's frightened face into sharp relief.

'I've waited a long time for this, Jackie,' he said softly. 'First you did me out of fifty thousand bonus money because of that café of yours, then your stupid sister Annabel was too lily-livered to play ball on the blackmail plot. Now you've lost me my place in Barbados and a life of luxury out there, all because your husband can't keep his nose out of my affairs. So you have to pay for it.'

Jackie's knuckles whitened as she steadied herself against the damp, mossy wall of the pillbox.

'Don't bother,' he said, amused. 'You can't get away and you're in the middle of nowhere. Where would you go? Wander about the dark woods all night?'

'Yes,' screamed Jackie inside her head. Anything was better than this. What was he going to do with her? Her terrified mind veered away. What about her babies ... and Barney? What did Tom have in mind for them?

*Sorry to say your beautiful wife is not feeling too comfortable at the moment. But, tit for tat, we have a few old scores to settle. You took away what I wanted, so I've taken what you want. And she's not coming home any time soon. I don't get mad Barney, I get even. Bye.*

Tom pressed 'send' and watched the message go. He smiled at Jackie. 'Not going home anytime soon.' He repeated the text message to her. The whisky bottle was nearly at his mouth when the realisation of what he had done hit him. When Barney received that text and knew for sure that Tom was holding his wife, their location could be traced.

He put the bottle down and switched off his phone, considering the situation. What to do? They couldn't stay here. He wasn't going to wait around like some sitting duck for Barney Anderson to walk in and find them. If it had just been Barney he wouldn't have minded. He would have enjoyed taking a swing at him and knocking him down. But, knowing Barney, he would arrive with a vanload of police and Tom wasn't waiting around for that.

They would have to move – and quickly. He remembered a building in the centre of York that had a cellar, built centuries ago in Roman times. He used to love playing in it when he was a boy. His uncle had owned it. It was deep underground and soundproof. It started underneath a shop which had been empty since the owner went bankrupt some months ago. He could take Jackie there and no one would find them.

To Tom's crazed mind, the plan was perfect. He hauled Jackie to her feet and retied her hands. 'We're going for another little drive,' he told her, and pushed her towards the pillbox doorway.

# CHAPTER 35

B arney stared at Tom's text on his phone, his hand shaking with emotion.

*Tit for tat*, he read. Tom had taken Jackie. Where were they and what did Tom intend to do with her? If he harmed her in any way...

He wasted no time and dialled 999. After a distracted conversation with the police, he telephoned Walter at Claygate.

Walter was appalled and was inclined to blame himself. 'She asked me specially to try and stop you from taking on the Allsthwaite campaign. She didn't want us to have anything to do with it, what with Tom Young at the back of it, an' all. I wouldn't listen to her.' Walter's voice cracked. 'I said it was about time we put a real spoke in his wheel and let him know he can't intimidate everybody in this city. I said I admired you for doing it. And now he's... I'm coming over right now.'

Walter put down the phone before Barney could explain about the police coming. Grabbing the van keys, he raced across to the barn where Ellie was potting up a batch of chutney. 'Tom Young's got Jackie. I'm going to Barney's now,' he gabbled and jumped into his van. The key turned in the ignition but the engine would not fire. With every attempt, the battery died a little more until it was completely flat.

Cursing his luck, the world and every white van that was ever made, Walter got out and slammed the door. Looking around, he spotted Rose and Arthur down in his former hayfield grooming their alpacas. He shouted and waved at them to come up to the house but they just stood there looking blankly at each other and then at Walter.

Cursing sisters, their partners, alpacas, Tom Young and all things mechanical, Walter ran at speed across the fields. 'Come quick,' he shouted. 'I need that van of yours. Never mind them bloody alpacas and their fancy fur coats. Get yourselves up here now.'

The panic in his voice reached them and they dropped their brushes and started running to meet him. 'What's up, Walter?' Rose was the first to reach him.

'Tom Young … he's kidnapped Jackie from the café and he's holding her somewhere. I've just had Barney on the phone. I've got to get over to his house but the bloody battery's flat on me van. Can I take yours? We'll have to search for her. He's evil. God knows what he could do to her – and the twins are due any time.'

Rose grabbed Walter's arm. 'Calm down, lad. Panicking like this won't get us anywhere.'

'You don't understand…'

'Yes, I do,' Rose said firmly. 'I understand you're her dad and you're frantic and, to my way of thinking, in no state to drive.'

Walter was about to protest.

'And so,' Rose went on, 'we'll come with you, me an' Arthur. We can help with the search. Come on, lad, no time to lose.'

\*\*\*

Half an hour later Walter, Rose and Arthur arrived at Acaster Malbis. Two police cars were parked outside, blue lights flashing. A policeman was guarding Barney's door.

Inside, a white-faced Barney sat at the dining room table alongside a police officer, both looking at a computer screen. The officer was busily tapping the keyboard and checking the map on the screen. With an effort, Walter contained himself and watched as the two men quietly conferred.

'It's somewhere just north of Allsthwaite village,' said the officer. He moved the mouse around a small area on the screen. 'Just here is woodland, I think.' At a particular spot, the red locator balloon began flashing. He divided the screen in half and brought up the Ordnance Survey map of the area. He was right. It was identified as Akers Wood.

'Akers Wood, near Allsthwaite,' Barney shouted, turning away from the screen and facing the newcomers. 'That's where he's got her. He's texted from there. Come on, let's get going. My wife's out there in the freezing cold with that...' Words failed him as he headed for the door.

A policeman stopped his progress. 'Leave this to us, sir. He's obviously dangerous and the situation could need careful handling. We'll keep you informed at every stage.'

Barney fixed him with a stare. 'If you think I'm sitting here whilst Tom Young makes off with my wife...'

'Aye, an' my bloody daughter,' added Walter. 'We're going and that's that. Come on, Barney, we've got the van outside. We'll follow this lot and find Jackie.'

Short of arresting all four of them there was not much the officer could do.

'All right,' he agreed, 'but just follow the officers' cars and don't interfere with the operation. We want Mrs Anderson back in one piece.'

On this chilling note, they made their way out into the night, Arthur driving the van and following the police cars.

Twenty minutes later, passing through Allsthwaite, the village streets, quiet in the cold December night, Barney looked wistfully out of the window. 'If only...'

'You did what you had to do, lad,' Rose said stoutly. 'Someone has to stand up to these big conglomerates. Look how we got turfed out of our holding there. We'd ha' still been there but for Bookwood Developments and their grand schemes to ruin the village.'

'If you'd ha' read your letter from them in the first place...' rejoined Walter.

'Oh, don't start,' Barney said sharply. 'This is not the time, but I wish now…'

Leaving the cosily lit homes of Allsthwaite behind, they followed the police cars out into the darkness of the open country lanes. Two miles further on, Akers Wood began. The police car lights were dimmed and they slowed down to a crawling pace, looking for the spot the GPS had pinpointed. Abruptly the brake lights slammed on as the computer identified the spot to their right.

Almost driving into the back of the police, Arthur stood hard on the brakes, squealing to a halt an inch from the bumper of the car in front.

'Well, if he's here, he'll have heard that,' Rose said crossly. 'Couldn't you have managed it better than that, Arthur?'

'He just stopped, sudden-like,' Arthur defended himself.

Barney and Walter had already jumped out and were treading as quietly as possible in the wake of the police officers into the edge of the woods. The red balloon on the GPS device in the officer's hand indicated they were at the spot. Silently they looked about them, flashing their torches around the woodland.

'There!' gasped Barney quietly. 'Among the brambles. Is that a bit of a building?'

Torchlight followed where Barney was pointing. Behind the tangle of overgrown brambles and nettles, the outline of a building could be seen. Motioning everyone to keep back, the two officers in charge moved stealthily around the building, their torches almost covered to reveal only a tiny pencil of light. Barney and Walter waited in agonised impatience.

After some minutes, the brightness of torchlight shone out again, as the officers made their way back towards them. 'Too late,' said the one holding the GPS.

Barney staggered and Walter caught him before he fell to the ground.

'No, it's all right,' the officer apologised. 'Sorry, I mean it's too late. They've gone from here. They've been here, all right.

This is the spot. It's an old World War Two pillbox – overgrown now, as you can just about see, but they were here. The ground inside is freshly disturbed. But if he's still got her, he's taken her somewhere else.'

'And that could be bloody anywhere,' said Walter angrily, hanging on tightly to Barney.

The officer shrugged helplessly. 'It could. Come on, let's get out of here, and go back to Acaster Malbis. There's nothing for us here. Forensics can take over now.'

\*\*\*

Jackie was not in good shape. The journey from Akers Wood back to the centre of York had tried her resources almost to their limit. With her hands still tied behind her, she lay on her side on the back seat of Tom's car, her face pressed into the black leather, hardly able to breathe.

When they arrived at their destination at the back of the shop, he pulled her out of the car and half-carried her down a flight of steps and along a stone passageway that opened out into a network of cold, dank cellars deep underneath the city. Depositing her on the damp floor, Tom untied her hands and ripped the tape from her mouth.

'You can scream here all you like, Mrs Anderson,' he said loudly. 'No one will hear you, only your echo bouncing around the walls. You try it.'

Jackie trembled in the darkness of the cellar. 'What now?' she thought. He was mad, she knew that now. With the loss of the Allsthwaite plan, he had completely lost his mind. Mad and dangerous. Did he intend to kill her and her babies too? 'Oh, Barney, where are you?'

Tom smacked his lips as he took another drink. 'I used to come here as a boy, you know,' he said conversationally. 'Yes, I did. I loved it here. Still do. It's quiet and peaceful and there's no one to bother you. No one will bother us, Jackie. The shop's empty … no one there … hasn't been for months. It's just you

… and me.'

He laughed and flicked her cheek with his finger. Jackie flinched in the darkness; she had not seen it coming. 'You and me, Mrs Anderson, and not a Barney in sight. Now if you are very nice to me … very, very nice to me, you might get out of here…'

Jackie's blood ran cold. No, he couldn't possibly be thinking of sex now in a place like this. But he was drunk and barking mad. He could think of anything and she knew he had a voracious sexual appetite – any girl, anywhere, she had heard.

She mustn't panic. She tried to remember what she had seen and read about hostage situations. That was it: befriend your captor, get him on your side. He would be far less likely to harm you then. But did that apply to madmen?

Wanting to put some distance between them, Jackie cautiously backed away from Tom. She felt a popping sensation in her body and fluid slowly trickled down her legs. It dawned on her that her waters had broken; the babies would soon be on the way.

'Tom,' she began softly. 'I know things have not gone so well for you lately.'

Tom Young laughed harshly and flung the empty whisky bottle at the cellar wall. A shard bounced off and sliced into Jackie's arm. She gasped and felt around it in the dark, her hand coming away sticky with blood.

'No, lovely Jackie, things have not "gone so well", as you so beautifully understate the matter. Things have gone bloody awfully, if you must know. I've been dropped by Bookwood Developments, lost a king's ransom and now seem condemned to live out my life in this poxy city, working with the idiot members of the Trades Council. How's that for not going so well?' he mocked.

'The thing is, Tom…' Jackie hesitated. Would it make things worse if she mentioned her waters breaking? She needed the hospital; she couldn't give birth here.

'The thing is, Tom,' he mocked her again. 'Well, *here's the thing, Tom.* You and your family between you have ruined my life and someone has to pay for it.'

'The thing is, Tom,' Jackie tried to keep the mounting panic out of her voice. 'My waters have broken and my babies are on the way.'

Jackie didn't know what reaction she had been expecting to this, but Tom's wild, hysterical laughter was not on her list. He laughed loudly and long, holding his sides and rolling in the dirt of the cellar floor.

'She's having a baby – no, not a baby … *babies* – right here, in the cellar.'

Sharp pain jabbed deep inside Jackie. She gasped and closed her eyes. This was it. This was the start. 'Oh, dear God, not here, not like this. Please…'

***

The police hauled in Tom's secretary to unlock the office of the Trades Council and provide a list of all the members and their premises. The frightened girl recounted how Tom had been in angry mood that morning and had dismissed her after lunch. She had last seen him brooding over an uneaten sandwich and a glass of whisky. She was horrified to learn that he had abducted Jackie Anderson from the Café Paradise, but could provide no further information to them.

Plain-clothes and uniformed police began the slow process of door-to-door enquiries in and around the city. Officers were sent to interview every member of the Trades Council, but no new information came from in their efforts.

As the evening advanced, Barney and Walter waited at home at Acaster Malbis, racking their brains and trying to envisage any of Tom's haunts that had not already been searched. Rose made tea and tried to persuade them to eat something, but they brushed aside the offer.

'I couldn't get it down, Rose, I'm sorry,' said Barney. Returning obsessively again to Tom's whereabouts, he added,

'The police are checking everywhere they can think of and every person he has spoken to in his life, but so far nothing. Either Tom knows somewhere we don't or, worst of all, he's taken her right away, out of York.' He put his head in his hands, groaning at this agonising thought.

'I know this city as well as Tom Young does,' said Walter, 'and I can't think of anywhere the police haven't already looked. But there has to be somewhere. If he was at Akers Wood two hours ago, he's keeping local. Maybe he knows of other Second World War huts that we don't. There's bound to be more of 'em. Someone will know. There'll be records…'

Rose put a hand on his shoulder. 'Hang on a minute. Something you said just then … keeping local… What was it?' Reaching back into her memory, Rose sank down onto a chair and thought carefully. 'Walter, when Tom was a lad, he used to help out at old Simon Fisher's shop on Goodramgate. Do you remember?'

Walter stared at her uncomprehendingly. 'Simon Fisher's? Him that had that big hardware shop? Aye, I remember old Simon. Don't remember Tom Young helping out, though. Since when did he help anyone?'

'Don't split hairs,' Rose said irritably. 'He didn't just help out. I think he was related to old Simon and he used to stay with him as a boy. Then, as he got older, he worked for him on a Saturday.'

Walter huffed in exasperation. 'This going down memory lane is all very nice, Rose, but what the bloody hell's it got to do with owt now? Who cares who Tom Young had a Saturday job with?'

Rose stared into the distance, taking her mind back to Simon Fisher's shop forty years ago. 'There's a bloody great cellar below that shop. I bet nobody remembers it now, 'cept Tom. It opens out to two or three rooms, as I recall.'

Walter's eyes narrowed to a gimlet stare. 'Goodramgate. Aye, I remember now.'

'So do I,' Barney joined in excitedly. 'The shop's empty. The owner went bankrupt a few months ago. We've been handling his affairs at the practice. And you say there's a massive cellar down there? If Tom knows it well, it might be the first place he would think of in a hurry. He knew he couldn't stay in Akers Wood once he'd sent that text. He'd know we'd find him there.'

Barney kissed Rose soundly and turned to the police officer at the door. 'Goodramgate. That's where he might be. Hell, what was the shop called?'

'Graham's Hardware,' said Rose.

'That's it! The sign's still up. No one's taken it over yet. You can't miss it.'

\*\*\*

Christmas revellers thronged the streets of York and half-scared tourists followed the ghost tour guide down the dark snickelways and cobbled streets of the ancient Shambles. On Goodramgate, a police car glided to a halt outside Graham's Hardware and switched off its lights. Further down, two more pulled in and a group of plain-clothes detectives strolled casually down the street.

At Graham's Hardware, uniformed officers kept watch outside. A key was quietly slipped into the lock and the group of men went inside. By the light of a pencil torch, they stole through the shop and into the room at the back. Flashing the torchlight around the room, they saw the cellar entrance had recently been opened, judging by the disturbance of the dust on the floor.

Quietly they lifted the trapdoor. The cold, dank air rose up to meet them. In the darkness they listened and waited but no sounds came up to meet them. Motioning for his uniformed colleagues to follow, the lead detective descended the cellar steps. He stood in the darkness and listened intently. To his surprise, he heard faint sounds of laughter coming from another part of the cellar. As his eyes grew accustomed to the gloom, he detected a faint light in the distance. He nodded to the officers behind him and switched off his torch.

Slowly and soundlessly they made their way through the rooms of the cellar, the glow of light ahead guiding them towards the laughter. As they drew near, the tone of the laughter changed and took on a crazed, manic note. Creeping closer, the detective peered cautiously into the last room. Dimly, he could see a figure prone on the floor, groaning in pain, and someone standing over her laughing uncontrollably.

In a moment they were on him, struggling to restrain the crazed Tom. Taken by surprise, he made a fight of it. It took three officers to stop him kicking and spitting before they could get the handcuffs on. One of the policemen, a judo expert, took the legs from under Tom and they half-dragged, half-carried him out of the cellar and into the waiting police van.

Inside the cage, Tom continued to kick, keeping up a stream of vicious invective against the police, the Andersons, the Breckenridges, Bookwood Developments, the Trades Council and all its members.

Down in the cellar, Jackie was gently helped up the steps to her family who were gathered at the door. Outside, the police were clearing the gathering crowds away from the police cars and ambulances. Paramedics were standing by with a trolley and blankets and quickly whisked Jackie away to the maternity unit. Barney and Walter followed behind in a police car, blue lights flashing.

# CHAPTER 36

Barney Anderson leant over the tiny cots in the special care baby unit and shook his head in wonderment at the new arrivals, Alice and Edward. Miraculously, they were perfect and unharmed in spite of their early entry into the world.

Reaching Jackie's room he found Kate there, holding her new baby. 'Meet Marcus,' she said, smiling broadly and proffering a tightly wrapped bundle.

Very gingerly Barney took the tiny baby and sat down on the bed. He looked down at Marcus. Big blue eyes, just like Stan's, looked up at him. 'Hello, Marcus Peterson,' he said softly. 'Another baby that was impatient to arrive, eh? You're a very handsome chip off the old block.'

The baby whimpered and Barney hastily handed him back to Kate. She took him tenderly, her face alight with love for her new son.

Barney laughed. 'How is poor Stan, by the way? I'll have to get over to see him now that our own little emergency is over.'

'It's nice to be known as "a little emergency",' smiled Jackie tiredly.

Just then the door opened and Stan, sitting in a wheelchair with his broken leg in plaster stuck out in front of him, was pushed in by George Montague.

'By gum, it's like a class reunion,' joked George. 'And Penny's outside too. Is there anyone left to run Café Paradise today?'

'I hope so,' laughed Jackie. 'I've a new café to pay for and I may be in here for a little while longer.'

'And at home for some time after that.' Barney was stern. 'You've been through a lot and the doctor says you have to rest, and I'm going to make sure you do.'

Jackie made a face. 'Between you and Dad, I won't be able to move a muscle, let alone look after the babies.'

'We'll be keeping a close eye on you in future,' said Barney. 'If you hadn't sloped off to the café and stayed so late…'

Seeing an argument was about to break out, Kate changed the subject. 'What's happening to Tom Young, anyway?' she asked.

'Barking bonkers, so I hear.' Barney was philosophical. 'I believe he's getting treatment but until he's judged sane he can't stand trial for abduction. I think he may be in the psychiatric hospital for some time to come.'

'I wonder what will happen to the Trades Council,' said George.

'I think it will be wound up and the members transferred to the Chamber of Trade and Commerce. It was Tom's grip on people that kept it alive in recent years. It'll be no great loss to the York business community.'

Penny put her head round the door and motioned to the three men. 'Come on, you lot. Can't you see you're wearing Jackie out? Let her get some rest and come back another day.'

'I can't. You're whisking me off to Lanzarote,' said George gloomily. 'Sea and sunshine.'

Everyone laughed as they trooped off down the corridor with Penny muttering darkly about Esmeralda and her many shortcomings. Only George could moan about sea and sunshine. How many people would love to be doing what George was doing? Couldn't he show just a little enthusiasm?

\*\*\*

Genevieve came to visit Jackie and her new niece and nephew

the next day, with Brian in tow. After they had been to visit the two blonde-haired infants, they sat by Jackie's bed and brought her up to date with their news.

Genevieve showed off the beautiful diamond ring Brian had bought for their engagement. 'We're getting married in the spring at St Denys's Church. You know, the medieval one in the centre of York. Mum and Dad have strong connections there. Juliette was married there as well.'

Jackie was delighted. 'But poor Monsieur Henri. I'm sure he had feelings for you himself, Genevieve. What will he do now?'

'Find a Frenchwoman who'll put up with him,' Brian said drily. 'I can't see any sensible English girl taking any of his nonsense.'

Jackie laughed and had to agree. She asked about their plans for a new home. 'We're hoping you'll let us rent the flat at Café Paradise for a while longer,' Brian said. 'That would give us time to save a bit more towards our own house and for me to build up my business in the area. I've made a lot of new connections already, but it may take a few months to get really established.' He smiled his deep, slow smile, his brown eyes crinkling at the corners. 'I've a lot to thank you and Barney for. Without Café Paradise I never would have met Genevieve.'

Things were getting better and better. Tom Young was off the scene for a long time to come. Jackie had gained two new babies and a new brother-in-law. All she wanted now was for the babies to gain enough weight so they could go home and life would be wonderful.

\*\*\*

Waking up from an afternoon nap, Jackie found Walter by her bedside looking down at her with such love in his eyes that she caught her breath. How she had fought with him over the years and nearly driven him to distraction, and Marilyn too. They had not deserved all the love and care this man had quietly given them. She sat up and took his hand. 'Dad, I'm sorry.'

Walter frowned and looked puzzled. 'Sorry. For what? What have you done now? You're in hospital. You can't possibly get into any mischief in here, can you?'

Jackie laughed. 'No, I can't. I just mean, I'm sorry for all the years Marilyn and I took you so much for granted and never really appreciated all you did for us and how much you loved us. You're one in a million and I'm so lucky that you're my dad.'

Walter blushed brick-red and shuffled in his chair. 'Oh … oh … get on with you, lass. Any dad would have done the same. And this time you have our Rose to thank for saving your skin. For once in her life she came in useful, and by gum, we're paying for it now. She's strutting about Claygate like she's one of her own peacocks. I'll never get rid of her now.'

'Ah.' Jackie tapped the side of her nose. 'You could be wrong there. I know something you don't know.'

Walter sat up, interested. 'You do? What?'

'A little bird told me … a little blue-eyed blonde…'

'Yes, yes, get on with it.' Walter was desperate for any change in Claygate's fortunes.

'A little bird,' Jackie repeated slowly, teasingly, 'said the land at Allsthwaite is going to be purchased by the village and returned to holdings again, thereby retaining their ancient character and green credentials in the village. The previous tenants will be invited to apply to return.'

A slow smile spread across Walter's face. It was going to be a grand Christmas after all. Rose and Arthur would soon return to Allsthwaite and Claygate would be a peaceful haven again for him, Ellie and Elvis to enjoy once more. And little Alice and Edward would soon be crawling about the place…

He kissed his daughter tenderly and took his leave. He couldn't wait to give Ellie and Elvis the good news. Happen he might share it with Rose and Arthur too.

# EPILOGUE

Christmas was over and Rose and Arthur had gone to stay with friends in Allsthwaite. On the cusp of the new year, Walter made his way to the cemetery of St Martin's Church. He tidied Marilyn's grave and placed a bunch of pink roses in the vase. Stepping back, he considered his handiwork. Yes, she would be pleased with those, although he could hear her saying crisply, 'Wasting your money on flowers for me.'

He smiled up at the sky. 'Enjoy them, Marilyn love. You never did in life, so take the chance now. I've come with all the news but I expect you already know it all. You're a grandmother. Who'd ha' thought it, our girl producing twins? That's my side of the family. Bet you didn't know that bit.

'Alice and Edward. They're right good 'uns, lively as anything already. We're going to have our hands full with them two. I'm sorry you're not here to watch 'em grow up, but at least we haven't grafted so hard all these years for nothing. They'll have a wonderful inheritance. Café Paradise is an amazing place. You should see it now. Well, I expect you can. Don't you think it's fantastic? That lass of ours has worked wonders with it and if her kids want to take it on, it's there for them. Or on the other hand if they fancy a career in the law, there's always Anderson & Cranton. What a future, eh? Maybe one of them will fancy farming at Claygate and taking on the vegbox scheme and Ellie's jams and chutneys. They just fly off the stall, you know.'

Walter paused a moment and looked quietly down at Marilyn's grave. 'I'm very happy with Ellie, Marilyn. We had our chance and we didn't take it. I'm not letting it slip through my fingers again. I hope you can be happy for us.'

He looked up at the sky again. 'And what about Annabel? That was a surprise. I thought an engagement was going to be a long way off but it made our Christmas to see her home with us and so happy with that David Hall. I can't wait to see them setting up home and shop in York soon.'

Lost in his own thoughts, he didn't hear Jackie approach. She slipped her arm through his and kissed his cheek. 'I thought I'd find you here. Were you telling her all the news?'

Walter nodded, unable to speak.

'I wonder what she'd make of us all now, Dad?' Jackie mused.

'She'd be proud,' he said simply. 'Everything she worked for, every scrimped and scraped penny, passed on to the next generation. What an inheritance to leave behind to two beautiful and talented daughters. And now you, in your turn…' He wiped a tear from his eye.

'A wonderful inheritance,' Jackie agreed, leading him away from the grave. 'And not only from Marilyn. I think a certain crabby old Walter Breckenridge might have had something to do with it too.'

'Cobblers,' said Walter.

Lightning Source UK Ltd.
Milton Keynes UK
UKHW02f1315131117
312671UK00006B/103/P